Janet McNulty

Book 2 in the Enchained Trilogy

Ensnared
Copyright © 2020 Janet McNulty

ISBN-10: 1-941488-92-7 (MMP Publishing)
ISBN-13: 978-1-941488-92-8

First Edition

This book is dedicated to those of you who have struggled, much like Noni does, between doing what is right and what others try to convince you to do. There is no shortage of people always telling you what to do, how to feel, and how to think. Just like Noni is forced to do, you have to make a choice, a very difficult choice: doing what you have been programmed to do and doing what you know to be right. It is not an easy choice to make, and standing up to the mob can be a lonely road, and so, this book is dedicated to you.

Contents

Chapter 1

Aftermath

"Renal! Renal, wake up!" I yell at him, lifting him up, trying to get him to open his eyes.

He moans.

I shake him a little, hoping that he will wake up soon as the alarms blare throughout Arel, alerting everyone to danger, as though they didn't already know.

"Renal!"

His eyes flutter open, blinking several times until he focuses them. "What happened?"

"You were unconscious," I reply.

After helping Sigal and the others leave the city, and hearing the explosions take place, I hurried back to where I had left Renal, hoping that he had not been near them or harmed. My wish had been granted. He still laid on the ground where I had left him, unconscious, and unaware of what had happened. Relief had flooded through me at finding him and knowing that he is okay, though I remembered to put my wristband back on before waking him.

"How long?" Renal asks me.

I shake my head. "Not sure."

"Did you see who struck me?"

I harden my face, putting on a mask so that he will not know that my next words are a lie.

"No."

He does not say anything as he rubs his head from where I had struck him, no doubt feeling the bump that forms and will be there for several days.

"I'm sorry," I say. "I should have been—"

"It doesn't matter," Renal says, taking a deep breath, and a pang of guilt strikes me for what I have done to him. "Sigal?"

"Gone."

Another explosion roars across the city as fire leaps for the starry sky, escaping their confines while doing as much damage as possible, followed by the terrified screams of its victims as they try, in vain, to escape.

"We have to go," I say to Renal and help him to his feet.

"This way!" he stops me when I run for the fires, pointing me in another direction.

I follow him through the darkened streets, listening to the windows close as we approach each new building, while curious eyes try to hide behind them, praying that we will not notice, or be too preoccupied to care. More arbiters line the street and we join them, running for the trap doors that lead to the underground tunnels which run beneath Arel. Renal stops at a detainment center and scans his bracelet, punching in a code. A door opens.

Together, we both jump through it, dropping to the tracks below. "In!" he yells at me, but he needn't have bothered since I have already strapped myself into one of the seats of the two-seater railcar. Our car speeds away just as more railcars appear and more arbiters drop into the tunnels behind us, answering the alarms. We charge though the tunnels, the wind whipping through my hair, causing my eyes to water, and despite my attempts to blink them away, the tears do not cease. As my body jerks to the left, we bank right, only to jerk to the right when we make a sharp left. My fingernails dig deep into my palms while I cling to my seat, afraid of falling out, even though my harness is fastened. Another sharp turn and our car decreases speed until coming to a sudden stop and flings my head forward before slamming it back into my headrest, giving me a sudden headache.

Feeling woozy, I unfasten my harness and toss it off me, jumping out of my seat, stumbling for a few steps as I regain my footing, and I chase after Renal, who has already reached the tunnel's exit. We take the metal steps two at a time and burst free of our underground tomb into a world filled with agonized screams, smothering smoke, and fires that melt the skin from our bodies. I stop, unable to comprehend the scene around me.

Thick, black smoke engulfs the street, cutting us off from the rest of the city, choking any unfortunate to be its victim as it weaves its way over rooftops, people, and the pavement, searching for another to imprison in its grasp. A man collapses next to me. Bending low, I lift him to his feet, placing his arm over my shoulder as I carry him away from the inferno amidst the cries of the medical transports that appear, ready to do what they must to save those they can.

"I'm okay," he coughs as I sit him on the sidewalk. "The children! They're still in there!"

My heart freezes from his words. For the first time, I take a closer look at the building that burns and the pit in my stomach opens wider, forming a ravine that will never be filled: the school is on fire.

"Get those waterpipes working!" Renal yells at a group of arbiters, and others rush forward to help put out the roaring blaze.

Time ceases its methodical step forward as I stare at the building that I had visited once as windows burst, sending shards of glass to those below who try to shield themselves from their fury, while others work in a frantic fashion to uncoil firehoses and spray water on the flames in a desperate attempt to put out what refuses to be vanquished. More shouts, more screams fill the air, but my fogged mind does not hear them as it focuses on the mournful cry of a child stuck on the second floor.

I race for the entrance of the school, charging across the ground and ignoring Renal's shouts as he tries to stop me. Flames burst through the scorched doorframe before being sucked back into the building itself, repeating the process twice as I run for them. Telling myself to think of the gauntlet, I count the seconds between each burst, timing my approach. I pause just outside the entrance as more flames spew from it. They dissipate. Seizing my chance, I leap through the doorway and dodge to the side, rolling across the ground just as another set of flames burst through the broken doors of the entrance in an effort to break free into the night air.

Smoke fills my lungs, causing them to seize and cough in an effort to expel the tainted air. The more I cough, the more I choke. I tear off my jacket and tie it around my face like a mask to help filter out the smoke, but it does little to ease my breathing. Looking around, I search for a stairwell that will take me to the second level, while holding my jacket to prevent it from slipping off my face because of the sweat that pours down my cheeks, streaming its way down my neck and shoulders.

"Hello!" I scream.

No answer.

"Anyone hear me?"

Thunder fills my ears, making them hurt from the noise and drowning out all else as I run my soot-covered hand against the wall, while bits of paint melt away from it, doing my best to navigate my way through the school. Smoky darkness broken by fire looms around me, threatening to take me. My foot bumps something and I trip, falling to my hands and knees, wincing as bits of mortar delve underneath the skin, cutting their way deeper into my flesh. As I look at what has caused me to fumble, I jump back from the charred face that stares back at me, its eyes filled with terror from the agonizing death the person has suffered.

A child's cry for help pierces the roaring of the fire, jolting me back into the present and my current predicament. I jump to my feet and rush forward, while feeling my way around with my hands and feet, not wanting to trip over another body, while ceiling panels crash around me, warning me of the danger I am in. A light breaks free of its hold. I leap to the side before it can strike me as it swings from the one remaining wire that holds onto it, desperate to keep it in its place.

Another cry for help.

"I'm coming!" I yell, but am unsure if anyone can hear me in this inferno.

A clearing lies ahead. I run for it, ignoring the heat and the smoke, hoping to make it to the stairwell that I know is down this way. Spit fills my jacket as it shoots from my mouth due to my panting and coughing, but I remain focused on my goal: the stairs.

A tremendous cracking sound fills the corridor, drowning the roars of the fire, and my arm hairs stand on end while goosebumps form, warning me of impending danger far worse than what I am in. I push harder, but before I take three more steps, the ceiling in front of me crashes as a support beam digs into the floor, and I jump back, avoiding its crushing weight, landing on my side as bits of insulation, dust, and embers float around me, mixing with the thickening smoke.

Stinging, burning pain engulfs my left forearm. With care, I raise it so that the light can touch it, revealing a severe burn and the bubbling, red and black skin it consists of. Grinding my teeth, I force myself to not think about the pain. I am an arbiter. I am strong and not subject to the whims of the flesh. Weakness is failure, and failure, right here, right now, means death.

I study the support beam that has fallen, barring my way, searching for a path around it, not willing to give up and sacrifice the people trapped here for my own sake. I spot it: a small, triangular opening just beneath the beam, just large enough for me to squeeze through. Repositioning my jacket around my nose and mouth, I charge for the opening, leaping over tiny flames that form a line, taunting me and telling me to turn back, but I ignore them and somersault on the floor once through. I turn back. The opening has disappeared, consumed by the fire as though mocking my efforts.

Plunged into darkness, with only the smoke for a companion, I search around me and find the stairwell leading to the second floor, each step littered with plaster, concrete, and every other matter of debris. I place my foot on the first step, crunching the plaster spread across it as I lift myself up, placing my other foot on the second step, moving with care, unsure of what to expect and uncertain about the sturdiness of the stairs themselves. My sweaty palm slips from the banister and I lose my balance for a moment, coughing as I go, pressing my jacket into my face.

A low whimper sounds above me.

Desperate, I hurry up the stairs, taking them two at a time, almost tumbling when my foot slips. Tears stream from my eyes as the smoke irritates them, making everything look blurred, and my rapid blinking does little to clear my vision, for each tear that is wiped away, two more take its place. Rubbing my face with the back of my hand and smearing soot on my skin as I do, I reach the part of the stairwell that curves and heads to the second level where nestled in a corner, head buried in his knees, sits one of the schoolchildren, his yellow uniform almost indistinguishable from the blackened debris around him.

He looks up and panics.

"It's okay," I say, pulling my jacket away from my face in an effort to calm him. "I'm here to help you."

"I'm scared," he says through tears.

Fear: the one thing that was never allowed at the training facility. If an arbiter feels fear, they are not fit to be an arbiter, or so I have been taught, and Molers always made it a point to remind recruits of what happens to them if they give in to fear.

I look into the boy's frightened eyes, realizing that I am also afraid—What if Renal learns that I knocked him out and helped Sigal? What if I burn to death or am crushed from the weight of the building collapsing around me?—but if I give into this basic emotion, no one will be here to help the boy. "I am too," I tell him in a soothing voice.

He blinks at me.

"Come on." I hold my hand out to him. "Take my hand."

The boy reaches for my outstretched hand and I grasp his, pulling him toward me.

"What about the others?"

"Others?"

The boy points up the stairs. "There are others trapped in a room."

For a split second, I consider leaving and carrying the boy out to safety, but my own conscience refuses to allow me to leave any who may still be trapped. "Take me to them," I tell him, wrapping my jacket around his nose and mouth.

He leads me up the stairs while bits of the paneling within the walls and ceiling fall around us, clacking on the linoleum floor, warning us that time grows short and our precious seconds tick by faster than we are able to move. The higher we go, the thicker the smoke becomes, and I bend low, hoping to escape it, but there is no way for me to crawl and carry him at the same time.

"That room there," says the boy.

After being tormented by the thundering of the fire that ravages the floor below, my ears ring in the unnatural silence of the second floor as we creep to the room where other survivors wait for rescue, encased in gloom and the gnawing feeling that soon we will be cremated. The boy reaches for the button that controls the door, but I smack his hand away, pushing him behind me. Feeling the cool touch of the door's fogged-glass exterior with the back of my hand, I conclude that it is safe to open it. I push the button next to it. Nothing happens. Frustrated, I hit the button again, but the door refuses to open, meaning that something has gone wrong with its mechanism.

I need to break the glass. "Wait here," I tell the boy, remembering seeing a plank of wood on the stairs.

He grabs my waistband in fear, but I push him back against the wall, forcing my touch to be gentle so as to reassure him.

"I'm coming back," I promise him.

With a doubtful look, he settles on the floor and wraps his arms around his knees. I dash off to the stairs, jumping down them, while clinging to the railing so as not to fall, and snatch the wood plank. A roaring sound fills my ears. Turning, I examine the bottom of the steps; the fire has reached the stairwell and will soon consume the second floor. Heart pounding, I race up the stairs, my boots beating the floor with harsh clomps as I charge up them and hurry down the hallway to the room where the boy waits for me.

"Stay back," I tell him, panting.

He stands behind me, but leans out, wanting to watch what I am about to do, forcing me to turn around, grab the jacket, and cover his face, shielding him from any glass that might fly.

"Leave it," I order the boy when he reaches up to remove my jacket from his face, and he places his hands back by his side.

Taking a deep breath, I pull the plank back and ram it into the glass door, turning my head so as not to get bits of it in my eyes. A small crack appears in its center. Frowning, I raise the plank again and smash it into the door over and over until more and more cracks appear, creating a musical sound of tingling glass as shards tumble to the floor.

"You okay?" I ask the boy, removing my jacket from his face and wrapping it around his nose and mouth once again.

He nods his head. I push him through the door, using the toe of my boot to remove the remaining bits of glass from the door frame.

"Hello?" I call, once through the door.

Three faces appear, all tear-stained and terrified.

"Come," I tell them, waving them to me.

The scraping of a desk against the floor snatches my attention, and I whirl around, finding a plebeian girl huddled in a corner, hiding behind a desk and its accompanying chair, her pale face smeared with soot and ash.

"Just leave her," says one of the children, but my glare silences her, and she recoils underneath it.

I approach the plebeian, but she scooches further away from me, frightened of my uniform, forcing me to reconsider my actions.

"Do you think you can coax her out?" I ask the boy I had found on the stairs.

He gives me a disbelieving expression, but does as asked, inching his way toward the girl. She pulls away from him, and for a moment, I consider leaving her, not liking such an option, but the boy holds his hand out to her—no words are spoken between them—and she takes it, allowing herself to be yanked from her corner and join the rest of us. I shove them through the door—glass crunching underneath our feet—and push them toward the stairs when a low creaking fills the hallway; its intensity builds around us.

"Get back!" I yell, jumping ahead of them and pushing them back to the room, through the door and away from the falling debris as the walls and ceiling crumble around us, barreling through the floor and to the inferno below.

Dust and smoke dance around us, choking us, and my lungs seize from the pollution, torn between allowing me to breathe or coughing to expel the smoke. I peek out the door. A giant hole is all that remains of the hallway, its ceiling, and its floor as fire winds its way upward, heading straight for us. We cannot go that way. Dismayed, I bow my head, believing that I have failed and that these children will die because of me. The boy puts his hand on mine, comforting me and shaming me because it should be me reassuring all of them.

A breeze caresses my neck, cooling the sweat that coats it and snapping my brain back into focus. Turning toward it, I notice an open window. Most times, the windows are kept shut, but sometimes a teacher will open one (they never open more than three or four inches) to allow fresh air in. I race to the window and peer outside where people dart about in a frantic state to put out the fire and arbiters attempt to establish order amidst the chaos.

I snatch the plank of wood from the floor where I had left it and pause before the window, gauging the amount of force needed to break the glass. The children gather around me.

"Turn away," I tell them and they obey.

With all the strength I have, I ram the plank into the window three times and watch as cracks form in the glass, spreading and growing with each strike until it bursts, sending shards below, and a gush of fresh air swoops into the classroom, pulling a few renegade flames from the hallway into the area, which disappear as quick as they arrive. I lean out, observing the distance to the ground. There is no jumping it.

As though reading my mind, the plebeian girl points at the ceiling above us at a series of Arelian flags, created by the students, that are attached to a cable stretching across the ceiling. I never noticed them until now. Thanking her, I stand upon a desk and reach up, snatching the line and ripping it free of its hold, coiling it around my arm as I gather it up.

Once back at the window, I call to the people below for help, but no one hears me. I spot Renal. I need to get his attention. Looking around for anything I can throw at him, I spot a tablet on a nearby desk and snatch it. I chuck it out the window like a frisbee and nick him in the foot. He jumps and looks right at me as I wave my arms and point at the children. No words are needed. He calls to a group of arbiters, ordering them to stand below the window and await my next move.

"All right"—I tie the cable around a heating pipe as I talk to the children—"I am going to lower each of you down to the people waiting below."

One of the children whimpers.

"I need you to be brave," I tell her.

"Like an arbiter," says another.

"Yes," I reply, "like an arbiter."

"Like you," the boy from the stairwell whispers and the others nod.

I pause for a second, touched by his words, having never thought of myself as brave before. I just don't want any of them to die. I tie the line around his waist, telling him to hold on as I help him out the window and lower him down. Once he reaches the ground, Renal takes him and tugs on the rope. I pull it up and tie it around another of the children, helping her out the window and lowering her to the ground like the boy before her. Minutes pass like hours, but I manage to free them from this prison of fire and smoke.

It is my turn. Unsure if the cable will support my weight, I tug on it, making certain the knot around the heating pipe will hold. It will have to do. I crawl out the window, snagging my shirt on a bit of glass and cutting my side. Wincing from the pain, I cling to the rope, lowering myself inch by inch, taking my time so as not to lose my grip, and plummet to the hard ground below. The line lurches. Fear rises within me and my heart beats against my chest as I realize that my knot is not holding.

I ease my way downward, breathing so hard that my lungs burn and my pulse thuds in my neck and ears, drowning the shouts aimed in my direction. The rope lurches again. I am only halfway down. I glance below me at the ground that seems so far away. The rope lurches for a third time. Weighing my options, all which end with me smashing into the pavement, I take in a deep breath to steady my nerves, accepting my fate and what awaits me if I fail to survive.

I let go just as the rope breaks free of the heating pipe. Air rushes by me, and for a moment, I believe that I am flying, until I crash into the ground below, landing on my side; the air in my lungs break free and I gasp for oxygen, curling into a ball from the ripping pain in my left shoulder.

Renal's strong arms seize me around my waist and help me to my feet. He wraps my good arm around his shoulders, allowing me to lean on him as he drags me to a medical transport.

"Bring her here," says a familiar voice and Natalie's face appears, ushering us to a gurney within the transport, and Renal places me on it with a gentleness I never thought he possessed.

"Her shoulder is dislocated," Natalie tells him. "Hold her still."

Renal obeys.

Before I have a chance to grasp what she plans to do, Natalie pushes my shoulder back into its socket and the pain courses through my body as I bite my tongue to refrain from crying out.

"Pain is weakness!" Molers' voice repeats in my head and memories of the times at the training facility when the instructors would beat us with switches until we no longer acknowledged physical pain flood my mind.

"You'll have to refrain from using that arm for a while," Natalie says as she places my arm in a sling. She looks at Renal's concerned face. "She'll be fine. Go, do your duty."

Renal leaves us alone, allowing Natalie to assess my wounds.

"Thank you," I tell her.

"It is my job," she says as she examines the cut on my side.

I have not seen her since the day I followed her to the plebeian quarters, and I find myself thinking about the mystery of the syringe and vial of medicine with instructions that had ended up in my coat pocket.

"Not for this," I say, taking a gamble and knowing what awaits me if I am wrong, yet cautious enough to choose my words with care, "but for earlier, back at the medical center."

"Again, I was just doing my job," replies Natalie, and I cannot tell if she understood my meaning or not, nor can I risk being more specific in case I have misjudged her.

"Of course," I say, keeping my voice low.

"I do appreciate your gratitude. It is nice to be thanked once in a while," Natalie says as she places gauze over my cut, securing it with medical tape. "Though we all must do our part for Arel."

I listen to her, to the tone within her voice, trying to determine if she speaks what she believes, or is testing me, as is the way in Arel: all must be assessed to determine their loyalty.

I remain calm, reserved, and keep my face impassive and my voice even, unsure if my gamble paid off, or buried me.

"I guess I owe you a debt," I say in a joking manner.

"Be careful," warns Natalie. "People have a way of collecting."

I chuckle at her statement. Such is our way.

"Here." Natalie places an oxygen mask over my face. "Breathe deep and slow." She glances outside and at the plebeian girl who stands alone among a stormy sea of rushing feet, anguished shouts, and blaring alarms, ignored by all while holding her arms close as she tries to comfort herself. I see it. A look of pity, the same one that I had seen on Mandi during the banquet, but before I have time to register its meaning, it is gone, and Natalie resumes her businesslike demeanor.

She steps out of the medical transport, but before she can close the door, I spot something painted on the ground that I had not noticed before: the symbol of Arel crossed out, almost like a warning. The doors to the transport slam shut and the vehicle jerks as it drives away with me on board, leaving me alone with my thoughts and to dwell upon everything that has transpired during my patrol.

Chapter 2

Chilling Consequence

An insistent knock on my door yanks me from a restless sleep as my mind desires to go back to that land of unconsciousness and ignorance, but the distant pounding in my ears breaks through the barrier, forcing me to open my eyes. I blink a couple of times to clear away the sand and focus on the ceiling above me with its panels of tarnished gray, each outlined by a black rimming—the color of my world. Arbiters are not encouraged to enjoy colors, like the vibrant bands of a rainbow after a spring rain, as they might evoke emotional responses, and we are to be emotionless beings.

I always liked the color red, not the bright color that blood brings, but more subdued, yet bold, letting the world know it exists and isn't just one small part in a sea of black uniforms. Cherries: their robust color is the shade I have always admired, and their life-giving fruit.

I remember the cherry tree that grew in the courtyard of the training facility. No one knew where it came from; none admitted to

planting it, but it appeared one day. In my fourth year, I spotted it—
it was no more than four inches tall—and I admired it for growing in a place that did not allow such frivolous luxuries to flourish.
Flowers, bushes, trees—all were forbidden within the facility. Arbiters are not to focus on frolicsome things, but keep their minds
on their duties and the protection of Arel; but this one cherry tree
managed to thrive in the very center of our courtyard, in the center
of where our drills were carried out, in an area known for its heat
and humidity. For ten years, I snuck it water, admiring its tenacity,
stubbornness, and beauty as it grew stronger. I remember the day it
first flowered, with beautiful, soft pink petals, and produced fruit as
though it mocked my gray surroundings, inviting me to be daring
like it was.

One night, I slipped down to the courtyard and plucked a ripe
cherry from the tree, marveling at its red color and savoring its tart
flavor, feeling pride and hoping that the water I gave it in its early life
helped it produce such delightful fruit. What I hadn't counted on
was being seen by someone else, by someone who despised anything
that could be considered good. When I awoke the next morning, all
that remained of that cherry tree was a lone stump, a reminder that
life is fleeting and that anything as wonderful as that tree can be
taken away in an instant. From then on, the shade of that one cherry
the tree allowed me to eat has been my favorite color.

The knocking stops and the door to my room slides open. Startled, I bolt upright and turn toward the door, ready to defend myself against this uninvited guest. Chase stands in my room, a worried look on his face.

"What's wrong?" I ask, throwing my blanket off me.

He does not answer.

"Gwen, she isn't…"

"She's fine," says Chase.

Before I can do anything, Chase rushes toward me and envelops me in those strong, yet gentle, arms of his, holding me close as

though he is afraid of losing me. My shoulder pains me and I push him away, but instead of being insulted, he lets me go, realizing that his intended comfort has caused me pain.

"I heard the explosions," he says, "and I was afraid that…"

"I'm fine," I tell him, reassuring him, and wondering where this newfound affection for me came from, or has he always had it since the time we were lost in the wildlands? I have never been able to get that time out of my head. "I should get dressed. I have a review today and have to answer for my actions."

Without being told, Chase goes to my closet and pulls out a pair of pressed pants, a fresh under shirt, and an ironed jacket. I pull the shirt I am wearing off, doing my best to keep my face placid despite the burning in my shoulder from each little movement. The doctor I had been assigned at the medical wing the night of the bombing had told me that it would take a minimum of six weeks for my shoulder to heal. I wish it would heal faster. I detest being helpless. I stand before Chase with my breasts exposed, not caring about privacy, since it never existed at the training facility, and I learned long ago not to feel embarrassed when exposed, but he never glances at them, choosing to avert his eyes instead, giving some semblance of decency, doing his best to be mindful of my current situation. He hands me the clean undershirt and I put it on, forcing myself past the gripping pain in my shoulder, demanding that it work and pull the cotton material over my chin until the built-in bra snuggles my breasts and the hem settles at the top of my hips.

Next, I pull on my pants with Chase still averting his eyes, while I ease the snug material over my buttocks, allowing the waistband to hug my middle, securing my undershirt beneath its prison. My jacket appears in front of me, and I take it from Chase's outstretched hand.

"Thank you," I whisper, putting my good arm through the sleeve and allowing Chase to pull the other sleeve over my injured one, being reminded of when he had to carry me through the wildlands because of my broken leg.

I reach for my sling, but he beats me to it, grabbing it from the chair I had flung it on before going to bed, and slips it around my arm, taking great care to not cause me to wince, not that I would display such weakness, and wraps the thick, padded strap around my shoulder, securing it in place. Before I can say anything, he picks up my boots and waves me to the only chair in the room. Knowing that he would not take a refusal for an answer, I sit and allow him to lace up my boots, until they are snug and do not wiggle. His fingers work with an efficiency I never thought a plebeian could possess, and after a couple of minutes, I am dressed and ready to report for duty.

"You didn't have to," I say. "I can put my own boots on."

Chase looks at me, his gray eyes filled with sympathy and... respect?

"I know," he replies, "but I wanted to."

He grabs the bobby pins sitting on the desk and motions for me to turn around. With delicate fingers, he lifts the strands of my long hair as it reflects the pale light in the room and twists them together, forming a bun. One by one, he sticks the pins in, securing the bun while making certain that each pin neither pulls nor tugs so as to cause any discomfort. Once done, he admires his handiwork, saying, "Now you look every bit the arbiter, and are ready for your review."

"How..."

"My former mistress used to have me help her with putting her hair up. Her hands didn't work well, and the slightest movement caused her pain. I help Gwen with her hair too."

Being helped with a simple task, such as getting dressed, is foreign to me. While at the training facility, we were never encouraged to seek assistance, much less accept it. If an arbiter cannot do things on their own, they are not worthy of defending Arel. My mind drifts back to when I was eleven and each recruit in my year had one arm tied behind their backs where they could not use it. We were to conduct our duties that day one-armed. Some, like Trevors, thrived and managed to do everything as though they were not handicapped at all, while others struggled. One recruit was unable to do the simplest of tasks, and upon Molers' orders, received a beating from one of the instructors. I watched as the recruit fell to the ground, doing her best to cover her head, but was unable to escape the torment brought down upon her.

In a rare moment of compassion, I ran to her and shoved the instructor aside, demanding that he stop before he killed her: one of my many mistakes. The instructor knocked me to the ground, kicking me in the stomach, and while I lay there with pebbles boring into my skin, he lashed me with his switch, stopping when Molers strolled by, his hands clasped behind his back as his lips curled into a sardonic smile, baring his teeth.

"Compassion, mercy, and sympathy are for the weak," he said. "If you cannot conduct yourselves with one arm tied behind your backs, how are you all going to be of any use if we are attacked and you are wounded? You must be able to push through your inabilities and your pain. Those who cannot are feeble and unfit to be arbiters. If your fellow recruit is dealt a punishment, watch them accept it because they deserve it for not being stronger. If you challenge their punishment, then you shall also be reprimanded." Molers bent low, placing his lips against my ear so that his hot, sticky breath stuck to my skin. "Is that understood?" he whispered to me.

"Yes, sir," I had replied.

His salacious grin implanted itself in my mind—an image I cannot rid myself of—as he stood up and nodded his head at the instructor. With one final strike, the switch lashed me across the side of my neck, implanting a red mark that lasted for four days. Afterward, both my arms were bound as two arbiters placed me in a straight-jacket.

"Because of your actions," Molers announced as he circled me, "you will spend the rest of the day confined in this jacket. No one is to help you. Any who do will suffer a worse fate."

Memories of sitting alone during mealtime with both my arms strapped down so that I could not use them flood my mind as the feeling of isolation wells within me, forcing me back to that moment as though it is happening now. That day, I ate like a dog, planting my face in my food and using my tongue to scoop up bits of peas and potatoes into my mouth, and when I had to use the bathroom, I urinated myself because I was unable to pull down my pants and use the toilet in any manner of dignity: a humiliation that overshadowed me for weeks.

"Hey," says Chase, bringing me back to the present. "What's wrong?"

"Nothing," I reply, not wanting to burden him with my past.

He reaches up and places a calloused hand on my cheek, using the lightest of pressure to force me to look at him and those gray eyes that hold no amount of loathing, anger, or hatred like they did the first time I ever saw them—not even pity. All that dwells within them is caring.

"I should be able to do all this myself," I say, remembering my training. "Weakness is…"

"You're not weak," Chase cuts me off. "It's okay to ask for help."

What changed? How did we go from being enemies who despised one another to caring about the other's well-being and helping them when we can?

"Why did you lie for me when they found us?" I ask; the question still lingers on my mind as he had never given me a satisfactory answer.

He turns to the window and the wall that lies outside it, dwarfing us, reminding us of the forbidden world beyond. "I heard them talking, your commander and the commandant. We plebeians know what Arel does to those they believe are useless, and your injuries were severe. Though your commander believed in your abilities to survive, the commandant wasn't so sure, so I lied. When they asked for my version of events, I told them that you saved us both and fought off an outsider, despite your physical weakness. I told them what they needed to hear so that you wouldn't be sent to the crematorium."

I stare at him, unable to process what he had told me.

"You should get going," Chase says, approaching the door, "before they notice your absence."

"Why?" I ask him again, my voice just above a murmur.

"You say that I am the reason that we are both alive today, but I never lied. You saved me."

I say nothing.

"Promise me that you will do what you need to, to survive." The door slides open and he disappears, allowing it to close with a soft thud, leaving me alone in my room, silhouetted by the faint light pouring through the window, broken only by the shadow of the wall.

Taking a deep breath to control the well of swirling emotions within me, I step to the door, forcing it to slide open and allow me passage, and stalk out of my room, stomping down the dim and empty corridor to the stairs to face what the day has asked of me. Commander Vye waits for me at the bottom step.

"I was about to send someone to get you," she quips.

"Sorry, ma'am," I say. "There is no excuse for my tardiness."

"Grab something quick to eat," says the commander. "We are expected at the review board within the hour."

Another review. I am not surprised. After the bombings, it makes sense that there would be a review of our actions, such is the norm in Arel; all arbiters must account for what they do to ensure that they serve Arel without hesitation or impunity.

I stroll into the dining room and bump into Anan. He glares at me—he never did like me, nor I him—and stalks away with a grunt, hurrying out the door and to his duties. Silence looms around me as arbiters finish their meals and hurry to report to their stations, while those who do not go on patrol until sundown either sit in the reading room to relax, go to the outdoor gymnasium for exercise, or sneak upstairs for some much-needed rest, all without speaking to one another. The bombings have frightened all of us. No one knows who was behind them, a mystery that engulfs us all, making each of us wonder if there is another target and who will be next.

I spot a bronze tray with egg fritters on it and snatch a couple, shoving them in my mouth and swallowing without bothering to chew them much. A glass appears by my hand. Looking down, I see Sheila holding it out to me with a frightened look on her face.

"Thank you," I say to her, taking the water and looking around to make certain no one watches us, but they are too preoccupied with their own affairs to notice us, much less care.

"Your shoulder…" she begins, and I pull her aside, away from everyone else.

"It'll be fine," I tell her.

"I saw the smoke and feared…"

"I'm fine," I reassure her. "I have to go now. You take care of yourself."

Sheila nods. Before I am able to take a step, she seizes my wrist and pulls me back, handing me a small bundle. "I saved this for you when you didn't come down for breakfast."

Puzzled, I take the bundle, unwrapping the faded blue cloth and revealing a blueberry muffin with a sugar crumble topping.

"Where did you get this?" I ask, since such a treat is never served at the manor.

"Commander Vye sent me to the market to fetch a few provisions for the next few days. There is a baker there who sometimes gives me yesterday's discards. I saved it for you."

"You shouldn't worry about me," I tell her, handing her back the muffin, but she refuses to take it as her lips settle in a firm line, displaying her resolve. "How about we share?"

Sheila nods.

I break the muffin into three big pieces and hand two of them to Sheila. "One is for Gwen," I tell her when she opens her mouth to protest, and she closes it, agreeing with my suggestion. The clatter of a plate hitting the table snatches my attention, and I must be going or suffer Commander Vye's wrath. Eating the muffin piece in two bites, I wipe the sugar crystals from my mouth and hurry to the entrance where both Commander Vye and Renal wait for me, much like they did the first time I was summoned to the Command Division for a review, except this time, something is different; this time, another arbiter waits with them. I study this arbiter and her regal stance as she stands with her feet shoulder-width apart and her hands by her sides, waiting for us to be ready to leave, her uniform pressed without a single wrinkle in it as though it has just been laundered.

Before I have a chance to ponder this new arbiter's presence, or why she is here as I have not seen her at the manor before, Commander Vye ushers me out the door. I obey without delay, followed by her, Renal, and our mysterious escort. Our brisk strides down the driveway are in tune with one another as our boots stomp on the pavement while we make our way to the railcar platform. Just like before, people pause in their activities to watch us as we hurry down the street in procession, never allowing their eyes to linger too long, lest they be stopped and questioned for their overabundant curiosity. One studies me as I stroll past, but his eyes dart to the side the moment he notices me watching him, and he runs off, signaling to his plebeian to hurry up. The hunched shoulders, wary stares, and hushed whispers shower me in the fear that has gripped the city because of the bombings.

The whine of a railcar rushes by us and I know that we are close to the platform, and just like last time, a lone car waits for us. As we hike up to the platform, we stroll by a group of children dressed in red uniforms, the future engineers of Arel, listening to their teacher describe the mathematics behind constructing the raised railways and the cars that glide along them, carting people throughout the city. Two students pick the pocket of another, and I seize the shoulder of one, getting his attention. He looks at me with frightened eyes and his mouth hangs open as he wonders what I will do to him, but I point at the item in his hand, and he gives it back to his fellow student. As I let go of his shoulder, Commander Vye gives me an odd glance, but says nothing as she steps into the empty railcar with

Renal, while the arbiter escorting us turns toward me and I hurry into the shuttle before she says anything.

We each sit down with several seats between us, none of us bothering to talk as silence is preferable, and the arbiter with us keeps a close eye on each of us, encouraging us to keep our mouths shut. The shuttle moves away from the platform and toward the inner part of Arel, heading for the central station, and the force of its movement slings me to the side as I stare out the glass that encompasses us and the tiny rainbow it forms from the small ray of the sun that pokes through the clouds. Lifting my eyes, I look out at the city and the smoldering rubble left behind from the domestic attacks, wondering how many had been injured and how many survived. What happened to the children from the school?

The shuttle passes over the central part of the eastern sector, over the walkways and the people who hurry down them, desperate to get to their destination, and I spot the school. Blackened brick litter the area as a huge hole engulfs the roof and an entire side of the building. Leaning closer to the glass, I watch as plebeians clear away the rubble and rebuild the outer exterior, proof of Tapiwa keeping her promise to ensure that repairs to the eastern sector would be made. The shuttle veers upward and to the left, allowing me to steal a glance over the wall and at the grassland beyond, and the veil of trees that lie further away, and my mind dwells upon the outsider that had helped Chase and me while we struggled to survive beyond the wall.

Our escort clears her throat, and I turn away from the glass, staring straight ahead, taking note of her watchful gaze upon me, one that would even make Commander Vye shrink underneath it. No words are needed to voice her disappointment. Her hardened eyes drill into me, delving deep into the inner depths of my soul as though she desires to know my thoughts, or perhaps she already does. Once she turns away, I look up at the sky and the rail that passes over us, casting a long shadow upon us before disappearing in the distance. A slight shift jostles me as the railcar switches tracks, bypassing the central hub and heading straight for the heart of Arel where the Command Division is.

Towering buildings surround us, dwarfing us as they stand tall, showcasing their glass towers that reflect the scenery around them, mirroring everything, letting every citizen know that this is Arel, the center of civilization, or so we're taught. A massive, square building looms ahead, hollowing out the pit that already fills my stomach, and beyond it are trails of smoke: the crematorium. The sinking feeling in my stomach grows as sweat coats my palms and the nervousness that I have managed to hold back bursts through without mercy, refusing to release me or allow me any sort of comfort.

Before we hit the building in front of us, the railcar dips, sinking below the skyline of the city and to the streets below where massive screens soar past us, pleading with us to buy the product advertised, while others portray the aftermath of the bombings, with Tapiwa's and Kumi's voices narrating over the images, speaking about our bravery and resolve, while vowing to bring the cowards responsible to justice. My body shifts as the shuttle slows to a stop, passing beneath copper archways that crisscross one another, until we reach the platform and the doors slide open with a baritone hiss. A few people try to board, thinking that it is a normal transport, but our escort shoos them away while the rest of us disembark, heading for the entrance.

I do not wait to be ushered to the glass elevator, having gone up it the last time I was here, and head straight for it with the others right behind me. Other arbiters hurry past us. A few of them glance in our direction, but turn away just as fast, resuming their duties and glad to not be in our position. As we glide upward to the topmost floor, I marvel at the luminescent streets below us that shine as though they have just been polished, allowing the diamonds embedded within them to cast tiny bursts of color in a ragged pattern that goes against the uniformity surrounding them, almost as though they are conducting their own form of rebellion against the conformity demanded of them. The elevator stops and we leave it, heading down a hallway with a glass wall on one side, allowing us to look out upon the city and its marvels: mirror-like glass buildings reflect the colorful sky and the city, making it appear double its actual size while railcars soar above it, adding to its majestic presence. Our escort leads us to a set of double doors, made with reinforced steel, with two guards on either side and one in the center who stops us the moment we reach them.

"State your business," he demands.

"Captain Ryals, serial number R21908, reporting with Commander Vye, Lieutenant Renal, and Arbiter Noni as requested," replies our escort, speaking for the first time.

Renal steps forward next. "Lieutenant Renal. Serial number R26389."

The guard's eyes flick over to Commander Vye, who walks toward him, head held high, her mouth set in a rigid line, while her eyes pierce through his body armor, causing him to take one step back.

"Commander Vye. Serial number V21923," she says in a stern voice, daring him to challenge her.

The man checks her information on the tablet within his hands, and his gaze turns toward me. For a moment, I am thrust back to the time I was first summoned here, forced to relive my shame from my first visit to the wall since being assigned to the eastern sector, and the same anxiety that had seized my stomach then threatens to cripple me again. Swallowing a wad of spit to force the lump forming in my throat away, I square my shoulders, straightening my posture, doing my best to give the guard my own piercing stare.

"Arbiter Noni," I say, keeping my voice firm, not allowing it to quiver or give away my anxiety. "Serial number N27461."

Once again, the guard checks his tablet, confirming my identity and that we are to be there. He waves his hand and one of the others hits a gold button encircled in bronze, forcing the steel doors to slide open, while our escort steps aside; she is not allowed within the tribunal chambers as only those summoned are.

Following Renal and Commander Vye, I step inside the darkened interior where a bright, white light shines down upon a podium, blocking the view of those sitting in judgement of our actions. I move my eyes, keeping my head still, trying to take in the scene around me (black walls with tapestries hanging from the ceiling, each with Arel's crest, unmoving even from the slightest draft), while ahead of me lies a long, raised bench with three high-ranking arbiters seated upon it, each with sour expressions. Unlike last time, I shiver from the judgmental atmosphere, despite the warmth of the air and the fact that I wear my full uniform.

Movement in a far corner catches my attention, and I turn my head without thinking, catching a glimpse of an ivory train with golden circles embroidered upon it before it creeps back into the shadows. Commander Vye clears her throat, and I flick my head forward, hoping that none of the tribunal have noticed my insolence, but a quick peek tells me that they did.

"Lieutenant Renal," says a drawn-out voice, and I look at the one it belongs to, noting that, like my commander, the woman has her head shaved, but unlike Commander Vye, her scowl could freeze molten metal.

Renal takes the podium, remaining at attention, and his face betrays none of the turmoil that might be reeling within his mind.

"You were on patrol when the attacks happened and when the school within the eastern sector was bombed," says the same member of the council.

"Yes, ma'am," answers Renal.

"Tell us, in your own words, what happened that night."

Renal takes a moment to inhale and let out a slow breath. "I was on patrol with Arbiter Noni when someone threw a rock at one of the loudspeakers in the main square. Arbiter Noni and I pursued the suspect and subdued him. At this time, an alert flashed on our wristbands. I told Arbiter Noni to take the suspect to detainment, while I went to see what the alert was about."

"You let her go alone with your detainee?" says another member of the council.

"Yes, sir," replies Renal. "She is more than capable of handling herself and we could not leave the suspect alone on the streets, nor could we take him with us to investigate what might have caused the alert to go off. So, I thought it best to split up for the moment. She is well-trained and I knew she could catch up afterwards."

"And what did you find?" asks the first member of the council.

"I found six citizens out after curfew, attempting to sneak out of the city."

"Can you identify them?"

"No."

It takes all my resolve not to jerk my head in Renal's direction and to keep my face impassive. He lied. Why would he do that? I know that he and Sigal were on friendly terms, perhaps they were friends, but anyone who opposes the law of Arel is considered an enemy of Arel and are to be dealt with accordingly. I think back to that night when I had caught up to him, but he had not seen me. He used Sigal's name, pleaded with him to not leave, to not put him in the position of taking him to a containment box. I think back to when Chase had lied to save my life. Is this why Renal refuses to tell the truth? To spare me? Why would he? He has no idea I was even there. As far as he knows, I found him after some mysterious stranger had knocked him out and Sigal and his family had escaped. Perhaps he is lying to protect himself, but that does not seem like Renal.

"No?" questions the third member of the council. "You did not get a good look at them? You have no idea who they are? You have been in the eastern sector for seven years and you're telling us that you cannot guess who they might have been?"

"I apologize to the council," says Renal. "It was dark and I was unable to see their faces or make out any defining characteristics. I understand my failure, and for that, I know I must be reprimanded."

"What did you do when you found them?" asks the first council member.

"I ordered them to stop," Renal replies.

"Did any of them speak?"

"No, ma'am."

Another lie. The memory of that night floods my mind, and I find myself thrust back into that alley listening to Renal plead with Sigal to not go, to not put him in the position of arresting him, while Sigal begged Renal to let his wife, daughter, and the others go and arrest only him if he must arrest someone. I hear the desperation in both their voices in my mind as though I am there now.

"What happened afterward?" demands the second member of the tribunal.

"Someone struck me on the head," answers Renal, "and I blacked out."

"Do you know who did it?"

"No."

"And afterward?"

"I woke up to Arbiter Noni informing me of a series of explosions that had rocked Arel. We headed for the nearest tunnel and took the railcar to the nearest bombing. There, Arbiter Noni entered the school and rescued some who were trapped inside."

"One of whom was a plebeian," says the first member of the council, and her dark undertone makes it clear what she thinks of my actions. A part of me wonders if she ever smiles or even knows how to work those muscles in her face. I'm guessing the answer is no.

"As arbiters, we are charged with protecting all within Arel," replies Renal. "Perhaps she had seen something. I'm sure this is what Arbiter Noni thought when she rescued her."

Why is he covering for me?

"Perhaps," says the same woman on the council, and I catch a glimpse of the pins on her collar, denoting her rank. "Is there anything else?"

"No."

"You may step down."

Renal stalks away from the podium, taking his place beside Commander Vye and stands at attention.

"Commander Vye," says the same female member of the tribunal, "you may step forward."

Commander Vye hurries to the podium, not bothering to glance in the judges' direction and steps upon it, the bright light making her uniform shine. Squaring her shoulders, she eyes the darkness before her, daring the people hiding within it to condemn her.

"You are the commander of the eastern sector, is that correct?"

"Yes." Commander Vye's sharp voice echoes around the chamber, causing my chest to vibrate and instilling fear within me.

"And Arbiter Noni is under your command?"

"Yes."

"Has she ever shown a tendency to sympathize for plebeians before?"

"Arbiter Noni follows the law."

"Answer the question," demands the council.

"I just did." The defiance in Commander Vye's voice overwhelms me. Never before have I heard her challenge someone above her rank, nor care about the consequences of doing so. Arbiters are to enforce the law and are never encouraged to show the slightest tendency toward rebellion.

"If you wish to have an official report about my arbiters' actions during the terrorist attacks, then you shall have it, but to subtly accuse one of them of disloyalty after having awarded her a medal for valor is insulting! You don't even have the courage to say what it is you think she has done!"

"Mind your tongue, commander," warns the first council member.

Commander Vye rethinks her words before opening her mouth again. "My arbiters put their lives on the line every day to defend this city and those within it, and that includes the plebeians. The law is clear: we are to protect those who dwell within Arel. No distinction is made between citizen or plebeian. Arbiter Noni and Lieutenant Renal have followed and upheld the laws of our great city, and yet, today, you treat them like common criminals!"

"You're dismissed!"

Commander Vye opens her mouth to speak, but rethinks her decision when one of the guards within the room shifts his position, readying his weapon should the need to use it arise. With one final glare at the tribunal, she spins on her heels and steps off the podium, her brisk steps clacking on the slate-colored tile floor as she walks back to where both Renal and I stand.

I swallow the second lump to form in my throat today, awaiting the inevitable.

"Arbiter Noni, take the podium."

Despite the fact that both Renal and Commander Vye accompany me in the room, I feel alone, isolated, as I step toward the podium and the singular, blinding light that bears down upon it, doing my best not to tug at my collar as sweat pools beneath it, causing it to itch. The singular sounds of my boots tapping the floor as I move closer to my inquisition fills my ears, stabbing the buzzing silence that engulfs them, mimicking my apprehensive mood. I place my right foot on the podium, lifting myself into the beam of light, and take my place in its center, placing the sweaty palm of my good hand on the rail before me.

"Arbiter Noni," begins the female member of the council who had first questioned Renal, "tell us, in your own words, what happened the night of the bombings."

"Madam Coun…" I squeak and stop, clearing my throat and willing my voice to be firm and void of emotion. "Madam Councilwoman," I begin again, my voice radiating off the walls as it resonates around me, "the night began as Lieutenant Renal says. We were on patrol when a man threw a rock at one of the loudspeakers. Since he was out after curfew, the lieutenant and I engaged pursuit and apprehended him. That was when our wristbands alerted us to trouble within the city. The lieutenant ordered me to take the suspect to the nearest detainment box while he investigated the summons. I did as commanded, and after the subject was secured, I searched for the lieutenant. I found him lying on the ground unconscious, and soon after, the first bomb went off."

"And did you see who had attacked him?" asks another on the council.

My mind goes back to that night, reminding me of how I had snuck up behind Renal and clubbed him with my own baton. I am the one who had attacked him, but I cannot admit that here. Such a betrayal would wound him.

"No, sir," I reply.

"Did you see who it was he had chanced upon?"

Sigal's face fills my mind's eye, but Renal had lied about seeing him—and why, I do not know—and I cannot contradict him, or he will be arrested and sentenced to the crematorium. "No, sir. No one was there when I found him."

"And after you found him?"

Afterward? Afterward, I helped Sigal and his family escape Arel, taking them to the hole that still remained in the wall, luring the guards away so that they could cross through it and into the wildlands. I am the traitor they seek.

"I shook him awake," I say. "We went to the tunnels and took a railcar to the school within the eastern sector that was on fire. When we reached it, I heard a child screaming, so I ran into the building."

"You just ran inside?" scoffs the female member of the tribunal.

My fist tightens around the cold steel bar within my hand, wishing to strike her for her condescending attitude.

"Yes, ma'am. I ran inside."

"Tell us why."

"Because that is my duty as an arbiter."

Motion in the far corner of the room attracts my attention again, and I turn toward it, peering into the shadows, doing my best to make out the faint outline of a person standing behind its veil, concealed from my view, but I feel eyes upon me, studying me, and reading my body language.

"What happened next?" asks another member of the council, thrusting me back into the present and away from my pondering.

"I found a boy hiding on the stairs. By the time I had reached him, the fire had already blocked the entrance, so we went upstairs to the second floor where I found three more children."

"You said children," interrupts the female member of the tribunal.

"That is what they are," I growl, unsure about her statement and where she is headed.

"I believe you mean two children and one plebeian," the woman continues.

My knuckle turns white as I clutch the bar in front of me, my anger rising, but I take a deep breath and exhale, calming myself and reminding myself that I must remain in control. She awaits my reply, but I remain silent, knowing that if I open my mouth, nothing good will come out of it.

"Well?" says the woman.

Knowing I will not be able to stay silent for much longer, I consider my words, but my anger refuses to be quelled and it forces my mouth to speak before logic and reason have a chance to stop me.

"Well, what?" I challenge her, the annoyance in my voice evident. "You asked me for my version of events, and that is what I am giving you, yet you stop me because I used a term you dislike? Yes, they were children! One may have been a plebeian, but none of them have reached the age of adulthood, so what else should I call them?"

I pause, staring at each of the three people sitting behind the bench, in the dark, safe in their own anonymity.

"You think me disloyal?" I demand.

"You did save the life of a plebeian instead of searching for more citizens," replies the woman.

"She might have witnessed something," I say. "And if she had, how could she tell us if I had allowed her to die?"

"A valid point," says one of the other members.

"Yes," continues the woman, "but we questioned her and she had seen nothing."

"Arbiter Noni had no way of knowing that," counters the other member of the council.

I have had enough of this, of being thought a quisling for doing my duty to Arel.

"I saved her, because as an arbiter, I am charged with protecting both plebeians and citizens. It is written in the law, or have you all forgotten that? If you think me disloyal, then give me a test!"

A sardonic grin crosses the woman's face as her white teeth reflect the light within the room, and the moment I see them, I wish I can recant my statement and take back my challenge, having realized that I have fallen into her trap.

"Yes," says the woman, "I believe a test is in order."

She snaps her fingers and the guard opens the door, allowing two arbiters to enter the chamber, dragging a small girl by the shoulders—her bare feet squeal as her toes slide across the polished tile—and dump her between me and the bench the tribunal sits at: the plebeian girl I had rescued. They had questioned her, all right, as the bruises on her small, pale face attest to. She lays on the floor, crying, her small shoulders hunched, but bobbing up and down with each sob. One of the arbiters kicks her, yelling at her to sit up. As she forces herself into a sitting position, I envision myself jumping over the bar I cling to and pummeling the arbiter as he terrorizes the girl, but one glance at Commander Vye and Renal stops me. I cannot win this scenario. I have brought this upon myself, and if I do as I wish, then we will all be dead. The council intends to kill this girl anyway, I see it on their faces, written within their ice-cold eyes.

"This is not the first time you have been in here, Arbiter Noni," says the woman.

One of the arbiters that had brought the girl inside the room places his sidearm next to her, out of her reach, and steps away with the other beside him. All eyes focus on me. I close my eyes. Please let this be a dream, a nightmare and nothing more, something I can wake from. My eyes open and my heart sinks, dropping into my stomach, weighing it down, as the reality of the situation slams into me, crushing me. This is no dream, and I have two choices: kill the girl, or sentence Renal, Commander Vye, and myself to the crematoriums, and the girl will die anyway.

She lifts her head; her mangled hair falls around her bony face, but parts enough so that her eyes can stare into mine, and I register the physical pain on her face; there are wounds that I cannot see, but severe enough where she will die an agonizing death. Her fate is sealed.

As I stare into her pain-ridden eyes, Chase's words echo through my mind: promise me that you will do what you need to, to survive. If only he knew what that meant, what I would be asked to do.

Summoning my resolve, I bite the inner corner of my lip to keep from screaming, to keep from shouting obscenities at everyone within the room, and step off the podium, away from its condemnatory light, and walk up to the girl, each step heavier than the last. Once I reach her, my gaze shifts from each member of the council, but I keep my face stolid, void of emotion, like theirs. A soft whimper jolts me from my stupor. I reach for the sidearm lying on the floor, and as its icy exterior touches my skin, I remember the first time I had killed a living creature. During my sixth year at the training facility, a knife had been placed in my hand and a live rabbit, tied up, squirmed in front of me. I had hesitated, unable to kill such an innocent creature who had done me no harm and whom I did not need to use for food, but refusal to follow orders is not tolerated, and a firm hand gripped mine, forcing me to swipe the sharp edge of the blade across the rabbit's throat. I cried as its warm blood covered my fingers and received a slap in return; but this girl is no rabbit, and yet here I am, about to take her life, feeling as though another's hand forces mine to act.

"Close your eyes," I whisper to her as I stand up with the weapon in my palm.

Suffocating silence surrounds me, choking me, while whispering to me to do as I am expected to, tempting me to save myself, but the girl's eyes plead with me to end it, to ease her suffering and let her go. She closes them and bows her head as her tangled hair drapes around her shoulders, while I aim for the back of her skull. I squeeze the trigger, and a single shot echoes around me. She falls to the floor.

Without a word, I drop the gun and stalk out of the inquisition room, pushing my way past the guards, refusing to allow them to stop me. Once out the door, I hurry down the carpeted hallway and past the glass windows that stretch from floor to ceiling, not bothering to look out them and at the people scurrying below, oblivious to what has just happened, to what I have done. A door to the restroom looms ahead of me and I charge for it, bursting through it, and I check the stalls to make sure that I am alone and lock the door, not wanting to be bothered. Rambling thoughts scurry though my mind, taunting me with their condemnation. Time passes—how long, I do not know—as I pace back and forth on the crimson floor littered with Arel's insignia as though it mocks me and the turmoil reeling within me, demanding to be released and loosed upon the world to unleash its fury on all it deems guilty.

My reflection stops me. Facing it, I look at the woman staring back at me, her irate and somber eyes filled with confusion and a desire to undo the last hour. I did as ordered. I did my duty. I... I am unworthy to live. I should have been executed, not her. Unable to control the rage within me, I ram my fist into the mirror, dealing out my punishment to the woman glaring back at me, and a scream bursts free from my mouth, drowning the hum of the lights above me.

Once I calm down, I examine my hand and the blood that oozes from a fresh cut. Automatic movements turn the water on, rinsing my hand, washing away the blood before I dry it on the towel that hangs from the wall. Straightening my uniform and regaining my composure, I relax my face, allowing a mask to be shown to the world as I step out of the restroom.

Commander Vye waits for me.

"What is their verdict?" I ask, my voice even.

"Come," she says. "We're going back to the manor."

Deemed loyal once again.

I follow Commander Vye to where Renal waits for us, and we all head to the elevator, taking it to the main floor and leave the building, blending in with the hurrying crowds as though nothing has happened, as though it is just another typical day in Arel.

We catch the first railcar back to the eastern sector—our escort has disappeared, having done her job and is no longer needed—and within an hour, we arrive at the platform where I had made my first arrest. It seems like such a long time ago now, but I am reminded that it has been less than a year. I remember the excitement I had at being commissioned as a full arbiter, but all I feel now is emptiness. Where has my wonderment gone?

I steal a glance at both Renal and Commander Vye, but neither of their faces betray any emotion, or any indication that we have just escaped being stripped of our ranks and sent to the crematoriums. Sometimes I wish to know what they are thinking, but always think better of it in the end. Not knowing someone's mind can be a blessing. Staring straight ahead, I mirror their composure, doing my best to act as though I do not care about what had happened at the Command Division; it is best if I pretend not to, but the image of the girl's pained eyes refuses to leave me alone, determined that I relive the moment over and over again.

We arrive back at the manor, and I stop the moment I walk through the door: Tapiwa waits for us, seated in a chair near the entrance.

"Afternoon," she greets us as the door slides shut behind us.

"President Tapiwa," says Commander Vye, doing her best to hide the note of surprise in her voice, but a small portion of it comes through. "What can we do for you?"

"I am here to speak with your young arbiter, here." Tapiwa points at me as she rises from her seat, her ivory train with golden circles embroidered on it matches the loose-fitting pants she wears, and my breath catches in my throat as I remember where I had seen it before: my hearing from this morning. It was her who had been standing in the shadows, watching the proceedings, and as I wonder what her motive for such a thing is, I also ponder how she arrived at the manor before us until… The presidential transport. That explains it. She must have taken it here the moment our hearing had ended and ordered the driver to hide the vehicle so that we would not see it upon our arrival, thus concealing her surprise for us. Such an act is a way to catch us off-guard, and it worked.

"You may use my office," offers Commander Vye, and Tapiwa nods her appreciation as she strolls down the corridor to my commander's one place of privacy.

Unsure of what to do, I remain where I am, apprehensive about one of our presidents being here, but bolt from my spot the moment Commander Vye hisses at me to follow her. I hurry down the hallway and burst into the room as Tapiwa positions herself in my commander's chair, making me uneasy, since I have never witnessed anyone, except Commander Vye, sitting in it. The colorless walls and floor may match the organized desk and it's bare, black top, but Tapiwa's ostentatious outfit makes its plain features seem out of place.

"It is a bit warm in here," comments Tapiwa, removing her fitted jacket and baring her shoulders, something I have never seen before, "isn't it?"

I remain silent. Arbiters are not allowed to comment on the warmth or chilliness of our environment; we are expected to adapt and to endure as these are trivial matters and our duties come first.

"Do relax, dear," says Tapiwa in a silky voice, but behind all the charm and her honeyed tone lies a lioness in waiting, crouched, poised, and ready to strike.

"You came here to see me, Madam President?"

"Yes," replies Tapiwa. "I must say that you made quite the statement at your congratulatory dinner."

"If I upset anyone there, that was not my intention. I understand if my rudeness requires me to make some sort of amends."

"So willing to prove yourself."

I cannot tell if she mocks me or is complimenting me, but her grin unnerves me.

"I heard about your hearing," says Tapiwa, her voice holding an ounce of concern. "Accusing you of neglecting your duties, and after I had pinned an award to your chest. The tribunal should have known better than to question your commitment to Arel, though you will understand that they must be allowed to come to their own conclusions."

"Yes, ma'am."

"Though I think you impressed them."

Impressed is not the term I would have used. Her flowery statements, vague sentences, and praising manner causes the hairs on the back of my neck to stand on end, and should I not have been wearing my jacket, I might have shivered from the chill breeze that emanates from her. I wish she would get to the point.

"President Tapiwa," I say, "permission to speak freely."

"By all means. We are friends here."

"When are you going to tell me why you are here?"

Tapiwa chuckles, showcasing her pearled teeth.

"I knew I liked you. So quick to embark on the next task. You are right, of course. I am here for a reason." She stands and looks out the window. "We have been having trouble in our mines. They are not producing like they should. Their quotas are down. Considering your actions on the wall during our last attack, and how you handled yourself during the terrorist attacks, I think you are best suited to deal with this crisis."

"You want me to go to the mines."

"Temporarily, of course. I would not ask you to take a permanent assignment there."

"Why me?" I ask. Something about this doesn't add up. "I am not a ranking arbiter. Perhaps someone with more experience, someone with..."

"You have received one of the highest honors that Arel can bestow upon a citizen. You have something that the current commander there does not."

"What about the other recipients? They must be more..."

"They are needed here, for the moment."

Needed. This explains why Tapiwa was at my hearing. She wanted to know how I would react and if I would do what was demanded of me. I must have passed on both counts. I am not needed at the mines; this is just another test, another way to measure my resolve, and if I do manage to help increase production, that will be an added bonus.

"I know I am asking much of you, Noni,"—Tapiwa faces me with affection, the sort a mother would display to her child—"but I need your help. If we do not meet our quotas, we could lose power and be left defenseless against our enemies. I'm not asking you to leave right now. You need a chance to heal first." She glances at the sling that holds my left arm and the feeling of having been set up wafts over me.

"Whatever you wish of me, Madam President," I say, my voice hollow, devoid of the very essence that makes us human, "I will do it."

"I have complete faith in you. I will need to okay this with your commander, as she has the final say, but I'm sure she will agree that this experience will be good for you. A chance to prove yourself. We will discuss this in more detail at a later date."

Yes, another chance to prove myself.

A commotion rises outside the door, and both Tapiwa and I rush out into the hallway to find Anan hovering over Gwen, squeezing her thin wrist, as she cowers on the floor, pleading with him to let her go.

"What is the meaning of all this!" demands Commander Vye, storming onto the scene, her face contorted in anger, ready to lash out at any who dare disturb the order within her home.

"I caught this wretch stealing from me," replies Anan.

"I didn't..." Gwen protests, but her pleas are cut short when

Anan backhands her. I start for her, but a firm grip seizes my good arm, holding me back, and when I look behind me, Renal's stern face moves side to side, warning me to not get involved.

"Stop!" commands Commander Vye and Anan steps away. She glares at Gwen, aware that Tapiwa watches with interest. "What did you steal?"

"I didn't steal anything!" whines Gwen.

"You lying little…" Anan begins, but Commander Vye seizes him by the throat and slams him into the wall.

"Do not disobey me again," she growls at him.

While everyone watches the exchange between the commander and Anan, Gwen reaches in her pocket, pulling out a small vial of cologne—arbiters are not supposed to have such luxuries or be worried about their body odor, but some allowances are made, and there are always a few who sneak in contraband—but before she can show it to those gathered around her, Chase appears from behind and snatches it from her, saying, "I took it!"

Commander Vye faces him, her dark eyes ready to set fire to the entire building, but her gaze is not what attracts my attention; Tapiwa's appears mystified before morphing into pleasure.

"You took it?" demands the commander.

"Yes," says Chase, and I wish he would stop talking, though I know why he takes the blame.

"Why?"

"No reason."

"Why would Anan say she had it?" Commander Vye points at Gwen.

"Because Anan is a known liar," says Chase.

"You little—" Anan lunges for Chase, but Commander Vye whips out her baton and hits him in the face with it.

"I told you that disobedience will not be tolerated," she says. She takes the bottle of cologne from Chase and turns it over in her hand, examining it as the creases within her forehead deepen with each second. "What were you doing with this?"

Anan clamps his mouth shut, not liking that everyone's focus is now on him.

"He says he stole it. Ask him."

"I thought you accused the girl of stealing."

Beads of sweat dot Anan's brow as his lies unravel around him, ensnaring him within his own trap while Commander Vye's words hang in the air.

"Maybe they both stole it."

"A plebeian"—Commander Vye holds out the half-used bottle of cologne—"would not have the means to procure such an item, but an arbiter, wishing to attract company, would."

Anan quivers under Commander Vye's stare.

"This sort of item is not allowed here and I do not like being lied to."

"But…" begins Anan.

"Get down to the basement and clean the sewer lines. You will scrub them by hand and not show your face until you are done." When he starts to protest, Commander Vye adds, "Or, perhaps you would like to spend the night with the president's guards? I'm sure they can make you more compliant."

"They wouldn't mind entertaining a guest," Tapiwa says, enjoying the spectacle.

Anan rises to his feet, salutes, and stalks away without a word.

"As for your punishment"—Commander Vye turns toward Chase—"you shall…"

"I think Arbiter Noni should decide," interrupts Tapiwa. "This is a perfect opportunity for her to learn another part of an arbiter's duties."

"As you wish." Commander Vye looks at me and Renal releases my arm. "What is your verdict?"

I share a look with Chase, not wanting to decide his fate; the plebeian girl's face haunts me and I see her within his determined face and within Gwen's terrified one. I hesitate, wanting to be anywhere but here, wishing this had not been thrust upon me, while the notion that all this had been orchestrated from the beginning gnaws at me, churning my stomach into knots, until I almost think I will vomit.

"Noni!"

Commander Vye's harsh tone jerks me into action.

"Theft is forbidden in Arel for both plebeians and citizens. Assuming this is his first offense..." my voice trails off as I try to think, desperate for a punishment that won't result in Chase's death—a first offense when it comes to stealing results in spending a week in a detention facility, while a second offense results in a broken hand, and execution for the third—but the crushing atmosphere enveloping me warns me that this will end only one way. "For a first offense," I begin again, "and considering his station, he should be sent to one of the agricultural sectors for a period of one month."

Arel has three agricultural sectors, none of which are in the main part of the city, where some of the most troublesome residents go. From sun up to sun down, they labor underneath the hot sun, tilling the land, pulling the weeds, or harvesting. Many never survive their sentence there, but Chase will have a better chance in such a place than at the mines, which is another place undesirables are sent, adding to my own trepidation at being asked to go there.

"A suitable punishment," says Tapiwa, and arbiters lead Chase away, brushing past us and out the door, while Gwen remains frozen on the floor, glaring at me; the loathing in her eyes ignites a fire that burns my skin as heat rises around my collar under her gaze. I have taken her brother away from her.

"You all are dismissed!" says Commander Vye, and the arbiters gathered around us disperse.

Heavy boots pound the wooden floors as those gathered leave as fast as they can, not wanting to be on the receiving end of our commander's anger, but amidst the ordered commotion, I do not move as a tumultuous sea of conflicting emotions rage within me, only to be stopped when I notice Tapiwa leaving and glimpse her vainglorious grin in the mirror as she walks past, telling me that none of this was an accident.

Chapter 3

Six Weeks Later

Six weeks have passed since the explosions, since the fire, since I helped Sigal escape with his family, and since my hearing; six weeks since Chase was sent to the agricultural areas, and his continued absence puzzles me as he should have returned two weeks ago when his month-long sentence had ended.

A line of glowing red fills the space above the wall, casting a warm glow on a wall within my room, making the interior glow with its ostentatious color, turning my walnut-colored skin a rosy shade. I glance out my window at the wall, at our protection and prison, watching the humanoid shapes stroll across the top, keeping watch for anything suspicious, for any activity outside that might mean another attack. Puppets, that is what they look like, parading around as their strings are pulled by their master, doing what they are told to do, with no thought of their own, no will to do otherwise.

As the orange orb of the sun peeks over the wall, causing the glow in my room to transform to a burnt orange before morphing into a bright yellow, like that of calla lilies, attempting to cast away

the shadow of the wall, but its gloomy presence remains, strength-
ened by the sun's light, ever present, ever watching, I think about
Chase forced to live in the outside world. The agricultural areas
are not within the heart of Arel, but outside the main wall, though
they are not far and have their own defenses, protected by arbiters
assigned there to keep our food reserves safe from predators. I remember a story told to me once while I was still a recruit. A band of
outsiders had attacked one of the three agricultural areas that Arel
has. They were starving and had been rewarded with bullets.

I stare beyond the wall at the grass beyond and the trees that lie
even further away, wondering where Sigal is. Did he and his family
find a safe place to live? Where have they gone? Did they join the
outsiders, preferring their way of life over ours? Did they find the
fabled city, one that is supposed to be a paradise? I hope they are
safe, that they find what they are searching for.

I snatch my towel, glad that my arm is no longer confined by
a sling, since my shoulder has healed, and head for the bathroom
where the showers are. It isn't a large area: four toilettes, four showers, and four sinks separated by dividers; if you aren't there early,
you have to wait your turn, just like at the training facility. I stroll
through the dim hallway and the door to the bathroom slides open
upon my approach, allowing me to step into its plain and musty interior, lit by the fluorescent lights that spark to life the moment they
sense my movement. Hanging my towel on one of the hooks next to
an empty shower, I step into the moist interior, ignoring the speck
of mildew growing in the seams, and turn on the water, allowing
its chilled essence to wash over me. The manor has two water heat-
ers, one for the showers and the other for everything else, but Commander Vye refuses to allow the heater for the showers to be turned
on—sometimes she makes an exception in the winter—stating that
she wants her arbiters to remain rigid, not softened by a few niceties. I prefer cold showers. Sometimes, they are the only way for me
to prove that I am alive.

As I snatch a bar of soap—shared, just like at the training facility—my mind drifts back to the plebeian girl at the tribunal and the woman who insisted I dispose of her to prove myself. A plethora of emotions, ones I am not used to acknowledging, boil to the surface and bombard me with their accusations, repeating over and over that I should have done more to save the girl. I slam the bar of soap into the side of the shower stall, breaking it in half and watch as bits of it crumble away, falling away from my palm and into the drain beneath my feet, disappearing as water rushes over them the way a river drowns the rocks within its sandy bed. I shut off the water and snatch my towel—gray, like everything else around here—and wrap it around myself as I braid my long hair so as to keep it out of my face.

Voices enter the room. Not wanting to speak to anyone, I hide in one of the shower stalls, thankful that the ones here have a curtain, unlike at the training facility. They grow louder and bounce off the tile walls, allowing me to overhear them.

"How do you know?" asks one.

"I overheard the commander," replies the other, and I recognize it as Anan's voice, my loathing for him simmering just below the surface. I never did think much of him, but when Sheila told me what he did to her, such dislike turned to abject hatred, and it's not just the female plebeians he harasses, but the female arbiters as well.

"And?"

"We're going to hit someplace tonight."

"Are you sure you overheard correctly?"

"You doubting me?" Anan's dark tone sends shivers down my spine while I squeeze myself against the shower wall, staying as silent as I can.

"No, it's… You haven't been on the commander's list of favorites lately."

"It's that dumb Noni. That bitch is going to get what's coming to her someday."

He hates me. The feeling is mutual.

"So tonight? Where?" asks the first.

"Some old guy's place," replies Anan. "His daughter, Mora, I think—"

Mora! I know that name!

"—was executed not long ago for smuggling people out of the city. Sounds like she was a plebeian lover. The arbiter council doesn't fully believe that he knew nothing, so they're searching the place tonight."

"Why not just execute him?"

I know why. After the bombings, things have been fragile within Arel. People are on edge, looking for any reason to blame those in authority for what happened, and despite the investigation, arbiters are no closer to learning who orchestrated the attacks, despite Kumi's speeches of how we will bring the perpetrators to justice. The people of Arel want answers, and there is talk that these bombings have rekindled a rebellious spirit, and the threat of another uprising permeates everything, overshadowing the façade of contentment.

"Who cares? At least we get to crack some skulls tonight."

"And you get to get away from the sewers," jokes the other, and I imagine Anan's irate scowl at such a statement. "I need to go," says the man, and he speeds out of the bathroom before Anan can retaliate.

A curtain closes, rattling the rings that hold it to the rod as the water turns on, and I slip out of my stall, glad that my bare feet make no noise as I creep to the door. Something glinting on a bench snatches my attention: Anan's wristband. I never wear mine in the shower and leave it in my room, just like most of us, but here is Anan's laying out in the open, and a devious thought enters my mind. I snatch the wristband and hurry out of the shower room, my feet padding on the floor as I rush to Anan's room at the end of the hall, my towel flapping open as I trot, threatening to fall off me. I reach his quarters and the door slides open, allowing me to slip inside. I don't have much time. I scan his wristband against the wall monitor and it flashes to life, greeting Anan and asking what he would like to do. Thinking fast, I give Mora's name and the day I first heard it, amazed at all the text and images that scroll across the screen. Arbiters can always access information, at least what hasn't been deemed classified or above our rank, but such inquiries are tracked, a thought that rolls through my mind as I clutch Anan's wristband.

I tap a video and it enlarges, showing a woman's battered face, her left eye swollen to the point of closing it, while her enlarged lip makes it impossible for her to speak with any clarity, and something deep within me tells me that this is Mora, the daughter of the man who spared me from being captured the night I had snuck out with Chase. He didn't have to, and yet, he did it anyway, refusing to turn me in when he had a chance. I close the video and tap another folder. Orders to search the place spring up, and I scan through it, looking for the time. Midnight.

I close the file and turn off the wall monitor. Time has gotten away from me and Anan will be done with his shower soon as arbiters are expected to be quick, since showers are for good hygiene, not lingering in. I hurry from Anan's room to the bathroom, hoping that no one enters the hallway while I do, having no idea how I would explain my presence and the fact that the wristband in my possession is not mine. The sounds of water spilling from a showerhead fill my ears, the most pleasant of music, as I step inside the room and head for the bench where Anan has placed his things. I put the wristband back, but it falls to the tile floor with a thump just as the water shuts off, and I dash behind a corner to the area where the toilets are, holding my breath, forcing myself not to gasp or utter a sound. I peek around the corner, watching as Anan wraps a gray towel, standard issue like mine, around his waist, and if I hadn't already known him, I might have thought his chiseled muscles, accentuated by the light reflecting off the water dripping down his black, smooth, hairless skin, pleasing to look at. My heart pounds against my chest as he picks up his wristband and studies it, wondering how it had fallen to the floor, but he shrugs his shoulders and slips it on, before leaving.

A slow, steady stream of air escapes my mouth as I slow my heart rate and calm myself before I rush to my room, after making certain that Anan is nowhere to be seen, and snatch my uniform, not caring if I wrinkle it or cause a few creases to form. There is something I must do and there isn't much time. I may not have been able to help that girl, but I can try to spare Mora's father from the wrath of Arel. Once dressed, I rush out of my room and stomp down the stairs, taking two at a time, ignoring the hollow sounds that fill the enclosed area around me as I hurry to the main floor. My right foot lands on the bottom step, and I stop, noticing Gwen in the foyer, sweeping the solid wood floor, reminding me of Sheila when I entered the manor for the first time. My heart sinks as sympathy festers within it, filling it, until it overflows with the knowledge that she is alone because of me.

No one is around, one of the quieter days within the manor, and a short peek down the hallway leading to Commander Vye's office verifies that she is occupied, as the closed door to her office indicates. I walk toward her in a more mature manner, wondering what I will say to her as words fumble through my raging mind in an effort to convince me that they can convey what my guilty subconsciousness wishes to reveal. I want to comfort her, reassure her that everything will be all right, that it is only for a little while and her brother will return, but my leaden feet drag on the floor, refusing to carry me the closer I get to her.

Her broom swishes across the floor, kicking up bits of dust as she piles it in the middle near where she had placed the dustpan, and I step around it, careful not to disturb it, reminded of Sheila and how I had kicked her pile of dirt, unconcerned about the extra work I had caused her to do.

"Gwen," I say, but she turns away, showing her back to me. "Gwen, I'm sorry about Chase."

"Leave me alone," Gwen's small voice cuts through me, slicing my heart and making me feel worse than I did a few moments ago.

"He'll be back."

The broom stops. Gwen faces me with a vengeful look on her face, something I thought she could never possess, but the anger burning within her gray eyes bore through me, invisible lasers carrying out her will.

"Back? You sent him to the agricultural district. Once there, you never leave. It's no different from the mines or the crematorium."

I look around as her voice echoes around me, but if anyone is close enough to overhear, they remain hidden.

"I'm sorry, Gwen, but I didn't have a choice."

"You always have a choice," she spits.

Do I? Loose strands of her hair drape across her face, reminding me of the night I had caught her out after curfew, the first time I ever saw her, and as she stares at me, the face of the plebeian girl from my hearing fills my mind again, bleeding and bruised with terrified, pleading eyes, begging me to release her. I may have had a choice then, but none of my decisions would have ended well. Even if I had not elected to do as was commanded of me, to execute her, she still would have been murdered along with Commander Vye and Renal. One life or three, that was my choice. What Tapiwa had made me do with Chase was another test to confirm my loyalty to Arel, and if I hadn't done what she had wanted, he would have been sent to a far worse place, and so would have Commander Vye. One life or two, that was my second choice for the day.

"Sometimes," I say, my voice soft, just above a whisper, desperate to hold back the burning sting of the tears threatening to break free, reminding me that I have not cried since my days within the training facility, since the day they had been beaten out of me, "no matter what we choose, all decisions lead to the same end."

Gwen's hardened eyes never leave mine and I envision her playing scenarios within her mind of what she would do to me to punish me, if she could.

"Just go."

A single tear escapes my eye as I step away from her and head for the door, wiping it away the second it rolls down my cheek: another soul destroyed by my hand. Sniffling and swallowing the wad of spit in my mouth in an effort to eradicate the lump in my throat, I straighten my jacket, squaring my shoulders and march out of the manor, obeying Gwen's request.

I reach the end of the driveway to the manor and glance around, noting the hunched shoulders of not just the plebeians, but also the citizens as well, as they hurry to their destination, not wanting to be caught away from home should another attack happen, the fear in their eyes evident. Some peek out from under the brim of their hats to look at me, while others trot across the street, wanting to get as far away from me as possible, something I have become accustomed to. The bell of the trolley dings as it speeds down the street, stopping long enough to allow passengers to either board or disembark, before continuing down the street, following the steel tracks laid before it.

Turning, I head for the center of the eastern sector, retracing my steps to the man's home, hoping that I can find it again without attracting attention. A man on a bike speeds past me, almost running into me as he peddles down the road, hurrying away from me and delving into the heart of this sector and its bustling activity, causing me to jump to the side, startled, and crash into a woman walking by me. She falls to the ground, losing her hold on the bag in her arms, and it lands on the cracked cement, spilling its contents to the horror of the woman as she watches everything unfold. Her brown eyes flick to me, wide and unblinking as she waits for me to decide her punishment. Rubbing my shoulder—though it's healed, it's still a bit sore and, of course, it is the one that I landed on, thus taking the full impact of my fall— I study the items on the sidewalk, wondering what she is doing with first aid kits, medicine, antibiotic cream, and medical tape, though I have an idea. We stare at one another a moment, me in my black uniform, complete with Arel's crest on the wristbands of my jacket, with my long hair pulled back into a bun, looking every bit the arbiter of Arel, while she freezes on the walk in a basic button-up shirt and trousers, not the sort of clothing one of the wealthier members of Arelian society would wear, meaning that she is of the lower class, wishes to go unnoticed, or both, looking at me as her eyes have still not blinked or left my gaze, while bits of her frayed hair—the sort of locks that detest humidity, heat, cold, any sort of weather, choosing to remain unruly at all times—float in the breeze, bouncing in a way that reminds me of a seesaw. I reach for a roll of medical tape, pondering it as the ribbed fibers brush against my palm.

"Where do you seem to be off to in such a hurry?" I ask, doing my duty as an arbiter, but trying to not sound so cold.

"No... nowhere," replies the woman, her voice shaking, "just heading to... to my mother's."

"Mother?"

An old term. Most people handed to a couple to be raised refer to their adoptive parents as "parental units". Arel learned that people need some sense of belonging and feeling loved, which is why they allow some to have the semblance of family, but they are not encouraged to become too attached.

"I was given to her when she was approved for her permit to adopt a child."

I consider her words. The only way to know for certain if she is telling the truth will be to take her to an information booth and have her palm scanned, but if it turns out she is lying, then I will have to detain her, which means those depending on her for these supplies will suffer. If I let her go and she gets caught by another arbiter, she will tell them of me, of that I have no doubt, which will result in my arrest. As I consider my options, Gwen's anger fills my mind, reminding me of what I had sentenced her brother to, and memories of the plebeian quarters—their fear, their desperation, and their hopelessness—waft over me, and I hand the medical tape to the frightened woman who takes it from me, unsure at first, and stuffs it back into her bag.

"You should be more careful," I tell her as we stand up.

Her head swivels around as she ponders over whether this is a trick or not, waiting for me to change my mind or for other arbiters to jump on us and take her to the Ministry of Justice.

"Have a good day," I tell her and walk away.

She remains frozen in her position for a moment before running off, getting as far away from me as she can.

I stroll down the sidewalk, retracing my steps from the night I evaded a drone while out after curfew and without authorization, ignoring the honking of horns, the bell of the trolley, the whistle of the railcar as it soars above everyone, and the incessant conversations of those brave enough to leave their homes for the day. I turn down an alley, making certain that no one watches me, while pretending to be doing my normal rounds. The dip in the hole-ridden pavement looks familiar, but it is difficult to tell in the bright sunlight when I remember seeing it in the dark of night. The constant stomping of footsteps on the walk just beyond the alley echo around me, circling me in waves as the noise reverberates off the brick sides of the buildings towering over me, sheltering me in their shadows as I make my way further in. I pause. Which way did I go? Closing my eyes, I picture that night in my mind, remembering my fear of being caught, my apprehension and desire to get away, and... a fence.

Looking around, I spot a dilapidated fence, run-down and decayed from neglect and horrid weather conditions, and I hurry toward it, crawling through the hole in it like I had that night, being careful not to tear my uniform, or else face the unnerving task of explaining such an infraction to Commander Vye. Once through, I hurry to the end of the alley, making certain that I keep my pace even, my posture erect, and act as though this is a routine investigation as no one dares question an arbiter, unless I act as though I have something to hide. I reach the edge of a building and join the meandering crowd as people rush by me, keeping their heads low and giving me some space, not wanting to bump into me or give me a reason to detain them. A woman's broad hat brushes the side of my temple as she walks by, unaware or unconcerned that her hat has just struck me, as she walks down the sidewalk, and I study the brim of her orange and green hat with a pink daisy in its center almost as wide as her pudgy hips.

The square.

I remember running across it and to another alley. Stepping off the walk, I trot across the street, avoiding the trolley as it roars down its tracks beeping at me to get out of its way, and for a moment, I am thrust back to my first day here when I had decided to hitch a ride on it in an effort to report to Commander Vye on time, with no such luck. Children's laughter catches my attention, and I notice a group of school children accompanied by their teachers out on an excursion, their yellow uniforms almost as bright as the sun as they glow in the daylight, walking across the street, when one of the girls in the back drops something. She turns around to get it. In horror, I watch as the trolley speeds down its track, not caring if a child is in its path as it hurries to get to its destination so that it can dump its passengers and get new ones.

I sprint for the girl. The trolley nears, but I push myself to go faster, my feet flying over the hole-ridden pavement as I charge through the menagerie of people who remain unaware of the girl's plight. The rumble of the trolley fills my ears, pushing all other extraneous sounds out of my mind as I focus on reaching the girl before it does, my heart pounding in my throat as I force my lungs to take in air, utilizing the oxygen to the best of my advantage. I shove someone out of my way, unconcerned about sending him flying, forcing him to let go of his paper-wrapped bundle that skitters across the ground, stopping when it hits the curb.

"Move!" I scream at another too busy talking to her friends to notice my desperation. She starts to say something, but clamps her mouth shut when she notices my uniform and the speed I am moving at.

Almost there.

The girl picks up her fallen object and looks up just in time to see the trolley coming for her, but she freezes. I quicken my pace, almost tripping as I run with my legs threatening to entangle themselves. The incessant beeping of the trolley warns those around us that something is wrong, but the girl refuses to move, rooted to her spot, holding a small spherical object in her tiny hands, her face contorted in fear. Her mouth opens in a scream just as I reach her, and I wrap my arms around her slender frame as I push her out of the way, and we both tumble across the ground; the trolley just misses us and continues down its track as though nothing has happened. I examine the girl, making certain that she is all right and not injured when her teacher rushes up to us.

"Bethany!" she scolds her. "How many times have you been told to look where you are going?"

I stand up, glaring at the woman, thinking her harsh words unnecessary. Even if the girl does need reminding, this isn't the time.

"I think the important thing is that she's okay," I say, and the teacher ceases her badgering of the whimpering girl.

"I meant no disrespect, arbiter, but this one tends to daydream and not pay attention," the teacher tells me.

I look at the girl as tears run down her cheek. She cannot be more than six years old.

"Are you injured?" I ask her.

"My knee hurts," she answers in a small voice, not bothering to look up from the ground.

I kneel down and inspect her knee. The material has worn through and droplets of blood dot her kneecap; it is a scrape, nothing more.

"It's just a scratch," I tell her in a gentle voice, dabbing her knee with the sleeve of my jacket, and scowling when I notice a tear. "You'll be fine. Let this be a reminder to always be aware of your surroundings and to look where you are going."

The girl nods and runs back to her classmates.

The teacher says nothing as she watches me, before turning to head back to her group of students, and as she leads them away, she steals one last look at me, but I am already headed to the other side of the square. Once I reach it, I set a brisk pace down the alley and meet a wall, its bricks different shapes and different sizes, making it stand out in Arel's society of conformity, and I stop, trying to picture how this place looked at night.

Did I turn left or right?

Once again, I close my eyes, trying to remember that night: the acrid smell in the air, the chilled damp permeating through my clothing and soaking my skin, the eerie silence, broken only by the whine of the drone and the shouts of the arbiters pursuing me. Left. I had turned left. I dash down the left fork of the alley, darting past shuttered windows and locked doors as my foot splashes in a small pool of water where the asphalt has crumbled away, forming a foot-sized hole. No one is around, allowing me to continue unhindered and without the worry of being seen. I walk faster, my heart skipping a beat as I near where I remember the man living, unsure of what I will say to him once I find him.

I come across a dead end, or what appears to be a dead end, and stop. Two doors loom before me, and I stare at them both, uncertain of which one to try. If I knock on the wrong one, I will need a plausible story for my being there, one that Commander Vye will believe in case the person who answers it complains. People can complain about what they believe to be unfair detainment by an arbiter, few do, but if the person behind the door does, I need to be prepared. Just when I think I have a good story, I start for the furthest door and stop the moment I hear a knob turn and hinges creak, afraid of being caught out here, since this is not my section to patrol today. I dart behind a corner. The door closest to me opens and out steps the same man who had helped me the night I had snuck out of the manor. He shuts his door and goes to the second one, the one I had first intended to knock on, opens it, and leaves.

Checking to make sure no one watches me, I step out of hiding and approach the second door with caution, pausing when I reach it, straining to listen to the sounds beyond it. I reach for the handle and twist, easing the door open and almost gawk at what I see: people strolling by talking, some running to catch a moving walkway, while others mosey down the walk, all unconcerned about me watching them. I am such a fool! There was a door here the entire time that led to another street, which I could have used that night, but I never tested it, assuming that it was someone's home; though, there could have been arbiters on the other side waiting for me, I remind myself.

I step through the doorway, closing it, and mingle with the crowd, matching their pace, stepping in time with them, as though we are all one as I follow after the man, keeping him in sight, but doing my best to not alert him to my presence. As I walk, I turn back, getting a better look at the mysterious door and the building it is attached to. Even from the outside, the door looks as though it goes to someone's dwelling and not to an alley. Who constructed it this way and why is a mystery, and one I will never learn the answer to, but it must be convenient for those who know of its existence. Reminding myself that I have a mission, I turn back around and hurry after the man who had saved me. He strolls with the crowd, following the wave of people, blending in, while remaining aware of what's around him, while I keep my distance, doing my best to pretend to be doing my rounds. He turns and heads to an entranceway, and I follow his movements, staying behind him as he walks through a door.

Hurrying, and not wanting to lose him, I shove my way through the crowded sidewalk, hiking up five stairs—the corner of the third one is missing as bits of it crumble away, demonstrating a desperate need for repair—and to the door at the top. I stare at the barrier in front of me, noting its color of dried blood. As my mind races with thoughts of how I must have been detected, I take the final step

toward the door and it slides open with a whoosh sound, only audible to those close to it, greeting me with a dark hole. Wary, I walk
inside, glancing at the sign above me that reads, "ES Dine In" and
wondering what I will find inside.

The distinct clatter of silverware on plates, shrouded by soft
murmurings as people converse over their meals, being careful to
keep their volume low, lest inquisitive ears pick up their sentiments,
greets me as the door closes behind me; my eyes roam the interi-
or of the restaurant, feeling out of place and how I do not belong,
despite the arbiters sitting at some of the tables, lined in neat rows
with the same amount of spacing on each side, consuming their
meals with little to no thought about my presence. Waiters move
from table to table, providing refreshments, only water is served to
the arbiters while the other patrons are allowed to indulge in more
delectable fare, dressed in matching uniforms of pale blue and each
with an apron tied around their waists. Though not horrifying, the
uniform atmosphere is not inviting, making me miss Sigal's place
and the boisterous activity that I always found there as he hopped
from table to table, giving every person that warm smile of his as he
talked about his food, while slipping dessert dishes to those who
weren't supposed to have any. Spotting a camera, I step to the side,
staying out of its line of site, my stomach turning in knots as I sneak
around, avoiding eye contact and the lights attached to the wall,
casting a bluish glow on the paisley floral paper, until I am underneath it and pull out the cord, unplugging it.

I scan those indulging in food, searching for the man I had followed here, and each moment I spend in this place, my chest tightens as I hope that I am not recognized by any of the arbiters here.
I spot him sitting next to a wall at a table for two, munching on a
bowl of pasta, almost as though he has been expecting me. Acting
casual, I migrate between chairs and tables, staying as close to the
perimeter as I can, until I reach him and sit down in the chair across
from him.

"Continue eating," I tell him.

He glances at me while holding his fork in midair encased in noodles as bits of white sauce drip from them, landing on the beige tablecloth. No words escape his mouth. No semblance of surprise fills his eyes as the intelligence behind them studies me, more bemused than anything else.

"I was wondering when you would find me," he says, placing the pasta in his mouth and speaking around it. "I had expected you before my lunch arrived. You'd think arbiters would be better trained."

He was expecting me!

"How..." I begin, but he cuts me off.

"You're not as good at hiding as you think you are."

I glare at him.

"Actually, I saw your shadow. When the sun is at a certain point in the sky, even when you think you are well-hidden in that alley, it will cast a faint shadow on the wall across from my door. Don't worry. I'm the only one who knows about it."

Despite the smugness of his response, and how much it irks me, I rein in my annoyance and anger at having been made a fool of and try to find the words to tell him about the planned raid, wondering how best to inform him, before realizing that there is no good way to say it, but before I can, a waiter rushes up to the table and places a glass of water on it, asking for my order. My mind goes blank. I have no idea what they serve here and the stale air carries no aroma of spices or tanginess, not like what Sigal's place had where my mouth salivated the moment I walked through the door. I have to order something. If I do not, it will look suspicious.

"Whatever I am allowed to eat," I say, holding up my wrist, allowing the man to scan the thin band around it, thus deleting funds from my allotment and cursing the fact that he showed up and can bear witness to my talking with the man across from me.

"Do you want the zucchini or asparagus."

"Surprise me," I say in a dry tone, indicating that I want to be left alone.

Insulted, but knowing it is not wise to upset an arbiter, the wait-er holds his tablet to his stomach, bows, and leaves.

"That wasn't…" begins the man.

"They're raiding your place tonight," I blurt out, while keeping my voice low.

The man puts his fork down, allowing it to sink into the bed of half-eaten noodles.

"When?"

"Midnight. They don't believe that you didn't know anything about your daughter's secret life—"

"You mean smuggling people out of Arel."

"—but are too afraid to just arrest you."

"That," replies the man, "is because of what I do for them."

"And what is that?"

"I'm an engineer."

Confusion must have filled my face because he chuckles.

"I don't wear the red uniform because I am not that kind of en-gineer. I build weapons for them, the ones that help you arbiters pro-tect us all from those who live outside, as well as fortify buildings."

"Not all of them are hospitable," I say, remembering the time my convoy had been attacked by barbarians.

"My dear, I am not so foolish as to think that they are. Some of them are just as our leaders describe them as: barbaric, cruel in-dividuals who thirst for war, but some are the opposite, and some-thing tells me you already knew that." He looks into my eyes, the way he did the night he prevented me from being caught out after curfew. "So, the killer now suffers from pity and doubt."

"I didn't come here…"

"Why did you come here?" asks the man.

"You saved my life that night. You could have turned me in."

"I'm afraid that was not possible. If I had, they would have searched my place for certain and found those banned books, among other things."

"Are you always this snarky?"

"A trait my late wife always complained about. Call it a bad habit if you will. Midnight you say?"

"Yes, and you can consider us even."

"I never entertained the thought of you owing me. I'm not sure how I am to get rid of all that contraband."

"I suggest you find a way."

The man frowns at my statement.

"There is one other thing," I say as the conversation from the night in the presidents' home enters my mind, "Mora is dead. They never sent her to the crematorium. They fed her to the dogs."

The man's cheeks twitch as he holds in the emotions whirling within him, willing his anger to remain confined, instead of bursting forth and making its presence known for all to see, but his eyes conceal nothing, and I read the pain written within them as he struggles to keep his composure.

He stands up, taking one last sip of his drink, before speaking again. "Do try the pasta. It's not bad for a last meal, but nothing compares to the linguine that Sigal served. How unfortunate that his place has been shut down due to health concerns."

I watch as the man disappears. Of course, Arelian officials used a cover story for Sigal's place being closed. It wouldn't do to let everyone know that he chose to leave the city and had succeeded in being smuggled out.

The waiter appears with my plate, smiling at a particular waitress as he exits the kitchen, giving her a flirtatious wink and giving me an idea as I know that I must do something to encourage him to remain silent about my presence here, because if he talks, I'll be sent to the crematorium and all record of my existence will be erased. He puts a ceramic plate with green edging encircling it in front of me with three bean salad, asparagus, and meatloaf, all in their own section on the plate and each a single serving, making me miss Sigal's overflowing platters of goodness, but before the waiter can step away, I snatch the collar of his shirt and yank him close, until my lips are against his earlobe. "If you tell anyone anything other than I ate alone, I will make certain that your life is a living hell, starting with that waitress over there."

His frightened eyes flicker over to the woman he had flirted with moments before, and judging by the quickening of his breaths, I know I have touched the correct pressure point.

"Do we have an understanding?" I ask.

He nods, and I release him, allowing him to run away and hide in the kitchen, leaving me alone with my meal, while a hollow void fills my stomach as my conscience chastises me for my actions: I have become Molers.

Chapter 4

Midnight

Alone lamp flickers in my room, casting eerie shadows on the wall, each one circling the one my body creates—monsters threatening to consume me—as I stand in front of the square window, looking out at the wall beyond, a pastime that has become all too common for me these days. Dark figures amble across it, making their rounds as they protect us from any attacks that might happen, and I remember the times I have spent on the wall, each one during an attack, and wonder if Chase is sitting up, right now, looking back at Arel, thinking of me the way I am thinking of him. Melancholy fills my heart as I remember that it was me who sent him to his current predicament—will Gwen ever forgive me? —and I snatch a handful of bobby pins from the black, oval-shaped bowl on my desk and wrap my hair up, twisting the long strands into a bun, securing them. A quick glance in the mirror and I know that I look every bit the arbiter I am supposed to, but my eyes appear soft, worried, not hard or unforgiving like so many of my colleagues.

My lamp flickers again, telling me that I will have to change the bulb soon, but as it dims and brightens in succession, its yellow glow makes my walnut-colored skin appear darker than it is, as shadows cross my eyes, giving me the appearance of a racoon, a thief in the night about to steal a man's life. But what choice do I have? I glance at the time: 25 minutes until midnight. The others will be waiting for me and I mustn't delay them. I snatch my belt, the same one Commander Vye had given me upon my arrival here, and wrap it around my waist, making sure that the baton is in its hold. A door in the hallway opens and closes, followed by another, and I know it is time for me to go. Taking a deep breath, I leave my room, walk down the hallway, and stomp down the stairs, taking my place with the others who have been chosen to go on this mission.

"All right," says Commander Vye, "you all know the drill. We will hit our target swiftly and leave nothing untouched. Our target is suspected of having conspired with a known traitor to Arel, but the council has decided that we need some proof of his treachery before we can proceed."

"And what if we find nothing?" I ask, doing my best to keep my voice unemotional.

"Considering the nature of this case, if we do not find any evidence of him having conspired against Arel, we will have to let him go, so be thorough in your search."

A few murmurs of "yes, ma'am" spread throughout those of us gathered.

I hear a small squeak next to me and glance in its direction, finding the door to the plebeian quarters opened with Sheila peeking through the slit, wondering what we are up to. She locks eyes with me and I shake my head, hoping that she understands my message, pleased when she closes the door.

"Noni," Commander Vye says, jerking my attention to her, "you will be taking point on this."

What? I am still a newbie, having only been an official arbiter for just shy of a year. This has to be another test, to prove, not just my loyalty, but to see how much I have learned, and if I will be capable of handling tough missions on my own, without her lead, or the help of any higher-ranking officer.

"Ma'am?" I say, not wanting this honor.

"This will be your mission to lead."

"Yes, ma'am," I say, garnering a few odd glances from the surrounding arbiters, and I notice Anan's envious gaze as he glares at me, wishing me harm, while Renal's encouraging gaze gives me the courage to step forward and do what is expected of me. I pace to the front of the room and look out at my fellow arbiters, all the color of night and each looking sharp in their black uniforms, each of them waiting for me to give the order, and I find myself thrown back to the day of the gauntlet, wondering if this is how we had all looked to Molers: hopeful, yet uncertain.

"We have our orders," I say. "Let's go."

The door to the outside opens as we all pass through it and I watch as arbiters, each standing erect with their shoulders squared as they stare straight ahead with no emotion, no ounce of uncertainty on their faces, marches out into the night air, blending in with the darkness, while my mind argues with itself in an effort to come to terms with my part in this raid. No sounds greet us as we march two by two through the damp streets of the eastern sector: no crickets, locusts, or grasshoppers; not even the dripping of water from the rooftops, due to the shower we had minutes before we left accompany us during our march. Pounding feet—that is all we have. I glance at Commander Vye in the front, silhouetted by the pale amber lights of the lamps on this moonless night, before craning my neck to catch a quick glimpse of the stars dotting the dark sky, twinkling as though they are curious about our excursion. Renal clears his throat, jerking me back to my mission, and I snap my eyes forward, keeping my face stern, emotionless, and robotic. This is not the time for admiring anything.

We turn a corner, taking a more direct path to the man's

home—I still do not know his name—than the one that led me there while escaping the drones and arbiters on duty the night I had snuck out. A small whine fills my ears, and I turn in its direction, finding a drone hovering next to us. Odd. We did not have one the last time we raided a citizen's home. Resuming my march, my mind ponders the drone's presence, jumping from possibility to possibility as I grapple with this change, wondering what it means and what will follow afterward. Commander Vye holds up her hand and we all stop, taking our places, prepared to do what we must to ensure the safety and security of Arel.

"Noni."

Commander Vye's voice slices through the still night, reminding me of how a hot knife cuts through butter, and I rush to her side, taking my place, knowing what she wants me to do as words are not needed. Obdurate eyes watch me, each unyielding, each void of a soul, and all waiting for me to do what is expected, what is my duty. I know what awaits me if I fail, if I refuse, and I feel Commander Vye's sharp gaze boiling my skin, causing sweat to form under my collar and beneath the waistband of my pants, as my internal temperature rises from all the pressure being pushed on me to complete one of Arel's most basic tasks for an arbiter: rooting out traitors. The thudding of my pulse in my ears and neck almost drowns out the high-pitched squeal of the drone hovering next to me as it also awaits my command, ready to broadcast it back to the command division. Steeling myself as moisture beads on the sleeves of my jacket, I wave the two carrying the battering ram over and signal for them to break down the door.

They rush over, holding the iron battering ram between them, and position themselves in front of the door, remaining silent as they lift the battering ram into the air and swing it at the door, causing it to burst open as it smashes into the wall behind it, creating an ear-splitting noise that reverberates around us, striking fear into any who hear it. Arbiters pour into the room. I remain outside, waiting for them to do their duty and search the place for any contraband, and indication that the man knew of his daughter's intentions and treachery. Once enough time has passed, I move from my spot and step through the door, finding myself surrounded by arbiters hurrying from one end of the room to the next, throwing books, pictures, shelves, knickknacks, and papers—they're really just foldable electronic screens that look like paper, an illusion that people respond to in a more favorable manner—to the floor, coating the rug in their disarray. Copying Commander Vye's stringent movements, my feet lead me through the melee as things crash next to them, while dust bunnies fly in the air, bombarding me, enticing me to sneeze.

"What is the meaning of this!" yells an irate voice as the man storms down the stairs from the upper level and into the chaos that has consumed his home as we do to it what we will, not caring if a trinket gets broken or if a framed picture is ruined by muddy boots stomping on it.

Commander Vye remains silent, directing her gaze toward me, telling me that this is my show and my responsibility to subdue any who challenge us.

"Seize him!" I say, and a couple of arbiters snatch the man, yanking him off the steps and over the railing, not caring if they harm him as they throw him to the floor facedown, restraining him.

"Mr...." I allow my voice to trail off because no one told me the man's name.

"Luther," Commander Vye says, the first time she has spoken since leaving the manor.

"Mr. Luther."

"I prefer Luther."

"Luther," I continue, clearing my throat and doing my best to sound as though I am in control, "we have reason to believe that you conspired with your daughter, Mora, in helping people to leave Arel, thus violating our laws and the safety of the Arelian people."

"Violated?" Luther looks at me, craning his neck so as to stare me in the eyes from his position on the floor. "I have just received word of my daughter's death and you accuse me of treason?"

For the first time, I spot the rolled-up notice in his hand, and I reach down, snatching it from his grip and unrolling it as words appear on the flexible screen, and I run my index finger down it, scrolling through it while scanning the words. It is a consolation letter from Arel, regretting to inform him that his daughter has passed due to unforeseen circumstances; it is a polite way of saying that she was executed. I toss the notice to the floor, allowing it to skid a little when it hits the hard surface and melts into the scattered items around it.

"So, you knew nothing of her activities?" I ask, maintaining my role as inquisitor.

"No."

"We shall see," I reply, using a phrase I have heard Molers use, and my tone reminds me of him, making me quiver inside as it seems that with each passing day, I become more like him.

Arbiters continue to ravage the place, knocking over a bookcase and ripping open cabinets while chucking anything they find onto the floor, stepping on books—the screen of one flickers at me, and I pick it up, opening the flap so that I can view the screen better while wondering what happened to the archaic volumes, ones with actual pages that had surrounded me during my first visit here—cookware, pottery, and pillows that had been torn down the center so that their stuffing poked out, all unconcerned that what had been a warm and inviting home has been transformed into a garbage heap. I chuck the book to the side and the crunch of broken glass meets my ears as it lands on the shattered surface of a coffee table. I wander the room, taking in every detail, every act of the arbiters around me, noting how Anan seems to be enjoying himself a bit too much, all while wondering what happened to the inflammatory books I had seen that night I was out after curfew. Did he suspect this would happen when he threw me out of his home and into the lonesome night? A few arbiters stomp down the metal stairs, having run up to the second floor after Luther had been subdued, shaking their heads, meaning that they found nothing that could be used to convict him.

Not sure when this fiasco will end, I meander to a corner of the room where a lone desk sits, covered in blueprints, pencils, and rulers that has not been touched yet and realize why he has not just been arrested. Picking up one of the blueprints, and remarking at the detail of the drawing, I recognize the presidential seal. I scoop up another one: it is a scale drawing of the council chambers. The more I rummage through them, the more I am convinced that Luther is the chief architect for the executive district, putting him in a position where he cannot just be gotten rid of, and if he also designs weapons for Arel, as he told me earlier, it makes him almost untouchable.

As I look over some of his blueprints, noting how accomplished of an engineer Luther must be, something catches my attention on the shelves nearby. I take a quick glance around the room, but no one watches me, too consumed in their own ordeal; not even the drone is focused on me. Reaching over, I tug on the item that has caught my notice and almost gasp when I see it: it's a book, not the electronic ones like at the manor that are dressed up to look like leather bound volumes, but an actual book with pages (yellowed and stained) made of paper. My mind races with possibilities of how I can prevent this from being discovered, but I have mere seconds, not enough time to think of a plan, unless…

An armoire sits next to the shelf in question. I move over to it and open one of its doors as it sits ajar by two inches as though someone had tried to close it in a hurry, but it never latched. Empty, except for a thin layer of pale dust outlining where something had been stored there moments before we arrived. Stealing another glance at those in the room, I prepare to knock the free-standing cupboard over, but am stopped by an arbiter marching up to me to give me an update.

"We have found nothing, ma'am," she says.

Perfect. I could not have planned this better, even if I had been given the time to do so. Hardening my facial features, and about to do something the second time today that will make me more like the person I loathe most, I grasp the armoire and chuck it to the side, its featherlight weight making it easy to do so, so that it smashes into the desk, breaking it and scattering the drawings everywhere, and they land on the soiled floor as ink bursts from a bottle and coats them. I take a step back, pleased that my antics helped conceal Luther's transgression, but it will not stay that way for long, unless I get everyone out of here. I need to play my part and do it so well that it convinces those surrounding me to not question my orders or motives. I spot a carpenter square on the floor, probably deposited there when I destroyed the desk, and snatch it, swinging it as I rush over to where Luther remains pinned on the floor, and I shove one of its rusty ends under his rounded, yet bony, chin, forcing him to look up at me.

"If I hear anything," I say, my voice cold and devoid of emotion, sending chills down my own spine, "about you owning contraband or committing treason, anything at all that indicates that you're guilty of helping your daughter violate our laws, there will be no trial for you, nor will you be sent to the Ministry of Justice. Only the crematoriums will be pleased that day. Understood?"

Luther nods his head as best he can with the edge of the square digging into his throat while the drone circles us, capturing every moment of my threat.

"This will be your only warning." I drop the carpenter square, and it clangs on the floor as it lands, sending a hollow and ominous sound throughout the home, filling my stomach with dread, and turn toward Commander Vye. "We're through here."

Without waiting to receive her approval, I leave, stepping through the door and stand at attention as I watch the other arbiters follow my example, and disappear down the alley, their black uniforms and skin concealing them from my view as the night blankets them with its darkness. Anan gives me a quick glare as he passes, but my scowl forces him to turn away, while Commander Vye is the last to leave. She nods in my direction and continues walking away, leaving me to take up the rear. My boots splash in water as I stroll through the alley and to the square, leaving me to believe that another short-lived shower had dumped rain while we were all inside performing our duty for Arel. Before I turn the corner, I pause, looking back at the doorway and the door that hangs at an odd angle on its hinges, swaying from the slightest breeze, trapped in a cage of conflicting emotions at war with one another, causing a slight wave of nausea to wash over me. The man could have given me up; he could have told them about how I had warned him earlier today, but he didn't, making this the second time he has saved my life and spared me from Arel's wrath.

The soft whine of the drone fills my ears, enveloping me in its annoyance as it hovers within arm's reach as its camera focuses on me. Willing myself to move on and let go of these musings, I turn toward the drone, staring straight into its coin-sized camera, and if a single gaze could cause the destruction of an object, the drone would be a pile of ashes. Knowing that I cannot destroy it, I release that desire and walk away, turning the corner and following after my fellow arbiters, while the nagging feeling of having become Molers for the second time today gnaws at me.

Chapter 5

Discontent

A yawn creeps up on me as I meander through the outer edges of the eastern sector near the wall, shrouded in its ever-present shadow, unable to escape its barrier, or its constant reminder of our place in this world. Our presidents and council tell us that the wall is for our protection, and like anyone raised in Arel, I believed them, until now, until I had been assigned outside of it for a time and met two of the inhabitants in the world beyond. The barbarian during the hunt did not seem like a terrible man, though he could have been for all I knew, but he had done me no harm, and had been captured by Commandant Paq for the sole purpose of being hunted down as though he were no more than a mere animal, meant to be the object of one man's entertainment; nor did the one who had helped Chase and me while we dangled over the edge of a hill strike me as someone who meant us harm. I do not know their names, a fact that never bothered me until now, but as the memory of them floats through my mind, refusing to allow me to forget them, I realize that they must have names, just like me.

A sliver of red appears on the upper arm of my uniform jacket, standing out amongst the black in stark contrast, as though the rising sun is trying to tell me that the world is not all darkness, as its vibrant sliver of light expands, snaking down my arm, until it reaches my feet and spreads to the buildings beside me, stretching up the dilapidated structures as it envelops them in a mixture of warm color tones, forming its own rainbow of reds, oranges, and yellows, all blending together, all separate, but one. I watch as the sun's light stretches up the building next to me, filling the cracked and grime-ridden panes of glass with its golden glow, mesmerizing me as it reflects off the sides of the structures, filling the void between them and the wall, enveloping me in its warm comfort, turning my usual walnut-colored skin tone amber. Glancing at the towering stone edifice beside me, I marvel at how the wall, always dark, always impending, now exhibits a honey color, that of clover honey, as though it has been rebirthed.

My mind drifts to Chase, alone, outside the wall among strangers, sentenced to a life of depravity, and my hope of seeing him again dissolves, replaced by determination. I will see him again, I tell myself in silence, not wanting to be overheard, and I will bring him back to Gwen, who still refuses to speak to me, not that I blame her.

My wristband chirps, and at first, I assume that it is telling me that my shift is almost over, which would be a relief, as night patrol is always the longest and most arduous shift to get through. I stop cold in my tracks when I realize that it isn't a reminder at all, but a summons: trouble brews and all available arbiters are needed. I sprint away from the wall, diving between two resident buildings, the corners of their foundation crumbling away, littering the uneven pavement with brick dust, and squeeze through the narrow space in an effort to reach the nearest information booth as fast as possible. I burst out the other end into a yellow beam of light, hurrying to the booth that lies 50 yards away. Once I reach it, panting, I place my palm on the scanner, allowing it to scan me, disregarding the information that appears on the screen as it flashes green, allowing me entrance into the tunnels below.

A small sound escapes my lips as I land between the steel tracks below, in front of a two-seater railcar, just like the one Renal and I had taken the first time I had been summoned to a riot, and my knees buckle, forcing me to outstretch my hands for support. Wincing from the force of the impact of my hands slamming into the semi smoothed-edged bumps of the concrete beneath me, I brush them on my pants and rush to the railcar, jumping into the first available seat and strap myself in. Another arbiter sits beside me. Startled, I glance in her direction, keeping my face impassive, while pretending that I knew she has been here the entire time. She straps herself in, her hands shaking as she buckles the harness, and I note the beads of sweat outlining her hairline as a few stray strands work themselves lose from her bun, framing her rectangular face. She does not look familiar, and I do not know her name. Perhaps she is from one of the other manors in the eastern sector. We share a look, each pretending not to be anxious before facing forward as the glass casing lowers, sealing up inside.

The railcar jets ahead. Air bursts free from my lungs, squeezed out by the harness as it digs into my torso, leaving impressions in my skin, despite the clothing I wear, while my back presses into the seat, held there by the force of the railcar's acceleration, and my nose flattens against my face, causing pressure to build up in my sinuses as though I have a sudden cold, giving me an instant headache in the center of my forehead.

Red flashing lights streak past us, mingled with fluorescent bars built into the stone walls, rendering rectangular beams of opalescent white broken by jagged crimson rays, stretching from the front of the car to the back as we are hurled down the tunnel. My body shifts to the right, causing the harness securing me to creak as it holds me in place, digging into my arm and causing it to go numb for a second, while we bank to the left. Another curve shifts me to the right before the tracks straighten out, convincing me that my brain will pop out of my head as pressure builds within it and the beginnings of a second headache starts to form, causing a vein to pulsate on the side of my temple in tune with my breathing, skipping and changing each time the railcar encounters another curve and I am thrown from side to side. I glance at my fellow passenger, noting the reflection of the car zipping down the grey, mirrorlike walls, but she remains statuesque, her wide eyes focused on the rails ahead of us as we speed through the never-ending tunnel.

An ear-piercing squeal reverberates around us, bouncing off the sanded and polished concrete walls of the tunnel, causing me to wince as my ears beg for relief, while sparks fly from the brakes, bringing us to a sudden stop. Once again, my harness creaks as it holds me in place as I am thrown forward, causing the straps to snap, my diaphragm begging for release as the belt cuts into it, wrenching the air from my lungs, before I am thrust backward and slam into the back of my seat with a force that radiates up my spine and swivels around my head. Before either of us have a chance to regain our breaths, the glass shield around us raises upward, allowing a rush of warm, metallic tasting air to rush inside as we break free of our cramped prison.

My fingers fumble as they unhook my harness, and I climb out of the railcar, holding onto the sides for support as I step onto solid ground, my legs wobbling, refusing to support me, while my mind grapples with the fact that my body is no longer strapped in a moving vessel, but is stationary. Retching catches my attention, and I turn my head, eyeing my fellow arbiter as she hunches over, expelling the meager contents of her stomach, forcing me to turn away, and give her some privacy as another railcar appears, releasing its occupants, both of whom experience just as much difficulty standing up as I had. Once the gagging sounds stop, I step beside her, placing a gentle hand on her shoulder, not wanting to startle her as I do my best to will my stomach to be a block of iron, while the acrid stench of vomit attacks my nose, causing it to want to bounce.

"It's okay," I whisper to her, leading her away from the railcar and the puddle of vomit and to the panels sliding open on a far wall, granting us access to body armor and weapons. "Just walk it off."

Once we reach the panels, she straightens up and thanks me as she reaches for a vest, and I do the same, yanking the thing off its hooks and strapping it around myself before snatching a semiautomatic weapon. My mind drifts back, for just a moment, to my first time being summoned to put down a riot, and I wish Renal was here with me, like he had been the last time, guiding me while calming my nerves with that encouraging smile of his. Forcing myself back into the present, I grab a helmet, noting how the cold lights above me turn the black, shiny surface a bright white, while my reflection casts an ominous shadow over it. The clicking of weapons being armed pulls me from my reverie, and I ram the helmet over my head, falling in line with the arbiters running up the stairs that have dropped down, beating them with our thunderous footsteps as we hike up to the world above and to what awaits us.

Snakelike trails of smoke float around me, encircling me once I reach the street above and jump into the sunlight, faded by black clouds of burning embers that swirl above me, billowing in the wind as they stretch for the sky and thin out enough to allow the yellow orb, turned red by the smoke, above us to show its face. Fires rage around us as they consume piles of trash, built on purpose to form a perimeter of sorts, filling the atmosphere with their angry roar, a noise muffled, somewhat, by my helmet. I whirl around, weapon at the ready, searching for any sign of rioters, but there are none. As I tread through the street, surrounded by my fellow arbiters, the raging fires imprison us in their sweltering heat, causing sweat to stream down my face and get in my eyes, fogging up my visor, while an ominous feeling burrows within the pit of my stomach, forcing my heart to sink and my breathing quicken.

Where is everybody?

Boots creep across the pavement, crushing glass, pebbles, and bits of paper that have escaped their torment in the unforgiving flames. No sounds. No people. Nothing seems to be here. The arbiter next to me coughs as the smoke gets through her helmet—they're not meant to filter out contaminants like smoke or pollution—and I glance at her before turning back to the emptiness before me, surrounded by my fellow arbiters, all of us on edge, all of us wondering where the rioters are as the space around us grows darker from the ever-growing clouds of smoke hovering in the air, suffocating us.

My foot brushes a metal plate, scooting it across the ground, revealing something drawn in red paint, now dulled and darkened by the ash settling over us. Bending low to take a closer look, my mind jumps back to the day of the explosions and the symbol drawn on the ground in front of the burning school: the crest of Arel, crossed out like before. I bolt upright, spinning around on my feet, searching for any threat, convinced that we are not alone and that this entire incident is by design. Before I can voice my suspicions, a grenade plops on the ground, several yards away from me, clacking as it skids to a halt before it ceases its movement, looking like a small ball waiting to be picked up.

"Get down!" someone yells as I jump back, grabbing the nearest arbiter and throwing us both to the ground; but before we land, the grenade explodes, creating a force that slams into my side, throwing me and the arbiter I had grabbed into the air. My mind whirls in confusion as my body appears to fly before it crashes into the ground. Coughing, I lay on my stomach a moment, gasping for air as my head buzzes from the noise and refuses to focus. As the madness continues, I force myself to my hands and knees as time slows around me, drowning the cries and shouts of those surrounding me as people burst from behind the burning piles of trash and attack any arbiter they see. I try to stand, but my legs refuse to support me at first, causing me to drop to the ground again as I shake my head, attempting to clear it.

A muffled yell pierces my ears, snapping me to attention. I turn in time to see a man with a plank heading straight for me, his eyes filled with murderous intent as he takes aim with me in his sights. Still on my knees, I rear up, seizing the plank and twisting it from his grip, forcing him to lose his balance and tumble to the ground. As he lays there, regaining his senses, I raise the plank and swing it at him, striking him in the head, and the sound of his skull cracking reaches my ears, telling me that he is no longer a threat.

My weapon.

Scrambling, I search the blackened debris, my gloved hands swiping the pavement in a desperate attempt to find anything I can use to defend myself. I see it. My weapon lies just out of reach. I dive for it, crawling across the soot-covered ground, and wrap my fingers around it as something wraps around my throat, digging into my airway, causing me to choke and to drop my weapon. Unable to breathe, my first impulse is to reach up and grip the rope around my throat, but I stop, remembering what an instructor at the training facility had said once: if you reach for what's around your neck, you can't fight back, and your attacker knows were your hands are.

My eyes bulge as the line around my neck tightens and the corner of my vision blackens from lack of oxygen. I jerk to the side, throwing my attacker off-balance, and as he recovers, I lunge for my weapon, seize it, and ram the barrel over my head, guessing the position of my opponent. The barrel meets resistance and the rope slackens. Seizing my chance, I twist around, flinging myself onto my back and jerking the rope out of my opponent's hands, while raising my weapon and squeezing the trigger. A shot rings out, euphoric music to my ears, and hits the man in the chest, and before he collapses to the ground, I spring to my feet.

Another psychotic scream fills the air, and I duck as a woman with a crazed look in her eyes charges me, forcing her to fly over my back and crash into the ground, sending bits of ash into the air. Without a second thought, without any mercy, I aim my weapon at her head and fire, not caring that bits of her brain mixed with

warm, crimson blood splatters my pants while the back of her head
bursts open, allowing the contents within to mix with the soot on
the pavement. Another rushes for me, and I raise my weapon like
a staff, blocking the man's attack and twist my weapon, forcing his
out of his grip, before dropping to the ground and sweeping his feet
out from under him. Surprised, he slams into the pavement and
scrambles for a discarded rod, the chosen weapon of another dead
rioter, but I pounce on him, seizing his arm and ramming my elbow
into his face, stunning him, before swinging my elbow back a second
time and plunging it into his neck. Gurgled choking escapes his lips
as he struggles for air before going limp.

A muffled roar reaches my ears as flames shooting out of a
flamethrower dance in front of my helmet, engulfing any it comes
into contact with, while its creator walks forward with slow, steady
steps, ignoring the anguished screams of those burning alive. One
humanoid inferno rushes for me, unaware of his actions as he tries
to put out the fire burning his flesh. Reacting in the manner I had
been trained, I point my weapon at him and fire, putting him out
of his misery. He sprawls on the ground, rolling through the smoldering embers before stopping and breathing his last. Surrounded
by a mixture of terrified screams and vengeful yells, my feet remain
rooted to the ground, unsure of where to go or what to do next as I
watch the chaos unfold around me with rebellious citizens and arbiters locked in conflict, each hoping to destroy the other. A flash of
movement catches my eye. Turning, I spot a woman trying to sneak
past me and reach for her, seizing her arm and twisting it behind
her back as I kick the back of her knee and force her into a sitting
position. She yells in pain and pleads with me to stop, but this is my
duty: to put down rioters and she is…

I stop.

For the first time, I notice it: the small roundedness of her abdomen, the distinct sign of a pregnancy, and an unregistered one at
that, meaning that, once again, the sterilization techniques of Arel

have failed. Craning her neck, the woman does her best to look up at me with her pleading eyes, but my helmet prevents her from seeing my face, but I see the raised scar of a mark burned into her left cheek for all to see as a reminder and a warning. Either she, or someone she knew who had been executed while she had been left alive, had tried to help a plebeian escape punishment, and this was her reward: to spend her life as an outcast, warning others of what happens if you do not conform to Arel's demands. Her hunched shoulders with a small pack strapped to them and jittery hands tell me that she is not part of this rebellion, but had decided to use it to escape: an offence met with death.

I release her.

"Go home," I tell her, but she shakes her head. I seize her shirt and haul her to her feet, shoving her away, when a metallic clink clacks against the street. Looking down, I discover that it's a small two-way radio, contraband and punishable by a sentence of five years in the fields or the mines. This is more than just a target of opportunity for her, but something she has been planning on doing for a while.

"Please…" she begs.

"What do you know of all this?" I demand, gripping the collar of her shirt.

"Nothing!" she wails. "I cannot stay here anymore." She looks at her bulging belly and I know what she means. Now that she is starting to show, it will be almost impossible for her to conceal her pregnancy, and she does not strike me as someone who has many friends willing to help her.

I stare at her, my heart torn between what I am trained to do and know I should do for the safety and security of Arel, though it means sentencing her and her unborn child to death, or helping her. Fear resides in her eyes as her mind races with the possibilities of my choices and what I might do, the same fear within the plebeian girl's eyes when I rescued her from the fire, and when she pleaded with me to end her suffering: both desperate to escape their torment.

Pounding boots rushing toward me makes my decision for me. I release the woman, whipping around and bringing my weapon up, ramming it into chest of an arbiter who had seen me with her and chose to do his duty for Arel. He staggers back, but remains on his feet. Before I finish him, he lunges, catching me around the middle and forcing me off my feet. I crash into the pavement, and the force of the impact forces me to gasp. Refusing to give up, I seize his arm and wrench it across his chest, forcing him to lose his balance, just as I roll, flinging him to the side. Twisting, I keep my grip firm as I bring my legs up, wrapping them around my opponent's torso and yank, pleased when I feel his shoulder pop out of its socket. Before I can get up, a low whistle echoes above us, and I roll on my side, covering my head with my hands just as an explosive device the size of a tube of toothpaste strikes the ground and detonates, scooting me across the ground and showering me with bits of debris that pelt my armor and helmet. Once the dust settles, I force myself to my feet and turn toward the arbiter that had charged the woman, but he remains on the ground with a metal rod poking out of his chest.

The woman!

Running to where I had left her, I find a bundle of loose clothing with a pack strapped around it. My gloved hands fly over the bits of asphalt and miniscule rocks that cover the small mound, clearing them away until the woman's head is revealed. I lift her up. She moans while clinging to my arm as I drag her away from the chaos, trying to think of what to do next as the wall is too far away, but perhaps…

Another small device detonates and the screams of those caught in its wrath fade as I cart the woman away from the square, using the shifting walls of black smoke to my advantage, allowing them to conceal us as I lead her to a place of temporary safety. A man rushes for us with a Molotov cocktail in his hand. Pushing the woman aside, but being careful to not hurt her, I reach for my weapon only to remember that I have dropped it. The man draws closer. Whipping out my baton, I revel in the snapping sound that cracks the air as I extend it to its full length. He swings at me, hoping to strike me with his explosive cocktail, but I drop to one knee and whip him in the stomach with my baton before swinging it again and jabbing him in the face. With my other hand, I grab his Molotov cocktail and ram it on his head, allowing the flammable liquid to spread down his face. While he runs away in agony, I hurry back to the pregnant woman and haul her back to her feet, but as I do, another rioter rushes for me, and I turn around, extending my leg, tripping my attacker, and as he falls forward, I twist again and ram my elbow into the back of his neck.

Engines alert me to a change in the chaos. Looking at the topmost level of Arel, I notice that the doors to the hangar are open and Arel's aircraft head straight for us. They are about to bomb their own people! A whistle sounds the signal for any arbiter in the area to seek shelter, and we do not have much time. I strengthen my grip on the woman's arm, dragging her away from the melee and to a sewer, knowing that it is our best bet for survival. Her feet stumble as she tries to keep up with my unforgiving pace, but I refuse to let her go, and drag her across the ground, until she regains her feet and jogs after me. Only 60 seconds until they reach us.

We reach the sewer. Dropping to my knees, I grip the grate, straining as I lift the solid iron bars away from the hole in the ground and slide it across the pavement, creating a grating noise that drowns the sound of the engines approaching from above. My muscles tired, I look at the black hole before me, unsure of how far the drop will be and hope that it is less than I fear.

"In!" I yell at the woman, but she backs away, knowing what I want her to do and afraid to go through with it.

Frustrated, and having no time to waste, I leap to my feet, seize the woman, and shove her through the hole and into the sewer, jumping in after her as the aircraft rush by overhead, dropping their explosives. A drumbeat of multiple explosions radiate above us, broken by the woman's screams, shaking the ground as it ripples through the solid earth, echoing around us and creating a cage of deafening gloom that penetrates our hearts and vibrates our chests, broken only by the bits of fire that rain down upon us, squeezing through the hole above, while I cover her, shielding her from its fury and wincing as a piece of scalding metal burns through my sleeve, leaving what will be a permanent mark on my skin.

Once again, time seems to stand still as we wait for the Arelian aircraft to finish dropping their weapons, but little by little, the thundering roars fade, replaced by shrieking silence, making me wish for the explosions as the ominous silence cuts through me. I release the woman who shivers in the sewer water, afraid to look up. I try placing a comforting hand on her shoulder, but she shakes me off, not wanting anything to do with me. Knowing what I must look like to her, dressed in body armor and with a helmet to conceal my face, I reach up and lift it off, allowing the woman to see me for the first time.

"You must stay here," I tell her, keeping my voice low and gentle so as not to startle her. She glances at me, her red eyes filled with tears that spill from the outer corners, leaving streaks of amber on her face that barrel their way through the soot covering it. "For now, at least."

"I need to get out," she says, her broken voice echoing around us, mixed with the constant trickling of murky, green water in the still sewers.

"Security is going to be tight after this," I say, pointing at the hole above and indicating what Arel's response will be to this chain of events.

"Just let me go," she pleads. "I have a friend outside the wall."

"You can't!" My voice stops her and we both glare at one another, each unwilling to yield. "Look," I say again as she lowers her face in dismay, and I remember the two-way radio she has, concluding that it must have been how she had communicated with her friend,

"I'll do what I can to help you, but for now, you need to stay here. Your baby's life depends on it."

She nods her head, accepting my orders.

"Do you have any food?" I ask.

"Enough for a few days," replies the woman.

"Don't come out, until I come for you."

I put my helmet back on and lift my arms up, leaping at the manhole above us and gripping its edge, ignoring the way it digs into my palms, despite the gloves I wear for protection.

"Why are you helping me?" asks the woman.

Unsure of how to respond, and not knowing why I am helping her either, I remain silent and lift myself through the manhole and into the world above where impenetrable barriers of smoke open before me, revealing an emptiness, filled with charred bodies and crumbling sides of what had once been livable residences, while hushed weeping reaches my ears. I glance back at the hole, searching for the grate, and when I find it, I drag it across the ground, stirring up embers that spring into the air and float around me, angered at being disturbed, until the iron bars thump in place, sealing the woman inside. As I meander through the remains of what had been a place for people to gather together, a single thought consumes my tortured mind: how am I going to help the woman?

Chapter 6

Smuggling

Lights out. The chimes that signal that it is time for all arbiters to be in their quarters and in bed, unless they are assigned to night patrol, rings throughout the manor, its soft ambience unfitting for such a place of rigorous exercise and unshakable rules. I turn off my lamp and wait, listening to the feet stomping in the hallway as arbiters hurry from the bathroom to their quarters, not wanting to be caught out of bed when the final chime sounds, an act met with swift punishment. Once the final door slides close and silence falls around me, I crouch next to my bed, feeling underneath it and the mesh wires that hold the thin mattress, until I find what my fingers search for, a slack wire. Scraping it with my index finger, I grasp it and tug on it, cursing at its refusal to come loose, until it pops free and jiggles the bed. Afraid that someone might have heard that, I stay still for a moment, counting the seconds as my heart thuds in my ears, causing them to ache, until it settles down, reassuring me that no one heard my infraction. Reaching back under the bed, I find another loose wire and yank it out. Holding the wires in the faint light spilling into my room from the quarter moon, I stare at the copper strings, wondering if my ruse will work, but I must risk it. I wrap the two wires together, twisting them in a way so that they form a bracelet. Once done, I hold it next to my wristband; it's not even close to being a match, but from a distance, it might fool someone, as long as they do not take a closer look. I wrap the copper wires around my wrist and place my wristband underneath my pillow, tugging the long sleeve of my shirt: dark like me, like my uniform, like the night, like my world.

I coil the rope I had stolen earlier from the garden shed after returning to the manor around me, draping it across my left shoulder so that it crosses in front of me at an angle like a fibrous sash before strapping a pouch around my waist, containing four pieces of meat that I had stolen from the kitchen, and head for my window, knowing that I cannot risk going out through the plebeian quarters like the time Chase and I had snuck out. With care, and always alert in case someone hears me, I slide my window open wide enough for me to slip through, and climb upon the desk, hoping that it does not rock beneath my weight, and slip outside, feet first until they dangle in the air. Hanging onto the ledge outside, I close my window, leaving it open a finger's width so that I can get back in, and take one last look at the pair of pears sitting on the desk, a treat for Sheila and Gwen, but Sheila never came, a thought that shrouds me with a thin veil of despondency, and I hope that she gets them.

Thrusting the thoughts aside, I look at the steel drain pipe on my left that is bolted into the side of the building, unsure if it will support my weight. There is only one way to find out. I plant my feet against the side of the building and twist as best I can so that I face the pipe and let go. My heat skips a beat as I fall and slam into the pipe. For a second, I fear that I will fall as my fingers slip against the metal, creating a screeching sound that pierces the still night, until I stop. My arms and legs pulsate in tune with my heartbeat as blood rushes through them, stirred by the fear of death, and I hang there for a second, convinced that someone heard me, but as the night remains undisturbed, confidence washes over me, and I slide down the drainpipe to the dewy ground below, landing with a squishy plop. Taking a quick look around, I race across the green area to the part of the fence with the loose boards that Chase had shown me at a time that seems so long ago.

Once through the fence, I crouch and wait. No arbiters. I sprint through the street, keeping to the shadows so that the few lights within the city will not reach me, darting down alleyways and side streets as I make my way to the square where the riot took place earlier, doing my best to stay silent, and avoiding the normal patrols. A faint whine catches my ears and I duck behind some garbage, staying as still as I can as a single drone hovers past, coming out once it disappears. Too close. I dash down a side street before veering down another alley, cursing at how long it takes me to navigate my way to the square.

The hum of a moving walkway catches my attention and an idea forms in my mind. Some of them have bars underneath for workmen to attach themselves to with a harness. I dart up a stairwell, sticking to the edges so as to avoid the range of the cameras, in case any of them still work, and pause at the railing that sits just below the first walkway, but before I go any farther, I rub my hands against the ground, scooping up what dirt I can and brushing them over my palms to soak up the sweat that has formed on them. Hoisting myself up, I balance on the railing, knowing that one false move will force me to plummet to my death, and bend my knees as I focus on the first bar attached to the underside of the causeway. I jump. My hands seize the bar and I tighten my grip, squeezing with such force that my fingers go numb as my feet dangle in the air, swinging back and forth from my momentum. I look down at the walk below me, wrapped in the murky light of the streetlamps as moths flitter about in confusion. As I reach for the next bar in front of me, I am reminded of my exercises at the training facility involving the monkey bars and how the instructors would force recruits to cross them over and over, until we could hold onto them no longer, and any who fell met a swift punishment.

One bar at a time, I ease my way across, my feet swinging back and forth in tune to each of my movements as sweat drips from my chin, while the hum of the walkway surrounds me, enveloping me in its mocking tune, daring me to let go. I grab another bar, willing myself to hang on, refusing to let go as I remind myself of the woman's fate should I fail to retrieve her from the sewer, repeating to myself that this is just another test of my endurance, another gauntlet. Halfway there. I reach for the next bar, but my hand slips and my stomach lurches into my chest as the fear of falling grips me, but I cling to the bar I dangle from as I stretch out again, wrapping my fingers around the other one before letting go of the previous. Time stands still as I go from bar to bar, until I reach the last one.

Voices stop me.

Above me are two arbiters who have decided to pause for a short conversation. I cannot make out the words, but I wish they would hurry up and leave. My arms strain from my weight as I hang in the air, waiting for them to end their conversation and move off, screaming at me to let go, while my mind reminds me of the consequences should I fail. Burning fatigue stretches from my wrists to my shoulders and through my chest, choking me with its viselike grip as it forms a cage around me, threatening to force me to release my hold on the bar as my arms shake from the strain. I cannot hold on for much longer. Quivering even more, my muscles start to relax against my commands, and I readjust my grip in an effort to keep from falling.

The two arbiters move off.

Relieved, I propel myself to the platform in front of me and land on it with a soft thump. As my arms thank me for letting them rest, I glance around, making certain no one heard me, before charging down the stairs and sprinting into the shadows, staying clear of the streetlamps as I run to the plaza. My breathing quickens when I reach the place of the latest riot, and I pause, taken aback by the remains of Arel's victory. At first, the lack of arbiters guarding the area surprises me, but as I meander through charred remains, spotting an upturned hand that resembles a charcoal claw more than an appendage, while covering my nose from the stench of cooked flesh left to spoil in the sun, I realize why no one is here. Who would be? The side of my boot brushes a tablet, scooting it across the ground with an eerie scrape. I pick it up, forgetting where I am as I turn the thing around, the chipped and scorched sides scratching my fingers while a cracked screen looks back at me, and I become lost in my own somber face staring back at me with blackened shadows creeping behind me, taunting me.

Taken aback, I step backward and stop the moment something cracks beneath my heel. A part of me does not wish to see what I have stepped on, but another part, the curious side, wins, and I turn my head, finding a ghoulish face staring at me with lifeless eyes bulging from the face as the skin around it has melted away, stripping away all its humanlike features, leaving a sunken cave where there should have been a nose. Judging by its small size, I surmise that the face used to be a child's, perhaps the very one whose tablet I have found.

Bile clogs my throat, and I cover my mouth in a desperate attempt to keep from vomiting as I hurry through the charred skeletons, doing my best to not trip over the broken pavement as death and sulfur seize my nostrils, invading them with their repugnant odor. I cannot stay here. I must get out, away from Arel's resolve to ensure that its citizens follow its structured way of life, and away from this reminder that I am sworn to obey it despite the costs. Not caring if I make noise, I run away, as far away from this open tomb as I can get, heading straight for the sewer and the grate that imprisons a citizen of Arel, whose only crime was getting pregnant.

The grate looms before me, and I drop to my knees in front of it, reaching between the bars and grabbing hold of it as I lift with all my strength, my already fatigued arms not wanting to obey my command, but forced to do so. Metal against concrete fills the atmosphere around me with its low rumble as I slide it to the side, revealing the darkened tunnels beneath. I hope the woman is still there.

"PSSSST!" I whisper, cringing as it echoes beneath me, bouncing off the concrete walls, threatening to warn all of Arel of my unwarranted presence here.

A face appears in the darkness and relief floods over me. Too much time has been wasted, and I must get her out of here. I unwrap the rope from around my torso and lower it into the sewer, not needing to tell the woman what to do as she grabs hold of the line, and I haul her up from the underbelly of Arel and into the open air. My arms feel as though they are on fire as I heave the woman out of the sewers and help her onto the pavement, my breaths in short gasps from the exertion.

"Come on," I say to her in a hushed voice, after scooting the grate back into position, and hurrying away from the exposed area.

I jog back through the hellish remains of the riot, slowing my pace when I notice that the woman struggles to keep up, and I grab hold of her, dragging her after me, knowing what will happen if we are caught. She gasps when she spots the child, but I yank her forward, forcing her to look away before she can give us away. The familiar whine of a drone reaches my ears, and I shove the woman into a doorway, putting my finger over my lips as my nerves threaten to paralyze me from the fear of being caught and only release me from their hold when the drone hovers past, unaware of our presence. We need to reach the wall, and we need to reach it now.

Searching my memories, I envision the schematics of the city which I had to learn as part of passing my written exams, while remembering what I know of the eastern sector's layout. Most of the buildings are close together, some just wide enough for a person to squeeze through if they walk sideways.

"This way," I tell the woman, hauling her behind me as I hurry down the walk and turn down an alley, before darting around a corner and charging into a side street.

My eyes roam around me as we run, checking for arbiters, while making certain that the woman has not fallen behind. Sweat streams down her cheeks as they puff in and out from her labored breathing, causing me to worry about the baby, and whether I am putting any strain on it by forcing the mother to run, but the moment concern threatens to overcome me, logic quells it, pushing it aside while reminding me of our situation. If I fail, the crematoriums will have new victims to claim. The woman trips over a dip in the broken pavement, and I stoop down to catch her, heaving her upright before she hits the ground, and she breathes a thank you.

We come to a gap between two residential structures, and I urge the woman to follow as I squeeze between them, shuffling sideways as the brick building towers over me, threatening to suffocate me, but I force myself to remain calm. The woman refuses at first, but the whistling of an arbiter on patrol springs her into actions, and she shoves her way into the space. Seconds drag as we ease our way through with her protruding belly touching the walls. Just a little further, I keep telling myself, over and over while remaining alert, afraid that at any moment we will be caught.

A gap appears ahead, and I stop the moment we reach it, peeking around the corner, looking left and right, my ears straining to hear any drones that might be about. Nothing. Urging the woman onward, we rush across the street and to the wall, its impenetrable constructions warning us to turn back. I run my fingers along the bumpy surface of the wall, feeling for anything unusual, while my heart slams against my ribcage as I stay concealed in the darkness, hoping that those on the wall will not see us, glad that they watch the wildlands beyond more than the city, and thankful that the latest riot had forced the commanding officers to pull arbiters from the wall and place them elsewhere. My fingers catch on something.

Pausing, I run my hands up and down the wall, feeling a tiny gap and know that I have found it: a door.

I open my pack and pull out the four pieces of meat I have in there, unwrapping them while making certain that no one is above us on the inner wall, and toss them over. No barking. Using my prybar, I manage to pop the lock and force the door open enough for a person to walk through and look inside, finding one dog scarfing the meat. I yank out my knife and creep up behind it, poised and ready to strike, like I had to while a recruit. In my 15th year, each recruit had to sneak up behind an aggressive dog while it was distracted by food. Those who failed had their throats ripped out by the canine's teeth. I had the misfortune of kicking a pebble, an innocuous thing on most occasions, but on this one, it alerted the dog to my presence, and it jumped at me, forcing me to land on my back. Only my quick action with a knife saved me that day, but not before sharp teeth latched themselves onto my arm.

I still my breathing as I stalk up behind the dog, listening for any others, while it devours the meat. Only one piece to go. Knowing I am running out of time, I leap at it and plunge my blade into its skull. It drops to the ground in a pool of its own blood without making a sound. Glancing around, I listen for others, wondering why there only seems to be the one wild dog. Perhaps it killed the others in this section; since they are kept in a starved state, such a thing is not unheard of. Footsteps above me startle me and I hug the wall, craning my neck to watch as a lone arbiter strolls past while stiffing a yawn, meaning he has been here a while. Once he has gone, I rush back to the doorway and motion for the woman to come through before jumping to the door on the outer wall and undoing its lock. I peek outside, not finding any sign of life.

"Here," I say, handing the woman my pouch with its meager supplies. It's not much, but it's the best I can do. "Stay low in the grass and let it cover you. Crawl if you have to, but go slow. If you move too fast, you might be seen."

The woman takes the pouch and straps it around herself. "Thank you," she whispers.

"You can…" I never get the chance to finish my sentence as she steps through the door.

Stillness wafts over me as I watch her crouch low in the grass, feeling her way through, determined to take her chances beyond the wall, even when all sense warns that it is a death sentence, but her fate if she remains will be just as final. Hollowness fills the empty caverns of my stomach as she disappears in the vegetation, but before I can shut the door, the night bursts into day, just for an instant, as an explosion thrusts me backward and rocks the earth. Landmines! Nowhere in my studies did we learn about them being anywhere outside of the wall.

After I regain my senses and the ringing in my ears dissipates, I bolt upright, thinking only of the woman, and I rush through the door into the field, not caring if I step on a mine. Swishing sounds accompany me as I run through the tall grass, shrouded by the night, fearing what I will find. A bloodied hand stops me. Pausing, I pick it up, cradling it as though it is a priceless treasure, and I know what awaits me if I go any further. The hand thumps as I drop it in the dirt and take five more steps forward, crushing the tall stalks of grass beneath me, ignoring the shouts that echo behind me along the wall. A mangled body, or what is left of one, lays on the ground, soaked in blood, it's red color visible in the night as it reflects the sliver of the moon above us. I drop to my knees and turn the woman over, cradling her as tears ease their way down my cheeks, something that has not happened in a long time. Her glazed eyes stare at me for a moment before rolling to the side, and her head drops and hangs to the side, reminding me of a dangling cord as it flops. Unable to grasp what has happened as despondency rears its ugly head and chastises me for my ineptitude, I lay the woman on the ground and close her eyes as it seems to be the right thing to do.

I have failed, again.

The terrified face of the girl I had killed to prove my loyalty to Arel fills my mind. My ears hear the distant screams of the wailing infant from the factory. Chase's sympathetic face upon seeing the scars on my back fills the void before me, and his lips move, mouthing the words he spoke to me not long ago: promise me that you will do what you need to, to survive.

Sheila and Gwen fill my mind.

"I will," I whisper to the darkness as angry shouts and unceasing barking reign over the once quiet atmosphere, threatening to overcome me.

I jump to my feet and sprint to the door, following the broken stalks of grass that mark the path I had tread moments before, until I reach the door and close it, knowing that the broken lock will be discovered at some point, but perhaps it won't be right away. Once through the door on the inner wall, I shut it and dart across the street to the crumbling buildings of the eastern sector.

"Over there!" shouts an arbiter.

I quicken my pace, refusing to turn around to see how many pursue me. A rectangular hole in the sidewalk is not far ahead, and there is no grate covering it. I charge for it, my feet pounding the pavement as I run, my lungs burning for air as I force them to inhale and exhale in tune to my speed, before dropping to the ground, sliding across it, and rolling into the hole where I drop into the sewer below. I gulp air and hold it as I wait for the sounds of those chasing me to pass. Once clear, I lift myself up and peek out, finding no sign of arbiters or drones. An inward struggle takes hold as my mind grapples with remaining in the sewer or risking everything to get back to the manor. I have to take the chance. Soon, the alarm will go off, and if I am discovered missing…

Jumping up, I heave myself out of the sewer and crouch low as I glance around for any sign of danger, but when I find none, I take off, darting down another alley while confusion reigns behind me.

Chapter 7

Sneaking In

Lights blare from the manor, illuminating the building as I crouch behind a thorny bush, observing the people darting about in response to the landmine going off, and I watch as each room glows from the single lamps within them turning on. Bedroom check. The knowledge of what will happen to me once my room is discovered empty floods my mind, jerking my heart into action, forcing it to race as my options appear one by one, each as dismal as the previous. I need to get to my room, or somewhere within the manor before my presence is discovered here in these bushes, hiding like a common criminal, letting all of Arel see that I have something to hide. I start to sprint to the building when a slender hand seizes my wrist, its gentle pressure forcing me to stop and dive back into the bushes as tiny thorns tear into my shirt and scratch my hand.

Sheila stares at me with wide, fearful eyes, placing her finger over her mouth, signaling for me to keep quiet. My mouth opens to ask her why she is here, what she is doing, but I clamp it shut, driving the incessant questions from my mind as this is not the time.

She must have snuck into my room and noticed that I was missing; sometimes she dropped off a pressed shirt or an extra set of towels that she had smuggled out of the laundry, showing me an extra bit of kindness and putting my feeble efforts at keeping her safe to shame. Before I can do anything else, she holds out my wristband to me, looking out for my well-being once again, when it should be me protecting her. Commander Vye's irate voice thunders over the green, screaming my name, and I know that my absence has been detected. I remove the coiled wires from around my wrist and take my wristband from Sheila's thin and smudged fingers and slip it on before jumping up and hurrying to the green, while clutching the makeshift bracelet in my sweaty palm, desperate for an excuse, anything that will sound plausible; in the back of my mind, I know that my punishment will be swift and severe as I have pushed Commander Vye's good graces to the limits.

"Noni!"

"Commander?" I say, trying to keep my voice from sounding too jittery, but it catches regardless of my attempts, revealing my fears.

"Why didn't you respond when I first called you?" she demands, her cheeks red with anger, giving color to her dark features, and I remember how when I first met her, I had wanted to be just like her: strong, iron-willed, and powerful.

"No excuse, ma'am," I reply, and anger radiates from her eyes, squashing what courage I have left, letting me know that I have more than failed her—I have disappointed her.

"Why are you not in bed?"

"I couldn't sleep, ma'am." It's a flimsy excuse and she sees right through it.

"And, so, you thought that you would just come out here to the gymnasium and work some of that energy off."

"Yes, ma'am."

Movement catches my eye, and I shift my gaze to the side to try and see the figure standing in a doorway, outlined by the light, but shrouded enough so that I cannot make out any details. Worry shackles my mind, but I must remain calm and hope that no one is aware of my exploits in the city.

Commander Vye stalks in front of me, the wheels within her mind turning, calculating, formulating a suitable punishment for my infraction as a warning to the others and as a testament to her authority.

"See that bar over there?"

I nod.

"Go to it."

Here it comes, my punishment. My feet squish the dew-topped blades of grass as I walk over to the bar hanging seven feet off the ground and jump for it, grasping hold of the cool iron rod, allowing myself to dangle in the air.

"Well? What are you waiting for?" Commander Vye's voice echoes off the lawn as more arbiters gather around me like they did the day I received a flogging for my negligence; now they can watch me be chastised again.

I heave myself up until my chin is over the bar before lowering myself down in a controlled motion so that I do not drop to the ground.

"Again." Commander Vye's chilled tone tears through me and the hollowed pit of my stomach expands.

Once more, I haul myself up, my already tired arms from hanging on the bars underneath the moving causeway screaming at me to stop, to give in to their demands for rest, but if I do, if I allow them to have their way, I will appear weak, and weakness means death. As I ease myself downward, my arms shaking from the exertion, I stare into my commander's brown and hardened eyes, daring her to look away, but she smiles instead.

"I did not tell you to stop," she says.

I pull myself up again, my feet hanging limp, unsure of what they should do as my biceps and pectoral muscles burn—what number am I on?—and warn me that they cannot keep this up for much longer, but this is a not about physical strength; it is a battle of wills, and I must defeat my commander's. Sheila's face pokes out from between two arbiters, worried and concerned that I will fail. I try to reassure her, but I cannot allow the others to see me looking at her, or they might use her against me. Arbiters are not supposed to have personal feelings or attachments, but mine have always crept through, even in the minutest of forms.

As I look away from Sheila, gray eyes stop me, holding my attention for a second, their tear-filled nature reminding me of a promise I had made: I had vowed to protect Chase's sister, and I cannot do that if I fail here and now. Three more pull-ups go by with my muscles begging me to stop, but I tighten my grip on the bar, digging my stubby nails into the heels of my hands, until drops of crimson blood trickles down my wrists, past the coiled wires stuffed under my sleeve. The blood's redness thrusts me back outside the wall and to the minefield I had not known was there, where the woman met death, and the weight of her mangled body cradled in my arms presses against my skin once more. She died because of my poor planning, and now I cannot ask her for her forgiveness. Forgiveness, a word I have never thought about until now. Arbiters do not seek redemption. We deal out Arel's punishment and are to be obeyed, just like we are to obey Arel, yet the nagging need for forgiveness continues to build within me, simmering the way a covered pot does before the lid is chucked aside from its contents boiling over.

"You may have won a commendation,"—Commander Vye steps around me, circling her prey, yanking me from my internal lashing—"but that does not give you the right to be out of bed after lights out, nor does it give you the right to do as you please. You are not above the law."

Our eyes meet as I lower myself down from another pull up, and I hope that my gaze is just as unforgiving as hers, as I have no desire to allow her the satisfaction of knowing that she has beaten me.

"You may let go."

I relax my hands. A moist film coats my shirt and pants as I land on my side, grunting from the impact, but I refuse to show any pain, even though my hip stings, telling me that I will have a purple bruise there in the morning.

Commander Vye's black boots tread in the grass, circling me, leaving their imprint in the murky, white light. "We have rules for a reason. Anyone who disobeys them will be met with swift punishment. Is that understood?"

"Yes, ma'am!" responds a chorus of voices as those gathered around us stand at attention.

"Dismissed."

"Just a moment."

My blood freezes within my veins as I remain on the ground in a fetal position, only daring to lift my head enough to peer at the person who has spoken, afraid of confirming what I don't want to be true. Molers steps out of the light, allowing himself to be seen, to be more than just a shadowy observer. His time at the munitions factory must have come to an end, much to my dismay.

"Is there something I can help you with, Master Arbiter?" The sarcasm in Commander Vye's voice does not go unnoticed, but Molers remains calm, poised, collected, a snake playing dead while it allows its prey to grow overconfident before it strikes.

"Isn't it convenient that Arbiter Noni is out here, alone, when the landmines outside the wall go off?"

Damn. Of course, he doesn't buy my story; though, I'm not certain that Commander Vye believes that I was out here exercising because I couldn't sleep; it was a lame story when I told it. There is only one thing I can do to convince them that I am telling the truth, and as my mind floats back to Sheila, I wonder how I would have made it this far without her quick wit and foresight. Thrusting my wrist outward, allowing my sleeve to fall back some, revealing my wristband, the one that had been assigned to me when I had received my commendation as arbiter, I glare at those around me, daring them to challenge me, to scan the bracelet, knowing what they will find.

"Go ahead," I say, my voice even and hard, the rebelliousness within it evident.

Renal steps forward with a scanner and runs the red beam over my wristband, watching the screen as it flashes green, telling him where I have been for the last few hours, or at least, where my wristband has been. He closes the scanner and looks at Commander Vye. "She's been here the entire time."

Molers' unforgiving glare bears down upon me, as though trying to read my innermost thoughts, my secrets, but I meet his gaze, daring him to challenge me. I know what he thinks: how convenient. He was never an easy one to fool, but right now he has no proof that I was anywhere but in the quad, but it does not stop him from making my night worse.

"Arbiter Noni is very confident of her abilities," says Molers, and my heart sinks, not liking where this is going. "Perhaps a test."

"We're done here," Commander Vye growls, angered at having her authority tested.

"Are we?" replies Molers in a silky manner, and my nerves explode from the calmness of his voice.

"You have no authority here," says Commander Vye.

Molers opens his mouth, but closes it when Renal shifts his stance, ready to step in, reminding me of the day I had stopped Molers from harming Sheila and how he had to step in to stop Molers from killing me. Again, I wonder about Renal's position here and if he is more than just an arbiter assigned to the eastern sector.

"As a recent assignee to this region, I would like to have my faith in its commander justified, and if you can't control one of your arbiters, then…" Molers allows his voice to trail off, and cold fear grips me.

He has been assigned here? Why? And his request was accepted?

For years, Molers has tried to get assigned to other parts of Arel, to get away from the training facility, but his requests had always been denied. Why approve his transfer now? The chilling thought that I had something to do with it wafts over me, causing me to shiver from its ominous implications. If I had not sentenced him to the munitions factory, he might still be at the training compound, but now he will be here, at the manor, able to watch my every move and torment me once again, as fate has chosen to be punitive by placing me back under his stifling presence.

"And just how can I reignite your faith in me," mocks Commander Vye, though a part of her feels threatened by Molers' accusations. If her authority is in question, she is in danger of disappearing, and she would not be the first commander to have vanished one night and have every semblance of their existence wiped clean.

"The trial of fears." A devious grins spreads across Molers' face as his words echo around me.

The trial of fears. I have heard of it. Every arbiter has. As a testament to their bravery and skill, recruits whose willingness to serve Arel are called into question are forced to face a maze filled with their deepest fears. They are locked in a building, or someplace, the location always changes, and forced to face five challenges. If they succeed, they are reinstated to their position; if they fail, they die, thus ridding Arel of a weak link.

Molers did not pick this task without reason. He does not trust me—he never has—and he covets Commander Vye's position. If I fail, I die, and my commander's ability to train future arbiters will be questioned, thus removing her from command. If I refuse to accept, I die and Commander Vye will be sent to the crematorium. Only one course of action provides the chance of sparing us both.

"I accept," I say.

Hands seize me, hauling me to my feet, and a glint of metal catches my attention: the coiled wires I had shoved under my sleeve have fallen onto the grass, a speck of rust tainting the slender blades of green. If they are discovered… The last thing I see before a black bag is shoved over my head is Renal stepping on the wires, concealing them from view, but whether it is by accident or on purpose is anyone's guess, and I haven't the luxury to ponder it. Stale spittle suffocates me as a thick canvas bag encircles my head, and other arbiters throw me into the back of a transport, the banging of the door slamming shut, sealing my fate, while reminding me of the finality of my decision.

Chapter 8

Trial of Fears

The edges of my boots scrape across a metal surface with raised bumps in it to provide traction, unsure of where to go or what to do as gloved hands shove me through a corridor, not caring if I stumble. Hot, sticky vapor from my rapid and anxious breaths cling to my cheeks and chin, forming their own mask underneath the bag strapped around me head, while sweat coats my hands, soaking the rope securing them. An old-fashioned thing for them to do, but Arel likes its mind games, and I had encountered many of them while at the training facility. The incessant thumps of my pulse in my ears heightens my already nervous senses, but fails to drown out the stomping of heavy-soled boots accompanying me to my doom. I knew Molers would get his revenge for what I did to him, and that I would have to face it someday; I had just hoped that it wouldn't be so soon. I should have been more careful.

The pace slows, and I am jerked to the side as a heavy door opens and the welded on hinges release low, drawn out creaks—a sign that they haven't been used in a while—and with a final shove in the middle of my shoulder blades, I am forced through the opening, causing my feet to entangle themselves, and I fall to the floor, landing on my bound hands, allowing my elbows to take the brunt of the impact. Grunting, I work the rope loose while a metallic thud reverberates around me, mocking my predicament and daring me to challenge it. They're free! Relieved to have my hands free, I yank the black bag off my head and drop it to the floor as I stand up while looking around, searching for clues as to where I am. Ethereal light surrounds me, plunging me into suffocating darkness, and as I turn around, my eyes roaming up and down the walls, noting the gigantic fans in the ceiling, I realize where I am: I'm back at the training facility. The training compound is full of areas set aside for training exercises, and this is one of them.

A high-pitched whine fills my right ear, forcing me to step back. A drone, no bigger than my fist, hovers beside me, capturing my worst moments on its tiny camera and transmitting it back to the viewing room, where I am certain Commandeer Vye and Molers are, waiting to see what my next move will be. I smile to myself, not surprised about the drone's presence. What happens here will either be used to instruct future recruits, or broadcast throughout Arel as a testament of its greatness, or both.

I walk forward, unsure of where else to go, and there must be a door around here somewhere. The hollow thumps of my boots on the metal floor trail after me, giving me the odd sensation of not being alone, yet I am certain that no one else is in here with me. Nerves on edge, I tread with care, unsure of what to expect or what I will be forced to face. The trial of fears is supposed to focus on the fears that the individual participant harbors, forcing him to face them. Sometimes, the ones in charge just choose some of the most cruel things they can think of that will entertain them, but if Molers is watching, then it will be a testament of how well I face my fears, because he knows them well.

A thin chain dangling from the ceiling catches on my shirt, hooking itself deep within the knitted fibers. As I try to untangle it, it pulls and tugs, yanking open a trap door above me, spilling its contents. A wave of squirming tarantulas overwhelm me, covering me in a sea of hairy legs and fangs, all angry at being disturbed and taking their ire out on me. Twisting and turning while bending over to keep them off my face—not that it worked as tiny stings inundate my cheeks—I wave my arms in a frantic motion, desperate to get the hairy beasts off me. Something slams into my side as I run into a rail, knocking the wind out of me, causing me to tumble, while the squirming vermin assault me. The drone hovers nearby, capturing my thrashing as I knock every last one of the tarantulas off me and they scatter, scurrying away, preferring the overreaching shadows over my frantic movements.

I pause. My face burns, my hands burn, and my neck burns, informing me that I have been either bitten, or have gotten some of their urticating hairs underneath my skin, causing an insatiable irritation that I just want to scratch, but I force my mind to focus on the end goal: completing the trials. This is just the first test. Spindly legs stretch out from my shoulder and I jump, flinging the one remaining tarantula off me and onto the metallic floor. It rears up on its hind legs, showing me its fangs in a threatening gesture, hoping to ward me off. Lifting my foot, I stomp on the disgusting creature, feeling it flatten underneath me and turn into jelly as I twist my heel from side to side. Once done, I stare into the camera of the drone, daring those watching to give me another test.

A door on the other side of the chamber opens, releasing its red light into the darkened area surrounding me. Apprehension wafts over me, but I head for it, knowing that I am to go this way, even though it means another trap. Any who do not continue forward in the trials are killed. Memories of another arbiter trapped in here, just like I am now, flood my mind as my fellow recruits and I were forced to watch his trials as part of a lesson. He never got past the second test: a series of electrified wires shooting out 20,000 volts of electricity, enough to fry anything. The man froze when faced with the possibility of being electrocuted. That was when a sniper's bullet killed him.

I stop. Without moving my head, I glance upward, remembering why I feel as though I am not alone—it's because I'm not. Snipers must be up there, above me, or on the same floor as me, ready to assassinate me should I refuse to engage in any of the tests. Giving into fear is never an option here, yet it is the hardest to conquer.

Growling emanates from the shadows before I step into the stream of red light. Peering into the dim glow hovering in the darkness beyond the reach of the red beam, I glimpse the outline of a cage, and the wild dog trapped inside it—its ribs poke through the skin as it has been kept in a starved state so that it will attack anyone it comes across—stares back at me, its yellow eyes taking in my toned form, sizing me up and how I am enough to feed him for a few days. I freeze. I have never liked the wild dogs kept in the space between the outer and inner walls surrounding Arel and still remember the time I had to kill one while a recruit. I never showed fear then, so why is this my second test? Molers must be toying with me. He would have told the ones in charge of these tests my fears, and since he was my instructor for 18 years, he knows them well and would have recommended this.

The cage opens. The dog charges me, saliva dripping from its bared fangs, snapping its jaws as its barks bounce off the concrete walls around me, causing my ears to ring. I dive out of the way and roll across the floor, but before I can regain a defensive posture, the dog snatches my foot between its powerful jaws and tears into the leather, while shaking its head from side to side with such force that I fear it will break my ankle. I roll onto my back and kick it in the face. The dog tightens its hold. As I scoot across the ground on my back, the thought that it will go for my throat shoves its way to the front of my mind, and I search for anything that can be used as a weapon, but I have been left with nothing.

The dog releases my foot. It leaps for me, but I roll across the icy floor, flinging my fists in a vain attempt to ward it off. I touch fur, but have no idea if it made an impact or not, so I continue to roll, until I no longer feel the dog on top of me. As I come to a stop, I rip off my shirt and crouch low, eyeing the dog as it paces in front of me, snarling, exposing its razorlike teeth, and my skin already feels the sensation of them ripping into my flesh, warning me of my very probable future. I wrap the ends of my shirt around my fists while never removing my eyes from the animal, poised and ready for its attack.

It lunges at me. I hold my shirt out in front of me, allowing the dog to bite into it, and while it snaps its jaws in an attempt to get to me, I jump up, flinging myself onto its back and wrap the rest of my shirt around its neck, squeezing as hard as I can while jerking its head into an odd angle. It rears up on its hind legs in an attempt to throw me off, but my grip remains firm as I wrap my legs around its midsection and continue to squeeze the life out of the animal. I feel a pop and the dog goes limp, crashing to the floor with me atop it. Seconds tick by as I refuse to move, unwilling to believe that it is dead, but the longer I remain here, the greater my chances of being killed by a sniper become.

The room ahead of me beckons me to walk toward it and step inside its tomb. Untangling myself form the dead dog, I step toward the open doorway, a moth to the flame, and enter its snare as its blood red light transforms my walnut-colored skin and black undershirt into a crimson fire. The door closes, sealing me inside.

Now what?

I spin around in a slow, methodical motion, scanning the walls from floor to ceiling, but all I see is red on smooth metal, except for a small rectangular shape that appears to be the access port to a circuit box. Before I can wonder why it is there, a tremendous bang mixed with a groan reverberates around me, filling me with dread as the grinding of gears rise in volume and the ceiling edges downward with panels breaking away to accommodate the walls inching their way inward, decreasing the size of the room and threatening to crush me. Being crushed to death: an abhorrent thought that gave me nightmares for a week once.

During my 11th year at the training facility, our instructors decided that it would be prudent to teach recruits what could happen if we were ever pinned down. Molers had been put in charge of the training exercise, and he took some amount of pleasure from tormenting us. He devised a chamber, similar to this one, where the walls closed in and the unfortunate victim trapped inside had to figure a way out. None of us were allowed to talk to each other, nor were we allowed to see within the room to prevent us from observing the chamber's secret escape.

"A test," I remember Molers saying to us before sending the first person in there, "of your resolve under pressure. You must learn to accept that death is imminent. No one escapes it. If you can master that one fear, you will be masters of yourselves."

The recruit sent in before me had panicked. His pleas for help, to be let out, mixed with his agonizing screams as he died, until they ceased, giving in to silence's dominance, still fill my ears to this day, almost as though I am there now. Flesh and flattened bone, glued to the walls by fresh blood, greeted me when Molers shoved me into the chamber. I froze when I stepped on the brains strewn across the floor, what was left of my fellow recruit and the only testament of his meager existence. That same fear freezes me now.

My heartbeat quickens and I start to hyperventilate as the ceiling and walls close in on me. This is about to be my tomb, and I had walked into its trap. Sweat pours down my face, getting in my eyes and forcing me to wipe them as I spin around, desperate to know what to do, how to escape as that fear from so long ago resurfaces and my nightmare becomes a reality.

"Just breathe, Noni!" Faya's voice echoes in my mind, almost as those she is here now, and I remember how as I panicked in the chamber Molers had put me in, her encouraging words filtered through the door, giving me the encouragement I needed to think of a way out of my predicament. She had received a slap for her efforts.

Breathe. Standing still within the shrinking room, I close my eyes and inhale, until my lungs can hold no more air before releasing it in a long, slow, and controlled breath, calming my heartrate and forcing my mind to think. When I open my eyes, they focus on the rectangular panel. The panel! Its wall has not moved.

I rush for it, shoving my stubby fingernails underneath it and pull at it, until I rip it from the wall, ignoring the blood dripping from one of my fingers as its nail tears away from my skin, exposing half of the skin underneath. Coiled wires hang from it, but that isn't what gets my attention: it's the open hole behind the wires just big enough to get an arm through, and the lever that lays beyond it that snatches my focus. I shove my arm through the opening, reaching for the lever, but my fingers come nowhere near it. Of course, they wouldn't let it be this easy.

A wall touches my foot, and my pulse quickens again. The temperature within the room has risen, or my body thinks it has, as sweat glints off my arms and trickles down my neck, forming its own path down my front as it crawls between my breasts and soaks my undershirt. The gears shift, creating a sound that thunders through the metal walls, warning me of a change in its plans. Squished into a room now the size of a closet, the walls cease moving, but not the ceiling: it increases its descent.

I seize the coiled wires and yank them free of their hold, pulling on them, until I have a long enough rope. Shoving my arm back through the hole, wires in hand, I fling one end at the lever, hoping to wrap it around the handle, but each attempt proves to be in vain as the wires slap it before smacking the floor. I try again, and again, but with the same outcome.

The ceiling closes in.

Panic threatens to take hold of me, forcing me to relive my past. I shove it aside, choosing to focus on Faya's old advice of breathing, when I remember Molers' words: death is imminent. Death is certain, but it doesn't have to be today. I jerk my makeshift rope back inside and search for anything that can be used as a hook as I hunch over to avoid being touched by the ceiling as it refuses to let me stand at my full height. The only other item in the room is the panel. I jump for it, grabbing it and bending it between my hands. It is pliable, more so than it should be. It will have to do. Slamming it on the floor, I bend the edges, rolling them up, until I have something that resembles a rod and smack the palm of my hand with it. It smarts. Good. Flattening out on the floor as the ceiling is now just three feet above me, I force one end of my rod up until it resembles a hook before tying the coiled wires around its flat edge.

I shove it all through the opening and fling it at the lever. Almost, but it bounces off. Desperate, and almost out of time, I shove my other arm through the hole and pull the hook back to me. Swinging it, I focus on the lever, releasing a controlled breath as I fling my makeshift hook at it again. It catches it. Bits of hair stick to my neck and face as I squish myself against the opening with my arms crammed through it when the ceiling touches my back. This is it.

I yank the rope.

The lever shifts to the other side as a click sounds, stopping the encroaching ceiling, and I pull my arms back into the room, releasing a sigh of relief. A trap door beneath me springs open, plunging me into a metallic tube, similar to a ventilation shaft, and I reach out, allowing my fingers the squeak against the sides as I try to grab on to something, while still maintaining my grip on the coiled wires. Darkness surrounds me as my mind races. What's next?

In answer to my question, water envelopes me as I drop from the tube and into a pool of water, deep enough to cushion my fall, and some of it rushes into my open mouth, going down my throat and causing me to cough, which results in me inhaling more water. Kicking, I swim to the surface, and relief washes over me when my head bursts through the surface, allowing me to breathe air, crisp, cool air, a welcomed change from the mustiness of the red chamber. The coiled wires float around me, resembling a water snake as it encircles me. With a final bang, my makeshift hook splashes into the water beside me and the trap door closes, sealing itself and denying me a way out.

Transparent walls surround me, allowing me to see into another room and in front of me, hovering in the air with its camera focused on every move I make, is a drone. I glare at it, knowing that people watch its transmission, debating what my next act will be and whether I will pass this test. A series of squeals reach my ears and water gushes from a hole in the ceiling, filling the room with its fury. Fear of drowning. Swimming has never been one of my strengths, so I avoid deep pools of water when I can, and Molers knows this.

The water rises, and within minutes, the glass chamber will be filled. Glancing around, I do not see any opening or access port, just seamless prison of glass. Taking a deep breath, I plunge beneath the surface and swim toward the bottom, hoping to find something—the water makes my surroundings appear to be dancing in front of me—but there is nothing I can use, no obvious means of escape. I hurry back to the surface, gasping for air, dismayed at how fast the water has risen. My focus turns back to the glass and the drone watching me. It must be the only way.

Snatching my hook from the water, I swim to the glass in front of me and bash it with its pointed edge, but all I receive for my efforts is the hook bending. It isn't rigid enough, nor strong enough on its own. I need a sharp edge. I study the lights above me and wonder if its supports will be enough to do what I need. There is just one problem: if the entire structure falls, I risk electrocuting myself. It is a gamble I must make.

I throw my hook around one of the supports for the light and yank on it. Nothing. Hoping the hook remains around the support, I climb the multicolored rope I have, knowing that the light's supports were never meant to hold 145 pounds of pure muscle. A part of me feels as though I have made no progress in my ascent as the seconds tick by and nothing happens.

The water continues to rise.

I bounce the rope, using my weight to jerk the bolts holding the support beam free. One splashes in the water. Again, I tug at it, desperate to get my hands on the metal support. Another bolt pops free and plunges into the water. With each passing second, the surface nears me, until water covers my toes and creeps up my foot to my ankle. I'm running out of time. I bounce on the rope again and again as the light shakes more and more from my movements. The final bolts pop free from their hold and splash in the water, and I plunge into the foaming liquid, followed by the metal support breaking free of the light as it splashes next to me with my hook. The light hangs at an odd angle, and foreboding builds within me as it sinks lower and lower to meet the rising water.

Snatching the rod, I coil my makeshift rope, pulling the hook within arm's reach, and ram the two together while wrapping the line around them, creating a club. The water has almost reached the ceiling. I hurry to the glass and ram my club into it. Hollow echoes vibrate throughout the water. I bash my club into the glass again, using the sharp point of the metal to try and weaken it. Nothing. Again, I ram it into the glass, screaming in frustration when a crack appears. Emboldened, I continue striking the glass in rapid succession, ignoring the burning fatigue within my muscles as the water reaches the ceiling and the dangling light. More cracks appear in the glass, stretching out like a spider's web as they increase, creating more fractures that spread into their own nest of jagged lines. I pull my arm back and deliver a final blow just the water touches the light, causing it to fizzle out. A jolt of electricity courses through me at the same moment the glass breaks, and I curl into a ball as water spills through the hole with me in its grasp.

Gasping for air, I roll across the floor and lay still in the puddle enveloping me as it stretches across the floor, while water drips from the exposed edges of the opening within the glass wall, allowing my chest to rise and fall, savoring each breath I take. The drone hovers above me. Annoyed, I whip my club at it and knock it into a wall where it crashes and shoots out tiny sparks before going dead. Within seconds, another drone appears, taking the previous one's place, and I burst out laughing, amused at how the people controlling them are so intent on observing my efforts to pass the trial of fears, and unable to control myself, even when my sides hurt. Those watching must think that I have lost my mind. I don't care. They aren't here. They can put up with me laughing until I am ready to continue.

Dancing light illuminates the darkened area around me, waving up and down the walls, as an orange glow brightens and dims as though it cannot make up its mind what it wants to do. Turing onto my stomach, I lift my head and see fire jettisoning from vents in the ground and the ceiling in rapid succession. My final test. I stand up, dropping my homemade club and amble over to the edges of the spewing flames; my feet plop on the floor, splashing droplets of water onto my already soaked pants. Each time fire bursts from a vent, a stentorian roar slams into the tomblike walls, bouncing from one to the other, pounding my ears with each echo and causing the miniscule hairs within them to vibrate so much that they itch.

One… two… three… four… five… six… seven… eight… nine… ten.

They are timed, just like in the gauntlet. Confused, I stare at the flames, unsure of why I am to face them again; I never feared them in the gauntlet. An uneasy feeling nudges the back of my mind, warning me to be careful, while the drone hovers behind me, ordering me to continue or face the consequences. The vent in front of me shoots out a wall of fire that lasts for ten seconds, but is enough to kill a person, before going dark. I run. Remembering the gauntlet, I have ten seconds to reach a safe space before the next series of flames begin.

One… two…

My fatigued muscles refuse to work, wanting nothing more than to rest, but I push them onward, demanding more from them, knowing what will happen if I give in to my body's demands.

Six... seven...

Almost there.

Ten!

I jump, landing in a pit as fire bursts from the second vent, and I cover my ears to drown out the roar as heat sears my back, causing my skin to burn and feel hot to the touch. It stops, and the count begins again.

I take off.

One... two...

My lungs work overtime as I breathe fast, in tune with my legs as they stretch before me, sprinting across the charred area to the next safe zone. I keep my focus straight ahead, not daring to look back, afraid that I might stumble if I take my eyes off the red line that marks the end of the fifth and final test. Smoke spews from the vents as an ominous rumble builds, intensifying with each passing second, causing my chest to vibrate in tune to its thunder. A wall of fire erupts behind me as I slide into the second safe zone. Staring ahead, I gauge the distance to the next safe zone, frowning when I realize that it is a greater distance than the previous two. I'll need to...

What the hell!

Something clatters on the floor next to me, shooting sparks in every direction as electricity courses through the metallic floor, and I jump to the side in an effort to avoid it, glad that my boots possess thick, rubber soles. Tapping it with the bottom of my boot, I realize that it is a net, but instead of a normal snare, it is electrified. Another one drops from above as the fires cease, and I leap out of the way, rolling across the floor, my mind racing, wondering what to do about this unforeseen part of the test. The creators of this trial changed the rules on me, chucking what I believed to be the only way to pass this test into the garbage, forcing me to consider another way, but I can think of nothing. I jump to my feet and bolt for the next safe zone—if you

can call it that—trying to count within my head until the next series
of flames, but I've lost my count and focus on running. An electrified
net crashes onto the floor in front of me, and I leap over it, stumbling
as I land, but I get back up, refusing to slow down.

I reach the safe zone and am about to jump in it when I notice
sparks zapping along the bottom: an electrified net lines it! The rumble begins again. Shifting from one foot to the other, I try to think of
what to do, but my mind refuses to work. Either I jump into the pit
with the net and risk electrocution, or I remain where I am and burn
to death. A nail scoots across the floor as my foot touches it. I pick
it up, wondering why a nail is here, but shove it aside—who knows
what this placed was used for before my trials—and fling the nail at
the pit walls, testing them. Nothing. An orange glow fills the void
within the vent closest to me, telling me that I have seconds to act,
and I lower myself into the pit, pressing my feet and hands against
the sides, holding myself above the net as it zaps from the drops of
sweat that fall from my chin. A deafening roar overtakes me, pounding my eardrums, forcing me to scream from its painful eruption as
I hold myself up, while the drone, my constant companion in this
hellish place, hovers below me, capturing every moment.

The fire stops. Silence whistles in my ears as I crawl out of the
pit, being careful not to touch the net beneath me, and I charge
across the final stretch while continuing the count in my head.

One... two... three...

Pure will drives me forward as I am determined to not fail, and
I think of Sheila, and Gwen. If I die here, who will protect them? I
think of my commander, knowing that if I die here, she will meet the
same fate. Besides, I have made it this far; I'll be damned if I fail now.

Four... five...

I push harder, my feet flying over the floor so fast that they look
like blurred smudges. A spark catches my attention.

Shit!

I stop just I plow into the electrified net stretched across the finish line. Pacing in front of it, I search for a way through, but there is none and the count has ended. The final rumble begins, warning me that my time has run out. I need an escape. There has to be a way past this! The overseers of the trials would have left some way for me to win; it is in the rules. I scan the floor and find nothing as the rumble intensifies. Swallowing the lump in my throat in an effort to stay calm, I look upward, for anything that might...

I see it!

An end of a rope dangles high above me, coiled on a platform. I notice the conveyor belt attached to the dais and follow its line back to a single button on the far wall. The whine of the drone fills my ears as it watches me, giving me an idea. I snatch it out of the air and chuck it across the open space, hitting the button that drops the platform, releasing the rope, but it is still too high up for me to reach. Heat encircles me as the ominous orange glow fills the vents, while a series of zaps bursts from the net that imprisons me. Bracing myself, I take a running leap for the rope, knowing that I have one chance to get it right. Fibers touch my hand, and I seize the line, not caring if my tight grip turns my fingers pale as I kick my feet, swinging back and forth in an effort to gain the momentum necessary to propel me over the net. With one final swing, my body drifts over the tangled web of electricity as fire spews from the vents, creating an impenetrable wall that cooks my skin, and I let go. My knees buckle from the impact as I land, forcing me to drop to the floor and somersault over the red finish line.

Snapping reverberates around me as the locks on the giant, steel door in front of me release their hold and it opens, allowing those on the other side to pass through. I glare at the faces surrounding me, looking for familiar ones, spotting Commander Vye, whose face appears to be a mixture of pride and relief, before settling on Molers' fuming eyes.

"Any more requests?" I ask him; my defiant tone does not go unnoticed.

He turns and stalks away, disappearing into the cold light of the corridor, salvaging what dignity he has left.

Chapter 9

A Summons

The bronze gates to the presidential palace loom before me as I approach them, marveling at the carvings upon them—of leaves folding over one another in a linear sort of pattern—that I had not paid much attention to the first time I had been invited here. Each ray of the sun brings out a different shade of red and orange as it shines upon the structure, forming a thin veil of color that resembles burnt smoke more than sunlight, and it changes my black uniform to an apricot color as I pass in front of it, strolling up to the arbiter standing guard, knowing full well that more are nearby should I, or anyone, try anything. He holds his hand out in front of me, stopping me. "State your business," he says in a growl.

"Arbiter Noni, serial number N27461, is here to see President Tapiwa," I say, standing at attention.

The arbiter scrolls through his pad and finds my name there, checking it off, before scanning the mark on the back of my neck, verifying my identity.

A metallic crunch echoes around me as the gates open, allowing me passage. The arbiter says nothing when they open, so I just continue onward and walk through into the courtyard beyond, having not been provided a transport like the last time I was here. More than a week has passed since my escapade in the trial of fears, but instead of being allowed to go back to my life as an arbiter, I received a summons last night; a plebeian had showed up just as my duty shift ended and handed me the request to appear before President Tapiwa before noon today. Not wanting to keep her waiting—it is never a good idea to ignore a presidential request—I made sure I left the manor right after sunrise. And so, here I am, a lone figure walking along the bisque-colored stones of the courtyard as they squeeze together, forming star-like patterns as the bits of glass mixed in them glint in the sunlight, making it look as though I am walking upon a sea of diamonds, heading up the triangular steps to the 20-foot-high copper-lined steel doors. I pause as the gates close behind me, feeling tiny in this stone square, and feeling alone. The last time I was here, Commander Vye was with me and her presence gave me strength, but now… now I must go alone as my mind focuses on one reason after another for the presidential summons. Why does Tapiwa want to see me?

Before I have time to dwell on scenario after scenario, a dark figure sprints down the marble steps, hurrying toward me, his aegean-colored pants billowing in the breeze created by his movements, resembling balloons around his legs more than an item of clothing. In a way, he looks like a blueberry rolling toward me. I inch my way closer to the steps, aware that the only reason this man is here is because it is his job to greet me, and as he comes closer, my mind recognizes him as the same man that greeted me, and the others, when I was here for the ceremony.

"Arbiter Noni!" Kelab, the Minister of Affairs, greets me. "You're here. Good. Good. Follow me."

He hurries back up the steps, but despite how fast his feet move, he doesn't cover much distance, since for every three of his steps, one of mine manages to keep pace. He should learn to walk with dignity and to stand tall and proud like us arbiters. As we go up the marble stairs and through the magnificent doors, the sun's light intensifies, shaking off the sleepiness of the morning, letting everyone know that now is the time to be awake. Like before, we pass under the dome, and like before, I find myself staring up at it and the paintings of glorious moments within Arel, wondering about them, about the past, about how the city was formed, and wondering if there was a time when dark-skinned and fair-skinned walked together as equals, instead of separated. I must have stopped walking because Kaleb clears his throat to shake me from my ponderings.

"My apologies," I say as I continue to follow him up the marble steps and the amber ribbons that weave their way through them, reminding me of endless rivers forming their own tangled web of illusion.

"It is magnificent," Kaleb says with a wink. "Now, come along. We mustn't keep President Tapiwa waiting."

His feet scuffle on the marble floor, squeaking as he hurries off with me walking behind him in a calm fashion, while moving my eyes around to take in the ornate engravings on the walls as they snake up from the floor to the ceiling, looking like candle sticks that are stuck in the wall and can come alive at any moment. I force myself to quit mesmerizing at the grandeur of the palace, though it is difficult, as this is only my second time in the presidential palace and its elegant acquisitions, and I hurry after Kaleb as he takes me up the first flight of stairs and to the two staircases that branch upward, veering to the one on the left.

Unable to contain myself, I place my palm on the railing, remembering that, when I was first here, Kaleb had said it was made out of Lala palm, and it is still just as smooth as the day it was first created. I remove my hand when Kaleb glances back in my direction, winking at me again as though I am some fresh-faced recruit. When we reach the top, the light dissipates into shadowed mystique as we stroll down the corridor and to an area that I assume is the private living space of the two presidents, but what catches my notice is not the change in atmosphere, but the portrait of a man, tall and proud, with an air of arrogance as he holds his chin high and looks down his nose at any unfortunate enough to cross the path below him, dawning the archway at the end.

"Our first president," says Kaleb, somehow knowing that my eyes have been drawn there. "Our current ones are descended from him: pure-blooded Arelians, fit to rule—govern us. Come. Come."

I keep my eyes on the portrait as chills go up and down my spine, making me wary of what lies ahead, and of Tapiwa's true intentions for summoning me here. Once through the archway, darkness overshadows us until we reach a burgundy door with a silver knocker with silver hinges, each with the Arelian insignia engraved on it, and the door handle shaped like a blazing fire that appears to burn as Kaleb opens the door, after giving a quick knock, and the light contained within the room spills out, enveloping me in its dissonance. I step through the doorway and into a room that seems to be from a different era, or place.

The ticking of a grandfather clock fills my ears as my boots cease to clack on the marble floor and sink into a Persian rug that stretches across the room, almost filling it to capacity, held down by bergère chairs, whose scarlet texture accentuate the wine-colored rug as flecks of gold and emerald threads weave their way throughout the rug itself, adding a splash of color to the ivory ceiling above us. I brush the arm of one of the chairs, remarking at its silkiness, and wondering where they acquired such a thing, but I cannot deny the elegance it lends the suite's outer room. As I observe every ounce of color, furniture, and the lighting, the one thing that strikes me as absent is President Tapiwa herself.

Kaleb gives me an embarrassed smile and excuses himself before hurrying to a mahogany door on the far side of the room, giving it a quick knock, before opening it and slipping inside, but despite his efforts to close it, the latch slips and the door swings open just for me to peer inside. I know I shouldn't, but curiosity gets the better of me, and I lean over to sneak a peek. A scurry of movement and shadows hurry around the room as a figure crawls off the bed and to a chair where a lilac-colored robe, made from the thinnest of materials, hangs, while a naked Kumi remains where he is, chuckling at the commotion, giving credence to the rumors about the nature of their relationship. As Kaleb and Tapiwa approach the door, I straighten back up, doing my best to pretend that I have not been snooping and that I am not interested in what goes on here.

"Noni," Tapiwa says through a honeyed smile, exposing her stark white teeth and the pearls within them, "it is good of you to come."

I flash a quick grin as both she and I know that anyone who refuses a presidential summons suffers the consequences.

"Thank you, Kaleb," Tapiwa says, dismissing her Minister of Affairs, and he bows, leaving without a sound.

"You must be wondering why I asked you here," she says as she strolls over to a desk that is built into the wall and presses a button, bringing up a monitor, her sheer robe leaving little to the imagination as to what lies underneath as it parts, almost allowing one of her breasts to spill out, but I remain silent. She is the president and I am nothing more than an arbiter. Outside the presidential palace, I have authority, but here, I am little more than a plebeian.

"I must say that you are an enigma, Noni. Your exploits in the trial of fears was quite the show and proof of how well-trained our arbiters are, and that I made the right choice."

She watched that? I know Molers had, and that all recruits at the training facility will be forced to watch it, but what is her interest in it?

"Your tenacity is what we need right now," Tapiwa continues. "Tell me, what caused you to demand the challenge?"

"The challenge was presented to me, and an arbiter never refuses a contest. To do so would be to admit failure." And, as we are often reminded, failure is death.

"Such bravery is what I need right now."

The monitor flashes to life and images appear. I study them, wondering where they are from and what this all means as the reports scroll across the screen, broken only by the intermittent flashes of people struggling to carry loads that weigh more than they do.

"As you will recall, I had asked you to go to the mines some time ago, but your shoulder needed time to heal after your exemplary actions during the bombings."

For a moment, I stand dumbfounded, until I remember that she had told me about the mines, and I had accepted, but so much has happened since that I had forgotten all about it.

"Yes, ma'am," I reply when I realize that one is expected of me, while administering an internal reprimand to myself for having forgotten all this, and how I was forced to sentence Chase to work in one of the agricultural sectors.

"We've been having a problem at the mines," continues Tapiwa. "Production is down, and it appears that Commandant Gant is having difficulty meeting quotas. Without the ore from the mines, we cannot power our homes or our businesses. Arel depends upon the ore for survival and way of life. It is vital for our existence that production increases. This much you know. However, it appears that there has also been some unrest at the mines. According to some reports, it appears that the workers there have this idea that they can be contrary. Such obstinance cannot be allowed, or we will all suffer."

"Then, perhaps someone should be sent there to remind Commandant Gant what failure means," I say, reiterating what I know she wants to hear, and what is expected of me.

A grin snakes across Tapiwa's face, making me feel as though I have just stepped into a trap, as an unnatural heat rises within me and settles around the base of my neck.

"That is where you come in."

I bite my tongue to keep from voicing the words that enter my mind.

"I want you to go to the mines. All I get from Commandant Gant are excuses, and what I want are results. I want you to observe the mines and do what is necessary to increase production."

"With all due respect," I begin, choosing my words with care, "should a more experienced arbiter be sent? I know very little about the mines."

"Your shoulder is healed, is it not?"

"It is."

"Most arbiters do not display your sense of strong will. I need someone who does not flinch when faced with an impossible task and who will see things through. Your actions in the trial of fears prove that you are willing to do what is necessary to accomplish a goal. That is what I need right now. I would not have considered you otherwise."

Though her words make sense, there is still a gnawing feeling in the pit of my stomach that she is not telling the entire truth behind her reasons for sending me and an ever-increasing suspicion that Molers challenging me to the trial of fears was no accident.

"Of course, you won't be going alone. A more experienced arbiter will be sent with you, to ensure that Commandant Gant heeds your authority. I will expect constant reports."

"Yes, ma'am," I reply, knowing that I am committed to this venture, whether I want to be or not.

"Are there any questions?"

Plenty, but I know that I cannot voice them here, so, I settle on one.

"When do I leave?"

"Tomorrow." Tapiwa presses another button on the desk and the door to the suite opens, allowing Kaleb inside.

"Madam President," he says with a bow.

"Kaleb," Tapiwa responds, "please see to it that our guest finds her way out."

Tomorrow? So soon? Questions burn within me, each wanting its own set of answers, but with the way Tapiwa turns her back on me and stares at the door leading to the bed chamber, I reconsider my initial desire to voice my mind and salute her before heading for the door, knowing that I have been dismissed.

"Good luck," she says as I leave, confirming that there is more going on here than just the simple task of addressing the lack of production at the mines.

Kaleb ushers me through the corridor, down the marble staircases and out the door in such a hurry that I do not remember setting foot outside as the bronze gate closes behind me and the arbiter standing guard glares at me, warning me to move along instead of loitering. Deciding it best to make myself scarce, I hurry down to the nearest railcar platform and hop on a train before the doors close, not paying much attention as we speed along, leaving the tall glass buildings with their pristine exteriors reflecting the backdrop of Arel for the more dilapidated, crumbling structures of the eastern sector.

Just like everyone else, when the railcar stops, I get off, not caring that people give me a wide berth so as not to end up on the receiving end of an arbiter's wrath. I cannot stop thinking about the task Tapiwa has charged me with. To not accept it will result in severe consequences, and not just for me; but I am not qualified, which makes me wonder what her true intentions are. Is she toying with me, or does she believe in my abilities? As my mind ponders over the morning's events, my feet lead me back to the manor, back to the place I have called home for over a year, and the front door—it's glass still green from mold growing in between the panes—slides open, allowing me to cross its threshold.

Sheila busies herself with scrubbing the spokes of the railing for the staircase and glances in my direction, flashing me a quick grin, but making certain that no one else notices. I return the gesture, but before I have time to hurry up to my room, Commander Vye calls me from her office.

"Noni, a word."

My heart skips a beat as I wonder what it is I must have done wrong to demand such a summons. I stalk over to her office, knowing that there is no getting out of whatever it is she wishes to speak with me about, and shut the door behind me as I step inside. She sits behind her desk, with all the items upon it either stacked or in neat little rows where nothing is out of place.

"Have a seat."

I do a double take. I have been summoned to Commandeer Vye's office before, but never asked to sit down. She keeps her eyes on me as she waits for me to take the only chair in the room, beside hers, so I sit down as ordered, still unsure of why I am here.

"How was your meeting with President Tapiwa?"

I do not bother asking how she knows about it. Of course, she knows about it. No one can receive a presidential summons and not have their commanding officer be aware of it as well.

"It went well," I say, being careful in my choice of words, unsure if this is a test or not.

"You do not sound convinced."

I could scold myself. Commander Vye always sees through me, despite my best attempts at hiding my true feelings about something.

"I have been ordered to go to the mines to get them in order," I say, still not believing it myself and grappling with the fact that such a task has been thrust upon me.

Commander Vye glances around as though she is afraid of being overheard before she opens her mouth again.

"Be wary of her."

"Ma'am?"

Again, Commander Vye looks around as though she is afraid of being overheard.

"The mines are dangerous, more so than the outposts. Few who go there, ever leave."

"How do you…"

"Another of my arbiters was sent there once, two years back. He never survived his first night."

"What?' I say without thinking, and the word is out of my mouth before I can stop it.

Commander Vye leans over her desk and speaks in a low voice.

"Tapiwa is more like a cat; she toys with people, sizing them up, before deciding what to do with them, and for some reason, she has taken a keen interest in you."

"May I ask why?"

"You made quite the impression at the ceremony and another impression in the aftermath of the attack, and a third when you defeated the trial of fears."

"Why would she watch…"

"All you need to concern yourself with is the fact that she did. Did she tell you anything else?"

"I will be accompanied by a more senior arbiter."

Commander Vye leans back in her chair as a pleased expression crosses her face. "When do you leave?"

"Tomorrow."

"Listen, and listen well, Noni: trust no one outside of these walls, except the senior arbiter that accompanies you. I mean it! Trust no one, but the arbiter that is with you."

"Commander," I say, getting the feeling that there is much more at stake than me being sent away for a temporary assignment, "is something wrong?"

"Much is happening that makes little sense. Keep your mind sharp. Keep your wits about you. And do not, under any circumstance, let your guard down. When you return, I will want to read the report you are to send to Tapiwa."

"Yes, commander."

"Dismissed."

Confused, I stand up, salute Commander Vye, and leave her office, wondering what just happened and why her words to me were so cryptic. What does she know that I do not? I feel like a pawn in a grander scheme, and it angers me. As the door shuts behind me, I spot Gwen carrying a tray into the kitchen. She takes one look in my direction and hurries away, refusing to acknowledge me, not that I blame her, I am the reason that her brother is no longer here, and as the memory of that incident fills me, my heart aches. I hope Chase is well and is allowed to return soon. Gwen shouldn't be alone.

A door closes upstairs, jerking me from my moment of self-pity, and I wander over to the stairs and go up to my room to prepare for what tomorrow brings.

Chapter 10

The Farms

My legs feel as though they have been bound in cement and scrunched up against my body to the point where their current position will now be permanent, as I try wiggling my toes inside my boots while the transport bounces up and down on the uneven dirt road. We have been on the road for a day, without stopping, except for the few instances where someone needed to relieve themselves. I try to look out the window, but there is little point in doing so as the blackness of night greets me, and with no moon, there is not even the tiniest of light to see anything. Pitch black. That it is.

I glance at Renal as he sits straight backed in the front seat with his eyes straight ahead. One can only imagine my relief when I saw Renal waiting at the main entrance to the manor with a single bag, ready to depart upon my say so. Commander Vye had told me to only trust the senior arbiter that accompanies me; somehow, she must have known it would be Renal, or she called in a few favors to ensure it would be him. Either way, I am pleased that he is with me, even though he hasn't said a single word.

I shift as best as I can, as a few pins and needles radiate through my legs from having been in the same position for hours, though my attempts at relieving the pressure on my knees proves to be futile as my back now hurts, which is soon mitigated the moment my head slams into the top of the vehicle as we roll over a deep pothole. Though my head now aches, I refrain from rubbing it as arbiters are supposed to be able to endure pain and discomfort. Be like Renal, I tell myself, as I straighten up and do my best to remain still and alert, just like Commander Vye had warned me to. Another jolt knocks me around as we hit another hole in the road, making me wish that this road was paved.

Before I have time to get back into my seat, a bright, white light shines into the dusty front window of the transport, illuminating every corner, every crevice, and showcasing just how grimy the seats are, making me wish that the darkness would come back just so I do not have to look at them. The brightness of the light forces me to shield my eyes as it blinds us all and the transport comes to a halt. I shift, trying to get a better look at where the light comes from.

"Remain still," Renal warns me as armed guards run up to the transport, pointing their weapons at us, and as they pass in front, blocking the spotlight, I notice the heavy artillery on top of a giant wall that impedes our desire to go forward, all of them armed and ready to fire upon any threats that come their way. Following Renal's advice, I sit up straight and clinch my muscles, ordering them to remain still, to not flinch or do anything that would give the guards cause to react with force.

A gloved fist bangs on the driver's window and the driver opens it. "State your business," demands the guard that the gloved fist belongs to.

"Arbiter Geril, serial number G76329," replies the driver, as his tattoo is scanned. "We are here at the behest of President Tapiwa."

A fist pounds on Renal's window while another knocks on mine. Together, Renal and I give our name and serial number and both of our tattoos on the back of our necks are scanned, verifying our identities.

"You may go inside," says the guard to the driver, "and park where you are told. Do as you are told. Any deviance will be met with force."

The driver puts the transport into gear and eases it forward as the gate swings outward, opening just enough for us to go in, and as the spotlight leaves us, I take the chance to sneak a peek at the giant wall surrounding whatever lies hidden inside, reminding me of Arel's wall that serves as a protective barrier from the outside wall, as well as a set of concrete bars designed to keep the inhabitants inside at all times. No one leaves. No one enters. That is how it is, and the same must be true here. The sound of tires upon gravel fill my ears as the engine reverberates in the vehicle, causing everything within me to resonate as the driver eases us inside, pulling into the designated spot marked for us. More guards surround us, their black helmets reflecting the lights around us, allowing no one to see their faces.

Renal opens his door and steps out of the transport. I do the same. The moment I touch the door handle, a bit of burnt red touches my hand, turning my walnut-colored skin crimson, and as I step out, I glance to the source of the light, noting that dawn has arrived as the sun peeks over the horizon, shedding the first rays of its magnificence on the world, but even though it should bring me warmth, all I feel is coldness as the barrels of weapons glare at me, ready to fire if their masters will it. Once again, I take my cue from Renal as he steps forward with slow deliberate steps, and I do the same, keeping my hands where they can be seen.

"Gentlemen, gentlemen," says a jovial voice as an arbiter steps forth with the stripes of a commandant on his shoulders.

The guards relax their weapons, but remain ready to respond should Renal or I try anything while the driver remains in the transport.

"You must be Arbiter Noni," the man says to me.

"Yes, sir," I reply, saluting him.

"Commandant Firth at your service," he introduces himself, "and…" He pauses as he looks at Renal.

"Lieutenant Renal."

"Welcome!" Commandant Firth waves his arms. "Come. Don't mind them"—he points at the guards who still watch us with icy stares, ready to attack us should we try anything—"they won't bite."

Something tells me that biting us is not what they have in mind, as we walk past the guards and their helmeted heads turn in our direction as we move, keeping their eyes fixed upon us.

With each step, the sun rises higher in the sky, turning the red dirt orange, before lighting up the sky enough for the dirt and the grass around us to shine bright in their natural colors. We follow Commandant Firth up a set of steps built into the side of a hill as he leads us into the compound, and as I reach the top, my eyes widen at the sight that lies before me: fields upon fields of crops stretch out before us, filling every inch of land as a massive wall surrounds it, that seems to stretch on for miles, and as I remain transfixed, the sun's rays move over the fields, lighting up tomatoes, corn, wheat, beans, carrot stalks, peppers, radishes, blueberries, strawberries, cherry trees, an apple grove, parsnips, and grape vines. Further onward are fences that circle around the crops as shapes strolls back and forth behind them and I wonder if they are livestock.

"Magnificent, isn't it?" says Commandant Firth.

"Yes, sir," I reply, unsure of what else to do.

"Welcome to the farms!"

Commandant Firth walks forward, finding some steps that lead down into the fields themselves, and both Renal and I follow, knowing what is expected of us.

"I must say that I was surprised to receive a special communication from President Tapiwa regarding your arrival, but I guess that it is important for even arbiters to know where their food comes from."

"I do as I am told," I say when I realize that Commandant Firth expects me to shed light upon my presence here, but in all honesty, I have no idea why I am here. Tapiwa said that I was to go to the mines. She never mentioned a detour to the farms, except... Chase is here. I had sent him here, and he had not returned to the manor, meaning that he should still be here. Does she know about him? Did she know about the incident that landed him here, and my lenient punishment as a way of sparing him?

Shadows move from the edges of the fields, closing in on the crops with their shovels, rakes, and scythes, and it take a moment before I realize that these are people, and the closer I look, the more I realize that they are plebeians and only plebeians. Some of the places I had gone to had a mixture of both plebeians and citizens who had broken Arelian law, but here, only plebeians work the fields while their overseers, Arelians in green uniforms, signifying that they work for the agricultural sector, walk the fields directing the plebian field hands. I watch as they move into the fields or the orchards and start weeding or chipping away at the hard dirt to make a space for a new plant, while arbiters line the edges—some wander through the fields as well—keeping watch on everyone and everything, ready to act should trouble arise.

Commandant Firth continues down the steps, which are nothing more than metal grates shoved into dug-out sections of the slight hill and filled in with loose gravel, mimicking steps, and our boots clomp with each step until we reach the rock-solid ground at the bottom.

"Here is where we grow the food that feeds all of Arel. The fields are plowed every season," Commandant Firth says as he leads us down a row of legumes while the sounds of shovels hitting dirt surround us, "crops are rotated—there is never a time when we are not toiling over the land."

"What about winter?" I ask.

Commandant Firth smiles, pleased that I asked a question, for which he can showcase how well he runs this place.

"Let me show you."

Renal and I follow the commandant to the edge of the field—a few eyes glance in our direction before diverting themselves back to their work, while hoping to go unnoticed—as he leads us down a path as the sun's warmth envelops us while we walk until we come to an overgrowth of apple trees and tall, transparent buildings, with beads of moisture covering their walls, allowing no one to peek inside at the treasures contained within. As the commandant approaches a doorway to one of these buildings, a plebeian opens it for him, allowing us through. It's as though I have just walked into a sauna, as an intense wave of moisture hits me, covering my uniform, causing little droplets of water to form on the sleeves of my jacket, but the moment the leaf of a plant touches my cheek, I pause. All around me are various plants, just like the ones outside, but are contained by pots and either hang from the ceiling or are on shelves. Lush, green leaves holding bountiful fruit surround me, plunging me into a sort of edible jungle, as I wander around the greenhouse, observing all the plants and the plebeians that tend them.

"These greenhouses," says Commandant Firth, "are what get us through the winter. They run year-round, and without them, the people of Arel would starve."

Renal gives the commandant a glance as though to warn him to not embellish his role in feeding Arel too much, and the commandant rethinks his words.

"We try to grow most of what we need outside, but sometimes, it isn't enough. This is one of thirty greenhouses. They are all climate controlled. There is a sprinkler system that runs through the ceiling here"—he points upward, and for the first time, I notice a series of pipes with sprinkler heads attached to them, lining the ceiling of the greenhouse—"which is on a timer. Every half hour, it turns on and waters the plants. The crops in here are tended every day and with the utmost of care."

Commandant Firth leads us to the other end of the greenhouse where a door is and through another door to the outside. The moment I cross the threshold, I cough from the sudden dryness of the air, but manage to swallow enough spit so as to moisten my throat and prevent myself from coughing anymore, as it can be seen as a sign of weakness and weakness is never permitted.

"The livestock we keep are contained over there," says Commandant Firth. "We have cows and chickens and we keep them separated."

The mooing of a cow grabs my attention and I turn in time to watch a plebeian pour water into a trough for it to drink from, while others go into the chicken coops with baskets, coming out a few minutes later with eggs.

"What is that over there?" I ask, pointing at a black building with no windows, no discernable doors, and looking as though uninvited guests are not welcomed.

"The slaughterhouse," says Commandant Firth. "We will not be going there."

It appears that I am not to see everything here. We walk underneath an arch of branches, hanging low from the apples that weigh it down, as the commandant leads us to another part of the massive farm, and I find myself glad to be in the shade and away from the increasing warmth of the sun. As we continue, something gnaws at me, and I find myself wondering where we are going. A quick peek at Renal tells me that he is also uneasy, as his eyes dart from vantage point to vantage point, but he never says anything, preferring the advantage of silence.

As we continue to follow Commandant Firth to an unknown part of the massive farm, I start to open my mouth to inquire where we are going when I notice a man, about my age, leaning over a shovel in the bright sunshine as he rams it into the ground, scooping away dirt. Is it? The hair, the build, it has to be Chase, but I cannot see his face. My heart skips, excited to know that he is alive, but angered at the fact that he is still here. Gwen has not stopped crying since he left, and I cannot bear the fact that she carries that loneliness with her. I open my mouth to ask about that area, just so the commandant will take us closer to Chase, but I needn't bother because it seems as though Commandant Firth can read my mind and diverts his trek through the apple grove to the field beyond and the man with the shovel. The closer we get, the more my heart pounds from excitement and fear. I take in a deliberate, yet slow, breath, willing my nerves to quiet themselves as I do not want to attract unwanted attention, but the closer we get, the harder it becomes.

An arbiter strolls past the man with the shovel and appears to say something to him. Curious, I stop, wondering what is going on, but before I can ponder the interaction between the arbiter and Chase, he runs off, throwing the shovel to the side—it kicks up a bit of dust as it hits the ground—and heads for the wall. He sprints, ignoring the shouts and the commands, but something about this seems off. The arbiter that had spoken to him just stands there watching the proceedings as Chase runs before it hits me: this is a setup. I start to open my mouth, start to yell, but Renal stops me.

"Escapee!" he shouts, which seems to force the surrounding arbiters into action, as though they were waiting for someone to say something.

I watch, helpless, as they raise their weapons and fire—no warning, nothing—and my heart stops as the man drops to the ground, unmoving. I cannot stay here as he lays dying. I can't... I take off, ignoring Renal's attempts to stop me, and stop as one of the guards flip the fallen man with his boot and come to a halt when I see the face. It's not Chase. Relieved, I release the air I have been holding in my lungs, glad that it is not him lying dead on the ground, but that relief turns to anger and bewilderment. This was meant for me. Every fiber in my being tells me that this little show was meant for me as a warning, a test, or both. My fists clench, but before I can go any further, Renal appears by my side and grips my arm, warning me to reign in my temper.

"You seem anxious," says Commandant Firth in a nonchalant tone, as though he has been studying my actions, and for a brief moment, I wonder whom he will be reporting this to. "Or is that relief I see."

"Fury," I reply. "Are you incapable of keeping your plebeians in line? One runs off and your arbiters act as though they are sleeping on the job. He should have been dealt with the moment he dropped his shovel."

The commandant studies my actions, but I keep the tone of my voice even, but harsh, the sort of harshness one expects an ar-biter to have, but I can tell he is not buying my response. To sell it, I stalk over to the dead plebeian on the ground. I have no idea who he is, but am convinced that he was told to run just so he could be sacrificed. With the commandant watching, I swing my foot back and ram it into the side of the dead plebeian's head, causing it to snap before approaching the commandant. "One less piece of plebeian trash is of no consequence, but your lack of control over this is disturbing. Perhaps I shall include this in my report to President Tapiwa."

The commandant's face twitches. If this was all for my benefit, Commandant Firth seems to not want any of it to reflect upon him.

"There will be no need. I will ensure that such an incident never happens again."

I keep my eyes planted on him, hoping to make him sweat un-derneath the uniform of his, but Renal cuts it short.

"Is there anything else, commandant? We do have a schedule to keep."

"Yes, of course," replies the commandant as he leads us away from the dead plebeian and back to where our transport is parked.

As we head back, curious eyes glance at us, making certain not to linger for too long as the people they belong to keep their mouths sealed, but unease flows over me as we march through the fields until we reach the steps. I do not wait to be told what to do and go up them in a hurry, making my way to the transport where the driver waits for both Renal and me.

"Thank you, Commandant," Renal says as we get inside the transport and the driver starts the engine.

Commandant Firth says nothing as the vehicle heads for the

gates, which open up enough to let us through, before sealing behind us, and as we drive away, the feeling that the artillery on the
wall remains trained on us refuses to leave me. I force myself to
remain facing forward, instead of sneaking a look back as the gates
disappear in the distance, but despite my anxiety about what the
mines will bring, only one thing remains on my mind: Chase, where
are you?

Chapter 11

The Mines

A few wisps of clouds brush the sun, darkening everything for a second until they pass, as the transport rolls into the mines, past armed guards ready to fire upon anyone who proves to be a threat. I remain facing forward, not wanting to appear too interested in the people working the mines, but curiosity keeps a tight hold on me, so I move my eyes toward the window for a quick peek. Worn eyes return my gaze, filled with hollow ambition, void of any desire to do more than what is required of them; their despondency gnaws at me, and a lump forms in my throat as I am reminded of the plebeian quarters where the same misery resides. A mural of wretched faces passes by my window, poised and positioned just so with grungy rags tied around their mouths in a pathetic attempt to prevent them from breathing in the choking clouds of dust, as though an artist placed them there to capture and convey just the right amount of emotional evocation. Sunken cheeks creep by the window as a man, coated in ashen dust, flicks his gaze toward the transport before jerking it away and going back to his work. I swallow another lump. The abasement of this place radiates from each person here, from the darkest corner deep within the mine to the brightest spot outside, but not even the sun can comfort this place as its light dwindles when it touches the dirt, unable to bring about any form of solace.

The transport stops. I take a quick look at Renal, who remains erect and unmoving, just like I have seen Commander Vye do so many times, before opening the door and stepping out of the protected interior of the vehicle and into my newest assignment. A man marches up to us, his quick steps leaving deep impressions within the sifting soil, surrounded by three guards dressed in full armor with helmets that conceal their faces. Remaining still, I make certain to not give the guards any excuse to shoot me. A woman's scream snaps my attention. I turn, unable to stop myself, and find a woman, a citizen, lying on the ground with her arms in front of her, begging the guard beating her with a switch to stop. I shift my foot to confront it when a hand grips my arm, stopping me; its force unnerves me, and I look up into the Renal's eyes, warning me to stay out of it.

"Welcome!" says the man marching up to us, and the creased lines of his black uniform stand out in the sunlight. "I am Commandant Gant, and you must be Arbiter Noni." He wraps my hand in his own and the grin on his face makes the misshapen dark spot on his ebony cheek—a sign that he has spent a fair amount of time outdoors—wrinkle.

"Thank you," I say, unsure of how to respond.

"This way," the commandant waves us forward, taking the lead as he walks further into the compound amidst a symphony of shovels hitting dirt, pickaxes striking rock, and the squeaking wheels of the mine carts ambling down their tracks, overloaded with treasures.

He leads us to a haphazard structure that looks as though it had been slapped together with little thought to safety or durability as its roof slumps in the middle from neglect, while the posts supporting the entrance tip inward toward each other. I study it a moment, doubtful if it will remain standing while we are inside, but Commandant Gant stomps through the sliding doors, encrusted with dirt, coloring them brown, and the rest of us follow. A few seconds pass for my eyes to adjust after being in the sunshine, and I twist on the spot, taking in the wall-sized monitors bursting with images of workers slumped over, weighted down by their tools, as they trudge into the darkened caverns of the underground in search of treasure coveted by Arel. The outside of the building may have appeared to be a hermit's humble dwelling, but the inside is awash in Arel's glorious technology, as arbiters sit in front of monitors, each with a headset on, speaking into it, communicating with the guards that patrol the mines, keeping a careful watch on those under their supervision. Inaudible messages meld with the whomp-whomp of the fan spinning above us in its meager attempt to stir the air to prevent the room from feeling hot.

A familiar face on a monitor catches my attention. Is that... It cannot be. Did he see me when I first pulled into the mines and follow me to the command center where he stands, trying to avoid the guards while waiting to see if he saw who he thinks he saw? But he is supposed to be...

"Arbiter Noni!"

I jerk away from the monitor, remembering where I am and why I am here as Commandant Gant's voice bursts through my all-consuming thoughts.

"Commandant," I say, having no idea what he had just asked me.

"The commandant," Renal says, saving me from embarrassment once again, "is interested to know your opinion on the worker's productivity."

I turn away from the monitor, from the face that seized my attention, formulating the words needed to appease the commandant—I do not want to appear as though I am taking over his job—while saving face in front of the others within the room.

"You have quite the setup here, commandant," I say in a pleasant voice, "but you know why I am here."

That answer should force Commandant Gant to repeat what he had said while I was distracted. It does. "As I was saying, we are a copper mine, and as you know, our productivity is down. The presidents are not happy, and if we fail to get productivity up…"

His voice trails off, but he doesn't need to finish his statement—we all know what happens to those who fail.

"At the present," continues Commandant Gant, "this mine produces about twenty thousand pounds of copper ore to send to the smelters. Presidents Kumi and Tapiwa wish that to increase to thirty thousand, which brings us to why you are here."

He says that last bit with doubt and disdain, which does not surprise me.

"I have a job to do," I say, "just like you."

"Yes, but…" begins Commandant Gant.

"Arbiter Noni may be young in years, but she has proven herself more than capable of the most harrowing of tasks," Renal interrupts, his tone carrying a sense of finality to this direction in the conversation, and once again, I wonder if he is more than just an arbiter assigned to the eastern sector like me. Such musings are cast aside as Commandant Gant steers the conversation back to my reason for being here.

"I'm questioning nothing. As you can see"—the commandant directs our attention to one of the monitors with images of workers, plebeians, and citizens together, filling a mine cart with bags full of ore or copper—"our workers move slowly and lack any sort of enthusiasm in performing their duty to Arel."

By the bony features on many of them, as their limbs lack muscle, making me wonder how these walking skeletons stand at all, I see why they have no enthusiasm.

"How much are they fed throughout the day?"

"A single ration," replies Commandant Gant.

"That should be increased," I say, my voice dispassionate, yet firm.

"Increased?" protests Commandant Gant, but Renal clears his throat, silencing the man.

"Yes, increased. You want them to perform intense manual labor for ten or twelve hours a day, yet you do not feed them enough. And each worker will be allowed a day of rest." Even in the training facility, recruits received one day a week that was their own with no drill, no studies, just relaxation.

"We cannot shut down this mine for a day."

"You won't. The mine will continue to operate seven days a week, but the workers will be divided into groups, and each group will be rotated so that everyone gets at least one day to rest."

"This is absurd!"

"Are you questioning Arbiter Noni's orders?" asks Renal, a dangerous edge to his voice, "and thereby questioning the presidents' themselves?"

Commandant Gant rethinks his words. "No, sir."

"Well, I think this is ridiculous! The workers are here to work. That is their job. They are just plebeians or people striped of their citizenship," says a cold, yet familiar voice, and I turn, wishing that the person speaking is not who I think she is, but disappointment has long been my companion.

Grelyn stands on the edges of the room, proud and defiant, believing that everyone should care about her opinion, and still acting as though she can do whatever she desires and get away with it, as was the case on most occasions at the training facility. Renal directs his annoyance toward her.

"Name. Rank," he demands, and Grelyn shrinks under his harsh tone.

"Grelyn, arbiter," she replies, keeping her voice devoid of fear, even though she takes a step back from Renal.

"Your business here?"

"I am here to help the workers navigate the mines and find abundant deposits of copper ore."

That makes sense, as much as I hate admitting it. With her ability to see in the dark, she is a valuable asset, and in a place such as this, she will have no trouble spotting rich deposits or helping the miners dig new tunnels.

"So, why are you not in the mines?" asks Renal.

"I am here to file a report." Grelyn falters underneath Renal's intense gaze.

"Report," commands Renal.

Grelyn swallows, knowing that she has taken on more than she can handle as Renal intends to make an example of her.

"Commandant Gant, we have encountered a blockage. We will need digging equipment to clear it out if we wish to access the rich deposits behind it."

"Understood," replies Commandant Gant.

Grelyn turns to leave, but Renal stops her.

"I think you are forgetting something."

Grelyn's glare could curdle milk, but she remains in control of her mouth, faces me and says, "My apologies, Arbiter Noni. It is not my place to question your authority here."

"Dismissed," Renal says, and Grelyn rushes out of the room, hurrying through the sliding doors and disappearing into the sunlight.

I release the breath that has been trapped in my lungs, kept there from the surprise of Grelyn's presence, and I have a feeling it will not be the last my surprises.

"Commandant Gant, I would like to see the rest of this facility."

Relieved, and pleased to feel important again, the commandant urges Renal and me to follow him through another door leading into the center of the mines itself.

"This is the sorting area," he says, his tone robotic, and I watch as three people struggle to push a mine cart—bits of rock drop off the top of its load—up a small rise where they tip it over and dump the contents. Others rush up and seize the misshapen lumps of rock, throwing them into different piles to be loaded into dump trucks, their soiled and bony fingers almost the same thickness as the rest of them. "Any ore found will be sent to the smelters, while the stuff deemed unusable is cast aside and dumped in the wildlands."

Renal and I follow behind Commandant Gant as he leads us

down a hill and toward the entrance to the mine. Vacant eyes look up from their work for a moment before casting themselves downward, pretending to have not been interested in our presence and hoping that we will ignore them. Movement causes me to look behind. For a moment, I believe that the same familiar person I saw on the monitors follows us, but I cannot be certain, nor can I show too much interest, as my place is here, and my duty is to complete the task assigned to me. Commandant Gant's voice drones on, not caring if anyone listens, concerned more with hearing himself talk, but amidst his prideful boasts of quality production, despite the fact that the reason I have been sent here proves otherwise, all my mind focuses on is the forlorn, wrinkled, and soiled faces before me trudging in and out of the mine shaft with apathy and death as their constant companions.

As though rooted to the ground, my feet refuse to move another step, forcing me to remain where I am, surrounded by the workers and their guards. The creaking of wheels draw my attention. Two workers trudge up the hill, pushing a grime encrusted mine cart, stopping when they reach the top and stepping away for a second, one second too long. The brake pops free, and the cart edges its way down the slope, picking up speed as it goes until it careens downward.

"Look out!" someone shouts.

Guards and workers dodge out of the way of the raging cart, missing it by seconds. Among the chaos, a man stands up, chucking his shovel to the ground where it plops in the lifeless dirt, before charging for the rails, his shredded pants flapping behind him, clearing themselves of metallic dust in a feeble attempt to cleanse themselves for this final act. He stops in the middle of the tracks. Shouts and yells for him to move rage all around me before silence crushes them, and helplessness takes its hold as we watch the cart crash into the man, crushing him, smearing his flesh and bones across the tracks—a poor testament of his meager existence—before skipping the tracks and overturning, where it slides on its side with debris shooting out of its bed until it stops. As the noon sun illuminates the fresh blood blanketing the tracks, people turn away, going back to their work, and the cold melody of their digging tools fill the air.

I stand frozen in time, staring at blood, reminded of the woman at the factory who chose death over a life of forced servitude, while memories of the infant she tried to protect inundate my mind, accusing me of being no better than the heartless guards joking about the man's final act of desperation. Someone speaks to me, but my ears do not transmit his words to my brain. The taunting, the laughing, their callous reaction to what has happened infuriates me, igniting a rage that has sat dormant for years, only surfacing when my survival depended on it; but it threatens to escape its imprisonment, desperate for justice, or is it revenge it wants?

A guard throws someone to the ground and I whirl around to see what is happening. He raises his switch and brings it down upon the poor victim, and as it strikes pale flesh, the face I had been seeing since I arrived, the face I thought I saw on the monitors, stares up at the guard in defiance: it is Chase. My feet charge across the dirt, kicking up poufs of silty sand, as they carry me across the embankment to where Chase lies on the ground with his arms around his face, protecting it from the guard's wrath. I plow into the guard, knocking him to the ground and stand over him, my feet shoulder width apart and my fists clenched, ready to fight.

"Striking a starved plebeian is easy," I say, "but if it is a challenge you want, why don't you face someone who can fight back."

After the words are out of my mouth, I scold myself for being so rash and making such a bold statement, but despite my second thoughts, I remain firm in my stance so that those watching remain unaware of the turmoil within me. The challenge has been made. Now, I must see it through.

The guard removes his helmet and I almost gasp at the face that greets me: Trevors. What is he doing here? Possibilities for his assignment here roil through my mind, each one dismissed, until I think of the only reason that makes sense, aside from the probability that this could be some sort of punishment: they must be grooming him to be a Marshal. When recruits graduate from the training facility, some are selected for specialized training to become Marshals. If this is the case, then Trevors' presence at the factory, as well as here, makes sense because Marshals in training are sent to the most troublesome regions of Arel to test their resolve before they are allowed to monitor other arbiters. My stomach sinks at the thought of Trevors being given the authority to arrest arbiters, but I push it aside. I must not think of it, nor can I ever voice my suspicions because those who do are never seen again, and there is no need to guess where they end up.

"No..." Chase begins to whisper in protest, but he receives a kick in the face from another guard, forcing him to be silent.

I refuse to look at him. I can't. My gaze must remain fixed on Trevors as I wait for him to either accept or refuse my challenge. My jaw goes numb from clenching it as Trevors makes up his mind. He chucks his helmet to the side and stands up, and it takes all my resolve not to shrink away from his overbearing height as he towers over me.

"I accept," growls Trevors, and a malicious smile spreads across his face.

Renal looks at me with worry in his eyes, but there is nothing he can do. I made the challenge. I must abide by it.

Commandant Gant waves at a handful of guards standing nearby and two appear, one on each side of Trevors and me, gripping our arms and leading us away.

"Take them to the pit."

I dislike the sound of that. Once again, hands shove me away, leading me to my fate, and I wonder if I will ever learn to control my emotions and my mouth, curious as to why neither of them have gotten me killed yet. Eyes watch us, enthralled by the spectacle and glad to have a break from their mundane tasks, but only one pair of eyes capture my attention; they are the only ones I care about: Chase watches, worry etched on his face, creasing his tanned brow, and he follows after me, unconcerned about the repercussions should he be noticed by the arbiters surrounding us. My boots shuffle across the soil, kicking up clouds of dust, coating their shiny, black exterior so that they look dull and worn, matching the footwear of the guards shoving me through the crowd. A crater appears before us, its edges jagged, jutting out in places as though it wishes to slice the air around it, while other parts of it are soft, smoothed down by time and a caressing hand.

Before I have a chance to see how deep it is, my captors throw me in, and I tumble down the walls of the crater, and despite my attempt at tucking in while I roll, my body bounces down the sides, leaving a trail of dust that waves in the wind as though in greeting, or perhaps as a marker of where I am so Trevors can find me with ease. A protruding rock slams into my side, causing me to wince and gasp for air, but I mustn't show weakness because it always means death. The rolling stops. I remain on the ground, willing the spinning within my head to cease as I try to catch my breath and ignore the pain in my side, feeling another bruise form on my body, a constant factor in my life. Something lands beside me. Knowing I cannot stay here, I lift myself up to my hands and knees before rising to my feet, stumbling as my legs wobble, still refusing to find their footing, desiring nothing more than to sit back down instead of being forced to support my weight. I widen my stance, forcing them hold me.

Trevors stands before me, and by the slight shift in his weight, I can tell that he is also a little dizzy and hope that perhaps he injured himself on the way down, but judging by the determined look on his face, I am not going to be that lucky. We stare at one another for a moment, each one waiting for the other to make a move, but I refuse to attack first, remembering what one of my instructors had always said: wait for your opponent to make the first move. I know Trevors. I know his impatience. If I can remain still long enough, he will attack first; he always does.

"Just a moment!" Renal's voice echoes across the mine. "There are some rules that must be established."

Such is the way. Arbiters are allowed to challenge other arbiters, but there are always rules put in place to prevent us from killing one another, or causing irreparable damage. Arel cannot have its arbiters mutilating each other.

Disappointment crosses Commandant Gant's face, but he remains silent, aware of the long-established rules and the consequences for breaking them.

"The fight ends when one of you taps out," says Renal. "Neither of you are to cause permanent harm to the other. Any of you who breaks this rule will be met with swift punishment. Understood?"

"Yes, sir," both Trevors and I say at the same time, acknowledging that we understand.

He charges me just like I knew he would. I sidestep, but Trevors anticipates my maneuver and his feet scrape across the dirt as he changes course to counter my dodge, and he wraps his arms around my waist, knocking me to the ground. My back slams into the pebbles and silt coating the ground as I grunt from the impact and from Trevors weight landing on top of me. A fist strikes the left side of my face. Another hits me in the temple. Dazed, and unable to breathe from Trevors crushing weight atop me, my mind races for an idea of what to do. He has always been bigger and stronger than me. His fist heads for me again, and I bring up my arm to block it, but he seizes my wrist and pins it above my head while squeezing his other hand around my throat. My mind panics from the lack of oxygen and I must...

Chase's face appears from the crowd watching us, dejected, convinced that I have lost before the fight even started, but it is all I need. Trevors leans in for the kill, within reach of my other arm.

Clenching my fist, but allowing one of my knuckles to poke out, I jab him in the throat, causing him to rear back and loosen his grip on my neck and pinned arm. Not wasting time, I bring up my leg, planting, my foot against the ground, and push, flipping myself over and flinging him off me. Trevors crashes into the ground on his side, still gasping for air. Before he can retaliate, I roll on my side and kick him in the mouth, but as I aim another kick for him, he snatches my foot, twists, and flips me over onto my stomach. He jumps up, and I swing my foot out, aiming for his knee, but I miss, catching him in the middle of his tibia. Unphased, Trevors pounces on me, seizing me by the back of the neck, while his other hand goes between my legs, lifting me high into the air as he stands up, ready to finish me.

My eyes widen in fear, taking in the hazy sky, while my back braces for what I know Trevors plans to do, and in my mind, I feel it break over his knee. My hands claw at his, but his firm grip remains strong, unrelenting, and it tightens as he prepares to finish me. I have failed. My body lifts and starts to plunge downward when a single shot rings out, echoing off the walls of the pit and the hollow caverns of the mine, and as I crane my head to get a look at who fired the gun, I find Renal standing on the edge of the pit with a weapon aimed at Trevors, ready to fire that life-ending bullet. I hang in the air, staring at the tannish sky as swirls of dust encircle us, waiting for Trevors to make his decision: let me go or die.

He throws me to the ground, and I roll across the dirt, coating my uniform in shiny specks of dust until my body comes to a halt. Lifting my head, I notice specks of blood dripping from a gash on Trevors right cheek where Renal's bullet grazed him as a warning. His malignant focus is on Renal, not me, as he shifts his anger to a different target. Trevors almost broke the rule to not cause permanent harm to his opponent; he knows this, but he doesn't care. As I lie on the ground, calculating my next move, Trevors refocuses his attention on me: we still have a match, and neither of us have tapped out. He is too strong for me, too big.

Think, Noni, I tell myself, trying to plan out a method of attack, tired of being on the defensive. "You might be smaller than your opponent, but you are more agile," I remember Mandi's words to me one day after I had lost a one-on-one match to someone twice my size. "Most rely on brute strength to win. You must rely on your mind; you must outthink your opponent."

What are his weaknesses? Every individual has a weakness. Trevors is overconfident, always believing he has won even before the battle begins, or that his prey is too weak to fight. How can I...

Trevors walks up to me, a smirk on his face, ready to make me pay for his lack of judgement, but every other step, he shifts his stance, and to the untrained eye, it looks as though it is nothing, but I see it for what it is: his right ankle pains him. He does a good job of concealing it, which is why I never noticed it before. Devising a plan, I remain where I am, pretending to be injured and unable to fight back. It works. Trevors marches up to me, leering over me, convinced that he is the victor, and just when he gets within arm's reach, I fling my arms at him, backhanding him and roll on the ground, turning myself around and hook my feet around his injured ankle, forcing him to his knees. Surprise and rage fill his face, but before he can react, I jump on his shoulders, wrapping my legs around his neck and fling him to the ground, and we both land on our backs with my legs still coiled around his throat with just enough pressure to force him to give up; though I remain aware of Renal's sharp gaze fixed on me, ready to put me down should I violate the rule about permanent harm. Trevors struggles against my hold, but I remain firm, unwilling to give up. His hand thumps the ground, and I release him.

Standing up, I glance around at the faces staring at me, each with a mixture of mild amusement and praise, until I find Chase's, who sighs with relief. I have won, but my victory is hollow as we all know that if Renal had not stepped in, Trevors would have killed me. Not waiting to be acknowledged, I climb up the side of the pit

and claw my way to the top, heaving myself over the edge, not waiting for, nor expecting, any help. Chase starts to move toward me,
but I shake my head at him, urging him to stay where he is so as not
to arouse suspicion.

"I challenge you!" yells Trevors, his voice reverberating around
us as he points at Renal.

In response to the challenge, Renal takes off his uniform jacket,
allowing the sweat that has built on his well-formed and black arms
to glisten in the bright sunlight as it evaporates, and tosses it aside,
and it lands in a crumpled heap in the dirt. Commandant Gant's
eyes widen in enjoyment at the spectacle as Renal slides down the
side of the pit and into its center, landing on his feet and keeping
his gaze fixed on Trevors. They circle one another for ten seconds,
a span of time that seems to stop the motion of the Earth as we all
watch with baited breath.

Trevors charges. Renal side-steps, holding his fist out, allowing
Trevors to run into it. When they part, Trevors holds his bloody
nose for a second before realizing that such an act might appear
weak. Renal glares at him, never speaking, never moving, his stoic
face revealing nothing as he awaits Trevors' next act. Trevors attacks again. Ducking and twisting at the same time, Renal rams the
point of his elbow into Trevors' stomach before seizing him around
the shoulders and flipping him onto his back where he lands with
a hard thump and miniscule clouds of dust spiral around him,
stretching upward into the air where they disperse in the wind.
Renal jumps to his feet and steps away, waiting for Trevors to get
up, toying with him.

Sitting up, Trevors takes his time getting to his feet, glaring at
Renal as he moves, wiping the blood pouring from his nose as he
does so, the hatred evident on his face. He paces in front of Renal,
who remains still, watching, never taking his eyes off him. Trevors
charges again, but Renal kicks him in the stomach before rounding
on him, seizing one of his arms and wrenching it behind his back,

while placing his own arm around Trevors' neck. Trevors struggles to get free at first, but the more he struggles, the more Renal tightens his grip before leaning forward and whispering in his ear. I watch, curious as to what Renal tells Trevors, when my old enemy from the training facility bows his head and goes limp, conceding the challenge. Renal releases him and climbs out of the pit, leaving Trevors to sulk in his own shame.

"Renal," I ask, allowing my curiosity to get the better of me, "what did you tell…" I stop speaking the moment Renal jerks his head in my direction and glares at me, bowing my own in acknowledgement of his authority.

"Commandant Gant," Renal says, putting his jacket back on, unconcerned about knocking the dust off his arms first, "you have your orders. Now, we would appreciate it if you would show us where we will be spending our stay here."

Commandant Gant waves one of the arbiters under his command over. "He will show you to your quarters."

As Renal and I follow the arbiter to another part of the mine, I glance at Chase one last time, wishing I could speak with him, but knowing that now is not the time. I will need to find him later, or perhaps he will find me.

Chapter 12

A Familiar Face

The sun dips below the edge of the mine, covering us all in the shadow of the mountain and the ghoulish glow of twilight as I mosey through the exposed eating area, my boots thumping on the rotted floorboards, while I make my way to the cast iron pot that stands as high as my waist where plebeians line up with tin bowls, all of them different shapes, waiting for a ladleful of soup. One by one, they hold their bent bowls out for their meager meal. I watch them for a moment, the sallow faces, the hollow eyes, all coated in grime and covered in a mishmash of rags that do not deserve to be called clothes. One woman glances at me before directing her curious gaze somewhere else, while holding her hand near her cheek in a feeble effort to cover the swollen welt on it. My gaze follows the line of dark and fair-skinned mixed together and the few eyes that look my way, filled with contempt: they all hate me, something that I have become used to since being commissioned.

Raucous laughter inundates the somber feeding area, spilling over from another where arbiters feast on beans (a common staple as they are easy to ship and cook), meat (dried and reconstituted for cooking), dried vegetables, and fresh greens. Fresh greens? How did they manage to get those here without spoilage? Their boisterous conversation mocks the somber and reserved manner of the workers who await a single bowlful of liquid detritus, unfit even for the rats that roam this place.

Snatching a bowl from the stack near the beginning of the line, I march to the pot, noticing that not even a small amount of steam escapes its rim, and shove the bowl in front of the server. He looks at me for a moment, unsure of what to do—the stench of his stain-ridden apron bombards my nostrils, and I will myself not to pull back or acknowledge the putrid smell as it will be a sign of weakness—waving it at him, indicating that he should fill it. The ladle scrapes the sides of the cast iron pot as he dips it in the slosh and scoops out a single serving of what passes for nutrition in this place, placing it in my outstretched bowl. I stare at the pail liquid with shreds of what must have been a carrot floating in it, accompanied by something thin, something long, something that... moves? I dip my pinky into the soup and brush it. The thing moves again, wiggling in agitation, and I realize that it is a maggot. Feeling the heat of the workers' stares, I lift the edge of the bowl to my face and take a sip before spitting out the liquid in an effort to expel its rusty aftertaste from my mouth, but it lingers on my taste buds, refusing to wane away. The maggot still squirms in its putrid broth, angered that I have disturbed its tranquil bath. I toss the bowl aside, allowing its contents to soak the grayed floorboards and drip through the tiny spaces to the silt beneath them.

This isn't the first time I have eaten a maggot, or something just as disgusting. In my 16th year as a recruit, we were brought into the mess hall for lunch, but instead of a substantial meal of cooked vegetables, eggs, and slices of roast beef, we found plates crawling with maggots that squirmed and wriggled as they crawled over one another, dropping onto the steel tables in an effort to escape to freedom.

Our instructors patrolled the room, their hardened faces not bothering to look at us, as we sat down in front of the plates infested with the very things that infest carcasses, our faces twitching in refusal to touch the slimy grubs.

"What are you waiting for?" yelled Molers' voice over the quiet whispering of grumbling recruits. "Are you not hungry?"

We knew what was expected of us. If we wished to escape this place, this new torment by our instructors, we had to eat the maggots, another test of our willingness to overcome our fears, endure something we find abhorrent, or face the consequences. One recruit pushed his plate of squirming garbage disposals and stood up, refusing to endure another moment of humiliation. Molers grinned when he did, and we all knew that deleterious smile of his well; he enjoyed making examples of recruits who refused to follow his instructions. He stormed over to the recruit with such speed that none of us had time to react, and kicked the feet of the recruit out from under him, forcing him back into the chair, where Molers held him down while seizing a fistful of maggots and shoved them into the recruit's mouth. Seconds crawled by as Molers forced the wriggling monsters into the recruit's mouth with him choking and coughing, his arms flailing in an effort to get Molers off him, to no effect. The singular tap of a baton against metal rang over the room, stopping Molers as another instructor motioned for him to release the recruit. Angered, but not daring to go against a higher-ranking officer, Molers stepped away, squashing the maggots that had escaped to the floor as he eyed each of us.

"If you wish to leave here," his voice bellowed, causing us to shrink under its wrath, "you will eat every last one of these maggots until none remain!"

That day, I shoved the repulsive horde of writhing larvae into my mouth, not bothering to chew as I swallowed, feeling them squirm as they went down and attempted to crawl back up out of my esophagus. Little by little, the maggots disappeared down our gullets, and I joined my recruits in the bathrooms later that day, leaning over a toilet and throwing up the grubs, repulsed as I watched them swim in the latrine's mixture of water and bile.

As the unpleasant memory fades, I empathize with the workers being forced to consume something that even the rodents refused to call edible. I motion for the man behind the cauldron to step aside, and I take a step back, lift my left leg, and kick the pot of filth over, watching as the filmy liquid washes over the dingy floorboards, seeping through the cracks and disappearing, leaving only the writhing mess of maggots as they twist and turn in agitation. Bewildered faces stare at me, watching every move I make, saddened that they will not be allowed to eat, even if their meal consists of questionable water that looks more like in belongs in a latrine and the dwellers of dirt and rotting flesh.

"Follow me," I say to them, my voice even and tight. After a few steps, I pause, realizing that no one has fallen in behind me. "Well?"

Two jump at my command and trail behind me, bowls in hand, as I march to the other end of the compound where the arbiters enjoy a lavish meal, and as the other workers overcome their fears and doubts, they join their compatriots. The guards on duty turn toward us, ready to order the workers back to their side of the camp, but my refusal to acknowledge their presence stops them; they know they must keep the workers in line, but they are aware that I am not to be questioned, so they allow me to be the one to break protocol, knowing that it is my ass in the end. Feet wrapped in the leather remains of what had once been shoes, kept together by pieces of cloth, stride across the black soil mixed with ore and nails that poke out of the ground, waiting to strike any unfortunate enough to step on them. When we reach the eating area of the arbiters, the laughter stops as their confused and irritated expressions glare back at us, but I march through them, ignoring the wall of black faces and uniforms that try to stop me.

"What is the meaning of this?" demands Commandant Gant.

"Commandant Gant," I say, my voice stern as I speak over him, acting as though his words are nothing more than a mere annoyance, "it appears that you do not understand my orders, so allow me to demonstrate." I keep my shoulders erect and my hardened gaze fixed upon the commandant, copying a technique that I have witnessed Commander Vye use all too often. "Fill their bowls," I say to the cook as his mouth hangs open and a spoon dangles in his loosened grip, threatening to drop to the ground, while he watches me, unsure of what to do.

"Now, see—"

"It appears that you do not understand what I meant when I said that the workers are to be fed," I say, interrupting the commandant's attempt at chastising me and snatch a bowl from the hands of one of the workers and shove it into his. "Eat it," I say, unnerved at how much I sound like Molers at this very moment, but remain firm in my resolve to reprimand the commandant, knowing that I will have earned his hatred, a common thing among arbiters.

He looks at it, not wanting to do as I have ordered.

"If you think this is fit for consumption, then eat it," I growl into his ear, "and then we will see the ones under your command eat it as well."

He lifts it to his lips, his venomous eyes wishing that I would die a horrible death; he just may get his wish, considering the volatile nature of an arbiter's existence. Only a few drops of the filmy liquid enter his mouth before the commandant spits it out, coughing and gagging from its putrefaction, and I would not be surprised if they had taken that water from a pool that had a corpse rotting in it.

"They are to be fed," I say to Commandant Gant, "and by the same food that you give your arbiters. If you refuse to eat it, then why should anyone else be forced to?"

"I don't recall seeing you eat their meal," Commandant Gant challenges me, and I notice Renal stand up from where he had been hiding amongst them, his ever watchful gaze focused on us.

I snatch another bowl from one of the workers, still filled with the stomach-churning soup, and drain it in one gulp, forcing myself to swallow it while refusing to show hesitation to the piece of human garbage standing before me, my eyes never wavering from his smug face. As the seconds pass between us, purposeful clomps radiate over the area as Renal walks up to us, standing behind me.

"You have your orders, commandant," he says, his voice low, but with a slight edge to it.

Commandant Gant steps back, salvaging what dignity he has left. "What are you waiting for?" he yells at the cook, who jumps from the commandant's harsh tone. "Feed them!"

I watch as Commandant Gant storms through the crowd and disappears into the fading light, catching a quick glimpse of Trevors, who turns away the moment he notices me looking at him. Feeling uncomfortable with all the faces gaping at me, and knowing that the only reason Commandant Gant obeyed me was because of Renal's presence, wondering, once again, if there is more to Renal than just an arbiter assigned to the eastern sector, I stalk out of the eating area, desperate to get away from everyone and their accusatory stares. My feet charge into the ever-growing darkness that envelops the mines, hurrying away from the crowded area filled with strangers and leading me up a steep slope. Unable to breathe, I push myself harder. My foot slips in the loose gravel on the hill, forcing me to my hands and knees, but I jump back up and continue my trek up the slope away from the judgmental faces and the constant watch over my actions, wishing I was back in the eastern sector under Commander Vye's tutelage, relegated to following orders instead of issuing commands. I miss the days of wandering through the wildlands with Chase. Though we struggled to understand one another, it was simpler when it was just him and me fighting to survive.

I reach the top and suck in a lungful of fresh air, not the stale, dust-filled breaths that cause one to choke, but invigorating crisp air that beckons me to leave all this behind and seek a new life elsewhere; but where would I go? I look around at the bushes surrounding me, their limbs only half-alive with faded, wrinkled leaves poking out, their edges browned. Arel looms in the distance, while sparkling lights catch my attention, and I watch them flicker, performing a sort of dance as people retire for the night, secure behind the walls of Arel. I imagine the arbiters along the wall, pacing back and forth in a feeble attempt to remain awake, when deep down, all they want is to be in their own beds like everyone else.

A low noise, reminding me of the white noise that fills my ears every so often, rises in the night. Curious, I search the star-filled sky, hoping to find the source of the noise, straining my eyes to see anything that doesn't belong. The noise grows stronger. My heart beats faster from the anticipation of learning the source of the sound just when three Arelian aircraft appear, zipping overhead and speeding toward the black horizon, away from the city, while I spin on my heels, trying to track them. Where are they going?

Gravel crunches behind me. I whirl around, ready to defend myself from an attack and stop the moment Chase's face materializes from the shadows. Unable to control my excitement upon seeing him, and forgetting that unwanted eyes might be watching us, I run to him, embracing him, glad when he puts his strong arms around me, not caring that silt covers them.

"Gwen…" he begins.

"She's fine," I whisper. "Sheila is watching over her, while I'm here." Silent moments pass between us before I speak the question on my mind. "Why are you here? You should be in the agricultural sector."

"I never made it there," Chase replies, his voice distant.

What? I know that an arbiter's recommended punishment does not have to be approved by the Ministry of Justice, but this punishment does not fit his offence. If he stays here much longer, he could die and… My trail of thought ceases when I realize that, until now, Faya had been the only person whom I was ever concerned about losing, but the thought of never seeing Chase again sickens me.

"What are you doing here?" asks Chase.

"I've been sent here by President Tapiwa to see why this mine's production quotas are low."

"That doesn't make any sense," says Chase.

"None of this makes sense," I reply. I know that there is no reason for a low-ranking arbiter, such as myself, to be given this amount of responsibility, not unless there is another purpose behind it, but I know the price of failure. "But I have to see it through."

"You're not exactly making friends," Chase chuckles.

"Arbiters do not have the luxury of friends." As a rule, we don't. Sometimes, an arbiter will find one or two they can trust, but, even then, we have to be careful. "Arbiters cannot trust anyone."

Chase places a gentle finger underneath my chin—its shedding skin scratches mine—forcing my eyes to look into his gray ones.

"I will never betray you."

A single tear escapes the corner of my right eye, despite my mental commands that it stop, and Chase wipes it away with his thumb.

"I thought I lost you in the trial of fears," he says.

"You saw that?"

"They televised it live. We were all forced to watch. A testament of Arel's greatness."

I know that any who are put through the trial of fears will be filmed, but that footage is for training purposes, or so I have always been told; though, I don't remember them ever televising one live.

"We should get back," says Chase.

"Please," I say to him, not wanting to face Commandant Gant's arbiters, or Trevors, "just a moment longer, before I have to face the wild dogs that run this mine."

Chase smiles and holds me close as we sit on the hill, bathed in faded star light, as even the moon decides to conceal itself and give us some privacy. How long we stay here is a mystery, but I don't care. Chase's presence is comforting, and for the first time, I feel... safe. A soft breeze caresses us as it floats past us, and as the moon peaks around a cloud, our fingers entwine. A few shouts from below jerk us out of our peaceful pose, and we jump to our feet, knowing what will happen if we are both caught out here. The shouts draw closer. I start to head toward them, ready to meet them, when Chase pulls me back behind a thicket.

"What are you…"

Chase places a finger over his lips, telling me to be silent.

Going against my arbiter pride, I listen to him, trusting his instincts over mine in this place as the hairs on the back of my neck stand on end, warning me that something is not right. Before the two men appear over the crest of the hill, Chase motions for me to move behind another thicket, one that is bushier and certain to conceal my presence.

"Whatever happens," he whispers to me, "don't come out."

I nod in agreement and crawl into the thick brush, disappearing into its thorny branches just as the two men appear.

"They said she came this way," one of them says in an irate tone.

She? Are they looking for me? I bury myself further into the brush, allowing its overlapping branches to hide me from the world, glad that my uniform allows me to blend in with the darkness, but when I see Chase crouch behind the other thicket, my heart quickens, fearing that he will be discovered. There is no telling what these two arbiters will do to him, but every frightening scenario I can think of runs through my mind. I watch as the two men search the area where Chase and I had been sitting moments before; their arbiter uniforms look silver in the moonlight, giving an eerie glow, making them seem more like ghosts instead of flesh and blood. Three more show up. I back further into the brush when the back heel of my right foot presses onto a stick, snapping it, it's crisp sound radiating around me, filling the still air and alerting them to my presence.

Dammit! I curse in my mind, scolding myself as my eyes remain on the five arbiters, wondering what they will do, though deep down, I know what their reaction will be. One motions for the others to go to the left side of the bush I am hiding in, and I know that they are aware of where I am. I shrink back even further, but my mind tells me that such a desperate act is useless.

Chase springs from behind the thicket he had crouched behind, startling the two men, but forcing them to stop before they discover me. I start to get up, not wanting him to take my punishment, but he glances in my direction as though he knows what I am about to do, and his pleading eyes force me to stay put, safe in obscurity and anonymity, with the branches of a bush as my shield.

"What are you doing here?" demands one of the men.

"Hunting rats," Chase replies in a tone that tells me that on any other night this would be the truth, as though he has spent his spare time hunting vermin.

"Our food wasn't good enough for you?" scoffs one of the others, but Chase remains quiet.

One of the men turns, pretending to be leaving when he whirls around and backhands Chase, knocking him to the ground. Chase gets to his knees, but another steps behind him and kicks him in the back, forcing him to his stomach. Angered, I press my heels into the ground and stand up, before dropping back into the bush's heart when I see Chase's pleading eyes staring at me, and once again, I wonder how it is he knows what I am about to do, but I remain still, clenching my fists in an effort to do as he wishes. All five men take turns kicking or punching Chase, until he lies in a crumpled heap in the black dirt with bits of metallic dust covering his cheeks and tousled hair. When they tire of their fun, they each spit on him before trudging back down the hill, where they join up with a handful of arbiters waiting for them, laughing to one another as they relive their torment of him, mocking his refusal to fight back.

I spring from the bush and rush toward Chase, afraid that the men might have killed him, and drop to my knees beside his limp body. My hand shaking, I reach out and press my fingers against his neck, feeling for a pulse, when his hand grasps my wrist. Relieved, I hug him, but stop when he winces and jump back, not wanting to cause him pain.

"I need to get you to the medical center," I say to him.

"No," he replies, trying to sit up, but the effort proves too much and he flops back down on the ground as blood drips from his nose.

"But you're…"

"They won't treat me."

Confused, my mind tries in vain to grapple with what he says. I have been sent to oversee this mine, and Renal has made it no secret that my authority is not to be challenged; so, if I tell the doctors here to treat Chase, they will.

"But…" I begin to argue, but Chase cuts me off again.

"Those men were not here for me. They were here for you!"

What? Why would they want to jump me unless… I've made another enemy. As I reflect on the last several minutes, I remember that one of them mentioned something about "she came this way", meaning that Chase's assessment is correct: they had been looking for me, and I am willing to bet that they didn't do it on their own.

"I need to get you out of here," I tell him, knowing that neither of us can remain here in the open.

He nods in agreement and I help him up as I wrap his arm around my shoulder and allow him to lean on me, using me to support his weight as he stands on his feet.

"Something tells me we've done this before," he jokes, and I chuckle with him, remembering the time we had been alone in the wildlands and he had carried me, much the same way I carry him now.

"We'll take it slow," I say.

"I don't remember you being so patient the last time."

I give him a gentle slap on the shoulder, amazed that Chase can find humor in a terrible situation, and he feigns feeling pain, causing me to feel guilty, but it fades the moment I see the grin on his face. Taking it one step at a time, we trudge down the hill—he hops a little as his ankle is sore from having it kicked—and I lean backward, with his weight upon me, in an effort to keep from sliding downward on the loose soil. Pebbles shift from their position and clack against one another as they bounce down the hill, disturbed by our feet sliding across the surface of the earth. My grip on Chase remains firm as I guide him back to the mine, unconcerned about the blood coating the shoulder of my jacket as I listen to his heavy breathing, worried that he might have a broken rib, but tell myself that it could be the exertion of the walk that is the reason. His foot slips on a loose rock and his balance falters, but I catch him, placing myself between him and the ragged ground, unwilling to allow him to experience any more injuries than he already has, and lift him back to his feet. He smiles at me in reassurance, but even the darkness fails to hide the concern on my face.

Once we reach the bottom of the hill, Chase directs me to turn left and we head for what appears to be a hole in the side of the mountain. At first, I refuse, still wanting to take him to the medical center, but his stubbornness wins as I realize that he knows more about this place than me. He leans more into me and my leg wobbles underneath his weight, but I force it to support us both, reminding myself that I am an arbiter and physical weakness is not allowed; I must be strong for him. We stick to the shadows, staying clear of the lamps placed throughout the camp, avoiding their amber light for fear of being discovered. Movement catches my attention and I pull us further into the darkness, hoping that it is enough to conceal us as an arbiter strolls by, his stride bored and stiff, as though he is daydreaming about being anywhere but here. Once he disappears, I released the air stuck within my lungs as I watch him, and drag Chase away from here, making our way to the tunnel entrance.

His feet plop on the ground, unable to support him much longer and refusing to work, causing him to lean even more on me, and my shoulder aches underneath his weight, but I ignore it, wanting nothing more than to get him to safety. A black hole looms before us as we approach the opening and step through it; the sounds of chatter in the distance and crickets cease as we delve inside the tunnel, going around a bend, until we are in a cavern the size of the training facility. I stop. Small fires dace around us, lighting us up with their soft glows that mingle with a string of lamps hanging from the cavern walls, strung together in a haphazard fashion and looking as though they might fall to the ground at any moment as they dangle at odd angles. Glancing around, goosebumps appear on my skin as untrusting eyes glare at me, accusing me of having harmed one of their own.

"Please," I say, my voice echoing off the walls, making me sound wraithlike, "he needs help."

Someone summons me over to him, pointing at a thin mattress, soiled and coated in grime, with the stuffing poking through areas where the once distinguishable plaid fabric had worn so thin that only threads remain. I carry Chase over to it—his feet drag on the ground, forming parallel lines as we go—and lay him on the mattress, being careful not to drop him, my heart aching as he moans from the pain, his eyes half-open and glazed over. A purple welt forms on his face and anger roils within me as I think back to the men who did this. I need medicine, something, and I jump up, but Chase's hand grips my wrist again, pulling me back down.

"You need something to treat you wounds," I say.

"The medical center will locked and won't be open up until morning. Please, Noni, if you go there now, you'll get caught and Commandant Gant won't care that President Tapiwa sent you here."

It seems that he doesn't care anyway.

"Don't any of you have any sort of first aid around here?" I demand of the people surrounding me.

A woman appears a few minutes later with a bowl full of strips of material torn from old shirts and blankets and a bottle of oil. It seems that the workers have their own supplies for treating injuries just like the recruits at the training facility did, reminding me of the days when I would tend the sores of other recruits, which they received during our arduous exercises. I take the tin bowl from her, thanking her, and unscrew the lid to the bottle of oil, releasing a pungent scent of pine and eucalyptus that saturates my nostrils and causes me to cough. A bowl of brown water appears beside me. Repulsed by the foul odor of the water, I hesitate to use it, but soon realize that there is nothing else, and as the woman instructs me on what to do, I take a strip of cloth, its frayed ends dropping miniscule threads, and douse it in the repugnant bowl of liquid before sprinkling drops of the oil on it and placing it against Chase's cheek. He squirms from its sting, but I hold him still and place his hand over the cloth, forcing him to hold it to his own cheek, while I lift his shirt and press the tips of my fingers against his ribs, using the lightest of pressure.

"Does this hurt?" I ask.

"Yes!" he snaps, and I scowl at him.

"You know what I mean. Are you having any trouble breathing?"

"No."

Just to be certain, I lean over him and place my ear against his chest, listening to him as he inhales and exhales, looking for any sign that he might be struggling to breathe, but it sounds normal. Either way, the morning will let me know if there is fluid building in his chest cavity or not because he will either be dead or still alive. I notice bruises along his stomach and follow them with my eyes, until I see a gash on Chase's left arm. I take the bottle of oil and coat the gash with it, assuming that it must be some sort of antiseptic, and it's all I have for the moment, before wrapping another strip of cloth around the cut, but my mind keeps dwelling on the fact that he needs medicine, and there is only one way to get it.

"You're good at this," murmurs Chase.

"They taught us how to do a field dressing," I say.

"Of course, they did."

I rest his arm by his side and start to stand up when he grabs my wrist and hangs on with a grip that I didn't think he could make in his current state, but that is not what stops me; his panicked eyes do.

"Chase..."

"You can't go," he says through a cough.

"You need something for that cut on your arm."

"They won't give it to you," he says, and repeats, "and if you're caught, they won't care that you were sent here by Tapiwa."

He's right. If I am caught stealing medicine from their hospital wing, it will be met with swift and severe punishment, and Renal will not be able to stop it, but the idea of doing nothing to help him troubles me, eating away at me, tearing away at the miniscule essences of humanity I have left.

"Please," he whispers, and his pleading look forces me to sit back down by his side, forgetting about the multitude of plebeian eyes that watch our exchange and the fact that any one of them could report this.

"Just rest," I tell him, dabbing the blood around the corner of his mouth and nose.

Unable to keep his eyes open any longer, Chase rolls his head to the side and falls asleep. Silence surrounds me as uneasy eyes observe every movement I make, but I ignore them, more concerned about Chase's recovery than the strangers around me. I take another look at his arm and know that if I do nothing, it will get infected and he could die, the thought of which rips my heart in two. I know I promised him that I would take care of Gwen, but I owe it to her to see to it that he makes it back to her. My eyes move toward the woman who had given me the bowl of water.

"Stay with him," I say to her.

She nods without speaking, and she does not need to say a word as her eyes say it all.

Rising to my feet, I take one last glance around the chamber and at the gloomy eyes observing my every move, bewildered by my concern for one of their own, but not questioning it, and head outside into the darkness, broken by the milky light of the moon as it pokes out from behind a cloud. I dash across the grainy soil for the center of the camp and where the medical center is, keeping my steps light and soft, making as little noise as possible.

A sentry appears and stops in front of me, lighting up a smoke—they're not supposed to as it is forbidden, but that doesn't stop them from doing it—and I dive behind a cart, hugging my knees close to me, hoping that he never notices my presence. The tip of the smoke lights up, a speck of orange in the night, as he inhales its filth, before releasing it, unconcerned about the possibility of anyone being out of bed past lights out. Why should he be? Everyone knows what will happen if they are caught—a fear that keeps them in line. I watch as he finishes his smoke, before flicking the butt to the ground and grinding it into the dirt with the ball of his foot. As he wanders off, I release the breath that I have been holding in my lungs before sprinting to my feet and dashing across the ground away from him and toward the medical center, which is nothing more than a lone, single-room building with a red cross painted on it.

I pause by the steps when I reach it, looking around to make certain that no one is there. Silence looms. The first step creaks under my weight when I place my foot on it, and I lift it off, afraid that someone might have heard it, but as I wait for the alarms and the shouts, only stillness greets me. I continue up the steps and to the door. Locked. I expected nothing less. I take a bobby pin from the bun in my hair and place it in the lock, glad that it is an old-fashioned one and not some coded keypad, twisting it around, until I feel the tumblers within it move and a tiny click sounds. Wasting no time, I push the door open, hurrying inside, and close it behind me.

I head for the cabinets, opening their glass doors, rifling through the bottles and canisters, looking for any sort of ointment similar to what recruits kept hidden in their rooms at the training facility. A short, round container the width of my palm catches my attention, and I snatch it, unscrewing its metallic lid, revealing a creamy, somewhat clear, and odorless substance. As I smile to myself, relief washes over me now that I have found something that should help heal his cuts and bruises. I start to put it in my pocket, but stop when I realize that if I take it, it will be discovered missing.

Frustrated, I rummage through drawers and shelves, looking for any sort of container that I can fill with the ointment. Just when I am about to give up, my hand knocks something over and a container of vials clatter to the floor, clinking as they scatter in the thin beam of moonlight spilling through the grime coated window. I clean up the vials, placing them back into their box, snatching one and scooping some ointment into it before shoving a cork into it to seal it. Tiptoeing to the door, I pause, listening for any sounds of boots crunching in the black gravel, unsure if a guard is outside or not. Nothing. Gambling that no one is out there, I pull the door open just enough, locking the latch as I leave, and close it behind me, scuffling off into the darkness before ducking next to a building, crouching in its ominous shadow.

After catching my breath, I jump up and freeze. Grelyn stands there between the buildings with her back to me, no doubt on night sentry. If she turns around and sees me, it is over. I'll be arrested for insubordination and theft of Arelian property. The best punishment I can hope for is a quick execution; the worst is reeducation. Unlike the reeducation that ordinary citizens go through, an arbiter's reeducation consists of being starved, flogged until the person has no more blood to spill, and thrown into a vat of boiling tar, until the flesh cooks off the body and the disgraced arbiter dies, suffering a slow and agonizing death. Such measures are saved for the most grievous of offenders and serve as a warning to other arbiters. Mercy is a luxury we are never afforded.

I duck back behind the building, but my foot slips, scraping the ground, making enough noise to force Grelyn to turn around. Hugging the wall, I hold my breath as I remain still, hoping that she doesn't approach, but the soft plops of her feet on the ground inform me that I will have no such luck. I creep along the side of the building, hugging its rough exterior as the silt coating it rubs off on my fingers and make my way to the other end where I round the corner just as Grelyn appears. She looks around, her unnatural blue eyes appearing to glow in the dark, and I fear that she might have seen me, but as she searches, I know that I have not been spotted. I continue pressing my back into the outbuilding's wall as I inch my way to the other corner and ease my way around it. I need a distraction. Bending low, I scoop up some pebbles and chuck them at a nearby window. As they pelt the glass, a series of tiny drumbeats, I sprint into the darkness, running as fast as I can away from the camp and toward the workers' quarters, not bothering to look back. I reach the entrance to the cavern and dart inside, startling its occupants, forcing me to put my finger to my lips, signaling for them to remain quiet.

Chase still lays on the soiled mattress, half-asleep, and I hurry over to him, dropping to my knees beside him as I yank the vial of ointment from my pocket. His eyes focus on me and he tries to speak, but I shush him while spreading the ointment over his cuts and bruises, being careful not to cause him any more pain. Though the ointment will help with the superficial wounds, it will do little for his bruised ribs, and my heart aches at not being able to do more for him.

"You helped me once," I whisper to him, answering his unspoken question and remembering the time when my leg was broken and we were both lost on the wilderness and how, without him, I never would have survived. He shifts and closes his eyes. While his chest rises and falls and soft snores escape his lips, I remain by his side, monitoring him, making sure that his injuries do not kill him, and though the night fades and morphs into morning, I never move.

Chapter 13

Entombed

President Tapiwa's face fills the viewscreen before me, allowing me to see the soft cracks in her plum-colored lips—she must have applied a fresh coat of lipstick just before the call took place—and the striations within her brown eyes as the shade of her irises change from dark to light before morphing into a darker tone again. Four weeks have passed since I first arrived here at the mines, and this is the first time she has bothered to check on my progress, and my mind dwells on the pessimistic view that such an act is not a good omen. In fact, for one of the presidents to check in is an unusual act. Most times, it is a superior officer within the corps.

I keep my face impassive, as though I am unconcerned about this new development, when in truth, heat forms around me, rising within me, causing the collar of my uniform jacket to sizzle as it touches my skin. My stomach jumps as butterflies wrestle within it, but I remain rigid and stoic. Emotions are not to be acknowledged, least of all fear. As Tapiwa continues talking, creases form on her brow as though she is disappointed that I am not cowering before her the way a citizen of Arel should, but if I do, it will be a sign of weakness. Keeping my arms planted by my side, I listen to what she says amidst the clanging of pickaxes, shovels, and hammers as they join the rail carts' creaking wheels, forming a constant melody of metal and rock opposing one another. It does not aggravate me as much as it did the first few days of my stay.

Commandant Gant stands to the side, visible, but silent, and my eyes glance at him for a second as he raises his heels an inch from the floor before placing them back down, displeased with the manner in which I have run this establishment. In addition to dictating that fresh, unspoiled food and water be fed to the workers, I instituted shift changes. Before, the workers toiled in the mines for 12 or 14 hours a day and their skeletal bodies could not keep up with the abuse. I decided that they would work in four-hour shifts, being allowed to rest for two hours afterward. Commandant Gant put up a fight, but my decision stood and Renal reminded him of his orders to follow my command. Two hours after his protests, I caught Commandant Gant leaving the outbuildings, sporting a bruise near his eye socket, followed by Renal. He glared at me as he stalked away, while Renal strolled past me without so much as a glance. To this day, I have no idea what their fight was about, but I have a feeling that it revolved around me and my proposed changes.

Four weeks since I set foot here. Four weeks of constant infighting with Commandant Gant. Four weeks of watching myself and reminding myself how every action I take is monitored. At least there is Chase. The other workers helped him through his shifts as he recovered from the beating, and I am grateful that he is a fast healer. We stole moments together under the cover of darkness and away from Grelyn's watchful eye, as she always searched for an opportunity to catch me breaking the law. Turning in a fellow arbiter is met with great rewards, so long as you can prove that they committed a violation. Failure results in both being executed. When accused of a crime, the suspect is deemed guilty regardless if he is innocent, but to prevent arbiters from turning in their rivals in an effort to further their careers, if an arbiter accuses another arbiter of a crime, they best be able to prove it, or suffer the consequences. This is the only thing that stops Grelyn from turning me in now, despite her suspicions, but Chase is the only friend I have here and I'll not abandon him to this place. Last night, we watched the stars—a first for me—and held one another, and he never moved, even when I fell asleep in his arms, only waking me before the sun peaked over the horizon so that we could sneak back to our quarters before everyone woke up.

"Arbiter Noni?"

My attention snaps back to the present, and I scold myself for allowing my mind to wander. Tapiwa stares at me, expecting an answer to a question I never heard her ask. My mind races as I try to think of a neutral response so that she will not suspect that I wasn't listening.

"Madam President…" I begin.

"What do you have to say for yourself?"

My mouth remains shut. What can I say? I have no idea what she asked me.

"It was the best course of action," I say, hoping that my response answers her inquiry.

"Best course?" The displeasure in Tapiwa's voice is unmistakable, and I fear what she will say next, what her orders will be.

"Ordering that they receive the same food as what you and your fellow arbiters eat. Ordering that they work in four-hour shifts, with a break of half that length before they go back to work. Ordering that they be treated for their injuries. Ordering that they receive adequate bedding and having a new well dug for them so that they can have clean water."

I remember that day. Disgusted by the water the woman had handed me to clean Chase's cuts with, I vowed to change that, and the next morning, I ordered Commandant Gant to have a new well built where the workers would be allowed to get uncontaminated water. My ears still ring from his tyrannical outburst. Tired of his refusal to listen, I snatched a shovel and started digging, despite the commandant's taunts, but those taunts ceased when workers joined me in digging the new well, and Commandant Gant's eyes widened as, one by one, workers, fair-skinned and dark-skinned alike, grabbed a shovel and dug into the earth by my side, and I never asked them to. The commandant had opened his mouth to speak, but Renal's constant presence reminded him of his place, and by evening, we had water—fresh, cool water.

"It's as though you have forgotten your training," Tapiwa continues.

So, this is the reason for the call. Commandant Gant must have sent a letter of complaint to her, forcing her to check up on my progress to see if it is true. My mind dwells on how unusual this is because, when an arbiter has such a complaint made about them by a superior officer, they are arrested. So why have I not been? I think back to the bruise on Commandant Gant's face.

Tired of this indirect method of chastising me, I snap at Tapiwa.

"Production is up, is it not?"

Tapiwa's eyes widen at my outburst, and I know that I have crossed a line, but I press onward, aware that I cannot retreat now.

"Madam President, you sent me here to increase production. When I arrived, all I found were half-dead corpses, not able-bodied workers. People need to be fed. They need clean water and a warm place to sleep. You give them these things, and they will work for you without question."

"They are just plebeians."

Anger rises within me at that statement, and I clench my jaw in an effort to keep it from breaking free of my hold, unsure of what to do with such resentment toward such a notion, since not long ago, I shared it.

"And the citizens that are here?" I say, my voice tight, almost a growl, as I force myself to keep it even and steady. "They are here doing penance and are to be reintegrated into Arelian society once they have served their sentence. Should they return as skeletons? Are we not merciful?"

Tapiwa studies me, her mind brewing as she ponders my words and the meaning behind them, as well as my true intentions. As I stare at her, another revelation strikes me: people are sent here to die, including those who are told that once their pay their debt, they'll be released. I should have seen this when I first came here. Arel forgives no one.

"Madam President," I say, "I did what I thought necessary to accomplish the task you have given me. You told me to increase production. I have done that. If you believe that I have failed in my assignment, then relieve me of it and send someone one else who is better equipped."

Tapiwa's facial expression softens, but I know that I am still on the verge of drowning in her anger if I do not rein in my rebelliousness.

"Production is up?" she asks Renal, who steps out of the shadows.

"Yes, ma'am," he replies, his voicing filling the communications room.

"How much?"

"Almost double."

Silence regains its hold over us as Tapiwa considers her next course of action.

"Leave us," she says to everyone in the room.

Chairs scoot back as arbiters stand up and stomp out of the room in obedience, but Commandant Gant hangs back, displeased with her command.

"Madam President," he begins, "perhaps I should…"

"Get out!" roars Tapiwa, her harsh voice forcing me to take half a step back from the viewscreen. "Disobey me again, commandant, and I will have your head served to me on a platter."

My stomach churns at her words, but a part of me believes that she would resort to such barbaric methods if pushed too far.

The door closes behind Commandant Gant as he leaves, sealing me inside the communications room with Tapiwa's gigantic face on the viewscreen for company.

"I knew after your exploits in the trial of fears that you were the perfect fit for this job, and it appears that I was correct. You have done well, Noni. I shall be recalling you soon."

"Thank you," I say.

"There is one matter I wish to discuss."

"Ma'am?"

"It appears that the workers have taken quite a liking toward you."

"I'm sure they view me in the same manner as any other arbiter."

A fake smile crosses Tapiwa's plum lips, and I know where she is going with this conversation.

"Commandant Gant disagrees. And I have to wonder if he is correct. The way those workers joined you in digging the well without being told—you, when the most seasoned commander there has to whip them into obedience—one could say that you might have their respect."

"They saw a way to serve themselves and no other. Respect is not an arbiter's desire, only service to Arel."

Tapiwa backs away from the screen on her end and my robotic answers seems to satisfy her for the moment.

"I'm pleased to hear it. Now, if there is no other…"

"Madam President," I say, interrupting her, something that is never done, but I have to; I have to get Chase out of here. She glares at me, not liking my forwardness, but I continue, since there is no backing down now. "Please pardon the interruption, but there is a plebeian here whom has been here longer than his sentence."

"They are not afforded the same guarantees as citizens."

Death is a guarantee and we all fall victim to its grasp.

"I understand, but I believe that he might be of better service in the eastern sector."

"Why is that?"

"He services my physical needs," I reply, keeping my voice even, hoping that she will believe that I have found a toy to satisfy me, as she must not suspect that I care about him. Such a thing is not unheard of in Arel; every master seems to have their favorite plebeian.

"Strong?"

"Yes, ma'am, and silent."

"The strong and silent type. Yes, they are fun to play with. Very well. You may take him with you," she says in a bored tone, as though she is a mother granting her child's feeble wish, believing that I will grow bored with my toy within a month. Her beliefs do not bother me, as long as I can get Chase away from this place and back to Gwen.

"Thank—"

President Tapiwa shuts off her viewscreen, severing the connection.

I blow out the rest of the air trapped in my lungs, as I stare at the black viewscreen with the words "no signal" floating on it, allowing them to empty to the point where they beg me to inhale again, glad that my conversation with Tapiwa is over. My mind wonders why she seemed in a foul mood when before she had always been sweet to me—a fake sort of sweetness, I remind myself, and once again, I ponder the real reason she had sent me here to begin with. None of it makes sense, unless…

Before I can finish that thought, an explosion shatters the earth, rattling the windows as plumes of black soil burst from within the mines, shooting out into the air, showering anyone unfortunate enough to be in its path, coating them in specks of glittery dust. I rush outside, knocking a chair over in my haste. Panic ensues as people dart about, desperate to get away from the mine, while Commandant Gant yells at the arbiters under his command, who in turn, shout at the fleeing workers. I race for the entrance to the mine, looking at the grim-ridden workers who run in the opposite direction; each glance at me in confusion as I rush past, unwilling to stop. Another thundering roar bursts from the mine, encased in a cloud of dust as it collapses, forcing me to stop and cover my face in an attempt to protect it from flying debris, but a few of the needle-sized pricks sting my skin, despite my efforts. I turn in circles, searching for a particular face, but cannot find him amidst the floating particles that twinkle in the sunlight, forming a veil around us, separating us from the outside world. I spot the woman who had helped me the night Chase took a beating for me and seize her arm, stopping her.

"Where is he?" I demand.

She points at the mine, knowing whom I refer to and hurries away, pausing only to assist another worker with a bloody gash on his leg. I turn toward the mine. Rubble stands between me and the only other friend I have in this world. Gwen needs him, and it is my fault that he is here and… I will never forgive myself for allowing him to die, not when I can prevent it. My eyes search every inch of the rubble, looking for anything that resembles a hole, a place where I can squeeze through. A man's deep and worried voice distracts me for a moment, and I turn to find Trevors going form worker to worker, demanding to know where Grelyn is, and my stomach sinks. She must be trapped in there as well. The strangled cries of a man in trouble reaches my ears, forcing me to turn back toward the mine. It is not Chase's voice, but it doesn't matter. He needs help, or he will die. Rubble tumbles from the top of the entrance to the bottom, kicking up pebbles and dust as it crashes to the ground, forming a small hole in the barrier big enough for a single person to squeeze through. I charge for it.

"Noni!"

Renal's voice echoes in my ears, drowning out the rumble of the earth beneath me, but I ignore him, knowing that if I do not act now, people will die, and it will be my fault. I reach the small opening and dive through it into a world of darkness and thick, suffocating air filled with powdery dirt, causing me to choke as I breathe. Coughing rattles my body as my lungs try to expel the pollution, but the more they try, the more I inhale the filth. Covering my mouth with my jacket sleeve, I feel my way around with my other hand as my eyes adjust to the darkness, watering and stinging from the particles floating around me, surrounding me in an attempt to impede my efforts. The toe of my boot catches on a fallen beam and I stumble, throwing my arms out in an effort to catch myself and grasp a broken support, clinging to it as I steady myself. A low rumble reverberates around me, warning me of the precariousness of my situation and how the mine could collapse at any moment.

"Help!" someone cries.

I follow the voice, ducking low to avoid the hanging boards and the splintered edges that snag my jacket. Forced to my hands and knees, I crawl through the loose dirt—some of it sneaks between my waistband and my skin and crawls downward, poking me as it goes—as bits of sharp rock slice my hands. The man calls again, and I quicken my pace, feeling my way through the murky darkness, doing my best not to dwell on the possibility that I will be entombed here if I fail. A ghost-like hand appears from the ashes and silt falls away from it in chunks as it raises up in an effort to reach out to me. Crawling, my knees scrap against rock, but I ignore the stinging pain as I reach for the hand and grab it, clutching it tight.

"Can you move?" I ask him.

The man nods.

Pleased, I yank him free from the mound of dirt covering him and help him to his hands and knees. He tries to say something, but I cut him off as I point to the exit and urge him to hurry. He clambers past me and I watch as he leaves, before turning back to the depth of the mine and the void it forms before me and crawl underneath a fallen support to an area where I can stand up. Creaking snaps around me, causing my heart to race and my breathing to quicken as the fear of being crushed to death sweeps over me, threatening to control me, but I force myself to remain calm as bits of dust and pebbles fall around me. Walking hunched over, I navigate my way through the tangled web of wooden planks and rock that bar my way. More coughing snatches my attention and I hurry toward it, finding a woman huddled in the darkness, frozen with fear. I try to lift her to her feet, but she slaps my hand away. I try again with the same result.

"We need to go," I tell her.

"I can't move," she says, her voice filled with fear.

A quick examination proves that she is not injured, but paralyzed from fear.

"We have to…"

"I can't."

More dust falls around us and I know we haven't much time. Doing the only thing I can think of, I raise my hand and slap her across the face, creating a sound that travels through the caverns, and she stares at me with wide eyes.

"Get up!" I yell at her. "This whole place will collapse around us, so get up and get to that hole!"

Shocked back into reality, the woman scrambles to her feet and edges her way to the only exit, being careful not to trip over any rocks. Grumbling echoes around me as more of the rubble shifts and an ominous feeling settles in my stomach, warning me that there isn't much time to find Chase. I maneuver through the darkness as silt clings to my face, working its way into the depths of my pores, mixing with the sweat dripping from my hairline to my chin. More dust drops from above, getting into my eyes, and I look down, rubbing them and blinking in an effort to clear them, thankful for the tears that form, washing them clean. When I can focus again, I look around, but only see the faint shapes of rock, dirt, and splintered support beams.

"Chase!" I call; my voice fades in the distance, and I wonder if he hears me.

Whispering catches my attention. I turn toward it, my feet fumbling over a raised mound of dirt that gives way under me, causing my leg to sink into it until it is halfway up my calf and I almost topple over. Steadying myself, I pull my leg free, ignoring the tickling sensation of the soil running down my pants, creating the sound of trickling water as it falls. The whispering grows louder. I squint in the darkness, trying to make sense of the shapes before me when I realize that I have stumbled upon two more workers. A clang sounds behind me, and I whirl around, straining to see what caused the noise, but find nothing. I do not know how much longer this shaft will hold before the rest of it caves in. Turning back to the humanoid shapes before me, I inch my way closer, and they come into view, their clothes and skin covered in silt, making them blend in with the dark surroundings.

A girl, not much younger than me, bends over a boy who appears to be her age, shaking him and whispering for him to get up, but he never moves. The feeling that something is not right ebbs its way into my mind and I kneel beside the boy, while the girl ignores me, and place my thumb on his neck, where his pulse should be. Nothing. The girl shakes him again and his head rolls to the side so that his vacant eyes stare into mine, confirming my suspicion. I have seen eyes like his before enough times to know when I am staring at a dead body. My eyes move to the girl who still tries in vain to get him to stand up, unwilling to believe that he is dead, and a lump forms in my throat as my heart aches for her, a feeling I have not experienced often, and am unsure of how to react to it. Placing my hands on her shoulder, I try to coax her to move, but she shoves me away.

"He's gone," I say to her in a gentle voice.

"No!" she screams, and I fear that her shrill voice will bring what is left of the mine down on top of us.

I seize her shoulders and shake her with such force that, for a moment, I fear that I have snapped her neck.

"He's gone! You can't help him! You need to help the ones you can and not worry about the ones you can't!"

Her saucer-sized eyes stare into mine, still unwilling to leave her friend, but knowing that she has to, and she gets up.

"Go that way"—I point in the direction of the only way out—"and hurry!"

She stumbles off in a daze and all I can do is hope that she makes it out. I turn back around and face the depths of the mine, my mind racing about, wondering where Chase is, afraid that he is lying underneath the weight of the cave in, losing his ability to breathe as he is crushed to death.

"Chase!" I yell. "CHASE!"

My pulse quickens and threatens to cause a vein to burst as I search for him in a frantic state, every gloomy scenario filling my mind as I delve deeper into the mine.

"Noni!"

I stop. "Chase?"

"Over here!"

I shove my way through fallen timbers and rocks, pushing rubble out of my way as I hurry to him. My heart thuds in my ears, pounding out the dead silence of the shaft, as I force my way to him, and the more his dark shape grows, the faster I move, desperate to get to him. A rock lays on his leg, pinning him, and I fear that it might be broken. Once I reach him, I drop to the ground, cringing as a sharp stone jabs my knee, but the pain dissipates in a moment as seeing Chase alive invigorates me.

"Are you hurt?" I ask, the worry evident in my voice.

"No, just stuck. I can't move the rock."

I scramble to my feet and move to the boulder, studying it, hoping that when I move it, it won't cause more rubble to crash down upon us, but in the end, decide that it is worth the risk as I cough once more on the hovering pollution.

"When I lift this, you'll need to move your leg. Can you do that?"

He nods.

Summoning all my strength, I brace my feet against the ground in a firm stance and tighten my abdominal muscles as I lift the flat stone as high as I can, until Chase can swing his leg free. He does and rolls to his side, away from the rock, and I let go, dropping it to the ground, and my arms thank me for the reprieve. Relieved that he is alive and unharmed, minus a few bruises, I wrap my arms around him in the biggest embrace I can manage, and he envelops me in his strong arms as well, pleased that I did not abandon him.

"I think, now, I am the one who owes you," he whispers.

I smile at his words, until a thought enters my mind.

"Are there others?"

"The woman with the blue eyes…"

"Grelyn?"

Chase looks at me and answers, "If that is her name."

"Where?"

"Down there," he points. "She was scouting for more ore and a possible new shaft when everything crashed around us."

"The way out is that way." I point in the direction of the opening I had come through and turn to head deeper into the mine.

Chase snatches my arm. "What are you doing?"

"I can't just leave her." I can't explain it, nor do I know why, but the need to rescue her, or at least try, takes hold of me, refusing to let go, despite our mutual hatred of each other.

"You can't go down there."

"I have to. I can't just leave her there to die. I'm going."

"You're not going alone."

"You need to go." The thought of him following me down there and dying tears at my heart, and how would I explain to Gwen that I am responsible for his death, that I failed to get him to safety when I had a chance? "I thought…" I swallow back a lump.

"I'm not leaving you down here alone," Chase says, the resolution in his voice evident, and I know that there is no forcing him to leave. "We'll do this together."

I concede, and he points in the direction of where Grelyn was last seen, allowing him to lead the way as he steps over a turned-over cart with one of its wheels still on the metal track that stretches deep within the mine, buried beneath rock and metal. Particles of dust drop from above, sprinkling my jacket and catching me in the eyes when I look up, forcing me to turn away in an effort to clean the grit out of them. As I blink them clear, a frozen face with an arm that appears to jut out of its mouth stares back at me, causing me to jump, but I regain my composure, not wanting to show fear. The terror within the person's eyes burn into my own, imprinting itself on my brain, and

I know that I will not forget this moment anytime soon. Imagining what this person must have felt when he realized that he was going to die, the same terror, the same fear courses through me, making me think of my own mortality—something I have never done before—as I trek after Chase, hoping that we reach Grelyn soon.

"What happened?" I asked, trying to break the eerie silence.

"We were digging, like we're supposed to, when everything collapsed around us."

"And Grelyn?"

"She was scouting up ahead, searching for high density ore deposits and where a good place to dig next might be." Chase turns toward me. "What's she to you?"

I have no answer. I do not like her. I cannot stand her. We both despise each other, but a part of me cannot leave her here to die, not if she is still alive.

"I..." My voice trails off, echoing in the darkness, growing faint as it bounces from wall to wall in the tunnel, disappearing the same way those who are still trapped in this mine have, reminding me of my selfishness for only wanting to save the ones I knew, forsaking the others to die a miserable death as they are crushed under the weight of rock and stone. "I hate her," I whisper.

Chase stares at me, at least I think he is staring at me, since the lack of light makes it difficult to see any defining feature other than his faint outline.

"I can't explain it," I say to his unspoken question, but one that I would ask myself if I were in his position. "She and I... we never got along at the training facility. She always taunted me, teased me, and proved that she is better than me. She is stronger and faster. I despise every part of her, but she is also an arbiter and I can't just leave her down here now that I know she might be trapped."

Chases says nothing. He points further ahead.

"This way. The mine shaft forked over here, and that is where I last saw her."

Another low rumble reverberates around us, causing my chest to vibrate, and an ominous feeling rises within me as the hairs on the back of my neck stand up on end, like they did the night the wall was attacked, the night I earned my medal, the night I proved to be no different than anyone else within Arel. I stop and seize Chase's arm as foreboding rises within me, and the broken support beams and rock walls shake with a rapid secession of thunder, causing my ears to beg for relief. Before either of us can react, strong arms shove both of us out of the way just as more of the tunnel ceiling collapses, filling the small space we had been in, leaving the thinnest of trails that even the tiniest of people would struggle to maneuver through. I crash onto the ground; my knee smacks into a protruding rock, slicing it and leaving a bruise, and I roll onto my back, grimacing as I force myself to ignore the pain, almost jumping when I see who has saved us: Trevors. He leers over us in his muscular glory, tall and proud as his eyes frown at us while his lips form a straight line.

"What are you doing here?" I ask, though the answer is obvious.

Grelyn is trapped in the mine, and despite how much I loathe him, and how much he detests me and relishes in exuding his authority to the point of abuse, there is one thing the he cares most about in this world, and she is trapped under a mound of black earth.

Trevors stalks off, refusing to answer me.

"Lead the way, plebeian."

The manner in which he utters the word incenses me and I jump to my feet, but Chase stops me from attacking Trevors, and in that moment, I am reminded that I once referred to him in the same callous manner. Chase struggles to get to his feet, but Trevors' impatience forces him to seize Chase by the shirt and push him onward. "Now!"

I realize now that he must have entered the mine with one goal, to save Grelyn, and he overheard Chase and me talking about her last known location, which explains why he saved Chase, but why did he save me? Just four weeks ago, he tried to kill me. He could have let me die in the mine and no one would have asked questions, but assumed that my own stupidity caused my demise. I seize his hand when he tries to push Chase again and my firm grip forces Trevors to look at me.

"Yelling at him is not going to help us find her any faster."

Trevors yanks his wrist from me with a scowl that could scare off a pack of ravenous wolves, but I remain firm in my stance with a similar glower on my face.

"This way," says Chase, breaking us up.

More dust drops from above as a few rocks tumble downward, rattling as they go and sending a series of clacks that echo around us with a mocking clap. We come upon a wall of rock, mishmashed together in a haphazard fashion, forming a tangled mess of wood, metal, and stone with black soil filling in the cracks, creating an impenetrable barrier, except at the bottom where a small hole remains, blocked by metal bars. We rush to it and investigate it further, and for a moment, Trevors forgets himself, losing his rigid composure as he screams Grelyn's name.

"Grelyn!"

A soft mumble escapes the tiny opening, telling us that she is alive.

Trevors races for the opening, but I stop him. "If you try to go through there, you'll cause the entire thing to fall down on top of you. You're too big, but I'm not," I say when he rounds on me, forcing him to pause and reconsider his actions, and he concedes, taking a step back. "I need you two to hold these bars up so that I can fit through there."

Trevors pushes Chase over to the bars and they bend low, each taking a set, and lift them up as much as they can to allow me to pass through the opening, but not so much that it causes more rubble to tumble downward. I get on my hands and knees and crawl through the black hole, going further into what could very well be my tomb, ignoring the claustrophobia that rises within me as sweat oozes down my neck and arms from the exertion of wriggling my way through a tight space. Something sharp tears at my jacket as I move forward, creating an eerie ripping sound, which causes my mind to envision every terrible thing that can go wrong at this very moment.

My pulse quickens, and I inhale until my lungs can hold no more air before releasing it in a long, slow breath, quieting my nerves as I feel my way through the short tunnel that the cave in has created. Dirt eases its way down the neck of my jacket, giving me a gritty massage as it worms its way down my back and cutting me in places as some of the knife-like particles mix in with the grainy soil. Suffocating air envelops me, strapping me in its own binding straightjacket as I move, allowing me no relief, even when I reach the end of the tunnel and enter into a chamber that resembles the room with the walls that move inward like those from the trial of fears, instead of a mineshaft.

"Grelyn!" I shout.

"Over here!"

A shape squirms in the distance, resembling a being from a story that Faya told my bunkmates and me once while we were still recruits. I never learned where she had heard it before, but suspected that she had discovered a banned book in the training facility's library—they sometimes were snuck in there despite regulations—and stole it. I shake off the memory. This is not the time for such things. As I crawl up to Grelyn, she clutches her side and tries her best not to look as though she is in pain, but the torment is written on her face, and she scoffs at my efforts, able to see me with ease, as though the place is well-lit due to her ability to see in the dark. Her bright, crystal blue eyes, which are as natural to her as a fish on dry land, glare at me, watching my every move, emanating a faint glow that unnerves me and reminds me of how a cat's eyes glow in the dark.

As another bout of rumbling and creaking sets in, warning us of the inevitability of being crushed to death if we do not hurry, I push aside my hatred for Grelyn and kneel by her side. She slaps my hands away when I try to look at the gash that her hand covers in an unsuccessful attempt to stop the bleeding. Angered by her actions, I scoot away from her and sit cross-legged.

"Alright. Fine," I say to her, my voice stern. "Get up yourself."

We have a staring contest for a few moments as she ponders whether I am just posturing.

I move to the small opening I had come through. "You're weak," I tell her. "If an arbiter cannot drag himself to safety, but must rely on others for help, then that arbiter should just put a bullet in his head because he is unfit to wear the uniform," I say, repeating Molers' words, which he had spoken on several occasions when he believed that recruits had been too lax in their discipline.

"You won't leave me here."

Tell that to Trix. I think back to the attack on the wall and how she had been slumped over on her knees near the edge and threatened to hurt Sheila, and how I kicked her over that edge to the wild dogs below. Not once have I thought about that incident, not until now, and I feel no guilt over it. I inch my way back to Grelyn and place my face right in front of hers so that she can smell my sweaty breath.

"Try me," I whisper. "You will not be the first that I've killed. Nor the last."

Grelyn tries to get up, but flops back down onto the hard ground, and I notice that her right ankle refuses to support her weight. It isn't swollen, so I doubt that it is broken, but it might be sprained, and with that gash in her side, she would be hard pressed to go anywhere.

"Are you going to help me?" she spits.

I grab one of her arms and punch her in the face, causing sticky, red blood to dribble from her nose. She wipes it with the back of her dirt encrusted hand, scowling at me.

"That's for being a bitch."

Before she can say or do anything, I grab one of her arms and drape it around my shoulder, lifting her up, all 170 pounds of rigid muscle, and drag her to the small opening. It will be tight, but she should fit, not that she has much choice. When we reach it, I urge her to go first, since we cannot get through there any other way. She goes without argument and crawls inside, struggling to move as she uses one arm to support herself and the other to hold her wound. As she hobbles in the same manner as a three-legged dog, I snatch her hurt ankle and squeeze, putting as much pressure on it as I can, as her strangled yelp hits my ears, sounding louder than it is because of the closeness of the space.

"Don't even think about kicking me in the face," I warn her.

She yanks her ankle from my grasp and continues onward, inching her way through the tiny opening with me right behind her, doing my best not to let the feeling of claustrophobia settle in as more rumbling echoes around us. The realization that this entire shaft could finish caving in at any moment settles in. Grelyn senses it too and picks up her pace, more concerned with escaping this dismal cavern instead of tormenting me, which I'm sure she plans to do later. Sweat and grime cover my hands, making them slip when I place them on the rocks. Digging them into the ground to coat them in dirt, and give them a bit of traction, I push myself forward with my legs as soil falls around me, blanketing me and mingling with the ever constant stream of perspiration that circles my neck and back. We reach the end. Grelyn and I both spill out of the opening and roll across the arid ground, gasping for any sort of air that is not polluted by the putrid stench of sweat and anger.

Once again, I grab Grelyn's arm and drape it around my shoulders, lifting her to her feet amidst the floating particles of dust that settles in my lungs with each breath I take. A tug almost forces me off-balance as Trevors takes her other arm and insists on carrying her himself, but I maintain my grip on her, knowing that it is best if we both carry her so that we can move faster.

"Together," I tell him, and he does not argue as he is more focused on her well-being over any sort of power struggle. "Chase, lead the way."

Chase scurries ahead as Grelyn scoffs, "I can see better than him."

"But you can't lift obstacles out of our way," I tell her, and she clamps her mouth shut, groaning as we move.

An ominous creak sounds as, behind us, a beam bends under the weight of the earth, until it breaks, snapping in half, and mounds of damp dirt spills into the shaft, filling it, threatening to engulf us. We run, hoisting Grelyn over a fallen beam that we had climbed over on our way to get her, trying not to choke on the suffocating atmosphere as filth fills our mouths, clogging our airways. Chase moves a boulder out of the way as Trevors and I scurry through the mine, ignoring the painful protests of Grelyn as each move bangs her injured ankle across the ground or stretches the gash on her side, and with each step, her blood soaks into my jacket, coating my skin. More thunderous roars rage around us as another beam, bent until it formed a u-shape, snaps, releasing the underground's fury upon us. Trevors loses his footing, almost taking all of us down with him, but before he falls, Chase steadies him, and they lock eyes for a moment as a silent agreement between them forms.

A speck of light reaches my eyes and my heart leaps for joy as the possibility of making it out alive becomes attainable—we just need to run. I jump over a dead body, and, together, Trevors and I hoist Grelyn up so that her feet do not catch on it as he leaps over it as well. The light grows larger as we race through the shaft, challenging death, daring it to stop us. More dirt spills into the mine, forming streams of mud and rock that scurry around our feet in one last attempt to prevent us from escaping. We reach our only exit.

As though our minds are one, Trevors, Chase, and I push Grelyn into the opening, and she disappears into the sunlight. I grab Chase and shove him into the hole, refusing to let him die down here. I turn toward Trevors, but before I can ask who will go through first, he seizes my jacket and pulls me backward—this is it; he is going to leave me here—and shoves me through the opening with all his strength, as Renal's arms grab mine and pulls me into the hot sunlight. Blinking as my eyes adjust to the overabundance of light, I whirl around, surprised that Trevors pushed me to safety, and watch as he crawls out, coated in grime and mud, just like the rest of us. He looks at me for a second and his mouth parts, as though he is about to say something, but he clamps it shut at the last moment and rushes to Grelyn, helping her to the medical wing of the compound.

"What were you thinking?" Renal demands, forcing me to look at him, worry etched on his face, and I wonder why as I realize that I have never seen him like this before.

"There were people in there," I reply, my voice small and quiet compared to the commotion around us.

"Workers."

"We are charged with protecting Arel," I say. "Are they not also a part of Arel?"

Renal's face softens and he glances around, afraid that someone might have seen the way he reacted to my brazenness and lack of common sense.

"Go. Get checked out by their doctor."

I salute him and stalk away, observing the people around me, the mass of workers that managed to escape, spotting the woman I had slapped in order to get her to move, and the arbiters tending to them, not in their usual harsh and cruel manner, but as though they want to make sure that they are not injured, as though they care. The change in their demeanor puzzles me. What changed them? My gaze settles on Chase, and I want to run to him, to make sure that he is okay, but he shakes his head, warning me away, and I agree with him: it's too dangerous. My feet shuffle across the ground as I mosey to the one-room medical center they have here, hoping that we can leave this place soon.

Chapter 14

Uprising

Reports litter the desk before me, staring back at me, mocking my attempts to read through them, as their figures, graphs, and charts overwhelm my brain, threatening to shut it down as I try to make sense of their meaning. Paperwork. I loathe it and had hoped to never spend much time doing it, but it appears that much of what I hoped for will never come to pass. Tapiwa put me in charge of making the mines more productive, and with that comes the ugly side of bookkeeping. I pick up a report, and the flimsy plastic-like material it is printed on wobbles in my hands. In reality, each of the reports are just tablet-sized computer screens that are as thin as paper and look like paper, but are miniature computers. Commandant Gant frowned when I asked him to bring me these tablets, because I should have been able to view all the reports on one, but I like having them spread out in front of me so that I can read them with ease and make comparisons, even if it makes this desk in a secluded corner of the command center, which has been loaned out to me among protests from the commandant, look like a jumbled mess. As I study the reports, I realize that production is up as ordered, and Tapiwa will be pleased, but to what end? Once I leave, Commandant Gant will go back to the way things were before I arrived, meaning that the workers will go back to their overworked and starved state.

Sighing, I open and close reports, sending them all to one file in an attempt to organize them into a single account for President Tapiwa, which I will be required to produce upon my return to Arel. Whispering reaches my ears, which stops the moment I look up to see what it is about, confirming that I am the subject of their conversation. Many within the mine will be glad to be rid of me, though I share their sentiments, since I have no desire to be here any longer than necessary. Tomorrow, Renal and I are to leave. Renal. Where is he? I have not seen him since this morning, something that makes my skin crawl and a well deepens within the darkest corners of my stomach as a portentous feeling settles in, filling me with dread and a forewarning that something terrible is about to happen. I shove it aside, not wanting to dwell on it, but it continues to gnaw at me, ebbing away at the illusion of safety that I choose to engage in. I transfer the reports into a single file and save it, sending it off to Tapiwa, but not before making a copy to give to Commander Vye, just like she had ordered me to.

"So—"

I close the reports as Commandant Gant walks up beside me and sits on the desk, causing it to creak under his weight, and faces me in a manner that seems innocent, but is meant to put me at unease.

"—this is your last night here."

I stare at him, keeping my facial expression blank, wondering why he is here or what he wants. He knows that I leave tomorrow, making his statement redundant and unnecessary.

"Any plans for when you return?"

What game is he playing? We are not friends, not that friendships are encouraged, but we are not even on amicable terms, and he knows it.

"I'll be continuing my duties in the eastern sector," I say, gathering up the paper-thin tablets and forming a neat stack with them.

Commandant Gant picks up one of the tablets and bends it between his hands. Though pliable and durable, they will break if enough pressure is applied or they are put through a fair amount of abuse, and I wonder if that is his intention as he continues to bend it, but before it cracks, he puts it back on the stack, taking extra care to make sure it is even and in line with the others. He places his hands back in his lap and looks at me with a facsimile of a smile, making me uneasy.

"Is there something you want, commandant?" I ask.

"No," he says, and I start to walk away, having grown tired of this charade, "but there is one thing."

I face him.

"You haven't seen Lieutenant Renal, have you? It appears that he has been absent all day."

Heat forms under my collar as my stomach sinks into a bottomless pit of despair. I try to keep my face impassive, but judging by the smirk on the commandant's face, he knows that he has me where he wants me.

"Not since this morning," I say, keeping my voice calm, unwilling to give him the satisfaction that he caught me off-guard.

"Pity. I was hoping to speak with him before you two leave."

"Commandant, if you'll excuse me, but I do have an early start in the morning and would like to get some rest before then."

He stands up, apologetic for having delayed me and keeping me from getting some sleep, but his demeanor says something else, something more sinister.

"Please, don't stay here on my account."

I salute him and leave, but before I am able to exit the building, Commandant Gant makes one last declaration.

"Sweet dreams," he says.

The night air rushes over me as I leave, thankful when the door shuts behind me, allowing me to take in a deep breath in order to calm my quaking nerves as a single thought dominates my mind, refusing to let me go: where is Renal? Worried that something terrible has happened to him, and chastising myself for not being more vigilant earlier, I hike across the compound to our sleeping quarters, ignoring everyone I pass. A few arbiters look in my direction as I rush past them, observing my movements, making me believe that they are watching me upon Commandant Gant's orders, but I shove my paranoia aside. It will not help me find Renal. Whispers and eyes follow me; I feel them, and the more I know they are there, the warmer the base of my neck becomes, causing pellet-sized beads of sweat to form, creating a glue-like substance that forces my jacket collar to stick to my skin.

I burst into Renal's room. Nothing. Turning on a light, I search for any sign of him, any indication that he has been here or where he might be, but all I find is a single cot with the blanket smoothed out and tucked under the mattress without even a smidgeon of a wrinkle; the nightstand left untouched with only the lamp on it; and a washbasin with a dry faucet, meaning that it has not been used in several hours, but no Renal. Worried, and unable to contain it, I sprint out of the room, looking all around, wondering where he could have gone, while Commandant Gant's smirk fills my mind, convincing me that none of this is by accident.

A noise stops me, forcing me to turn toward my own room. Is someone in there? I duck to the side, getting away from the windows, so that if anyone is in there, they cannot see me. Approaching with caution, I pull out my baton, ready to attack whoever is in my room, as I ease the door open and peer inside its dark interior and am greeted with a mirror image of Renal's quarters.

"Noni."

I freeze. Crouched in a corner where light would never touch him, is Renal. I put my baton away and close the door before rushing over to him. At first, I reach for a light, but stop, reconsidering my actions, as I remember the ill feeling I had when talking to Commandant Gant. Renal gets up and stumbles toward me, unable to stand on his own, forcing me to catch him so that he does not crash into the sink and injure himself even more. Blood drips from his face and onto my left arm, soaking into my jacket, and I gasp when I see the left side of his face so overcome by swelling that there are no discernable features. One eye is swollen shut, and more blood drips from his temple and trickles out of his right ear, but it is the injuries I cannot see that trouble me.

"You need to run!" His hoarse voice struggles to form the words and make himself heard, without attracting unwanted attention.

"What happened?" I ask, unable to stop my need to know.

"It was a trap. I should have known. He told me that there was a barbarian encampment nearby that he thought might be a threat to Arel, so I had him lead me to it. We took a transport, but there were others waiting for us when we got there. I don't know how I managed to get away, but not before they did this."

I help him up, but Renal shoves me away.

"Run! Go!"

"I'm not…"

"Commandant Gant intends to kill you. You need to get…"

"I'm not leaving without you." My firm voice stops him, and before he can protest further, I haul him to his feet, allowing him to lean on me for support. We navigate our way out of the room, my feet plopping on the floor underneath his weight as my legs threaten to give out on me, refusing to bear him as a burden, but I will them to remain strong; if they falter now, we both will die. I half-drag, half-carry him outside as more of his blood oozes down the sides of my jacket, soaking into the miniscule spaces between the fibers and woven threads, but I ignore its stickiness and warmth as I steer us toward where the transports are located. I pause.

"What's wrong?" gasps Renal.

Chase. I cannot leave him, but I cannot search for him with

Renal in his current state. He stares at me with his one good eye, a speck of white sticking out of his dark, bruised, and swollen face, and I want to tell him—I should tell him—but how can I? Torn between two people I do not wish to see dead, we inch our way to the transport area, while my mind wrestles with the choices before me, each one as terrible as the first, and I know that my conscience will not allow any of them to take place. Darkness shrouds us, protecting us the only way it can, by concealing our movements as we edge our way to the transports, sneaking past sentries, and away from the compound. We're almost there.

A door creaks open and boots stomp on wooden steps as they carry their owner outside for a smoke—a forbidden act—and Renal and I stop, staying as still as we can, hoping that we will go unnoticed. Renal leans even more into me, dragging my shoulder downward from his weight, but I hold onto him, refusing to let him fall to the ground. My heart pounds in my chest as I remain still, waiting, pleading in silent agony for the man to go back inside. With a final flick of his wrist, the soft glowing embers fling through the night, disappearing into nothingness, as he turns and vanishes behind the door into his quarters.

Trapped air escapes my lungs and I shake Renal, urging him to continue as I haul him across the compound, staying next to the shadowy wall bordering what has become our prison. He groans and I shush him, not wanting his vocal overtones to draw attention. Though the way seems clear, that does not mean that someone isn't nearby, that some arbiter or worker won't stumble upon us. We turn a corner. I can see them. The transports are close. Just a few more yards. I shift Renal, relieving the pressure on my shoulder and strengthening my grasp of him as his feet stumble over themselves, unsure of how to walk.

A figure steps out in front of us. My breath catches in my throat when I recognize the tall, muscular build, and the broad shoulders that straighten themselves with pride. Trevors steps into the dim light of a lamp spilling through a grime encrusted window as his unforgiving gaze drills into my surprised eyes, while I cling to Renal in a desperate attempt to prevent him from crashing onto the ore-infested soil. Our eyes remain locked as we each ponder who will make the next move, but Renal's dwindling state jerks us both into action as his head lulls to the side in his semiconscious state and jumbled words escape his lips, forming unintelligible nonsense.

As I lose my hold on Renal, Trevors swoops in and grabs him, lifting him up as though he weighs no more than a bag of flour, reminding me of the time at the training facility when all recruits had to carry a 25-pound bag of flour for four miles; if we dropped it, or if it opened, we were punished, but Trevors never faltered and reached the finish line first with his bag intact. He takes Renal from me and motions for me to follow him as he moves through the compound, slinking between buildings, carrying Renal with ease, and I trudge after him, unsure of his motives or why he is helping me.

We reach the transport area, and after making certain that no one is around, we dart across the space between the compound and the transports and crouch beside one. I test a door. Locked. Trevors points at another and hurries toward it; his giant feet create such soft steps that, for a moment, I find it difficult to believe that it is him, but shake myself out of my reverie and back to the present. I race after him, keeping my steps light and hunker next to him when he reaches his destination. He motions for me to try the door and I do without question. It opens. Thrilled, I pull it the rest of the way, taking care to not allow the door to creak as even the slightest noise sounds like utter chaos on such a still night.

Renal moans as we place him in the back seat, laying him down with care. After Trevors shuts the transport, I head for the driver's seat, unsure of where we will go, when I stop with my hand on the cool handle of the door and look back at the compound shrouded in a darkening mist, broken only by the harsh lights of the buildings that house the arbiters as figures pace back and forth, bored with their assigned duties. I yearn to go back there, yet my head orders me to leave, and as they battle one another for dominance, Trevors eyes me, wondering why I have not moved. I cannot leave Chase again. How will I tell Gwen that I abandoned her brother? How will I look Sheila in the eyes, knowing that I have a chance, here and now, to get us all out of here, and I left him? How will I look at myself?

A firm hand frees mine from the driver's door and I whip my head around, stopping when I see Trevors' face. On any other day, my first impulse would be to punch him, but something within his eyes stops me. He does not gloat. There is no brazenness, no cockiness, just understanding.

"Go," he says. "I'll stay with him."

I step back, but before I get far, my mouth opens and spills the words that jump to the forefront of my mind, never giving me a chance to stop them, to chain them up before they break free.

"You should come with us," I say, not understanding why I am offering him a chance to join me, "you and Grelyn."

"You're wasting time." Trevors' harsh voice jerks me into action. "And, Noni, after tonight, we're even."

I nod, acknowledging his statement before I turn and sprint into the darkness, back to the mining compound, back to Chase, to free him. I understand Trevors' words: I helped him rescue Grelyn and this is his way of repaying that debt. I race through the night, hunkering by the first outbuilding I come to and wait for the sentry to pass before jumping to my feet and darting across an opening to another outbuilding, making my way to the workers' quarters. Another arbiter paces back and forth just feet away from me as I peer around a corner and wait for her to turn back around, heading away from me. Her feet crunch the gravel in a bored manner as she skips in an effort to entertain herself, swings around, and stalks away with her indolent demeanor on full display for the stars.

I spring from my hiding place and race to the worker's quarters when the screeching sounds of a siren ring out, drowning the peaceful night with its call to action, waking anyone slumbering and forcing everyone outside. Frozen, my legs refuse to move as doors bang open and half-dressed arbiters run out of their quarters, tying their weapons' belt around their waist as they search for the reason for the sirens going off in the first place, while workers spill out of their quarters wanting answers to the same question.

"There she is!"

The same arbiter whom I had watched moments before who wished for some sort of excitement, points at me as she shouts.

I run. Arbiters surround me, thwarting me at every turn as spotlights dance behind them, hoping to find me. Dashing down a narrow passage, I push myself as fast as I can go, hoping to get away, but a group of arbiters block my path. My feet skid in the dirt, kicking up clouds of fine dust as I stop and turn in another direction, racing between two outbuildings, desperate to get away. I burst into an opening, and gasp the moment a hard object slams into my chest, knocking me backward, forcing the air out of my lungs. An arbiter leers over me with a sneer on his face and a baton in his hands. He raises it, ready to strike me again when I jut my feet out, entangling them around his ankle and twist, knocking him over, and as he crashes to the ground, I scramble to my feet and run, stumbling as I regain my balance.

Shouts well up around me as arbiters surround me and my mind races for a solution, but I think of nothing as my breaths come in gasps and turn another corner. An arbiter tackles me and we crash into the ground, and I cringe as pebbles work their way underneath my skin, scraping it away. I roll onto my back and fling my fists, catching someone in the jaw, receiving a kick to the stomach for my efforts as more hands seize me, jerking me to my feet and forcing me to the center of the compound as the spotlights focus their beams on my disgrace. A plastic tie is wrapped around my wrists, cinched so tight that it cuts into my skin and warm blood drips from them, leaving a miniscule trail in the sand behind me: bright red in the glittery black earth. A hand shoves me forward in an attempt to force me off-balance, but I regain my composure, much to the ire of the man who pushed me. In response, he sticks out his foot, tripping me, and I stumble to the ground, landing hard on my right shoulder, but I refuse to show any pain to give these bastards any satisfaction in seeing me suffer.

"What have we here?" Commandant Gant steps out from among the gathering crowd of arbiters and workers, stopping with the toes of his dusty boots just inches from my eyes as he stares down at me, gloating.

"Back to your quarters!" yells an arbiter.

"Let them stay," says Commandant Gant. "They should watch what happens to anyone who challenges my authority."

His authority? Does he think he is Arel now? I spit on his boots. A baton strikes me on the cheek in response as Commandant Gant raises his hand to stop it. He kneels down, placing his face in front of mine, allowing me to see the stubble on the dark skin of his upper lip.

"I told you that accidents happen in the mines."

As he stands up, I force myself to my feet, refusing to allow my spinning head to cause me to topple over as I recover from the latest blow to my face. The slow wave of nausea dissipates as I straighten myself, standing with an erect posture, refusing to show weakness. Displeased, Commandant Gant glares at me, but turns away when a commotion arises as someone pushes their way through the crowd, dragging someone by the shoulders, and my heart sinks into my stomach as Trevors appears with Renal, tossing him to the ground the way a person treats a piece of garbage.

"I caught this one trying to escape, sir," says Trevors.

Commandant Gant nods in approval.

I should have known. In a moment of weakness, I trusted Trevors and that trust has now gotten both me and Renal killed. I glare at him, but he ignores my glance as he stares straight ahead, unmoving and unfeeling, just like the Trevors I know and remember. I return my gaze to the commandant, challenging him, not allowing him the satisfaction of seeing me grovel.

"You came here and thought that you could change things," Commandant Gant says, speaking to the crowd more than me. "You thought that you could force us to share our water, our food with these workers. They are nothing and are not our equals, yet you"—he snatches a baton from one of the arbiters and points it at me—"would have them sit with us as though they are! These people are filth, replaceable, and it is time that you all learn your place. Conform or die."

The commandant stops in front of me, his nose almost touching mine. "Kneel," he hisses at me.

"No," I reply, my voice soft, but stern, and it carries over the still atmosphere that settles upon us all as eyes watch us, waiting to see who will concede to whom.

An arbiter walks up to me and kicks me in the back of my left knee, forcing me to the ground and my knees slam into the hard earth as gravel digs into them, leaving jagged impressions. The moment the arbiter's hand leaves my shoulder, I stand back up, rising to my full height in front of everyone and squaring my shoulders as best I can, despite my hands being tied. Infuriated, Commandant Gant strikes me in the side with his baton, but I remain standing.

"KNEEL!" he yells at me.

"No."

My resolute voice echoes around us, hovering over everyone present, far stronger, far superior to his irate demands. Though my face refuses to betray it, I am smiling on the inside, aware that I have won this battle of wills, because if I am to die, I will do so on my feet and not begging for my life to the likes of this coward.

The commandant snatches a pistol and aims it at me, but before he can squeeze the trigger, before can bring an end to my existence, a single voice, clear and loud, rings out over us all.

"STOP!"

Chase forces his way to the front and steps out into the clearing, his grungy clothes dropping bits of dust with each movement, and his gaze meets the commandant's, something that is unheard of, since plebeians are forbidden to look their masters in the eyes.

"Let her go," he says, his strong voice holding everyone's attention, including Renal's, who watches with his unswollen eye.

The commandant's black face turns red with fury. He turns the weapon from me and aims it at Chase. I dig my feet into the dirt, prepared to jump between them, but before either myself or the commandant can make a move, Trevors' voice stops us.

"Commandant, let me teach this refuse a lesson."

Commandant Gant lowers his weapon.

Worried, I watch as Trevors walks over to Chase who remains rigid, refusing to cower in fear, knowing that he is about receive a beating, adding more bruises to the pale outline of the ones that have almost healed. Every crunch in the dirt from Trevors' boots pierces my ears, and I start to move, but the commandant's hand stops me, and I watch in horror as Trevors bears down upon Chase, standing a head taller than him, and prepares to strike. Before anyone can react, Trevors shoves Chase into the gathered crowd and snatches the weapon of a nearby arbiter from its holster, twisting around and firing at the commandant, missing me and striking him in the shoulder.

All hell breaks loose.

The workers charge the arbiters, jumping on them and pulling them to the ground as they seize rocks and shovels, attacking any arbiter they see, while whistles screech into the night, drowned by the angry cries of the workers who have decided to no longer suffer Commandant Gant's abuses. Breaking glass stabs the chaos as a stone is thrown through it and its shards crash into the ground, breaking into smaller pieces and mingling with the black soil. The cries of an arbiter calling for reinforcements from Arel force me to glance through the hole in the window and the command center behind it as panicked arbiters ditch their consoles. One goes for the weapons locker. I watch as he hands automatic weapons to arbiters rushing past, yelling at them to put down the uprising.

Remembering Chase and Renal, I spin around, searching for them—Commandant Gant has disappeared—and spot Renal lying on the ground where Trevors had thrown him, struggling to move as people rush past him, kicking him with their feet, unaware of his injuries, or not caring. I run to him and land hard on my knees beside him. As I try to lift him up, the binding around my wrists remind me that I cannot move them. I need to free them. Desperate, I search for anything sharp that can be used while dodging the melee of workers and arbiters fighting one another, but all I find is grainy silt that continues to rise up my thighs as I sink into it. I yank at the binding, grimacing as it cuts deeper into my skin as I try to wrestle it from my wrists. Moist blood trickles down my hands, coating the chilled tips of my fingers with its warm essence, but the binding remains. Just when I think that I will have to break my thumbs to get it off, Trevors appears. I aim a kick at him, angered that he betrayed me, but he deflects it with ease and pins me on my stomach. A knife appears. Struggling, my feet slide in the loose soil as I try to wrestle my way out of Trevors grip when—the binding falls away from my wrists.

Rolling onto my back, I watch as Trevors puts his knife away and grabs Renal, lifting him onto his shoulders with ease, and runs to the nearest outbuilding.

"Come on!" he yells at me.

I follow after him and stop. Not far from me is Chase fighting with an arbiter while another stands a few yards behind him, raising his weapon and taking aim. I seize the nearest arbiter, jabbing my fist on the underside of his jaw while snatching his pistol from his holster. Blocking out the sounds of the chaos raging around me as arbiters shoot at any who come at them and workers scream and attack those that have abused them, I aim the weapon and fire. I hit my target just as Chase manages to get the upper hand on his opponent. I charge for him, shoving a worker out of my way, knowing that I should help him, but there are only two people here I care about.

An arbiter swings her baton at me. I duck, leaning back as far as I can, and fall to the ground, dodging the fatal blow. She whirls around and swings at me again. Rolling across the ground, blood-soaked earth coats my uniform as I avoid her attempt to end me. The baton strikes the ground near my head. I jerk to my left, rolling onto all fours before springing at her legs, catching her around the knees and knocking her to the ground. She grunts as she lands. I jump onto her stomach, straddling her. She whips her baton at me, but I lean to the side, avoiding its sharp sting, and grab hold of it, wrenching it from her hands before pressing it down upon her throat.

"Stop," I tell her, wishing she would stop struggling. She is one of me. An arbiter, doing her duty. "Please, stop!"

She goes for her sidearm, and my training kicks in, taking over my movements, and I ram the baton into her throat and twist, jerking her head at an odd angle and breaking her neck. Relaxing my hold, and consumed with guilt for what I have done, I sit up, staring at her lifeless form, knowing that I am the cause of her death—a senseless death.

"Noni!"

Chase's voice jerks me from my stupor. I spot a girl about Sheila's age struggling to break free from the grip of another arbiter, and I swing the baton, catching him in the back of his knee, forcing him to lose his footing. Before he stands back up, I whip the baton through the air and smash it into his face, breaking his jaw, as a single, bloodied tooth flies from his mouth and settles in the dirt before another's foot stomps on it, burying it. I jump up and run to Chase and grab hold of him, thrilled that he is alive and unhurt.

"The transports," I tell him, guessing that Trevors must have headed there, since I cannot find him near any of the outbuildings, and it is what I would do.

We run. Workers and arbiters locked in battle litter the area before us as we push our way through them, dodging around them to avoid getting caught in the workers' bloodlust. I veer to the left, dragging Chase behind me, as a man puts the sharp end of a pick through the skull of an arbiter, splitting the cranium open and spilling its contents all over the blood-soaked soil. One by one, the arbiters fall, outnumbered and overpowered by the wrath of the workers, and as their numbers dwindle, the deafening shouts and screams dissipate, but I refuse to stop, wanting only to get away, to get Chase and Renal to safety.

A force slams into me, knocking me off my feet, and I roll across the ground as the sticky soil glues itself to my uniform, coating me in its horrifying entanglement of human entrails. Chase tackles my assailant, but he flings him off, throwing Chase to the ground and kicking him in the stomach, causing him to cough and gag for air. As I regain focus, Commandant Gant's face bears down upon me, full of rage and with murder in his eyes as blood oozes from the wound in his shoulder, but he refuses to acknowledge it and the pain it must be causing him.

He pulls out his pistol and fires a single shot—the noise echoes across the field, causing those nearby to stop and watch us—just as I move, and a warm sting grazes the right side of my neck, but I haven't time to consider my blessings. I face him. The commandant pulls the trigger once more, but all he receives for his efforts is a clicking sound. His clip is empty. Pleased, a devious grin crosses my lips. I charge him. Commandant Gant dodges out of the way, but I spin on my heels and barrel into his side, forcing him to the ground and wrench his arm behind his back as he throws dirt into my face, forcing me to jump back. I scoot backward, blinking and rubbing my eyes to clear them.

The commandant rushes me, but Chase appears, wrapping his arms around the man's leg. He slams his boot into Chase's face, but Chase's efforts did what he meant them to do: buy me time. I get on my hands and knees, focusing on my enemy, and spring for him, catching his left leg and ripping it out from under him. He slams into the ground on his back, releasing a groan. Tightening my grip, I twist the commandant's leg, dislocating his knee before jumping away. We face each other, each loathing the other as those nearest us close in, watching and waiting, forgetting that they had been locked in their own battles, and I realize that the one person they want to punish most is him.

"What are you waiting for?" Commandant Gant screams at a group of arbiters that have joined the workers to watch our fight.

They turn and leave, and my eyes widen as the workers gathered around us allow them to, since I had expected them to kill him.

"You fucking cowards!" screams Commandant Gant.

He glares at me, but I remain poised, ready for his next move. Commandant Gant lunges for me. I block his attack, wrapping an arm underneath his wounded shoulder and pressing a finger into the bloodied hole, ignoring his anguished screams that fill my ears before I break his collar bone and fling him to the ground like the piece of refuse that he is. Hatred takes over me as I lower myself to one knee beside him and grab the collar of his shirt, lifting him up so that I can look him in the eye before finishing him. Scooping up the broken handle of a shovel, I ready myself for what I must do, but stop when I see Chase's worried face and the look that shrouds it—the look that conveys he does not know me.

"Do it," urges Commandant Gant. "Follow your training."

I stare at him and the blood pooling around him. Is this who I want to be? Eighteen years of training, of being beaten and whipped into the perfect arbiter, commands me to kill the commandant and take his place as the chief officer of the mines, but if I do, what then? He deserves to pay for what he did to Renal and for how he has treated the people here. I scan the crowd. They want blood. A part of me understands their lust for it, nor can I stop it. The commandant will die tonight, but not by my hand.

I drop the shovel handle and it lands in the silt with a soft thump, sending a miniscule cloud of dust in the night air to float away, unaware of the death surrounding it.

"You were right, commandant, accidents do happen in the mines."

I step away from him and pause in front of the first worker I see. "He's yours."

Those that had gathered around us close in on the commandant and he disappears behind a hailstorm of raised fists and vengeful kicks as they unleash their wrath upon him, dealing out their form of justice. I turn away. No sorrow fills me over his demise, but a part of me wonders if I should have tried to help him live, and I remind myself that this is my world; this is what I am—a dealer of death. Chase's hand settles on my shoulder with the gentlest touch, causing me to jump, until I realize it is him, and his sympathetic eyes bury themselves within mine in an attempt to comfort me.

A low rumble rises in the distant night, cloaked by darkness and mystery, and the hairs on my arms and legs stand on end, sensing an encroaching danger as my heart beats faster from the impulse to run, but I remain still, studying the dark sky, listening, and waiting. The grumble morphs into a small whine that turns into a horrendous screech, as three aircraft zip past above us, scanning us. The Arelian fleet. Commandant Gant's cries for assistance had gotten through. I rush to one of the loudspeaker towers and rip the mic out of its hold, pressing the button on the side and screaming into it.

"RUN!"

People turn and look at me, while some flee, knowing what is to come next.

"Just run!" I scream into the mic, and my shrill voice echoes throughout the mine, filling it with panic. "Run for the wildlands and its hills! Go anywhere! Get out! NOW!"

Three Arelian aircraft fly low over the mines in formation, and I drop the mic, fleeing the area as fast as I can as explosives fall from the sky, detonating upon impact, showering everyone in fire, dirt, and a deafening blast that causes my ears to ring. As the dust settles, I stand alone by the loudspeaker, coated in grime, as I look around in a daze, searching for Chase, but all I find in the smoky haze are shadows, some running, some stumbling, others wandering in a stupor—ghosts in the night. Worry seizes me. Where is he? Did the bombs kill him? Scenario after scenario enters my mind, each worse than the other, and just as the image of Chase lying on the ground with his arms splayed and intestines hanging out of his mangled and charred body grips me, my voice pushes his name through my mouth in a desperate attempt to find him.

"CHASE!" My wild movements force me to run in circles, shouting his name, the desperation in my voice evident. "CHASE!"

No answer. I cannot find him. He's… Renal. Remembering that he is alone with Trevors and unable to defend himself, I rein in my emotions, but tears seep through my tempestuous barrier and ease their way down my cheeks, leaving streaks in the grime on my face, and I turn away, heading for the transports.

"NONI!"

Chase! I whip around, finding him crawling out from underneath a pile of rubble, and run to him, grabbing hold of him, refusing to let him go. His arms embrace me with the same unwillingness to let me go.

"Are you hurt?" he asks, and I smile, releasing a silly laugh, thinking that it is I who should be asking him the same question.

"Are you?" My fingers wipe the blood dribbling from a cut on the left side of his temple. The screeching intensifies. "We need to run!" I tell him.

We hurry away from the loudspeaker, joining the others who are desperate to escape the wrath of the Arelian fleet—Arel never allows dissonance to go unpunished—our hands clasped together, squeezing the blood out of one another as we refuse to let the other go. We race through the mine, dodging others as more bombs drop from the sky, spewing their vengeance on those unfortunate enough to be in their path, filling the darkness with fiery light, making us appear as nothing more than silhouettes in the night. Our feet rush over the ground, sinking into the soft earth, but we refuse to stop. More aircraft pass over us. An arbiter stumbles beside me. Letting go of Chase, I hurry to her and help her up, and she thanks me before scurrying away. We are all at the mercy of Arel now. I rush back to Chase and we take off again, not daring to look back as more explosions shatter the mine behind us, sending plumes of rock and ore high into the sky that arcs and rains down upon us as we try to escape, causing me to cringe as pebbles stab the base of my neck.

Movement catches my eye. Turning, I see Grelyn struggling to crawl out from underneath the bodies of two men that have her pinned to the ground. She gets about halfway out when the screeching starts again, as orange spots of light appear in the night and repetitive popping reach my ears. They're using their Gatling guns. Grelyn will never get free in time. I show her plight to Chase, and we race over to her, each grabbing hold of the bodies that weigh her down and haul them off her, allowing her to crawl to freedom. The planes draw nearer. Each of us charge away from the open area and to an outbuilding where we dive to the ground and crawl underneath just as the aircraft pass over us and bullets riddle the ground, leaving tiny craters, and the side of the building, filling it with holes. I start to move, but Grelyn snatches my arm and pulls me back.

"They're coming back," she says.

Though all I see is darkness, Grelyn sees the planes as though it is daylight, and I allow her to prevent me from going into harm's way. "Where's Trevors?"

"We got separated," she replies.

"Where's Renal?" I ask her.

"Don't worry about your friend."

I glare at her, incensed by her lack of concern for Renal, but remind myself that we have bigger problems, as the aircraft pass over us, releasing a hailstorm of gunfire that cuts down anyone in their path, not caring who gets killed so long as the uprising is put down.

"When I say," says Grelyn, "run and head for the west end of the compound." She cranes her head, looking up at the sky, her unnatural blue eyes seeming to glow, making her appear almost catlike. "Now!"

We all crawl out from under the building and jump to our feet, running as fast as we can away from the mine, away from the screams, and away from the fires. Chase and I link hands again, not wanting to get separated. More explosions, more fire threaten to overtake us as dirt mixed with bits of what used to be living people continue to fly through the air, pelting us with their fury. I lose sight of Grelyn. She always was a faster runner than me. My lungs threaten to give out on me as my legs start to turn to rubber, but I push forward, determined to escape this nightmare. I glance at Chase and he looks back at me as we try to encourage one another. Our feet pound the earth as the sounds of the night drain away from me, growing silent, overtaken by the screech of an Arelian aircraft closing in for the kill, and time stops around me, allowing me to observe every ounce of suffering of the people around me, and I feel as though I'm not moving at all, but instead am trapped on an ever-turning wheel.

My legs continue to propel me forward, despite the sensation of not moving as the bombs draw closer. I mouth Chase's name, but before I can finish, an explosion sounds behind us, and its shockwave propels us into the air, causing me to fly, turning over and over, until I crash into the ground, rolling across its slimy ooze, made that way from the blood of those around me. When my mind stops spinning, when my body stops moving, I am on my stomach with my arms stretched out in front of me and my hair nothing more than a tangled mess, covering the back of my neck. I lift my head. Chase lies a few feet away from me, unmoving.

"Chase," I whisper.

No answer. I reach for him and try crawling to him, but pain grips me and I am unable to move, to go to him, as darkness closes in around me, and my mind threatens to shut down. Consciousness eludes me, and slips away, and as I rest my head in the dirt, allowing bits of it to fill my ear, the last thing I see this night is the toe of a boot, with bits of flesh and blood on it, inches from my face.

Chapter 15

Veiled Words

Pale pink sunlight swarms over me as I sit by the wall-sized window, staring out at the meandering crowds in the street below, little ants scurrying about to get to where they need to go, unaware of my solitude, of my heart pounding in my chest, desperate to break through my ribcage as my pulse races from nervousness.

The last week is a blur, and its multitude of events blend together, forming strange memories, memories that I cannot sort through or decipher what is real and what is imagined. My lungs fill themselves with the circulated air of the building, glad to be free of the staleness of quarantine. Quarantine—that is what they told me it was, but it felt more like a form of interrogation by placing me alone in a room with just a cot, a toilet, and a sink, permitted to see no one and waiting to see when I would crack and lose my mind. I wonder if they did the same to Renal, if he is even alive. What happened to Chase? To Trevors? Or Grelyn?

My head rests against the cool glass, pressing into it until it aches from the pressure, but I ignore it as I watch the people below.

A boy in a white uniform with the emblem of the council on his back darts down a walkway just one floor below me. Any near him dart out of his way, aware of the law: council business shall not be infringed. He runs to the other end of the walkway, his white uniform glowing in the fain sunlight, and disappears through a set of glass doors that open and close as he passes by. The moment he is out of sight, I turn back to the people beneath me as they resume their business, wondering how much longer I am to be kept waiting.

A slight cough diverts my attention, and I shift my head to glance at the Marshal that had brought me to the Command Division to be interrogated about what had happened at the mines. The Marshal stares straight ahead, hoping that no one heard his slight cough, and I turn back to the window and my musing about the day-to-day activities of the crowds below, allowing him his peace of mind. Sickness is weakness, weakness is failure, and failure is death. This is my world. My gaze shifts to the wall and the horizon beyond it as I wonder about the people who live in the wildlands. Does failure also mean death for them? My mind wanders to the barbarian who had helped Chase and me when we were lost in the wilderness, and once again—I have lost count of how many times this has happened—I wonder what became of him.

A tremendous clang fills the hallway as the black, steel doors open, allowing someone to step through them, and I jump to my feet, standing at attention, while the Marshal accompanying me does the same. My veins feel as though they are going to burst as my pulse thumps so loud that my ears are unable to hear anything else, as I strain my eyes to see who has been released, almost jumping when I see Renal's familiar face. He stops in the corridor, salutes the arbiters standing guard, and walks off, not bothering to glance in my direction as he walks past, and the joy I feel upon seeing him alive and well dissipates.

"Arbiter Noni," says one of the arbiters by the door, while the two beside him remain at their post.

My lead feet drag themselves across the carpet, stirring up some static electricity, as I force them to carry me to the room beyond the overbearing doors, apprehensive about what will greet me once I cross the threshold into its dark underbelly, making me wonder if I am about to pass into Hades. The memory of me finding a book, a real one buried deep within the vaults of the training facility—it must had been overlooked when the others were burned so long ago—fills my mind as I remember reading the forbidden text, learning about the mythical underworld for the first time. An instructor had caught me with it and struck me in the face with it after snatching the book from my hands. Is this what the people in that book felt, I wonder as I stare into the empty abyss beyond the steel doors. The arbiter that had called my name clears his throat, impatient for me to hurry into the interrogation chamber, and I pick up my pace, pausing a moment as I steel my nerves and inhale until my lungs can hold no more: Hades has no hold on me.

As the darkness swallows me, the doors close, sealing shut, forbidding me from ever leaving this place, but I remain rigid in my posture, determined to not show the slightest indication of fear as I step toward the podium, draped in a beam of white light. I take my place at the dais, blinking in the light as I face the high table before me and the three arbiters seated behind it.

"State your name, serial number, and your business here," says the one in the middle.

"Arbiter Noni, serial number N27461," I reply, "and you summoned me here." The defiance in my voice rings throughout the chamber, and a part of me wishes I could take it back, while another tells me to let them hear it.

"You're a bold one," says one of the council members with a dark edge to his voice.

I glare at him, refusing to avert my gaze or allow him the satisfaction of thinking that he had intimidated me.

"You have been summoned here because of recent events at the mines," says the one who had spoken first. "Care to explain?"

"What am I supposed to explain?" I ask, unsure of where the arbiter council is going with this.

"Of your actions there."

"Perhaps you can be more specific," I say, growing impatient at this roundabout way of asking me what had happened.

Silence rings in my ears as I wait for one of them to speak, but when no one does, I open my mouth. "There was a rebellion and you put it down."

"You do not sound pleased."

"People died," I say.

"Plebeians," scoffs one of the council members.

"People!" I shout, not caring if my actions seem rebellious. They have already made up their minds about me, and this entire interrogation seems like a smokescreen for something else. "Citizens and arbiters alike died when you sent the Arelian aircraft to put down a rebellion that was triggered by Commandant Gant's shortsightedness."

The three arbiters behind the table converse among themselves in hushed tones, while my anger rises and boils over, and before I stop myself, my mouth opens and speaks what I have been wanting answers to since the Marshal brought me to the command division.

"Why don't you tell me why I am really here? Or are you all too much of a cow—"

"NONI!" Commander Vye's voice cuts me off as it reverberates around the chamber, saying my name in an endless array of echoes. I look around for her, but cannot find her in the darkness, though a part of me is comforted by the knowledge that she is here.

The members of the tribunal ignore my outburst as well as hers and silence engulfs us as we wait to see who will break it first.

"You were sent to the mines to increase production, were you not?" asks one of the members of the tribunal.

"Yes," I say, my voice clear and even as I try to keep control over my emotions.

"And did you?"

"Yes, sir," I reply. "Production had doubled."

"And just before you were to return to Arel, the riot took place."

"Yes."

"And do you know what happened to Commandant Gant?"

"He must have died in the bombing," I say.

Frowns appear on the faces before me.

"Are you aware of the report that Commandant Gant sent to Arel, concerning you?" asks one of my interrogators.

"No, sir," I reply, though I am not surprised that he had sent one.

"He expressed concern about your friendliness toward the workers."

"I made sure that they had food to eat, clean water to drink, and were able to rest when necessary."

"And why concern yourself with such a replaceable commodity?"

Replaceable? My eyes narrow as I stare at him, wishing I could wrap my fingers around his throat, but I clench my fists instead in an effort to control myself.

"I was charged with increasing production. When I arrived at the mines, I learned that Commandant Gant treated it more like his own private governance, instead of doing his job. I made the decision I did because when people are fed and rested, they are better able to perform the duties asked of them. You ensure that the arbiters under your command have adequate food and water so that they can perform their duties. Why should it be any different for the workers at the mines? Did I not increase production?"

"And what of the riot?"

"That rests on Commandant Gant's shoulders. His continued refusal to accept my temporary command bred discontent and discord."

"And he did not try to have you executed?"

"He did, after he tried to have Arbiter Renal murdered," I reply, "but Arbiter Trevors stopped him."

"Some say that you led the riot, that the workers of the mine followed you," the arbiter on the far right of the table accuses me.

"Some say that Presidents Kumi and Tapiwa are involved in an incestuous affair, but do we believe them? No. Rumors are unreliable." Afterthought scolds me for bringing up what no one in Arel is supposed to mention: the strange relationship between the presidents of Arel.

"You dare…"

"If you have reliable witnesses," I say, "then, please, present them."

The members of the tribunal whisper among themselves before facing me again. "Arbiter Noni," one speaks for all of them, "your version of events have been collaborated by Arbiters Renal, Trevors, and Grelyn, who all agree that Commandant Gant disobeyed a direct order and tried to have you executed, that he and some under his command had been secretly subverting the will of Arel. However, this is not the first time you have been brought before us."

Something tells me it will not be the last.

"In the last year," continues the one speaking, "your continued defiance, disrespect, and contumacy stain the Martial Diplomatic Corps. Therefore, you are to be remanded…"

"That will do." Tapiwa steps out of the shadows, startling all of us, and I wonder how long she has been standing there, and I have the feeling that this is not the first time she has watched such proceedings, as I think back to the days after the bombing within the city and the day I was forced to execute the plebeian girl I had saved from a fire. It seems so long ago, but it also seems like just a moment ago.

"Madam President," says a member of the tribunal, "we did not know you were here."

"Of course not. I doubt you can see much beyond your own noses," says Tapiwa.

"Madam President, this arbiter—"

"—was obeying my orders," finishes Tapiwa.

Deft movement catches my attention, and I notice as members of the presidential guard take their place around the room to ensure President Tapiwa's safety, just as curious as everyone else as to why she is here.

"Leave us," orders Tapiwa.

"But, Madam President…" protests one of the members of the tribunal.

"Now." The coldness in Tapiwa's voice sends a shiver down my back as everyone within the interrogation room leaves through the steel doors, until it is just me and her.

"I have to say, Noni, that you never disappoint."

I clamp my mouth shut, wishing now more than ever that I never brought up that rumor about her relationship with Kumi. She could execute me right now and no one would question it.

She paces in front of me and stops to study my face, to see if I react to her statement, but I keep my face emotionless like an arbiter is supposed to.

"It appears that you have had quite an experience at the mines."

"I have failed you, Madam President," I say, my voice even and the tone calm. "You sent me there to ensure that production increased, and instead, I have lost the mines and the damage is irreparable. For that, I know that I must—"

"Silence!"

I bite my tongue to keep from speaking, not wanting to anger her any further, though my mind bursts with questions as to why she lowered herself to come here. It is rare for one of the presidents of Arel to interfere in arbiter matters, and it has only happened once, that I can remember, back before Tapiwa and Kumi were the presidents, back when we had just one, when their father had decided to stop the execution of an arbiter. Why he did is still a mystery, but as president, he never had to explain his actions, not even to the Arelian council.

"Tell me, in your own words, what happened at the mines."

I swallow the miniscule amount of saliva left in my mouth to moisten my sandpaper throat so that my voice will be clear.

"Commandant Gant was displeased at me being sent there. He saw it as a threat."

"He refused to obey your orders."

"No, ma'am. Lieutenant Renal saw to it that he complied, but his displeasure was evident. The night of the riot, Commandant Gant had set a trap for Lieutenant Renal and left him for dead, but he managed to make it back to the mines to warn me. I tried to get him out of there, but Commandant Gant's men found us."

"Why did you not contact the Command Division within Arel?" Tapiwa asks.

"Because I could not trust the arbiter stationed in the communications room to not intercept the message. I had reason to believe that they were loyal to Commandant Gant."

Tapiwa's steady steps echo around me as she circles the podium, a shadow in the darkness surrounding me and an abysmal companion to my increasing feeling of being alone as foreboding wells within me, warning me to be mindful of what I say.

"You believed that he had his own agenda."

"Yes, ma'am."

"And after he caught you and Lieutenant Renal trying to escape, that is when he tried to execute you?"

"Yes, ma'am."

"Why did he fail?"

"Arbiter Trevors stopped him."

"Why would he do that?"

"I do not know, ma'am."

"And afterward?"

"Commandant Gant fired his weapon and the workers rioted against him and his men. I tried to get Lieutenant Renal out of there, but it was Arbiter Trevors and Arbiter Grelyn who saved us both. After the Arelian fleet arrived and the bombs fell… I have no memory of what occurred afterward."

"Considering how close you were to one of the impacts, I'm not surprised. Arbiter Grelyn testified that she carried you to safety."

Grelyn saved me? I think back to that night, to the last thing that I saw—bloodied boots standing in front of my eyes. Why would Grelyn help me? She loathes me, a sentiment that I share toward her. The perplexity on my face must have showed because Tapiwa stares at me, studying me, wondering if I am weak, if I have allowed my emotions to rule me, or perhaps she is waiting for me to contradict Grelyn's statement. I remain silent, thinking it best to not say anything, and Tapiwa continues her pacing around me as she questions me.

"Some witnesses reported that you seemed more concerned with rescuing a certain plebeian."

I freeze. What does she know? What witnesses? Was it Grelyn who told her, trying to sow doubt about my loyalties while she sealed her dedication to Arel by rescuing a fellow arbiter?

"In all the chaos, I may have forgotten myself and tried to hang on to a replaceable item."

I force the words out, hating myself for referring to Chase as replaceable.

"So, the news that he died in the bombing will not sadden you then."

My stomach drops, and if it could have torn itself away from my body to crash onto the hard floor, it would have, followed by the ever-increasing emptiness choking my heart, which stops for a second as Tapiwa's words permeate through my brain, their full meaning striking me where it hurts most. I cannot see my face, but assume that the blood drains from it as my mind refuses to accept the reality that Chase is gone and that I have failed to save an innocent person once again. Tapiwa stops in front of me and stares into my eyes, studying my reaction, and I know that I must say something, that I must pretend that I am unaffected by such unfortunate news. I look right at her, meeting her gaze, forcing myself to harden my voice and my nerves.

"No, ma'am," my constricted voice circles around us, dissipating with each echo.

"Even though you desired to have him for yourself."

"He was just a plebeian. I can find another to service the same need."

Tapiwa seems pleased by my answer, while deep down, I want to scream, to take my rage out on her and slam her skull into the table ahead of me, but I remain stoic with my arms by my side and my feet should-width apart, waiting to be dismissed.

"I find it interesting that workers rioted after Commandant Gant tried to execute you. His actions were a violation of the law, but it wasn't until after he tried to execute you that they rioted. One could wonder if, perhaps, they felt some sort of loyalty toward you."

"Perhaps they saw an opportunity and took advantage of the situation."

"Perhaps, but your actions do not go unnoticed, not even by the lowest of our society. You did ensure that they had adequate food and water."

"A matter of prudence. For the workers to be effective in their duties, they need physical strength, and that is achieved through adequate food, water, and rest, in addition to physical exercise. I needed them to dig more, so I needed them to be strong."

"And if you had to do it all over again, would you do it differently?"

"If you ask me to."

Tapiwa walks off, disappearing in the shadows, as she tells me, "You may go."

Before I can take a single step, her voice stops me, and I look into the darkened veil surrounding me, unable to see her, but I know that she watches me.

"One other thing: if you ever bring up those rumors about my brother and me again, I'll execute you myself."

A door closes and the lock echoes around me, informing me that I am alone, and I remain in the single beam of white light for a moment, trying to rein in my emotions that want to burst free, aware that I cannot display them here. Knowing that I cannot stay here, I mosey to the steel door and open it, stepping away from this room and deeper into my prison.

The three arbiters outside the door glance at me for a moment before turning away: two of them on either side of the door, while the third, the one who demands you name and serial number, steps aside, allowing me to pass, and as I walk by, I glance at his face: stern, emotionless, disciplined, and… inhuman. He does not care that a knife has just pierced my heart—I cannot figure out why I feel this way, nor can I describe it—and why should he be concerned? He is an arbiter, meant to uphold the law; he is what I should be.

A single raindrop hits the window in front of me, a soft thump that snatches my attention as though it mocks me, or perhaps it is trying to console me, to tell me that it shares my sentiments. Before the arbiters around me have time to wonder why I have not left, I stroll down the hall, my feet flopping on the red carpet stretched out before me, leaving imprints that last for a moment before disappearing, like the lives of so many within Arel. I near the elevator, and before I am able to enter its conclave, hands seize me, yanking me away from the elevator, away from the light, and pin me in a darkened corner away from prying eyes. I try to fight, but a harsh voice begs me to keep silent while his hands render me unable to move.

"What did you tell them in there?" demands Trevors, and for the first time, I realize that it is him who has stopped me from leaving.

"What was expected," I tell him.

He presses his face against mine. "What did you tell them?" he growls.

Why does he care? What was the verdict concerning his actions during the riot? He had to have been cleared of any wrongdoing, because if the ruling had been otherwise, Trevors would be on his way to the crematorium right now. But where is Grelyn?

"That you prevented Commandant Gant from executing both Renal and me, and that without your help, or Grelyn's, we would not be here now."

He relaxes his hold on me.

"Why would you do that?" he asks.

"Because it is the truth."

"Nobody cares about the truth. You do what will benefit you, or die."

"Is that why you stopped Commandant Gant from executing me? Or why Grelyn carried me to safety after the bombs hit?"

Trevors looks away, not wanting to meet my gaze, and despite my attempts at reading his body language, I cannot decipher what he is thinking or why he is so concerned about my testimony.

"Where is Grelyn?" I ask.

"She was sent back to that outpost, or so I'm told."

"I'm sorry." I know what she means to him, and despite the torture they put me through at the training facility, they do care about each other, and they must have hoped to have had similar assignments.

My sympathy angers him, and Trevors rams his arm against my chest, pinning me to the wall as his hardened gaze locks me in its cage.

"You helped her in the mine, and now we have helped you. We are even, understand?"

I nod my head, and he releases me. As Trevors walks away, two words escape my lips in a voice so soft, it almost seems like a dream, or the essence of a dream.

"Thank you."

"Watch yourself, Noni. Gratitude is weakness."

"Or strength," I protest. "Humility takes courage."

Trevors blows air out of his nostrils and stalks off, rounding a corner and disappearing from sight.

Relieved that he is gone, I step into the elevator and allow its glass enclosure to carry me down to the lobby so that I may leave this place. I squeeze through the doors before they open all the way, desperate to get out and to get away from here, and I burst outside into the steady stream of rain as a somber roll of thunder reverberates above me. Uniformed crowds, each in their assigned colors (red, green, yellow, white, and blue) stroll past me in tune to one another, unconcerned about the news I had received earlier and oblivious to the turmoil within me. Tapiwa's words repeat themselves in my mind.

So, the news that he died in the bombing will not sadden you then.

Gone. Just like that, he is gone, and no one will mourn him; no one will care, except for the cries of a small girl who has lost everything. Renal is safe, but Chase is no more. Rain drops from the sky, coating me in its misery, as it soaks through my clothes and my skin, delivering a slight chill, but the coolness does not register as my mind remains in a somber fog, unable to think, unable to process the activity around me. A man bumps into me and apologizes as he hurries away, hoping that I will not retaliate. I stare at him, my eyes glazed and unfocused, as water drips from my nose onto my lips and runs down my chin to my neck where it disappears beneath my collar. Only the automatic movements of my feet propel me forward in a jerky stride. I blink my eyes over and over to prevent myself from crying, but the tears break free and mingle with the raindrops that hit my face, making me glad that the weather turned gloomy after all. It can disguise my shame. The reflective surface of a building forces me to stop and study my reflection; at least, I think it is me, but all I see is a lone arbiter, a woman with swollen, red eyes, beaten until she is hollow, just a shell of her former self, while those around her wish she would get out of their way.

A man walks up behind me, blurred from the tears struggling to escape their prison, but I remain still, not caring if he is another arbiter coming to arrest me. My will has escaped me. My desire to get out from the rain has vanished. My carnal need to silence the tumultuous hunger that now grips my stomach has evaporated. The man nears. I remain rooted in my spot, an obstacle on the sidewalk for others to navigate around as I grapple with this empty feeling that has trapped me in its clutches, refusing to release me, when the realization that this must be grief strikes me, something I have never experienced before. The man grabs me, whipping me around until I face him, and his face seems familiar, but my brain refuses to dig through my memory to discover why that is.

"Come with me," says the familiar voice, and I allow him to lead me away. Together we walk down the sidewalk with him pretending to need my assistance, while I follow in a saddened stupor, shrouded in the drizzling rain.

Chapter 16

Fog

The man leads me toward a café covered with overarching umbrellas that stretch out over the tables in an effort to keep the rain off the customers that brave dreary weather for a hot beverage, when others would have chosen to stay home. My feet plop in the tiny puddles in automatic motion, not bothering to rebel or wonder why this man is talking to me, and though I try to focus on his words, my mind rebels as I stare at my hands, imagining them coated in sticky, red blood that oozes down my wrists and beneath the sleeves of my soaked jacket—my conscience injecting its own form of punishment. I may not have killed Chase, but it is my fault that he is gone. And Gwen. Poor Gwen. How will I tell her? Moisture trickles down my face past my ear, and I reach up to wipe the bits of rainwater away, pausing to study my wet fingers, and, once again, I see bright blood on them: the blood of the infant I was forced to murder, the blood of the barbarians that attacked the wall, the blood of the girl I could not save, and now Chase's. My hands seem to bathe in blood and not by choice.

A jumbled blur of words meet my ears, meshed together and forming unintelligible sentences, as I remain in my saddened stupor, staring at the man with a blank look on my face, unable to process what he says. He continues talking, glancing to the side at those who watch us, giving us odd glances, wondering why I seem to be so uninterested in what he says. My head cocks to the side as I stare at him, wondering who he is, when faint memories fill my mind in an effort to shock me back to my present situation. He is the man who had prevented me from being captured the night Chase and I had snuck out. He is the man whom I had warned when Commander Vye had planned on searching his place. His name is Luther.

He steps closer, until he can whisper to me without being overheard. "Pretend to be interested or we will both be punished. Do you think that no one is watching you?"

A test. Such is the way of life in Arel. We are always tested to see if we are worthy of existence, of Arel's benevolence. I flick my eyes to a passerby and the judgmental expression on her face as she debates whether it is worth reporting my lack of enthusiasm in performing my duties. Citizens can report arbiters who appear to not want to do their job, but such an act is not without risk. If it is deemed a false report, the informer disappears. Even if the report is found to be true, sometimes the informer and the arbiter in question both disappear, finding their way to the crematorium,—Arel cannot allow the people within her walls to have even the slightest inkling that her arbiters disagree with her—but there is the rare occasion where the informer is rewarded for their trouble, which is why some choose to risk it, like how this woman ponders its worth this very second.

"When did you last see it?" I ask in a hollow voice, hoping that my ears had picked up enough of what Luther had said. Whether they had or not does not matter as he plays along with the first sentence to exit my mouth for the last several minutes.

"It was here," he says, holding his hand out as the soft drizzle of rain coats it, and I notice a bit of hair on his knuckles for the very first time.

"Was there anyone nearby at the time?" I ask, beginning to fall into my role as an arbiter again.

"Not that I noticed."

"Describe the object in question."

"It was a shoulder bag. Gray in color."

"You'll have to come with me to file a report and…"

My voice trails off as I look across the street and see Mandi and wonder why she is here. Her presence is not that unusual, since even instructors at the training facility sometimes receive orders that require them to leave anywhere from a few hours to a few weeks, but that is not what strikes me as odd: her cautious behavior does. She looks over her shoulder for a moment and eyes each person that strolls past her as though she suspects them of watching her. I am about to turn away when Natalie appears. She hurries up to Mandi and walks past her. Neither say a word to each other, but I watch as Mandi slips a small wrapped package to her, which Natalie conceals underneath her jacket, small enough that it does not leave even the slightest of bulges. Before my gaze can follow her, Luther's grunting jerks me back to his ruse.

"…and make sure you disclose if there was anything in there of importance to the security of Arel. There should be an information booth over there."

A pleased expression crosses Luther's face, happy that I seem to be going along and allowing him to save me once again, though why he is doing this I have not figured out. I lead him to an information booth so that a formal report can be filed, as is regulation, hoping that he has planned this far ahead when something else catches my attention. A citizen and his plebeian hurry down the walk, toward one of the moving walkways, an act that is not unusual, except that the citizen seems to be helping the plebeian carry something, which is peculiar. I watch them for a minute, wondering what they are doing and hoping that I am not jumping to conclusions, but the bits of anxiety surrounding their actions is odd as they hurry to a support pillar for the moving walkway above them. I turn toward Luther.

"Get everyone out of here."

The urgency in my voice stops him from questioning me, and he rushes back to the outdoor café, yelling at people seated underneath the oversized umbrellas to leave, while I run toward the two suspicious men.

"Hey!" I shout at them.

One looks at me before turning away and urging the other to hurry up.

"Stop!" I scream, picking up my pace and rushing down the walk, ignoring the rain as it stabs my cold cheeks. "HALT!"

The two men set their burden down at the base of one of the supports for the causeway. One runs away, while the other faces me with a tenacious expression, determined to do what he has come here to do. I shove people out of my way in an effort to get to him as he faces me, daring me to try and stop him from performing his task.

A burst of light blinds me for a moment as intense heat wafts over me, and my feet leave the pavement as an explosive force propels me backward. My body slams into the ground, and I inhale, desperate for air, as muffled screams surround me, while ash, burning embers, and metal chunks land on the ground around me, enclosing me in their prison of death, as meandering feet shuffle past, unsure of where to go or what to do. Pain grips my left elbow, telling me that it bore the brunt of the impact when I landed. Lifting myself up, I shake my head, wishing that the muffled sounds would go away, that my ears would clear up, but I haven't time to wait for the ringing to dissipate as a woman runs toward me in a panic, unaware that I lie in her path. I roll out of the way just as her foot strikes the ground near where my head had been. I lift myself to all fours and stop. Next to me are two children in blue uniforms, one is missing a face, while the other has a hole in his chest from shrapnel and stares at the gloomy sky with vacant eyes, the eyes of death. My hand shakes as I close his eyes, allowing him the illusion of sleeping.

More people rush past, tripping over the rubble on the ground, and I jump to my feet to help them. At first, they recoil from me, afraid that I intend to arrest them, which puzzles me; arbiters are to protect Arel and her citizens, not harm them, and my mind drifts back to my first day in the eastern sector and the fear in people's eyes when they saw my uniform, forcing me to wonder if more goes on than we are told in training.

"Are you okay?" I ask one of them, forcing myself back to the present. They both nod.

"Get to the nearest medical center," I tell them as I help one of them to his feet, and they both run off.

I head for the epicenter of the explosion, determined to help any who might have been caught in its wrath, but I only take two steps when three of the gears from the moving walkway break free of their hold and crash onto the ground in rapid secession, creating an earsplitting sound that breaks through the ringing in my ears. I drop to the ground, covering my head as more shrapnel careens toward me, pelting the pavement around me. In a daze, I rise to my feet, detached as I watch more people flee the chaos while pieces of the moving walkway strike the ground around me, creating a metallic melody of doom and despair, while flames wrap themselves around the remaining support beams, determined to take them down. Wisps of hair float past me as a woman runs away, her frizzy perm having broken free of the yellow and green bandanna she has tied around her head. My body remains rooted there as swirling trails of smoke dance around me, beckoning me to succumb to their choking fumes, telling me that there is no need to flee or fear for my life, and I stand there, watching them until…

A hand touches my shoulder, and I snap back to the present, regaining my senses. Luther stands there, urging me to move. Just then, sharp clicks reach my ears, surrounded by the roar of the fire spreading across the pavement from the grease that drips from the gears that work the conveyor belt, alerting me to danger. I look up in time to see another gear drop from above, and I plow into Luther, tackling him to the ground, as I force us both out of the way, and the gear crashes into the ground, cracking the pavement and breaking into two. Once it's still, I look at Luther and he nods to my unspoken question, letting me know that he is unharmed.

"Everyone," I yell at the top of my lungs, putting a strain on my voice box, "get out of here! Head to the nearest medical center! If you can walk, help someone who can't!"

I hear a cry for help. Without thinking, I run to it with Luther right behind me, and we find a man with his right leg pinned underneath a beam.

"Are you all right?" I ask.

"I can't move my leg," he says in short gasps as he chokes on the smoke.

"Help me," I tell Luther.

Together, we grab one end of the beam and heave it off the man's leg, but the moment we do, blood spurts from his thigh, shooting into the air, warning me that he has bigger problems. We drop the beam and I run to the man, pressing my hands on the wound, but they slip as blood pools around them, refusing to stop trying to break free of the man's arteries. Luther reaches for the man's shoulder, knowing that we have to get him to a medical transport or he will die, but he stops when a shrill voice screams, "Don't move him!"

Natalie rushes up to us, and at first, I am puzzled to see her, before remembering that I had seen her moments before the explosion; she must have heard it, and being a nurse, came to help. She kneels beside me, studying the man's wound and the force with which the blood gushes from his leg.

"Give me your belt," she says to Luther, who obeys, yanking his belt free of their loops and handing it to her.

"Keep putting pressure on that wound," she tells me as she wraps the belt around the man's thigh, above the gaping hole in his leg, and cinches it so tight that it almost cuts into his leg, forming a tourniquet. More chucks of metal fall around us, warning us of the danger we are in. Natalie reaches up and pulls three bobby pins from her hair.

"When I tell you," she says to me, "remove your hands."

I nod my head in agreement.

"Now!"

I remove my hands, and both Luther and I watch as Natalie shoves her hands into the man's wound, pulling on the damaged artery and placing the bobby pins above the nick.

"We need to get him to a medical center now," she says, taking one of the man's arms and lifting him up, looking more like a butcher in her medical uniform as bright red blood stains the front, adding more gloom to the macabre scene around us.

"Help her," I tell Luther, and he obeys.

I watch them haul the man away to safety, hoping that he makes it to a medical center in time, before turning back to the melee behind me, knowing that more people might be trapped. Whimpering catches my attention, and I rush to it, finding a plebeian crouched underneath some fallen pipes, clutching a bundle that her master must have sent her to fetch.

"Give me your hand!"

She stares sat me, too afraid to move. The conveyor belt slips from its hold. There isn't much time before it crashes to the ground, just like the gears that run it had already done. Realizing that I need to coax her out, I crouch down until I am eye level with her, keeping my face soft and inviting.

"I promise I won't hurt you."

I hold my hand out to her. She studies it, debating if I am toying with her, and each second that passes, the conveyor belt sinks lower and lower as the fires continue to consume the other support beams, crippling them, causing them to buckle. Voices in my head urge me to leave her, to think of my own self-preservation, but I remain crouched next to a frightened woman, hoping that she will move, but determined to not leave her. I move my hand, urging her to take it, and she does, grasping it with a tighter grip than I thought possible for her slim arms to possess. With a yank, I whip her out from underneath the pipes and away from the dangling conveyor belt, pushing her away from the fray and toward a medical transport that has appeared, while other arbiters show up, each grabbing an injured person and dragging them to safety. A man rushes up to us, screaming at the woman for dropping her bundle, but I seize his arm and turn him so he faces me.

"Take her to a medical transport," I growl at him, my face matching my desire to seek revenge for the devastation caused here today.

He holds his hands up in submission, and I release him, watching his every move as he takes his plebeian to the nearest medical transport, before spotting Luther, who studies me as he helps someone else to a group of medical personnel. When my gaze meets his, I spot Mandi giving orders to a group of people in white uniforms, and not far from her is Renal, issuing instructions to the arbiters who have just arrived, reminding me that, in my desperation to help others, I never heard the sirens of the medical transports or noticed my wristband flashing, summoning all available arbiters to this place.

A cough snatches my attention, and I run toward it, finding a girl trying to crawl away from the suffocating smoke, her red uniform having turned brown from the ash. She looks up at me when I reach her and collapses. I grab her before she hits the ground and lift her up, cradling her in my arms as her head rolls to the side, but before I get any further, I stop. Painted in red is the symbol of Arel with a line through it, and anger rises within me, swelling to the point where I want to scratch that symbol off the metal it rests upon, but the harsh cough from the girl in my arms forces me to contain myself. Turning, I hurry away from the fires, away from the crushing smoke, and away from the falling debris, with the girl cradled in my arms, ignoring the rain and its failed attempts to wash the soot off my face. Doctors take the girl from my arms before I am able to reach the closest medical transport, their pristine, white uniforms standing out in the smoky mist that surrounds us.

"Noni." Renal hurries up to me.

"Lieutenant," I say standing at attention, "I traced two suspects here. One got away. The other died in the explosion. There are more wounded in there, we should…"

He shouts orders at a group of arbiters and they run off into the direction I had pointed in.

"Are you okay?" he asks me.

"I'm fine."

"Get that looked at." He points at a cut on the side of my fore-head; I didn't even notice it until he pointed it out, and I reach up to touch the droplets of blood that ooze from it.

"Lieutenant, I…"

"That's an order." He waves a man in a white uniform over. Before I have time to protest, the doctor whisks me away to a medical transport and assesses my wound, giving me a complete lookover, and asking me questions about how I feel, if I have a headache, if I feel weak, while flashing a soft light in my eyes to test my pupils' reaction.

"There's some ringing in my ears," I tell him.

He picks up a medical scanner and runs it around my head, fo-cusing on my ears, while I sit up, determined to not show weakness, but my heart knows that it is a façade, as I watch two men in white uniforms administer CPR on a younger man that looks to be about my age, reminding me of the news I had received earlier. It is time for me to tell Gwen.

"No damage to the ear drum," he says, which is a relief, though the ringing isn't as bad now. "The ringing should pass within a day or two. If it doesn't, have your commander send you to the nearest medical facility."

The distinct whine of a drone reaches my ears, mimicking the annoyance that plagues them. I turn my head, much to the ire of the doctor as he applies an ointment to the cut on my head, causing me to wince from the sting, and fixes a bandage over it. The drone hovers nearby, capturing everything on its camera, but the more I watch it, the angrier I become by its presence and the knowledge that what it films will be used in future videos to recruits, citizens, and plebeians about the greatness of Arel. As it spins, capturing everything it can on its tiny camera, I swat at it, knocking it to the ground, and watch as it skids across the pavement, sending out miniscule sparks as a few pieces break away from it.

"If you feel any dizziness or suffer from headaches, visit a medical facility immediately," says the doctor, dismissing me.

I thank him and jump out of the medical transport, focusing my attention on the area where the bomb had gone off. The fire crews focus a hose on a set of flames, putting out the last fire, and all that remains is a charred mess, resembling a black hole more than a piece of impeccable engineering. Most of the wounded have been carted away, leaving only the dead to be disposed of, as they lay piled in a corner, awaiting a transport that will cart their bodies to the crematorium. As the commotion dies down, a mixture of emotions reel within me, each clambering for my attention, but pushed aside by another, more powerful feeling.

"Arbiter Noni."

Renal stands behind me with the door to a transport open.

"You can take this back to the manor."

"I can help," I tell him.

"It's not a suggestion."

His even tone unnerves me, and I wonder where his friendliness has gone, until I spot another drone hovering behind him, recording every second for posterity. Why doesn't he want me here? Does he not believe that I can do my job as an arbiter? Have I not proven myself?

"I can walk," I say.

Renal opens the door wider, indicating for me to get in. Knowing better than to argue further, I amble over to the transport and pause when I see who is inside it: Grelyn.

"She is on her way to her outpost," says Renal. "You can catch a ride with her."

Not liking this at all, and still wondering why Renal is so intent on getting me away from here, I get inside the transport and take my place in the back seat next to Grelyn. She never glances in my direction, which suits me just fine.

"What about the girl or the man…" I begin to ask, but Renal shushes me, though it is not the harshness within his tone that catches me off guard, but the fear I sense in it. I clamp my mouth shut.

"Take Arbiter Noni back to her post in the eastern sector," Renal says to the driver, "and then take Arbiter Grelyn back to her assigned outpost."

The driver salutes him and Renal shuts the door, sealing me inside in the most uncomfortable situation I have ever been in. As the vehicle pulls away, I spot Luther speaking to another arbiter, and we lock eyes for a moment before the transport turns down a road and he disappears.

Neither Grelyn, nor I, speak to one another, choosing silence over pathetic quibbling. It's just as well. Anything we say to each other could be reported to one of our superiors by the driver. I lean my head against the glass, allowing the vibrations of the moving transport to tickle my inner ear as I glance out the tinted window at the empty streets, disconcerted by the lack of bustling activity. No one wants to be on the streets at this time. Not that I blame them. I'm certain that an emergency curfew has been put in place. I shift my gaze to the overcast sky above me, watching the drops of rain fall toward me and strike the window, making muffled ticking sounds on the glass as the vehicle rumbles along the road, taking the curves with caution.

The lulling sound of the engine, shifting from a soft purr to a resounding roar each time the gears change, almost tricks me into closing my eyes, but they remain open, too afraid to miss anything, while my mind wanders miles away, chasing a ghost and wondering how I will tell Chase's sister the terrible news. A tickle forms in the back of my throat as warm tears threaten to escape my eyes, forcing me to swallow in an effort to stop them. I cannot allow them into the open to betray me. One by one, the buildings pass by us, becoming more rusted, more dilapidated the further away from the center of Arel we go. I watch as the pristine siding transforms into crumbling brick and rotted wood, cursing when one of the wheels hits a pothole, telling me that we have entered the eastern sector, and all its decrepit glory. The rain picks up as we drive down the street, alone among a crumbling graveyard, the only sign of life on this dismal day, and my heart sinks the closer we get to the manor, to Molers. With one final turn, the transport pulls in front of the gate that marks the driveway going to the manor. Not a word is said when the driver stops the vehicle, and I open the door to step out.

"You shouldn't concern yourself with others," Grelyn says to me, breaking the silence, stopping me—and why she does is a mystery— but I face her, tired of her always acting as though she is better than me.

"If I hadn't, you'd be buried in a mine."

I slam the door and mosey up the drive, following its twisting nature to the rundown building that has been deemed fit to house the arbiters charged with protecting this section of Arel. The familiar yellowed glass door slides open when I approach it, looking more pitiful than it did my first day here, and as I step inside, dread weighs my stomach down with its apprehensive nature, making me want to run away, but I ignore its pleas, knowing that I must face what comes next.

Darkness surrounds me as the door closes, putting me at unease, but I ignore it and walk through the entrance, past the staircase where I had first seen Sheila sweeping up paint chips—another pile is there now from the always peeling paint—heading... I don't know where. Images of burning corpses run through my mind, replacing the wall paper coated in mold as it drops away from the walls, and I reach out to one who steps toward me with fear and torment etched on his face as flames engulf his body, boiling his flesh from his bones, striking my nostrils with its putrid odor, causing my stomach to churn and push its contents against my esophagus. I try to hold it back, to will my body to obey my command, but vomit explodes from my mouth and sprays the floor. When finished, I find myself in the dim hallway of the manor staring at the bile that has escaped my mouth, though its stale orange color does little to make the soiled rug look less attractive. Soft footsteps capture my attention, and I look up into the comforting eyes of Sheila.

"I'll... I'll clean this up," I tell her, embarrassed to have vomited in front of her—a sign of weakness.

Instead of being angry with me, she drops the dish towel in her hands and embraces me in a giant hug, not caring if bits of vomit drop from my chin to her grungy shirt, and I hold her tight, pleased to see her again, to see the face of someone who cares about my well-being, glad that she is safe. I study her pale face, glad that she was not anywhere near the bombing, and notice a yellow mark on her cheek, the mark of an old bruise still in the midst of healing. My fingers brush it, but she pulls back.

"Don't worry about it."

"Who did this?" I demand.

"Anan," she replies.

All the pain I have experienced today transforms into anger, a wild beast thirsting for revenge and starved for retribution. Having never liked Anan to begin with, I envision the things I wish to do to him, to make him suffer in the same manner he has caused others to, but I stop myself, remembering that I am no better.

Sheila pulls me from my internal wrestling as she places a bony hand on mine, her pale skin contrasting with my walnut-color shade.

"Gwen is going to be thrilled that her brother is back."

My face falls. How am I going to tell her what Tapiwa had told me? She despised me before I left, and she will have every right to hate me even more: his death is my doing.

"There is something I need to tell you both."

Before Sheila can ask me what it is, and before I can elaborate, a harsh bang echoes throughout the manor, rattling the doors and windows, and I'm afraid that some of the glass might break.

"Hide," I hiss at her, afraid of what approaches us.

She darts away, rounding a corner as Molers enters the hallway and finds me hunched over with a pool of vomit by my feet and a few splatters on my boots.

He snorts. "You always did have a weak constitution"—he steps toward me—"unable to withstand the harshest of environments."

I straighten myself, determined to not show fear as it will only encourage him, hardening my face, shoving all thoughts of Chase, the bombing, Gwen's loss, and Sheila's bruise aside.

"Tell me," he says, putting his face inches from mine, allowing me to smell the stale leftovers of his lunch, "what did happen at the mines?"

I glare at him, refusing to answer, unsure of what he knew, or pretended to know. Molers always seems to know things, but how he gets his information is a mystery, but one of his favorite tactics is to pretend to know everything so as to scare his victim into talking.

"You are not my commanding officer," I reply in a cold tone.

"Don't test me, Noni. You know what happens when you do."

I know what happens. The vapor from his breath moistens my skin, thrusting me back to my earliest memory of him. It was my seventh year. If a recruit managed to pass the first tests of their strength and resolve, they were introduced to Molers, who not only excelled at breaking people's spirits so that they could be molded into perfect drones, always willing to do as they are told, but he enjoyed it as well. Power drives him. Nothing makes Molers happier than proving that he is more powerful than you. On this particular day, I had asked him why we were to obey his orders, and he saw it as a challenge, one to be met head on and subdued. In response to my boldness, Molers punched me in the stomach until I vomited, but I soiled his boots, angering him even more. To teach me a lesson, he grabbed me by the back of the head and shoved my face into the bile—I still remember the acrid smell smothering my nose and bits of it went into my nostrils and my mouth, staining my tongue with its acid taste—causing me to choke and gag as I fought for air. I don't know what possessed me, but I had grabbed a stick and sliced the back of his hand with its uneven edge, forcing him to let go, and if it hadn't been for the commandant stepping in at that moment, I'm certain it would have been the end of me.

"I'm not the same frightened recruit that you taught back at the training facility," I say to him.

A smile creeps across his face. "I'm sure you're not."

"Is there a problem here?" Renal stands in the hallway, having snuck in without either of us knowing, putting himself between me and Molers just like last time when Molers tried to choke me.

"No, sir," Molers says as he stands up. "Shouldn't you be at the Command Division?"

"The commander of that region is handling it and has relieved me of my post, for the moment, not that any of it is your concern," replies Renal.

The commander's decision is prudent. Though Renal has healed from the beating he received at the hands of Commandant Gant's men, he is far from ready for duty.

"I heard you were quite the mess when they recovered you from the mines," taunts Molers.

"Why don't you challenge me and find out?" Renal says, closing the distance between them, "or do you prefer those you view as weak because you lack the strength to defeat a real challenge?"

Molers' eyes darken as a scowl covers his face, but before he can respond, Commander Vye steps out of her office and stops the moment she sees us. Her eyes settle upon me.

"Noni! Get in my office."

"She should report to—"

"I didn't ask you!" Commander Vye cuts Molers off.

I do as I am told, but keep a watchful eye on Molers and Commander Vye, sensing a power struggle between them and wonder what had happened while I was gone.

She turns to Renal. "You should go rest."

Renal salutes her and steps away, but he doesn't go far, choosing to remain close in case Molers tries something.

"And you," she turns toward Molers, "don't you have someplace to be?"

Molers salutes her, but his disdain for her is evident, and stalks off, leaving through the front door.

Not wanting to give Commander Vye a reason to take her frustrations out on me, I hurry into her office and stand at attention in front of her desk, waiting for her to sit in the only chair in the room. She does so, in the same manner that she had on my first day within the eastern sector, making me wonder if I had disappointed her, and I remember how I once wanted to be as strong as her. Such memories remind me that I have failed, again.

"You have yet to file your report on your time outside the wall and to clarify what happened at the mines."

"How am I supposed to do that when I have been called to the council for questioning, or when I am busy helping those caught in the midst of a bombing?"

I could bite my tongue for allowing myself to talk to her in such a manner, but I no longer care if my attitude angers her. I am tired of being yelled at, of being talked down to, of being expected to kiss the behind of everyone in a more powerful position than me out of fear of punishment. Silence looms between us, broken only by the pattering of the rain as the sky darkens beyond the window, threatening to send another storm our way, causing Commander Vye to appear as a silhouette in shadow—a panther waiting to strike. Only the whites of her eyes can be seen.

"I see you haven't lost any of your balkiness," she growls.

"My apologies, commander," I say, realizing that Commander

Vye does not deserve my anger. She did not murder Chase or those people at the mine, nor is she responsible for the bombing.

"I expressed my concerns to Tapiwa about sending you there on your own, but she refused to listen."

"Did you not believe in me?" I ask without permission, sounding like a child and feeling inadequate.

"I have complete faith in you, Noni," replies Commander Vye, "but you weren't ready. The outside world is harsh, crueler than what we have here within the walls of Arel. I don't know what games Tapiwa is playing, but—I know I've told you this before—be careful."

I say nothing. What can I say? Her concern is genuine and it throws me off-guard.

"What happened at the mines?"

"Commandant Gant treated it like his own... city with him as the president. He did not like me being stationed there and viewed me as a threat."

"I'm sure he did."

"He did not like the changes that I proposed."

"Changes, such as, making sure the workers there had adequate food and water? Some might view that as going soft."

"It was logical."

"Explain it then."

I'm being tested. "The workers were overworked and half-starved. No one, not even the healthiest individual, can work in those conditions without adequate food and water. If you want them to perform, then you need to give them what they need. I did what I had to in order to increase production."

Commander Vye rises to her feet and glances out the window for a moment, watching the rain as it falls from the sky and streams down the grimy glass, leaving clear streaks that form vertical rivers in the dirt.

"And the plebeian boy?"

A lump forms in my throat as a stinging tickle takes its hold on it, threatening to force me to release the tears I have been holding back all day, waiting for when I am alone and allowed a moment of privacy. How does she… Of course, she knows. Tapiwa might have told her of his demise to test her knowledge of our relationship, of my fondness for him. I swallow back the tears, forming the words I need to say, hoping that my voice sounds even and unemotional.

"We all have our needs."

She faces me, studying me, reading my body language as I will myself not to cry, not to show weakness or any sign that I am undeserving of being an arbiter.

"I suggest you put that same amount of candor in your report."

"Yes, ma'am."

"File your report in the morning, and when you're done, meet me on the green. For now, go get some rest."

"Yes, ma'am." I salute her and leave her office, wondering why she wants me to meet her on the green tomorrow.

As I make my way to the stairs, I glance around for Sheila, but find no sign of her. The first step creaks when I place my foot on it, causing me to wince, even though I'm not sneaking around, but I hate making so much noise. My hand catches the nick in the railing as I make my way upstairs, pricking my skin, but I don't register it as the tears build in the back of my throat and well in my eyes, blurring my vision. I need to get to my room, to a place where I will not be seen. I reach the end of the upstairs hallway and hurry to the door to my room, desperate to get away from potential prying eyes. The door slides open with a soft whoosh and I rush inside, stopping the moment I see the figure sitting on my bed, almost losing what little control I have left over my actions and emotions.

Chase!

We lock eyes, and disbelief wafts over me, making me light-headed as I refuse to believe what my eyes see: Chase sitting on the bed, causing no wrinkle to form on the blanket, with his hands folded in his lap.

"They told me to wait here for you," he says, his voice calm and controlled as he struggles not to betray his thoughts, and feelings.

A soft thud sounds behind me as the door to my room closes. Tapiwa lied to me. As I think back to our conversation and the way she questioned me, it becomes clear: she wanted to know if I am the heartless arbiter I should be, or if I have become like so many that had disappeared before me, and so she lied and measured my reaction. Did I pass, bitch? Something moist touches my cheek as the tears I have held back all day break free of their prison and gush forth, stinging my eyes and turning them red. Chase hurries to me and wipes them off my cheek with a gentle touch before they can drip past my chin, and I charge into his arms, wanting nothing more than to be held by him, elated that he is alive and not hurt, considering the last memory I have of him is of me trying to get to him after the Arelian aircraft destroyed the mine.

"I thought they had executed you," he whispers to me.

"Gwen," my mouth speaks her name as it pops into my head.

"Sheila saw me being led in here," replies Chase. "I'm sure she has told Gwen, but I haven't seen her yet."

As I bury myself into his arms with a multitude of emotions reeling through me in a swarm, each wanting to be acknowledged, a sense of peace fills me, but so does anger, anger toward the game Tapiwa played at my expense.

Chapter 17

A Warning

A dull orange glow peeks through the bottom of the shade with a reddish tinge to it, painting a straight line on the wall near the door. It glows brighter by the second before fizzling out as dark clouds cover the sun's feeble attempt at lighting up our world, blocking its warmth, and forbidding anyone from looking upon its magnificence. Chase's steady breathing lulls me back into a half slumber, and I close my eyes, relishing in the sound of the air entering and leaving his lungs, comforted by his presence and glad that he is here, instead of… I stop myself from thinking about it, still incensed at Tapiwa's cruel trick, though I am not surprised by it. Such is our way, the way of Arel. My head settles on his chest as I listen to the rhythm of his heart, unwilling to move, not wanting this peaceful moment to end, wishing that it would continue forever as I remember my relief upon seeing him alive. The night passed in a minute, or so it seems, and instead of wasting it talking about little nuances in an awkward attempt to pass the time, we laid on my bed with his arm around me and my head on his chest, content to just be together, and no words passed between us, because they will never capture what this simple moment has given us.

A door closes in the hallway, warning me that I must get up with its harsh thud, but I do not budge, as the heavy boots stomp down the hallway, heading for the stairs and hurrying down them. Chase stirs. I know that I must get up. I know that I cannot escape the aftermath of yesterday's bombing. I know that I must face whatever today chooses to throw at me, and so, I sit up, refusing to give in to my desires, and place my feet on the bare floor, allowing its touch of chillness to tickle them. I glance at Chase as he opens his eyes, wondering if he had watched me sleep during those long nights in the wilderness when we were forced to depend on one another for survival, wondering what he thought and if he felt any sort of relief at seeing that I still breathed. A bit of hair drops across his forehead as he shifts position, and I brush it away with the tips of my fingers, remembering the night at the mines when I stayed by him after he had taken a beating for me. The memory of it causes my heart to ache as I wonder why he sacrificed so much to save me, and how I have done nothing to earn it.

Another door shuts, warning me to get dressed, or risk the inevitable consequences of being tardy. Chase sits up as I step over to the closet to pick out a fresh uniform, cringing when I see the wrinkles in my pants from having slept in them.

"You should go," I say, a melancholy tone in my voice.

"I don't want to."

I do not want him to either, but if he remains much longer, others may talk, they may whisper about how my liking for him is more than infatuation, and they would be correct, but we cannot just think of ourselves; I have Sheila to consider, and he has Gwen.

"I have to report for duty, and Gwen must be anxious to see you."

Upon hearing Gwen's name, Chase stands up, knowing that we cannot stay here all day, as Arel requires our complete obedience. He heads for the door, but I stop him.

"Wait. There can be no questions."

As though reading my mind, Chase pulls off his shirt, exposing his well-formed pectorals, and unzips his pants so that they hang from his waist, threatening to fall off. Still not pleased with his attempt at a disheveled look, I reach for his hair, burying my fingers within their silky strands, and ruffle it, until he looks like a madman. To complete the charade, I pull off my clothes until I am in my undershirt, just in case any prying eyes are watching, and considering Tapiwa's deception, I know they are.

Chase's hand moves to the door, but I stop him. "Promise me, that you will do what you have to, to survive."

His gray eyes bury themselves within mine. "Only if you promise to do the same."

I smile at him, and the door slides open, allowing him into the hallway, and he ambles to the stairs with his shirt dragging on the floor as he keeps his head bowed low, pretending to feel shame at what we want others to believe he was forced to do. To add credence to the masquerade, I linger in the doorframe, allowing the cold metal of its frame to touch my bottom. The cold stare of another hits me, telling me that my suspicions are correct, as I glance away from the stairs where Chase's form disappears, and find Anan's malevolent face glaring at me with disgust. His eyes scan up and down my body, and I scowl back at him, daring him to try something, to give me a reason to shove my knee where it will impede him from fulfilling his duties for the day. With a rude gesture of my own, I turn and go back into my room, allowing the door to shut behind me, glad to be back in my own sanctuary.

A ray of light spills through the window, landing on the uniforms hanging in my closet, before more clouds smother it, snuffing out its existence, and I release a huge sigh, knowing that the time has come for me to face yesterday's aftermath. I snatch a pair of pants and pull them on, allowing the fabric to hug every curvature of my body, like it was designed to do, and tuck the hem of my undershirt into the waistband. A hollow face captures my attention as strands of black, silky hair escape their bun and wrap around the narrow chin, and I stare back at it, intrigued, but also saddened. Sadness fills the face before me, and several seconds go by before I recognize it as my own. Gone is the wonder I once possessed, replaced with doubt, anger, and a sullen disposition.

Who am I? Am I still Noni, the fresh recruit who desired above all else to be a good arbiter and to protect Arel? But what am I protecting Arel from? I am not naïve enough to believe that the outside world does not wish us harm; of course, some do, but who protects us from a leadership that uses fear and intimidation to keep people in line? Loyalty through fear—that is what Arel is about. So, who am I? What am I?

My wristband chirps, reminding me of the time, and that I must get going, and after everything that has happened, I do not wish to give my superiors another reason to doubt my commitment to my duties. I rip out the bobby pins that hold the disheveled bun—I had not bothered taking my hair out last night, as my joy at seeing Chase alive overruled everything else—and run a brush through my hair, before setting it up in a new bun, in accordance with regulations, and checking the mirror to make sure that not one strand is out of place. Another warning from my wristband propels me out the door as I snatch a fresh jacket from its hangar and shove my arms through the sleeves while hurrying down the hallway and down the stairs, zipping it closed as I reach the bottom step, making certain to avoid the right corner as it crumbles beneath anyone's weight—another sign of the desperate state of repairs needed for the manor.

I rush into the dining room, making certain to grab a tablet that I can use to write the report I have yet to file—there is always a tablet or two sitting in the front room for any arbiter to use, so long as they return it—and take my place by the table, sitting down to eat, and a plebeian places a plate in front of me with eggs, a fruit salad (a mixture of sliced strawberries, apples, and papaya), and mashed garbanzo beans (not the most appetizing, but it is food, and I am famished), and I dig my fork into them, shoving the gritty substance into my mouth, just glad to have something to eat. My first day here, we had to wait for Commander Vye to arrive before we could eat, but not every meal rests upon ceremony, since arbiters work different shifts and, sometimes, she is unable to make it, an increasing habit of hers.

I enter my credentials on the tablet and proceed to write up my report as I eat, hoping to accomplish two tasks in one sitting. My fork stops midbite when a familiar shape stalks into the room, causing a harsh chill to crawl up my back, freezing me and preventing me from moving. Molers sits beside me. Forcing myself to act normal, I shove a forkful of egg into my mouth. Sheila's head pokes out from behind the doorway leading to the kitchen, but she ducks back into the shadows when she sees Molers.

"I hear that you had quite the day yesterday," Molers comments, and I wonder where he is going with this statement, and why he is talking to me in the first place.

"It will all be in my report," I reply, trying to keep the nervousness out of my voice, as I continue to type. Molers always made me uneasy, and this moment is no exception.

"Yes, I noticed that you have not written it yet."

"That was Commander Vye's decision," I reply, trying to finish my breakfast and report as fast as I can, so that I can get away from him.

"She seems to make a lot of independent decisions," Molers says, and I look up from my report.

"I'm not sure what you mean."

"Of course not. You've been away."

"Is there something I can do for you, Master Arbiter?" I ask, growing annoyed.

"You can tell me what happened in the mines." Molers leans closer so that I can smell the coffee he had drunk earlier. Arbiters are not supposed to drink coffee, but that does not stop them, and Molers is no exception to this.

"You can read Lieutenant Renal's report," I reply, as I continue to type and eat at the same time.

"I did…"

Of course, he has. I wonder what Renal left out of his report that has forced Molers to ply me for information.

"…and it appears that he does not remember much after you found him."

I place my fork in the center of my empty plate and the soft, singular clink echoes around the two of us, sounding louder than it is, as a multitude of reasons, each as wild as the previous, run through my mind as to why Renal would leave so much out of his report. Though injured, he was conscious for most of what had happened, and well-aware of Commandant Gants' demise.

"If there is something you wish to know," I say, "quit playing the coward and ask."

Molers' nostrils flare from my blatant disregard to his rank and obvious disrespect toward him.

"I think you already know."

"I'm afraid I don't."

"You were there when the uprising took place. I want to know why it happened."

Why does he care? My heart skips a beat, but I will it to contain itself, to not exhibit any sign of anxiety, to not give credence to any of Molers' suspicions.

"They are workers. Workers always rebel."

"You never read any of Commandant Gant's reports, did you?"

Now, I wish I had thought to, though I doubt that I have the security clearance to gain access to a superior officer's report.

"He mentioned you several times," continues Molers, "about how you seemed to have a soft spot for the workers and how you gained their trust."

"I had nothing to do with the uprising, if that is what you are implying." Deep down, I wonder if that is true.

"We shall see."

I finish the last few sentences of my report and stand up, grabbing my empty plate.

"A plebeian can clean that up," says Molers.

For a split second, I wonder if this is another test of his, but decide that I do not care if it is; I want to get away from him.

"An arbiter's duty is to maintain order at all times. A dirty plate left to gather ants and flies is the opposite of that, or do you not agree?"

"Someday, Noni, you and I will have that one-on-one."

"I look forward to it."

The moment the words exit my mouth, I wish I had not said them, but it is too late; they have been spoken. Maintaining a stern composure, I carry my plate to the kitchen and deposit it in the sink where a plebeian busies herself with washing the dishes. For a moment, she is surprised by my actions, but does not question them as I walk over to a bowl full of green apples and take three of them. Not wanting to walk past Molers, I exit the kitchen through its other doorway and head for the hallway, to the door that leads to the plebeian quarters, hoping to sneak down there and give these apples to Sheila. Making certain that the corridor is empty, I creep over to the door, and as I place my hand on the cold handle, a hiss reaches my ears, causing me to jerk my head to the right. Sheila stands behind a corner, waving me over, and I hurry to her, hoping that no one decides to walk by at that moment.

I give her a hug, glad to see that she is okay, and feeling guilty for not taking more time to talk with her yesterday. She buries her face into me as I wrap my protective arms around her, not wanting to leave her here alone all day, but knowing that I have no choice.

"Are you all right?" I ask her.

She nods. "I was worried about you. I heard about the uprising in the mines and how you had gotten hurt and…"

"Shh," I soothe her, doing my best to comfort her. "It's my job to protect you."

She looks at me with somber eyes, and I wonder what has happened to her in my absence.

"Here"—I hand her the apples—"take these. One for each of you. Can you…"

"I'll see that they get them," Sheila replies, knowing that two of the apples go to Chase and Gwen.

"How is Gwen?" I ask.

"She doesn't blame you anymore."

She should. It is my fault that Chase was almost killed and that she was almost left without a brother.

"You must be careful, Noni," Sheila warns me. "Molers wants Commander Vye's position here, and… if he gets it…"

The mention of Commander Vye's name reminds me that I was supposed to meet her on the green this morning. Damn! I forgot all about it.

"Don't worry about it," I tell her. "Keep your head down. Where will you be this evening?"

"Cleaning the showers."

"I'll see you then."

I give her one last hug before letting her go.

"Be careful."

"Always," I tell her before she scampers away. When I turn to head to the double doors leading to the green, I spot Anan. He darts into another room when my eyes meet his, and the uneasy feeling that he might have seen my interaction with Sheila fills me with dread, but I haven't time to dwell on it: Commander Vye awaits my presence.

I hurry to the green, rushing out of the double glass doors and to the grassy area in time to spot Commander Vye as she finishes a pushup. Always training. Such is the arbiter way; and her constant display of physical prowess serves as a reminder and an example for the rest of us. I stalk across the grass as its tiny blades leave moist stripes on my boots that reflect the opulent light of the sun as it tries to break free of the clouds' clutches. She spots me and stands up, brushing the grass from her hands before she grabs her jacket from a bench and puts it on.

"You wished to see me, commander," I say.

"You filed your report?"

"Yes, ma'am."

Commander Vye nods her head in approval, but her eyes look away as though something troubling plagues her mind, and my vanity wonders if it is about me.

"Is something bothering you, commander?" I ask, breaking the terse silence and wondering why she has asked me out here instead of her office. Does she believe that the walls have ears? What happened while I was gone?

"Tell me what happened at the mines."

This seems to be the subject of the day. First Molers, and now she wants to know what happened there, making me even more curious as to what took place in my absence.

"Commandant Gant was not thrilled about my presence," I reply.

"Surprising," she says in a sarcastic tone.

I ignore her and continue. "The mines were pitiful. Starved workers were beaten in an effort to force them to push carts that were too heavy for the strongest of arbiters."

"And?"

"I was sent there to increase production and that is what I did."

"How?"

Something tells me that Commander Vye already knows how I succeeded, but I must answer her. She is my commanding officer and trying to keep secrets when she is already aware of the truth will only result in my imprisonment.

"I ordered that the workers be given adequate food and water, and that they work in shifts, so that they can get adequate rest."

"An unusual solution."

"It was necessary."

"Explain."

"If you want the best from people, sometimes you must treat them with kindness."

Commander Vye eyes me, studying me with that hawk-like gaze of hers, as though she can see inside me and see the depths of my tattered soul.

"That is not a sentiment that is taught to arbiters."

"Permission to speak freely," I say.

"Granted."

"The workers were skeletons. How can any sane person expect them to work in the mines without adequate food, water, and rest? If you want the people of Arel to perform their duties, they must be given what they need to live, or they will die."

"More workers could have been sent to the mines," says Commander Vye.

For what? A lifetime of despair where they choke on ore dust until their lungs turn black and they die, suffocating on the mucus that builds and collects within them? I keep this to myself. I cannot show anger. I cannot show compassion.

"I hadn't time to wait for a new supply of workers. President Tapiwa was explicit in what she wanted and what the price of failure would be. I was sent to those mines with no knowledge of the situation or what to expect. I did what I had to, to survive."

"As do we all," mumbles Commander Vye, and I do not believe I was meant to hear her. "And Commandant Gant's reaction?" she asks.

"He tried to have me killed my first night there."

Commander Vye's jaw clenches as her face tightens in anger, and I watch her struggle to hold it in, to keep from releasing it in front of me. She must always possess an air of control, and she knows it.

"How is it you managed to escape this attempt on your life?"

I consider my answer. Should I tell her the truth, or lie? She will see through a lie. One should never underestimate Commander Vye's intelligence or powers of perception. A half-truth then. That should suffice.

"A worker stepped in."

"You let him take what was meant for you?"

"It was either him or me. Commandant Gant's goons seemed more entertained by this fool's actions, so I let them do with him what they willed, and slipped away."

"Why would a worker help you?"

I look Commander Vye square in the eye, steeling my nerves and my face so that she cannot read it.

"I do not know. Perhaps he just wanted to die."

"After the attack on Renal, what happened?"

"I tried to get him out, but Commandant Gant's men found us. He called everyone from their beds to witness my execution, but it was stopped by the uprising."

I leave out Trevors' part in all this. I have no idea what Renal put in his report, or what Trevors and Grelyn put in theirs, but there is one thing I am certain of, none of them mentioned stopping Commandant Gant from executing me then and there. It goes against the arbiter way. We are taught to defend Arel, that death is inevitable, and that saving someone else at the expense of Arel's greatness is weakness. None of them would want to appear weak; appearing weak gets you killed, and judging by the satisfied look on Commander Vye's face, I have made the correct choice.

"And afterward?" she asks.

"An explosion went off near me, rendering me unconscious," I reply. "I remember nothing, until I woke up in a medical room."

Molers appears on the green, taking one look at us, and the tension between him and my commander fills the entire space, suffocating me and making me want to run away, before he stalks off.

"Commander," I ask, "what is going on? Molers knew about the uprising, details that were in the reports, and he read Commandant Gant's reports to Arel."

"How do you know this?"

"He told me."

"When?"

"Breakfast."

A flicker of concern fills Commander Vye's eyes, but it disappears before I have time to register it and to ponder its meaning, replaced by her stern face, the stoicness that she shows the world so that none know what secrets she holds, or the heart that beats within her chest.

"You remember, before you left, how I told you to be careful?" she says.

I nod.

"I am telling you again. Watch yourself, Noni. Things are different here, and you managed to catch the eye of one of our presidents, which puts a target on your back."

"Yes, ma'am."

"Is there anything in your report that I need to know about?"

"No, ma'am. Everything I have told you is what is in the report."

"Keep it that way."

"Is there anything else, ma'am?"

"We are to go to the crematoriums. It was not my idea, but has been ordered by President Tapiwa herself."

I take a step back. No one goes to the crematoriums, unless they are being sent there to die or be forgotten. There are arbiters assigned there, but they are ones thought of as unfit to serve anywhere else, so they are sent to the crematoriums to rot, until they are thrown into the fires that burn there.

"While we are there, you will keep your tongue silent and only speak when spoken to, understood?"

"Yes, ma'am."

Commander Vye grabs my shoulder and forces me to look into her worried eyes, and for the first time, I think of her as human, as someone with emotions, hopes, and dreams, and as someone who fears loss.

"Do not do anything rash. You leave that to me."

"Understood."

"We leave in ten minutes."

Commander Vye walks off, leaving impressions in the grass that disappear the way a handprint vanishes from a piece of foam, leaving me alone on the green to stew in the portentous feeling that settles in my stomach.

Chapter 18

The Crematoriums

Giant flues loom ahead of us, spewing plumes of putrid smoke into the dismal air, surrounding us with death as the transport we are in eases its way toward the gate guarding the crematoriums. I try to look ahead, but pull back when Commander Vye glares at me, giving me a reprimanding look, and a reminder that I am to behave with the utmost of courtesy. Now is not the time for curiosity or stubbornness. No one comes to the crematoriums unless they have been sentenced here, and the fact that Tapiwa wants me to visit this place fills me with trepidation and questions. The transport lurches to a halt, and I am flung forward as guards approach the vehicle with their weapons raised, ready to fire upon us if we prove to be troublesome. The driver rolls down his window and motions for the rest of us to do the same. The moment a small crack appears in mine, I gag, and my throat seizes from the smell of burning flesh, but this is different from the time I was on the wall and forced to use black fire on those who tried to invade Arel. This smell is constant, never ending, acrid in its makeup,

257

clothed in decay, and accompanied by death itself. I imagine a dark figure cloaked in tattered rags with his face covered, ashamed of being seen, of being known as the reaper, as the bringer of death. Such stories are forbidden in Arel; we tell them anyway. The older recruits would tell the younger ones these forbidden tales, and they would tell those who came after them, and so the stories survived, regardless of the presidential decree.

An armed guard appears at my window, and I look at my reflection within the visor of his helmet, reminding myself to keep my expressions neutral. He raises a scanner, and I know what is expected of me, so I lower my head, exposing the back of my neck and the tattoo that resides there. The scanner beeps, and he walks away, satisfied with what comes up on the screen. With a soft jostle, the transport creeps into the compound and parks a few feet beyond the gate.

Commander Vye gets out, and I do the same, not wanting to be scolded for being too slow. I follow behind her, heading for a giant, steel door that is blacker than my uniform, sneaking a peek behind me, wondering why the driver has not also gotten out, but instead stays within the safety of the transport. My stomach lurches and a deep, never-ending pit builds within it, growing by the second as my heart races and my pulse throbs in my neck. I do not understand why my nerves are spiking, why they are trying to warn me of impending danger. I glance back again at the driver, but Commander Vye clears her throat, forcing me to whip my head back into place so that I face forward, but I cannot help myself; I want to look around, to see where I am being taken, to know more about this ominous place that we all try to avoid, so I glance at the smokestacks and the black essence that spews from them.

Something lands on the edge of my nose. Unable to stop myself, I brush it off and stare at a piece of gray ash on the tip of my middle finger, sitting there as though it has been invited to stay for a while. Soon, I find myself surrounded by what appears to be soiled snowflakes, but the air is too warm for such a thing and they do not melt when touched. It's charcoal dust, or so I think. Ash falls from above, coughed into the air by the giant smokestacks, coating my uniform and my hair, and as I look up to study them further, one slips through my parted lips and settles on my tongue. As I taste its chalkiness, a sick realization takes hold of me: the ash surrounding me are the remains of human corpses that have been incinerated in the fires that burn night and day here. I am surrounded by death.

A hand rams into my back, in between my shoulder blades, and shoves me forward, causing me to almost stumble.

"Keep going!" yells one of the guards.

I start to turn to challenge him, but Commander Vye places a firm grip on my arm, stopping me. She shakes her head, and I obey her unspoken command. Let her handle it.

I had thought the mines a terrible place, but this is different. In the mines, there was some semblance of life, even if it was subdued and submissive, but here, there is nothing, not even the sound of crickets.

Harsh clacking sounds emanate around us as the doors swing open, beckoning us to enter and warning us that there is no escape from this place of hell. As they come to a stop, boiling heat smacks me in the face, causing me to sweat, and the desire to run away comes over me, urging me to flee, to escape to a place of safety, but I remain where I am, unwilling to show fear or weakness. I am an arbiter. I am Noni. I do not run from fear. I embrace it.

Inhaling as deep as I can—the sun pokes through the clouds for a second as though to say good-bye before disappearing again—I step forward, ahead of Commander Vye, and delve into the dark chambers of foreboding and despair, ready to face the fires of hell and to overcome whatever challenge has been laid before me. Once inside, I find myself in darkness, save for an orange glow at the bottom of a circular staircase. Even the sun dares not enter this place, blocked by the terror that lies deep within, as though an invisible wall prevents it from stepping even one inch into its realm.

A guard motions for us to go down the stairs.

We obey. Together, Commander Vye and I step onto the first step, and the lack of a metallic ring surprises me, as though even sound itself is too afraid to exist here. One fateful step at a time, I descend further into the darkness, heading for the orange luminescence before me, a moth unable to resist the glow of a lamp, and steel myself, commanding my anxiety to leave me, as it will only get me killed. I try to look around, to find a route for escape, but the black walls blend in with the darkness so well, that I feel as though I am encased in a hole, one that could well be my final resting place. The silence surrounding me makes me want to scream, to yell, to beg for mercy, but I clamp my mouth shut. Pleading only brings death.

I reach the bottom of the stairs and stand before another giant doorway, and as soon as I step off it, a deafening roar strikes me, filling my ears with its thunder and smashing the wall of silence that has imprisoned me. I want to cover my ears, unable to handle this amount of noise, but I mustn't show weakness. I must be like Commander Vye, who stands proud and unyielding, conveying no amount of fear or submissiveness, but is resolute in her pursuit of seeing this task through. Squaring my shoulders, I straighten my posture, emulating her and refusing to bow before this place and the unknown that awaits me on the other side of this doorway.

I walk forward and step into the orange light as though I am being born for a second time, passing from darkness into light, but this light brings no joy or hope; it is the sharp blade of the reaper's chosen weapon. Fires loom ahead of me, stretching from the floor to the ceiling, demanding more fuel, only to be satiated by naked corpses that inch their way toward them on a conveyor belt. One by one, they drop into the flames, and I watch as these soulless vessels are disposed of, having become nothing more than a common piece of garbage, a waste of space that is best disposed of. Unable to peel my eyes away, I stalk forward until a rail stops me, forcing me to stand still with my mouth parted, watching the hypnotic motion of bodies making their way to their final destination. Dumped, like rotted food, not even afforded the decency of a proper farewell.

Someone shoves a handkerchief in front of my face, forcing me from my stupor, and for the first time, the putrid smell of decay pierces my nose, embedding itself into my brain as a permanent fixture, a parasite I will never be rid of, and with each breath I take, that odor morphs into an acrid film on my tongue, reminding me of stale meat that has sat out too long and was allowed to go green. The memory of Molers forcing me to eat spoiled meat just to prove a point flashes in my mind. I vomited for the next 12 hours after that. From then on, I only ate meat that smelled fresh. The handkerchief hops up and down in front of me, reminding me of where I am, and I look up at the arbiter handing it to me, while her other hand holds another piece of cloth over her nose and mouth. None of the armed guards have such a thing over their face, but perhaps they can no longer smell it, or their helmets block it enough to make it bearable. She waves the cloth at me again, and I shake my head at her, refusing what temporary comfort it could provide. Commander Vye's sharp eyes watch me, taking in my refusal of the cloth, and she takes the material she had placed around her face and drops it on the floor, not wanting to be outshone by someone under her command.

The arbiter in charge motions for us to follow him, and as we do, I notice movement in the shadows. People, condemned to a worse fate than burning in the ravenous fires, place bodies on the conveyor belts, choosing to hide in the shadows than face the shame of what they are forced to do. The hollow expressions on their faces unnerve me. Whatever humanity they possessed before coming here has been stripped from them, turning them into automatons who do the bidding of their master. Loud voices echo from behind us, and I swing around to see what the commotion is about. A man refuses to lift another corpse onto the conveyor belt. Without a single word, a guard raises his weapon and puts a hole in the man's head, and before his body touches the floor, other workers swoop in and strip him of his clothes before dumping him on the belt. The belt carries him to me, allowing me to get a good look at him, reminding me of just how fleeting everything is, and as I watch his body be carried to the fire, the feeling that his dead eyes stare straight into mine morphs into a warning that wafts over me.

Commander Vye snaps her fingers, jerking me from my moment of silent wondering, and I hurry after her as she follows the guard guiding us. He leads us through the maze of conveyor belts and the people in the shadows stripping bodies of the possessions they had in life. We shove our way past them, ignoring them as they do their job. My shoulder bumps into a man holding a shirt coated in gray dust, masking its once vibrant blue color, with a tear stretching from the armpit of the left sleeve to the bottom of the hem, followed by blood, turned brown from oxidation. My mouth starts to apologize for bumping into him, but I stop myself, before I give myself away. I am an arbiter and not supposed to care if I disturb someone in their work, but that isn't what stops me.

His hollow eyes, bleak and soulless just like this place, stare past me, as though he does not see me, almost as though I am nothing more than a ghost to him, stop me, eating away at me until they have devoured the last bit of my humanity. He says nothing, makes no noise, and gives no indication that he knows I am here as his hands remove the pants from the body in front of him, flopping it around with ease, as though he has done this hundreds of times. I glance around me. A bubble of indistinguishable noises roar so loud that my ears become deaf to everything else around me while dark figures remain focused on their task, surrounded by moving shadows traveling into dancing light, wanting to be seen instead of forgotten. I am alone. Cut off—lost in a sweltering ravine, the only guest death has invited to a feast of burned flesh and putrid decay.

I cannot move. Despair greeted me at the mines, but this is not despair—it's hopelessness. Chained to the ground, I remain where

I am among those stripping the bodies, dressed in my black uniform as though I am death, as though I am the reaper who has condemned them all to such a horrendous fate. This is why Tapiwa wanted me to be brought here. This is a reminder of where I will end up if I disobey Arel's commands. The squeaking wheels of the conveyor belt pull me from my stupor, forcing me to look at the body of a woman as it passes by me on its way to the fires. Her eyes, clouded from death, stare at me, accusing me of being her executioner, of condemning her to burn in heartless fires instead of giving her a proper farewell. Without thinking, I reach up and place my index and middle finger on her eyes, closing them so that she will not have to look at the soot-covered ceiling or at the terrifying flames that are always hungry. Perhaps she can dream before she is burned, floating on waves of serenity. The conveyor belt carries her corpse to the flames and dumps it without a second thought, and I wonder who she was and what crime she committed to end up here.

An alarm blares, its incessant beeping pounds my eardrums, making me want to cover them, but I dare not to. I am an arbiter, not a terrified child. Everyone moves to the side as the alarm sounds, and I do the same, while looking at the flashing red lights that circles us, warning us of something that is coming. A hole in the ceiling opens up, allowing me to see into the silo above it, but before I can ponder what it is, a wave of corpses plummet from the hole and to the floor, adding to the pile of death's children, forming little mountains. Some of the bodies roll from the top all the way to the bottom, like rocks on a mountain, but instead of a roaring thunder, the only noise they make is that of soft thuds. One stops by my foot, and I look down at it, while my heart skips a couple of beats. For a moment, I believe that it is Sheila lying on the cold concrete floor in front of me, but as I study the girl's face, I realize that it is not Sheila—the pit in my stomach dissipates as this fact sinks in—but a girl about her age, who looks a lot like her. Fresh bruises cover her body, and her face is still swollen from having been struck; she is no more than a few hours deceased. Swallowing a lump that has lodged itself in my throat, I pull my foot away from the girl's body and step back, moving away from her and toward Commander Vye, all the while reminding myself that Sheila is back at the manor, alive and waiting for me.

Commander Vye gives me a reprimanding look for dawdling, and I glance away, unable to meet her unforgiving gaze. She turns back toward the guard guiding us, and I follow her, taking one last glance at the girl's corpse—someone is already stripping it—and the foreboding notion that builds within me, unnerving me. We reach a patch of light, and relief floods over me, glad to be away from the darkness and its cold residents. A woman stands on a platform in the orange beam of light with her hands on her hips, close to her weapon, watching us as we come toward her.

"Welcome," she says to Commander Vye and me, "to hell."

She steps away from the light, though it seems to follow her no matter where she goes, accentuating her stocky features, putting her burly muscles on full display, letting everyone here know that she is in charge. No one watches her, except for me and Commander Vye. Not even the guards escorting us bother looking at this woman. My eyes stay glued to her, watching her every move as she stalks to a set of stairs in a regal manner, and an ominous feeling geminates in my stomach, growing by the second as each of her steps echoes around us, drowning the roars of the fires behind us as though they too are afraid of this woman. Thoughts about what she had done to get assigned to this place rush through my mind, each worse than the last because she must have done something unforgivable. Why would anyone want to be assigned here? Unless…

"My name," the woman says as she steps off the platform, each word leaving her mouth at the exact moment her foot stomps on a step, "is Commander Aeron."

Shit.

There isn't an arbiter in Arel who does not know that name.

Even Commander Vye's cheeks twitch upon hearing the name: it is synonymous with death and carnage. It is rumored that she has marks on her body, one for every enemy she has killed; her body must be coated in tattoos by now. Though against regulation, the arbiter council decided to allow her this one bit of deviancy because of what she is able to accomplish. Everywhere her names goes, fear precedes it while death follows. Aeron—Aeron the Butcher. Stories were told to the recruits in the training facility, and the recruits repeated the stories among themselves, where they grew and evolved, or remained true to the original. As I watch her stride in front of the arbiters under her command, what I had once thought of as embellished tales told to frighten us into submission look more realistic by the second.

When she was a recruit, she murdered her roommates—all of them. She never gave a justification for such an act. When the warden on her floor saw her come out in the morning coated in blood, he rushed into the room to see what had happened and found a room covered in entrails, blood, bits of bone, severed fingers, two eyeballs, a dissected brain (if you could call it that, since it had been cut into thin strips that were woven together to form a sort of rope), bits of teeth, and a flab of skin that looked as though it had been fileted. The warden demanded to know what had happened, but all she did was stare at him, a predator sizing up its prey, with a sardonic grin on her face. She was put in detainment, but the council decided to let her live, to nurture her dark nature for their own purposes. I remember an older recruit telling me this story and he demonstrated every part of it. I did not sleep for a week, and it still haunts me even now.

Her murderous ways did not stop there. There is another story about her first assignment at one of our outposts. It was attacked by barbarians, and over 100 arbiters were killed, but not Aeron. It is said that the commandant of her outpost panicked and left his post, and that she took charge. She turned the battle around and forced the barbarians to flee back into the wildlands where they belonged, but not before sending a message. She had managed to capture their leader. To ensure that they never attacked again, Aeron strung him up on a pole just outside the outpost where all could see, unconcerned that someone might take a shot at her, and gutted him; she ripped out his intestines and chopped them into smaller pieces, throwing each piece at the barbarians watching from the trees, yelling at them to take the pieces back to their village, her blood soaked uniform instilling fear into any who watched. The body hung out there for weeks, but Aeron never allowed it to be taken down, even when its putrid smell made any unfortunate enough to be nearby vomit.

Sometime later, she was tasked with cleaning out the very settlement that the attackers had come from. If Arel wanted to make a point, they succeeded. Aeron not only attacked it, making sure that the barbarians who lived there were forced to leave, she made sure that they would never reside there again. She ordered their fields to be salted so that their crops would die, but that is not the worst of it: every man, woman, and child was tied to a post and left to die the most agonizing death. A trail of bodies, left out to rot, stretched from the settlement to the outpost, and it is said that she walked among the carnage, pleased with her handiwork—an artist and her painting. As I ponder the stories told of her, I can't help but wonder why she is here?

Commander Aeron steps in front of me, and I feel her cold eyes scrutinizing me, taking in every detail of my posture, every twitch, every uncontrollable spasm that her gaze brings out. A smirk crosses her face, telling me that she is pleased by the fear that her very presence instills. I do my best to keep my eyes straight ahead and keep my focus on something in the background as an incessant amount of warmth builds around my neck, stretching down my back and to my waist as droplets of sweat form, causing my uniform jacket and undershirt to cling to me, forming some sort of seal. I want to move. I want to get away from her, but I cannot. If I do, it will show weakness and weakness is never tolerated.

"You must be Arbiter Noni," Commander Aeron says in a stern voice, and I smell the decayed bits of meat, that she must have eaten hours before my arrival, on her breath.

I remain silent. There is no point in saying anything. She knows who I am. She knew before I arrived here. This entire venture was arranged by Tapiwa, and now I know why: it is a warning, a warning of what will happen to me if I continue to show mercy toward those Arel has deemed expendable.

"Well?" snaps Commander Aeron.

"You have not asked me a question, commander," I reply. She hasn't. What did she expect me to say? Yes, I'm Noni and you're a tyrannical bitch? Such a reply will get me sent straight into the fires. Chase's words echo through my mind: do what you have to, to survive. I keep repeating them, reminding myself of the promise I had made to him earlier, and to Sheila and Gwen. If anything happens to me, a far worse fate will befall to them.

"What do you think of my empire?" Commander Aeron asks.

"Empire?" I reply, unsure of what to say, but knowing that no one in Arel has an empire, except for the two presidents, and to say otherwise is punishable by death.

"My domain then." Commander Aeron bears down upon me as I take in her well-formed muscles that are twice the size of mine, and I know that she can crush me with one blow if I anger her, but I cannot stand her arrogance. This is all a test. I know it is. A test to see if I will break, if I will succumb to the fear that the crematoriums always instill in people, but seeing it now, seeing how the people here act like mindless drones as they throw corpses—the remains of individuals who once had hopes, wants, and desires—into the blazing inferno that hungers for more, my fear turns to anger, which transforms into defiance. I refuse to be broken, to allow this woman and her gruesome reputation to force me to coil into a ball, begging for mercy.

"Perhaps you need to see more of it," Commander Aeron says.

She motions for us to follow her and both Commander Vye and I do. Workers work in wanton repetition as they continue to strip lifeless bodies of their meager possessions before tossing them onto the conveyor belt for their final farewell. Debilitating heat singes my skin and smoke spews from the chimneys, leaking into the chamber, causing any who breathe it to choke, assuming the smell of rot hasn't already suffocated them, though my sense of smell no longer detects it, having become used to the death surrounding me.

As Commander Aeron leads us to another part of the crematorium, I do my best to keep my face emotionless, devoid of any humanity, otherwise I risk being outed as a dissenter, but inside, my heart aches for the souls condemned to this place. Whatever humanity they had before coming here has been stolen from them. Despite my efforts, I turn my head to watch as a man collapses from exhaustion, and like the one earlier, those next to him lift him up, and dump him on the conveyor belt. He screams in terror as he is carried to the fire. He tries to claw his way off the belt, but bony hands push him back down, refusing him mercy, and his screams morph into agony as he is dumped into the fires, before being silenced forever, and death's cold hand grips my back, warning me that I will be next if I am not careful.

We turn away from the fires, heading for a tunnel. Wild thoughts run through my mind as we trek down the metallic tube with charred grime crawling up the sides as though it is alive, forming whimsical patterns in a place devoid of beauty. The roar of the fires echo through the tunnel, forming a metallic drumbeat that pounds against my eardrums, causing my pulse to change its rhythm to this new melody of doom. Commander Aeron continues down the tunnel as the lights fade to a dim glow, making me feel as though I have been buried alive beneath the ground, and a new wave of anxiety courses through me as I wonder what she is up to. We turn another corner and enter a room with a giant wheel on it: its barbaric shape and sharpened spokes causing my stomach to leap as the dark figure of a person comes into view. Without warning, lights turn on, causing me to squint until my eyes become accustomed to the sudden brightness.

"This," says Commander Aeron to Commander Vye and me, "is Shamie."

I take a closer look at the man on the gigantic wheel. Blood drips from where the shackles have restrained him, and his swollen face only allows one eye to look at his spectators as he turns his head for a moment before going limp. Beneath the bruises and cuts on his body from where he has been beaten over and over again, I spot what had once been toned muscles, the muscles of an arbiter. The haircut, the physique, it is reminiscent of someone who was once like me, and I find myself wondering what he did to be sent down here.

"Shamie was an arbiter," Commander Aeron continues, enjoying every moment of the man's misery, "but he made one simple mistake: the mistake of believing that he could go against the rule of Arel. So, he was sent here to me."

Commander Aeron waves her hand and another arbiter brings her a torch. With horror, I realize what she intends to do with it and clench my fists, debating with myself over whether I should stop her or not, but if I do, I will be put on that wheel. Now I know why she is here, why she is overseeing the crematoriums: she asked for such an assignment because it grants her the ability to torment others without judgement or repercussions. Commander Aeron enjoys the misery of others and gets a certain amount of pleasure from being the deliverer of their misfortune. She lights the torch and holds it to the man's flesh, cackling as he screams from the agony of his flesh boiling away from his bones as he writhes in pain and pulls against his restraints in a futile attempt to break free, before yanking the torch away from him.

A quick glance at Commander Vye's clenched face tells me that she is as disgusted as I am, but Commander Aeron isn't finished with me.

She turns toward me, holding the torch out to me. "Perhaps you should give it a try."

I remain still, refusing to take it.

"It's quite simple," Commander Aeron says to me in a low tone. "You just press it against him and watch him burn."

The ease with which she explains this to me causes my stomach to churn. She holds it up to the man again, placing the tip of the torch on his left cheek before turning it on. Blue flames erupt from the nozzle, engulfing his cheek as the skin bubbles and cooks, filling the room with the smell of his cooking flesh, and a lump forms in the back of my throat, warning me that I am about to expel the contents of my stomach as Commander Aeron releases a malevolent laugh.

Unable to withstand it any longer, I step forward and reach my hand out for the cresset, doing my best to keep my face impassive and not betray the disgust that I feel toward this vile woman and her methods. Pleased, Commander Aeron turns off the flambeau and hands it to me, thinking that she has convinced me to be just like her. My fingers wrap around the warm base of the torch, tingling as they clench it, not wanting to drop it, and I take it from her, studying its blackened tip while working up the courage to do what I know must be done. The man on the wheel looks at me with his one good eye, pleading with me to end it, to let him go and face the unknown, and I am reminded of the woman at Commandant Paq's outpost as she lay in a pool of her own blood, wishing for her own suffering to end, and how I granted her wish. I try to give the man a little bit of comfort before I help him, not caring what he did to be sentenced to this place. No arbiter deserves to be tortured like this. They deserve a quick death, regardless of their crime.

Commander Aeron's sharp eyes burn into my back as she waits for me to turn on the torch and administer my form of punishment. I give a slight nod to the man stretched across the wheel, and he closes his eye, mouthing the words "thank you", and turns away.

With my free hand, I grab his nose and mouth, squeezing them shut so that he cannot breathe, keeping my grip firm as his body struggles against my grip.

"Shh," I say in a quiet voice, trying to soothe him, and he relaxes, allowing me to bestow upon him his one last wish.

He goes limp.

I remove my hand from his gaping mouth, trying not to look at the lifeless stare in his eye as it clouds over, unable to focus anymore. Stunned silence wells up around me, seething until it morphs into diabolical hatred.

Commander Aeron makes a move for me, but I whip around, holding the torch in front of me, ready to turn it on and burn her face off if necessary, and she stops, unwilling to be on the receiving end of the very punishment she administers to others. I glare at her, daring her to try it, daring her to make one false move, to give me any excuse to attack her. The bringer of carnage and death is what she may have been in the past, but those stories are old, and it's time for a new one to be told. Assured that she will not try anything, I use the butt of the torch to break the man's shackles loose, relishing in the clanging noise that reverberates around us with each strike. His metal cuffs break apart, falling to the ground, and I toss the torch aside, no longer needing it. Unconcerned about the others in the room, I grab the lifeless man and hoist him off the giant wheel, carting him to the doorway and into the metallic tunnel of sweltering filth and rotted flesh as I drag him to the belts. His feet leave streaks in the moist soot on the ground as I haul him away. No one stops me. Perhaps they are too afraid of what Commander Aeron will do to them if they interfere with her plans; or maybe they are too stunned by my actions to even consider stopping me. I don't care. I will not allow Commander Aeron to desecrate his body like she has done to so many before him. The least I can do is make sure that he is disposed of in proper fashion and cannot be tormented anymore.

Sunken eyes glance up from their work and watch as I walk past with the body of a former arbiter in my arms, no longer devoid of life, but instead, they watch me with intent, being filled with resolution for the first time in a long while. The tunnel morphs into a chamber of smoke and fire, and the hum of the conveyor belts greet me as an old friend. My arms tire from holding the man's corpse, but I refuse to let go, ordering my hands to retain their grip, and to not drop him. As I reach the belts, a hand reaches for the body in my arms, and I smack them away. No one is stripping this man of his possessions. My harsh glare causes the one who had tried to grab him to step back and sink away into the shadows like a wraith, while the gears of the conveyor belts squeal as they turn, unwilling to stop in their mission to deliver bodies to the ravenous flames behind me. Guards and workers alike watch, paused in their work, as though time itself has stopped, as they watch me place the man on the conveyor belt, not like a person tossing away a piece of garbage, but as a friend saying farewell.

"I'm sorry," I whisper into the dead man's ear while closing his one good eye with the tip of my index finger before he is carted away.

Stepping back, I salute him as a fellow arbiter, giving him the farewell he deserves, and I watch as he is carried to the flames and dumped into the inferno without a single tear to mourn his passing. Feeling the stares of others on me, (a mixture of confusion, pride, and disgust) I shift from my spot and consider the consequences of my actions. Commander Aeron will not allow me to get away with this.

The clanging of a piece of metal falling to the ground forces me to turn around, and in a far corner, away from the fires, the tunnel, and the conveyor belts, are the shadows of people hoping to go unnoticed. I hurry toward them as the workers and guards go back to their duties, unsure of what else they should do. I race to the area where the noise came from, blocking out the shouts of my name and the roar of the fires, as my swift movements force the sweltering, stagnant air to dry the film of sweat on my face. Dodging around a corner, I reach a grate that appears to go to a ventilation shaft. It hangs at an angle from its hinges, and as I inspect it further, I find a missing screw laying on the soot-covered ground, having just been pried loose. A shuffling sound comes from inside the shaft. I grab the grate and yank it free, revealing five silhouettes in the darkness, having frozen themselves as they all stare at me in fear. Each carries a small bundle in their hands. They're running away.

"NONI!"

My name echoes through this chamber of death, stopping me cold. My punishment awaits, and I can save myself by turning these five in, but if I do… the punishment for trying to escape Arel is execution, and their deaths will be on my hands. I examine the shaft, feeling the air that comes through it, knowing that they must have put some thought into this plan. As I look around, I realize that the crematoriums have one weakness: air needs to be brought in from the outside, meaning that the ventilation shaft is the one way out that is not guarded.

"NONI!"

My name strikes my ears again, warning me to hurry as I struggle with helping them or protecting myself, but as I continue to consider my options, I think of the woman I had tried to save, or the girl whom I was forced to execute, and Sigal and his family, who managed to escape Arel because of me. If I turn them in, then Commander Aeron and Tapiwa have won. I will have become what they want me to be: a mindless drone that obeys without question and kills without impunity.

"Do you know how to get to the eastern sector?" I ask, knowing that they will not get far on their own.

One nods.

"Go to the plaza there. There will be a series of barrels with garbage in them. Hide in them. I will meet you there, tonight."

I put the grate back in position, but one of them stops me.

"They will know you helped us."

"Not if you go now," I reply. Commander Vye's voice draws near and my time for getting them away from here draws short.

"I saw what you did. They will not let you go without punishment," says the man. "You must turn one of us in." He starts to crawl out of the shaft, but a woman stops him, begging him to stay with her, but he places a gentle palm on her cheek and kisses her. "Do as the arbiter says."

Before anyone can react, he jumps out of the shaft and grabs the grate from me, placing it back in position.

"Go!" he says to the others who crawl away, knowing that there is no going back now.

Commander Vye's voice is feet from us, and at any moment, she will round the corner.

Before I have a chance to think of a plan, the man punches me in the face, forcing my training to kick in, and I seize his fist, wringing his arm behind his back and press him into the ground, immobilizing him.

"What is the meaning of this?" demands Commander Vye when she finds me.

The man cranes his head to look at me, pleading with me to think of the others first; if I don't go along with his plan, we are all dead.

"I caught this filth," I say, doing my best to make my voice as harsh as I can, "trying to escape."

Commander Aeron appears with two of her guards. "What is going on here?"

"You can thank Arbiter Noni for discovering a weakness in your domain," replies Commander Vye with smugness.

Commander Aeron's eyes go from me to the man as she realizes what he was trying to do. She marches up to him and backhands him.

"You thought you could just leave?"

He spits in her face.

Infuriated, Commander Aeron shoves me aside, forcing me to land on my side, snatching him from me and throws him to the floor, kicking him in the stomach and ribs over and over, until I lose count, and he is left a mangled mess, coughing and spitting up blood. With one final bit of rage, she lifts her foot high into the air and brings her heavy boot upon his head, crushing his skull, grinning as blood and bits of his brain spurt on to the ash surrounding him. Without a word, the guards with her pick the man's body up and throw him on a conveyor belt to the fires, while I picture myself strangling the life from her to stop her from harming someone else. I press my hands in the ash, allowing it to coat them, as I bend my knees, ready to strike.

"And you, you little..." Commander Aeron rounds on me, but I cut her off.

"You asked me what I think of your domain," I say, changing the subject and forcing her to take a step back in surprise.

She folds her arms, waiting for me to praise her, to tell her how well she runs this place and to commend her for her efforts.

"It is a dump," I reply, "ruled by a sadistic bitch whose glory days of protecting Arel through a horde of carnage are well behind her, having been replaced as a caretaker of filth."

Commander Aeron's smug face contorts into rage. She charges me, bringing her fist up to strike, but before I can defend myself, before anyone else can react, a hand snatches her wrist, stopping her in mid-swing. Commander Vye's stern face glares at Commander Aeron, refusing to release her hold on the commander's wrist.

"No one touches my arbiter without my consent," Commander Vye says through gritted teeth, and I imagine her muscles bulging underneath her uniform, the same muscles I witnessed lift her as she performed an endless amount of pullups when I first arrived in the eastern sector. I have always suspected her of being an unyielding individual, and I am about to find out just how unyielding she is.

Commander Aeron glares at Commander Vye, and I step away, knowing what is about to happen.

Another fist flies at Commander Vye, and she dodges it, landing a blow of her own on Commander Aeron's face. Commander Vye swings again, but misses, receiving a knee in the stomach as a reward. I watch, unsure of what to do, as the two wrestle with one another. A part of me wants to help my commander, but if I do, and she wins, it will invalidate her victory; she must defeat Commander Aeron on her own, or be forever marred by my influence. The two become veiled by an onslaught of fists and feet as they move toward the fire, unaware of how close they are to it.

Commander Aeron fakes an attack and my commander falls for it, realizing her mistake too late as she is knocked to the floor with a grunt. Dazed, Commander Vye almost doesn't see the boot coming straight for her head, but she rolls out of the way just in time and the boot slams into the blackened floor, missing her. Before her opponent can do anything, Commander Vye charges her, catching her around the middle, and forcing her to take a few steps backward, but Commander Aeron's strength is not to be underestimated, as she lifts Commander Vye up, throwing her over a conveyor belt, where she crashes into the floor with a gasp. She lifts herself up, but limps, meaning that my commander has injured her ankle, but she refuses to let it stop her.

The two eye one another with the conveyor belt between them, carrying more bodies to the inferno. Commander Aeron lunges for Commander Vye, but Commander Vye seizes her wrists and drags her over the conveyor belt, knocking two bodies off in the process, and slams her into another belt with her hands around her throat. Commander Aeron reaches for the hands around her throat before flinging her knee into Commander Vye's stomach, forcing her to loosen her grip. Seizing her chance, she charges again, but Commander Vye swerves out of the way, causing Commander Aeron to roll over her back and grunt as she slams into the conveyor belt and the air is knocked out of her.

Once again, a flurry of movement envelops them, each striking and dodging the other as they move even closer to the fire that will consume us all one day. No one moves. No one dares. We all watch, waiting for one to come out the victor. Terror overwhelms me when Commander Aeron wraps her arm around Commander Vye's windpipe, choking the life from her, and my commander struggles to break free. This is it. If she dies, I die too because Commander Aeron will never let me leave alive, not after being challenged by my commander and by me. I want to turn away, to not witness the inevitable, but I can't, and I keep my eyes on Commander Vye as she gives one last attempt to get free before going limp.

Triumphant, Commander Aeron releases her hold and stands up, but the moment she does, Commander Vye drops to the ground, rolls onto her back, and rams her foot into Commander Aeron's calf, causing her to drop to one knee. In one swift series of movement, Commander Vye jumps up and kicks at Commander Aeron, who catches her foot and twists, forcing her back to the floor. Limping, Commander Aeron stands up, grabbing Commander Vye by the face and forcing her to her feet, so that she can look her in the eyes as she kills her. A knife appears in her hand, one that she probably kept hidden in her sleeve, and she thrusts it at Commander Vye, but Commander Vye dodges, twists around, and swings her leg, striking Commander Aeron in the center of her chest, forcing her into the wall of flames behind her, where she is consumed by her favorite method of punishment.

Victorious, Commander Vye stands in front of the blazing fire, a menacing dark shape shrouded by dancing orange and yellow light with swirls of smoke weaving in between her legs, daring any within the chamber to challenge her. No one moves. Not even the guards dare to defy her. Secured in her victory, she turns toward me.

"We're done here."

Wasting no time, I hurry after her as we head back to the stairs that will lead us to the outside world and to our transport. Though none of the guards have stopped us, there will be hell to pay, of that I am certain.

Chapter 19

Hello Darkness

The final chime sounds as the lights turn off throughout the manor, leaving only a few to illuminate the darkness that spreads throughout the dilapidated building, making the mold infested rugs appear to be possessed by black ghosts, whose only goal is to snatch any victim unfortunate enough to cross their path. The last bits of rustling move past my door as a few arbiters who have tried to stay up past lights-out realize that they need to get in their rooms before their indiscretion is discovered. I wait for the final five footsteps to cease thumping on the wooden floors before sitting up in bed, doing my best to not let the springs in my mattress squeak. While listening for anything that might prove my undoing, I put on my boots, lacing them up tight, having already gotten dressed before laying in my bed and pretending to be asleep. As I straighten up, I place my wristband on the desk.

I open my door, wishing that it was quieter as it slides open, noting how every sound seems exaggerated when one is trying to not make any noise. A quick peek up and down the hallway proves that no one has heard me. Good. I let my eyes linger on Amal's room. He stared at me the entire time during dinner as though he knew I was planning something—a treasonous act—and it took all my willpower to not allow his suspicions to get to me. He has always been an ass and I never liked him, and he never appreciated my spurning of his affections, nor my threats to be his undoing; and he seems to be rather cozy with Molers, another thing I will have to watch out for.

I slip out of my room, keeping an eye on Amal's door, hoping that he won't come out and catch me sneaking away. My door closes with a soft hiss behind me as I creep down the dim hallway, moving from faint lamplight to faint lamplight—a thief in the night. I reach the stairs and ease my foot on the first step, doing my best to not make it creak as I tiptoe downward, with my ears alert, listening for any sign that someone is up. As I near the fourth step from the top, I step over it, clinging to the rail so as not to fall down, avoiding its incessant creak whenever someone puts their weight on it. The silence surrounds me, suffocating me as I peak around the corner, making certain that I am alone.

A cough resonates from far down the hallway, pounding my ears the way a hammer strikes a nail, striking the stiff silence and tearing an irreparable slit into its veil. It's Molers. Sweat forms around my neck and back, soaking my shirt as his heavy boots draw nearer. What is he doing up? Lights out is supposed to apply to everyone. I remember a previous conversation I overheard between him and Commander Vye and how he insinuated that she will not remain commander of the eastern sector for long; that is something he covets for himself. I hurry back up the stairs, jumping over the creaky step and dash behind a corner as he appears at the bottom of the stairwell. He flips on the light, and I shrink back into the shadows, hoping to meld with them and go unnoticed as he studies the steps. My heart tries to jump into my throat and break free of its prison as it beats, warning me that I am about to be caught, and that I was a fool to think that I could sneak out at night.

"Master Arbiter!" Renal steps out of the shadows and stalks up to Molers with that commanding presence of his, and I shrink into the shadows even more. "It's lights out."

"Lieutenant," growls Molers, and I know he is still angry from the time Renal prevented him from choking me to death.

"Explain yourself," commands Renal.

"I do not answer to you."

"You are not on night rotation, while I am."

"If I were a commander, you would not be speaking to me in such a manner," Molers threatens.

"There is a reason why you are not one. Now answer me"— Renal closes the distance between him and Molers, forcing Molers to take a step back—"why are you still up?"

"I thought I heard a noise."

"Let's go."

Molers gives Renal a quizzical look.

"If you heard something and an arbiter is out of bed after hours, then we should find out. So, go. See what your noise was."

I slink away, delving further into the shadows, wondering if I will be able to make it to my room before Molers reaches the top step.

Renal snatches Molers' arm as he starts up the stairs.

"And you better pray that there is another arbiter out of bed up there, or it will be the worse for you."

Molers steps back down to the bottom.

"You will not be protected by Commander Vye forever," he says.

Renal grins, a secretive grin, the sort where the person smiling at you knows something that you do not, and they relish that fact and look forward to the day they can explain it to you, and Molers shrinks away, realizing his mistake.

"You are free to challenge me anytime."

Molers remains silent.

"Since you are having trouble sleeping," Renal begins, "I suggest tiring out those muscles of yours. There was a sewage leakage in the back earlier today. Clean it up."

Incensed, but knowing better than to push Renal, Molers salutes him and stalks away.

"And if any harm comes to that plebeian out there, I'll give you tenfold what he receives," Renal says, forcing Molers to pause for a moment before disappearing.

I push myself against the grainy wall, trying to control my heart-rate as Renal cranes his neck, looking up the stairs for anything out of place before shutting off the light and leaving me alone in the darkness with my worries.

Chase!

When Commander Vye and I returned to the manor, an arbiter informed her of a sewage leak that had sprung, and she sent Chase to clean it up and fix it. He's been out there all afternoon and now will be out there all night with Molers. What if Molers harms him? I start to think of how I can help him when my mind reminds me of my real purpose for sneaking out tonight. I have to help those from the crematoriums, the ones I promised to help. Chase will be fine, I remind myself. Renal did just threaten Molers if any harm comes to him. But why would Renal concern himself with the well-being of a plebeian?

Such questions will have to wait. Valuable time has been wasted due to Molers' nosiness. I hurry down the stairs, jumping over the fourth step from the top, and dash around the corner, heading for the door that goes to the plebeian quarters. Musty light illuminates the cracked door, causing my skin to glow a pale yellow as I reach it. Glancing around to make sure no one watches me, I open the door, slipping inside, shutting it behind me and sealing myself in the murky darkness beyond. I creep down the stairs to the bottom where two cobweb-coated lights spread their weak beam on the floor. A hand touches me when I reach the bottom step, and I almost jump before remembering that it is Sheila. Somehow, she knew what I was planning when I returned to the manor today and refused to take no for an answer. Now, more than ever, I am glad she is here because she gives me the strength to continue in my mission, even though it should be me encouraging her.

"You're late," she whispers.

"There was a delay," I say. "Is…"

"They're all asleep," she replies, referring to the other plebeians down here, and I hear faint snores coming from the rooms.

"Is it all clear?" I ask.

"Yes," she replies. "No one is outside. You should be safe until you get to the fence."

I give her a hug, knowing how much she risks.

"Thank you."

She smiles at me.

I start down the corridor, but Sheila hangs onto my hand, pulling me back. "Here." She places a wristband in my hand.

"Where…"

"It's Amal's," she replies. "I saw the way he was staring at you earlier and you can't get caught without one."

Something clicks in my mind as I realize what she planned, and I scold myself for not thinking of it earlier, but Sheila has. We are tracked by our wristbands, and if I wear Amal's into the city at night, it will make any who bother to check his whereabouts think that he is the one sneaking around the city, while mine is tucked underneath my mattress.

"You clever little thief," I whisper, proud of her and of how she has already, even for someone so young, thought about a way to save me should anyone want to scan my wristband and know where I have been. "How did you…"

"He tends to leave it in the showers."

"I'll be back before sunrise. Meet me in my room, if you can, but only if it's safe."

She nods.

I give her one last hug and send her off to bed, wishing that there was a way to keep her out of all this, but I know that I can't.

Once Sheila has disappeared into her room, I hurry down the musty corridor, almost choking on the moist air that fills every crevice and the odor of rotted wood, coated in mold, heading for the window that Chase had shown me the night we both had snuck out.

I lift myself up and force my way through the tight space, wincing as the ends of exposed nails tear into my skin just enough to leave a burning sting. Once through, I crouch behind some bushes, listening to the night and its silence, except for the soft scrape of a shovel scooping up the mess left by the sewage leak. I have to time this just right. As I peek around the branches and watch Molers and Chase shovel up sewage, neither looking at the other as the atmosphere around them intensifies, I position my feet underneath me, ready to spring into action as I watch, and wait for the right moment. They both bend low, turning their backs to me, to scoop up more of the mess. I burst from the bushes and sprint across the moist grass to the fence that surrounds the manor and its iron bars imprisoning me, and shift the loose bar so that I can squeeze through, disappearing behind it and into the cloak of night just as Molers straightens up.

My heart pounds in my chest, threatening to burst free as my anxiety increases, as the knowledge of what will happen to me should I be caught fills my mind. I shove it aside. I cannot allow it to weaken my resolve or force me to abandon those people from the crematorium. They depend on me. I hurry across the damp street, my soft footfalls releasing faint echoes behind me, and to the nearest alleyway, darting down it before turning a corner down another alley that leads to the main plaza. The hum of the walkways greet my ears as I near the main plaza and its haunting emptiness as ghoulish shadows stretch across it, broken only by the arbiters on duty. Their rhythmic footsteps click on the pavement in tune to their methodical pacing as they wander the area, searching for any violators. I spot the barrels on the other side of the plaza, but an arbiter paces near them. Theses is no way for me to get to them without being seen, unless…

Steam whistles from a nearby pipe stretching up the side of one of the ramshackle buildings next to me. On closer inspection, I can see the rusted metal, having corroded from the constant dampness in the air, passage of time, and lack of repairs. With a little pressure, I can break it, giving myself the distraction I need to coerce the arbiter to leave his position by the barrels. I grip the pipe—my hands make squishing sounds as droplets of water squeeze their way out from between my skin and the metal, mixed with my sweat—and pull, grimacing as a screeching noise echoes around me, causing a rat to scurry away. I have only seconds. Once the pipe breaks and steam shoots out of it, howling its fury at me, I dart away, around a corner, and duck behind a pile of crates overflowing with rotted vegetable scraps and waste.

The arbiter's gaze jerks in my direction, focusing on the pipe, and he hurries over to it, crossing the plaza in five steps, rushing down the alley and to the pipe I had forced free of its hold, bending low to examine it. I seize my chance. Sprinting from my hiding spot, I cross the plaza, hoping that no other arbiter spots me, and reach the barrels, taking a quick glance behind me to make sure that the one arbiter I had spotted still busied himself with my handiwork. His back is to me still. Good.

I lift the top off one of the barrels, hoping that the crematorium escapees are there and that this is not a trap. As I remove the lid, frightened eyes stare back at me, blinking away the dust I have stirred, and I breathe a sigh of relief. I motion for the woman inside to come out. While the arbiter remains occupied, I pop the top off the other barrel, revealing another of the escapees, and he hurries out of the cramped space, relieved to be freed from it. They help me open the other barrels and release those hiding inside. I motion for them to follow me. As I search for the best way to leave, I spot the arbiter, staring right at us. We've been noticed.

"Go!" I yell at the escapees, and shove them around another corner, down another alleyway, but it is blocked, ending in a dead end.

Shit!

The arbiter calls for help, and we only have minutes before more arrive, if not less, and he stands between us and possible freedom. I snatch the scarf one of the escapees wears and tie it around my face so that only my eyes are visible, and jump out from behind the corner just as the arbiter reaches us, tackling him. We slam into the wall of the building next to us, and he grunts as the wind is knocked out of him, but I am not fast enough to block his swing at me. His fists collides with my cheek, dazing me, but before he can swing again, I duck out of the way, and ram the point of my elbow into his jaw.

He snatches my hair, yanking me backward, and as his other arm wraps around me, I seize it, bringing it toward me as I throw my body forward and fling him over me. He crashes into the pavement, but kicks me in the stomach before I can subdue him. Forced to gasp for air, I never notice the knife until it slashes me across the right side of my abdomen, burning as it slices into me, and as the pain grips me, I shove it aside, focusing on my opponent. The glint of his knife flashes before me as he brings it toward me again, but I catch it and force his hand back until his wrist breaks, while ramming my foot into the back of his knee, knocking him to the ground. I grab the knife out of his hand, and in one swift motion, shove it into his chest, while placing my hand over his mouth and nose, so that he cannot take a final breath.

Frozen, I stare at the body of my fellow arbiter, dead by my hands, and for what? Because I wanted to be a hero? To save people I don't even know? The knife is still in my blood-soaked hand. I throw it down the alley, away from me, not wanting to be a part of this terribleness any longer, wishing that this was all a dream, but it's not, and now I must make a choice. Eyes stare back at me, wondering what my next move will be as footsteps approach. One life or many: that was my choice. I know I must go, that I must get these people out of here, or we will all be put to death, so I steel myself, locking away my emotions, exhibiting the unfeeling nature that all arbiters are expected to possess.

"Let's go," I tell the eyes staring at me as blood soaks my shirt.

They scurry out into the open, and I lead them into the plaza, hugging the sides, and darting from one edge of a building to another, until we reach another alleyway, and I motion for them to go down it. They move fast, with me in the lead, setting the pace, clutching my wound and breathing hard as fatigue threatens to overtake me. I'm bleeding more than I would like, and don't know how much time I have until my body quits. Amal's wristband lights up. The alarm has been sounded. The body has been found. I hurry down the alleyway, jumping over discarded shoes and mop handles, with my charges right behind me, until we run into a fence. Motioning for them to jump over it, I hold my hands out, helping the weaker ones, before hopping the fence myself, but as I do, the world spins, and I crash into the ground, landing on my side, as burning needles spread from my wound and sweep over my whole torso. Grime-coated hands grab me, helping me to my feet, and for the first time, I notice the concern of the ones I chose to help, but not the sort of concern one has when their life is in danger and they fear its end; this concern was for me, for my life.

"Come on," I say to them as I haul myself to my feet, swaying from the exertion.

We cannot go to the wall, but there is one place we can go to, if he'll help us.

Shouts and whistles echo around us as we navigate our way through the maze of alleys, and the buildings surrounding us remain dark, as the occupants prefer pretending that they hear nothing, rather than risk their own well-being to satisfy their curiosity. After a few more turns, we reach the narrow pathway that leads toward Luther's. Pressing myself against the rough brick of the building, I step sideways, feeling the air being whisked away as my inevitable doom encloses in on me, suffocating me. One by one, we ease our way through the narrow space between towering buildings, and I flinch as my shirt catches on the porous brick, snagging it and twisting it around me, while I try to put pressure on my wound as blood squirts between my fingers.

Almost there. Just a few more steps. My chest heaves as my breathing quickens, and I feel as though I might pass out, but I mustn't—I need to remain conscious, or these people will be caught. I pop out from the narrow space between the buildings and find myself facing the familiar fork that led me to Luther's that night Chase and I had snuck out. Once the others have freed themselves from the claustrophobic-inducing space, I urge them to follow me down the left side of the fork until we reach the dead end. For a moment, I pause, taking in the steps leading to Luther's and the door shrouded in darkness, remarking at how it has remained unchanged, but now isn't the time for musings. Before any of them can ask me where to go next, I rip the scarf from around my face and knock on the door, not too loud, so as not to attract unwanted attention, but loud enough to wake him up. No one stirs. No lights turn on. I knock again, more forceful, but still trying to be quiet. Worry seizes me as the belief that I have just led us all to our end, or another trap, controls my mind, but before I can act on it, or allow it to control me, the latch on the door pops and it opens, allowing a pair of brown eyes to peek out at me, and the moment I see them, I recognize the sharp mind behind them, and my shoulders sag in relief.

"We need your help," I whisper, still clutching my wound.

Luther takes one look at my bleeding abdomen and the people huddled around me and waves us inside, closing the door in silence, refusing to allow the night's self-proclaimed guardians to enter.

Luther takes my arm and leads me to a table with a single lamp on it and overflowing with contraband books, one of which lay open to a page with the words "The Rights of Man" on the top in fancy script that I had not seen before. I grimace as I sit down and a burning, stinging pain grips my knife wound and more blood soaks into my shirt. It's not deep, but it bleeds as though it is.

"Shut the drapes," Luther tells the others, "and make sure that they are sealed tight."

Within moments, all the windows are closed off, refusing to allow even the most prying of eyes a glimpse into the secrets within this home. Luther turns on the lamp, allowing its weak, yellow light to create a small dome around us at the table as he places some bandages, antibiotic ointment, a bowl of water, and a towel on its nicked surface. A part of me wonders whom he had paid to get the ointment and bandages, as they are also considered contraband; Arel didn't want her people to be too independent, otherwise they might get ideas. I lift my shirt up, not caring if the others see my naked body—it's not as though no one has seen it, since privacy is a foreign notion among arbiters—and dip the towel in the bowl of water before dabbing it on my wound to wipe away the blood. As I examine it in the faint light, I can see that it isn't too deep, but will require stitches.

"Seems like you got yourself into a bit of trouble," comments Luther.

I glare at him. Nothing like stating the obvious. It doesn't take a genius to figure out that I have gotten myself into a situation that I no longer know how to control.

"Do you have any thread and a needle?"

Without a word, Luther goes to a drawer in the room and pulls out a spool of thread and a small, wooden box with a floral design etched into it and places them on the table in front of me. Before he shuts the drawer, I manage to catch a glimpse of a scrap of blue paisley fabric and a pin cushion and wonder if that had been something used by his wife before she died. I grab the box and open it, revealing needles, and thread one, knowing full well that what comes next is going to be a bitch. Stitch by stitch, I push the needle through my skin, gritting my teeth each time the needle pierces me and droplets of blood coat my fingers, making them slippery.

"They taught you well at that training facility," mutters Luther. "Not even one utterance of discomfort leaves your mouth as you stab yourself with that needle."

My eyes meet his, and I watch him as he studies me as though I am a spectacle meant to be observed and not a human being, but as I also study his face, I remember that he has a reason not to trust arbiters and to view them as specimens, fighting machines that possess no humanity, only the skills to subdue a riotous population, and a fighting force meant to carry out orders, not question them: only one fate awaits those who start to wonder if such a life is worthwhile.

"Back at the training facility," I begin, not knowing why I tell them this, "we are taught to ignore pain. Before we are five, our instructors swat our hands with a metal pipe until we no longer flinch or utter a sound. If you cry, you are considered weak. Weakness is…"

"…failure, and failure is death," Luther finishes in a drawn-out tone. "They cannot stay here." He glances at the people surrounding us, wondering what is to become of them.

"I know," I whisper as I finish the last stich and tie off the thread. It looks like a mess, as though an untrained hand tried to stitch themselves up, and… well… it's true. But it will have to do. As I try to find the right words to ask for help from a man I do not know well, but trust more than anyone else at this moment, I place some ointment on my wound with its zigzag stich job and cover it with a clean bandage. "I need to get them out."

"No one leaves Arel," says Luther.

"You know that's not true."

"Well, it seems that you have cut off your only way out."

I don't have time for these games. Leaning on the table so that I can look into his eyes, I keep my voice low so that the others cannot hear me.

"Something tells me that you know another way out of the city."

"An act that is met with one end," says Luther.

Before I can think of what to say, I notice a flask for the first time and the aroma of alcohol, and a picture of a young woman, vibrant, full of life, and unafraid. Luther hadn't been asleep like I had first thought; he had been up, reminiscing, remembering when his daughter had been alive, before she had been taken to the crematorium to be burned as though she were trash whose only value was that as fuel for a never-ending fire.

"If you want to honor her memory," I say, pointing at the photograph, "help us."

"Don't you—"

"What was she arrested for?" I challenge him. "You know full well she was doing exactly what I am trying to do now. You have a chance to carry on her work, or you can sit here wallowing in your own grief and self-pity, shaming her and her memory." I stop myself, wondering where this emotion comes from, where these words are coming from. I have never acted like this before. What has changed?

He cocks his head to the side as though seeing me for the first time.

"The fierceness is still there," he muses. "The unwillingness to give into fear is still there, but so is something else. Some sort of conviction that you don't even realize has already settled in the small semblance of a soul you have managed to maintain, despite their attempts to beat it out of you." He leans in closer, until his freckled nose almost touches mine, as his eyes pry into the depths of my mind, of my innermost thoughts, the secrets I hide, but he finds them, finds where they are buried, and I cannot tear myself away from him as I find myself hypnotized by his unwavering gaze.

"Ah, yes, the killer is still there, but tempered with mercy. What happened to you, to make you go against your programming?"

"I was at the crematorium today," I reply. There is no point in lying to him.

"As a warning, I'm sure." He sits back in his chair. "And despite that warning, you have decided to smuggle them out."

For a moment, I think it strange to be talking about these people as though they are not here, but my mind reminds me that I have always talked about others as though they could not hear me, unconcerned about their feelings. They know that our lives are in Luther's hands right now, and at any moment, he or I could turn them in. For all they know, this could be an elaborate setup.

I open my mouth to speak, but I have no answer for Luther's unspoken question. I don't know why I am helping them, nor do I know the real reason I helped him earlier when his place was scheduled to be searched. I have no explanation for my actions, except this feeling, deep down that people ought to be allowed to make their own choices in life, instead of being forced into a situation that is not of their choosing, a life of burning the bodies of those who were once alive, but were executed for asking questions… or the life of an arbiter, never allowed to have children, to love or feel loved, or to know happiness.

"And once you get them outside the city," continues Luther, "what then? Their chance of survival is slim. Most likely they will be killed by the barbarians within a day."

"Not all barbarians are evil," I say, remembering the one who had helped Chase and me when we were lost in the wildlands. He could have killed us, but chose to save us instead, and I never thanked him. Will I see him again?

Luther studies me as I ponder that moment, allowing that memory to fill me, and wonder what happened to the one barbarian that prevented Chase from falling to his death, and a part of me wonders if he can read my thoughts.

"It does not bother you that they might die out there?"

"They will be killed if they stay here," I say, my voice firm. I glance at the desperate and frightened eyes watching us, too afraid to speak. "If people wish to leave Arel and take their chances in the wildlands, that is their choice to make. Who am I to stop them?"

A smile creeps across Luther's lips, as though he is pleased with himself, and I wish I could read him as well as he seems to be able to read me.

"You've just passed your first lesson."

Lesson? What lesson? Was this whole conversation nothing more than a test? I am sick to death of tests. I am tired of always having my loyalty and my convictions questioned. Once again, I open my mouth to say something to him, but he raises his hand and silences me as he stands and stalks over to a cabinet, pulling out a paper map, and places it on the table in front of me. Intrigued, I stare at it, having not seen one in a long time. Arel does not use paper maps. Everything is on a tablet or holographic. The very thought of using paper seems foreign and archaic. The last time I saw a paper map was when I had snuck into Mandi's office one night.

It was my tenth year, and I had been looking for snacks, having been forced to skip dinner, a punishment for one of my many indiscretions. Knowing that some of the instructors at the training facility stored extra treats in their offices—something that is forbidden, but they do it anyway—I had snuck into hers, hoping to find something I could eat, that would stop the incessant growling of my stomach.

Upon opening the bottom drawer of her desk, I found a strange piece of paper, folded up with care, and my curiosity forced me to forget about the meal I had missed. I had just pulled it out and unfolded it, recognizing it as a map, when Mandi walked in and caught me, causing me to drop the map and step back in fear, expecting to be punished for snooping, but she never said a word, never raised her voice. Instead, Mandi took the map, folded it, and placed it back in its drawer, before walking to a bookcase, where she pulled out a couple of books, revealing an apple. She had handed it to me and sent me along my way. I remember hurrying back to my room, eating the apple as I went and disposing of the core in one of the trash chutes, relieved that she had spared me from more punishment. I never spoke of the incident to anyone, and had forgotten about it, until now.

Luther stretches the map before me, placing the lamp in its center.

"There are some abandoned tunnels that run underneath Arel. They are abandoned sewers, and some serve as drains during the rainy season. Few know about them."

"How many?"

"Huh?"

"How many know about them?" I ask again.

"Four," replies Luther. "Two are dead. One is on the council. And you are talking with the fourth." He places a finger on the map, tracing a line. "There is a tunnel that runs through here. You can access it at the western side of the supply store. It is hidden, so you should be safe from prying eyes. The tunnel will take you outside the wall. After that, you are on your own."

"Where outside the wall, and how far?" I ask.

"There is only one way to find out," replies Luther.

I study the map, memorizing the path that Luther has shown me. He hands me the map, but I wave it away. At the training facility, recruits were expected to memorize any layout they were shown, any bit of weaponry, or any bit of instruction upon the first introduction to it. Failure to do so…

"You best get going," says Luther. "The sun will be up soon."

He's right. I've wasted too much time here. The arbiters chasing us should have given up by now. They will report the incident, but not that they lost us, because that would be a poor reflection upon them. Instead, they will make up some story about how it was a false alarm, or will pull people from their homes, saying that they were the perpetrators. A part of me feels terrible about the innocent who will suffer tonight because of me, but what can I do? My choices are to save the ones I have here with me, whom I promised to help, or turn them, Luther, and myself in, to spare a few from being accused of a crime they never committed. Damned if I do, and damned if I don't.

But I have made my choice.

I turn to the people with me. "Let's go," I say to them, and go to the door, hoping that I can uphold my promise and get back to the manor before sunrise.

We hurry outside, making as little noise as possible, for fear of arousing suspicion and attracting unwanted attention. We only have one chance to get this right. Failure means certain death. Once outside in the cool, night air, Luther locks the door behind us, leaving us to our fate, and the mercy of the darkness.

"This way," I say, heading back the way we came. I know a shortcut to the supply store; I just hope that the arbiters on duty do not know of it as well. We follow the cramped alley that leads to Luther's back to its beginning, but before reaching it, I dive down a small space between two buildings, pressing my back against one as I step sideways, exhaling more than breathing in in an attempt to squeeze my way through as bits of crumbling brick fall downward, pelting me on the top of my head before rolling down my shoulders and arms, their clacks causing me to cringe as the slightest sound seems louder than a mortar shell detonating. Craning my neck, I look back at the people with me, watching them struggle as they scoot sideways, trying not to become stuck between two dilapidated buildings that could very well become their grave. Focus, I tell myself, and continue easing my way to the other side, ignoring the snags on my shirt and hoping that the threads do not get pulled out.

We reach the end, and each of us suck in a lungful of air, glad to be out of the cramped and suffocating space that I had pushed us through. Checking my bearings, I realize that we are not far from the supply shack, and I motion for them to follow after me. Within seconds, one of them steps in a puddle, forcing me to whip around and glare at him, reprimanding him with my cold stare, as the sound of splashing water echoes around us and mingles with the hum of a drone. I push them into the shadows once more as the drone draws closer, hoping that it doesn't notice it and that it will hover past, but it stops next to us, floating in the air as its sensors work overtime to try and determine what had drawn its attention in the first place.

Pounding thuds in my ears as my heart beats against my chest and I gulp back air, willing the drone to conclude that nothing is here. Just when I think that we are done for, it flies away, but we haven't time to be relieved. I hurry down the alley before darting down another, looking back every so often to make sure that my charges are with me. We're almost there. Just a little bit farther.

I stop.

The supply store is across the street. Peeking around the corner, I search for any signs that an arbiter is nearby, but see nothing, though there is the chance that a couple of them are hiding out of sight just waiting for someone to make the mistake of being out after curfew, but we have to risk it. There is no turning back now. I dart across the street with them behind me and we all hunker by the side of the of the supply store, listening for any indication that our presence has been noticed, that our indiscretion has been realized.

Nothing.

Taking it as a good omen, I search around the supply store, looking for the entrance to the tunnel that Luther had shown me, growing more frustrated by the second as I find nothing. Could he have lied to me? Did he send me on a fool's errand to save himself? Will arbiters show up at any moment to arrest us? Scolding myself for allowing my mind to consider one dire scenario after another— if Luther had wanted to betray me, he could have done it at any moment before now—I tap my foot against the pavement, using the heal of my boot to listen for any difference in the thumping, and stop when a hollow sound reaches my ears. Tucked away in a little nook on the exterior of the supply store is a manhole cover, covered over by debris and garbage, thought of as little more than an abandoned metal plaque, and treated as nothing more than an afterthought. I try to pry it up, but it refuses to budge, having not been opened in so long. It has rusted shut.

"Help me" I whisper to the others.

They each bend low and pick up an edge of the cover, and together, we force it loose—bits of copper rust break free, being carted away by the breeze—and scoot the cover over, until the opening beneath it is revealed. The hollow darkness below unnerves me, but I spot the faint glint of light against what must be the rung of a ladder, and all I can do is hope that it is still intact enough for us to use it. I motion for them to enter the tunnel, and they do so without complaint, as I keep watch for signs of danger and move some of the garbage in front of the opening in an effort to disguise its presence. Once they have each disappeared below ground, it is my turn to venture into the unknown.

I place my right foot on the top rung, jerking it back as it slips on the grime that has coated it due to neglect and lack of use; I steel my nerves, knowing that I must make this descent, and I place my foot on it again, shifting it, until it feels firm below me. I place my other foot on the next rung of the ladder and lower myself into the hole, delving into the darkness, as though I am a miner searching for treasure, and continue feeling my way downward, as grime coats my hands, causing me to grip the ladder even tighter, and relief floods through me when I reach the bottom and the familiar sound of my boots hitting a hard surface reaches my ears, but the moment is short-lived as the musty air strangles my lungs, forcing me to cough, until I become used to it.

Enveloped in darkness' shroud, I call the map that Luther had shown me earlier to my mind, envisioning it, remembering it and what direction we need to go in. I just hope I can navigate in pitch blackness. My anxiety builds, threatening to overtake me and turn me into a frightened child that is too scared to leave his place of hiding, even if it means certain death, but I cannot give in to the carnal nature of humanity, because if I do, we all die, and I will have broken my promise.

"Follow me," I whisper, keeping my voice low, but the steel walls of the tunnel reverberate my words and they grow by the second as they echo down the empty expanse before us.

As I feel my way through the darkness, slime coats my fingers, making them about as useful as a wet bar of soap that refuses to remain in your grip, and my hand slips off the wall, causing me to lose my balance and stumble in the mucky sludge that coats the tunnel floor, and I cringe as bits of it drip down the inside of my boots. Refusing to give up, I straighten myself as best I can, though the top of my head smacks the tunnel ceiling, forcing me to hunch over, and make my way through its mysterious forebodings, looking back every so often.

Sometimes, I think I can make out the faint outline of people behind me, but it is so dark, that I cannot be sure if it isn't just a product of my imagination. Step by step, we trudge through the stagnant mixture of mud, water, and waste as it tries to hold onto our feet and prevent us from moving onward, but we mustn't let it succeed. The further we go, the gnawing feeling that we will never reach the end of this tunnel tears at me as precious seconds tick by, and I start to panic, to think that I have made a mistake and gone in the wrong direction, dooming us all, until my nose detects a change in the air. The musty odor that has plagued me since I entered this tomb, changes as a small hint of freshness lingers within it, beckoning us forward, telling me that we are close. My pace quickens, as hope washes over me. We have to be close; I just hope that we are far enough beyond the wall that we are not spotted by the arbiters guarding it.

Something smacks me in the face, bringing me to a halt as I regain my senses and feel around, trying to determine what has stopped me, but the cold feeling of steel, despite the grime crusted on it, tells me that I have reached a ladder. This is the moment of truth. There is no going back. I climb the ladder, clinging to it as though it is my life saver, and ascend through the dark opening above me, until my head bangs into a metal barrier, causing bits of dirt to fall away and splash in the water below. This must be the way out. I push against it, but just like I had feared, it refuses to budge, except there is no way for another person to squeeze in here to help me open it, meaning I will have to do it myself. Feeling the eyes of my charges on me, waiting for me to give them their freedom, I climb higher on the ladder, until I am on the second to last step and hunched so far over that my knees touch my chest.

I ram my back into the manhole cover. Nothing. I ram myself into it again, hearing a small pop, but it still refuses to allow us passage. The feeling of claustrophobia threatens to overtake me as I remain hunched in this cramped space with sweat pouring down my chin and dripping onto my shirt, while my breathing quickens from the fear of failing settling in. Memories of the woman I had tried to help escape Arel course through my mind, and for a moment, I am back there, clutching her mangled body in the middle of a minefield, while the dogs' incessant barking warn me that I will be their next meal as punishment for my failure. Guilt grips my shoulders as I remember how I had led her to her death in my efforts to help her, and how I was responsible for her fate, but it doesn't have to be the same outcome here.

Right here, right now, I can make certain that the people with me have their chance at a better life. What they do afterward, is up to them, but I will not let them die here in this sewer full of waste, as though they are refuse themselves, not wanted, never missed, and deemed unworthy of a chance at life. Summoning all my strength, I push hard with my legs and slam my back into the metal barrier above me, ignoring the pain that seizes it and the marks it will leave, and push with every ounce of strength I have, until it moves. I refuse to stop, refuse to slacken my efforts, but push even harder as cool air slips between the cracks and dust rains down around me, coating my sweaty face, but I do not care. I cannot stop. I cannot quit. With another great push, I throw myself into the manhole cover, and it pops free, releasing a tremendous clang as it flies upward and lands on the ground, teetering on the edge of the opening, but I straighten up and push it to the side, glad to be free of the imprisoning darkness of the tunnel.

I glance around, overjoyed at seeing the tall grass around me, obscuring my view of the wall, meaning that those on it will be hard pressed to see my bit of rebellion, and the trees are not far. Laughter begins to emanate from me, but I stop myself, reminding myself that this is not the time. Hauling myself out of the opening, I lean over on my hands and knees, urging them to hurry up as a faint glow appears on the horizon, warning me that my time is short. One by one, I help them out of the darkness, and watch as they snake through the grass and into the jungle of trees beside us. No words pass between us. There is no time, nor is there any need. I watch as they disappear, wondering what will become of them, where they will go, and remember that none of us ever know what the future holds, but we can decide what happens in the present.

The glow on the horizon grows brighter, reminding me that I must get back to the manor before the sun is up. I jump into the hole, and pull the manhole cover over it, sealing it once more, as I bury myself in the darkness, but it doesn't seem so oppressive anymore, as thoughts and half-plans work their way through my mind, giving me ideas, ideas that Arel tries to trample into submission.

I hurry through the streets, not caring if I run into arbiters on duty. I haven't time to worry about it, or to be cautious. If I fail to get back into the manor by sunrise, my time on this earth will come to a close. Punishment is always swift in Arel, and dissonance is never tolerated. Windows remain shuttered, and the streets empty, with only the echo of silence for comfort, as I turn down street after street making my way to the manor. Almost there. I turn another corner and come out on the street leading to the manor, and the memory of me riding on the back of a trolley in an effort to not be late on my first day in the eastern sector rushes into my mind, but I shunt it aside.

The sun pokes over the horizon as I crawl through the fence, doing my best not to tear my clothing on the loose bar that I have moved to the side so that I can squeeze through. The thudding of shovels delving into sludge hits my ears, telling me that Chase and Molers are still cleaning up the sewage that has leaked and covered the atrium. Once through the fence, I place the bar back in place, hoping that its indiscretion continues to go unnoticed, and dart across the lawn, using the long shadows of the building as they try to preserve what twilight is left, before the sun has a chance to rip it away from them.

Before I reach the shelter of the thorny branches of a coveted bush, Chase spots me, and our eyes lock for a moment, but Molers must have seen the sudden change in his gaze because he turns in my direction, but before he spots me, Chase scoops up a handful of sewage and chucks it into Molers' face. Enraged, Molers rounds on him, closing the distance between them in two steps, swinging his fists, and knocking Chase to the ground. I stop. My heart aches as Chase plows into the sewage and it covers him, coating his clothing, making him look like some sort of mud creature, as he tries to regain his footing, but Molers leers over him, bending low and placing his knee in the middle of Chase's back. My feet shift and take a step toward him, but the harsh hiss from Sheila as she holds the basement window open—she must have stayed up waiting for me, watching for me, and noticed me standing frozen in the middle of the grass, unable to tear my eyes away from Chase's plight—and Chase shaking his head, like he did at the mines when the guards jumped him, force me to stop, breaking my heart into two as I struggle between the two paths placed before me.

A blur of movement catches my attention, sparing me from making a choice I could never live with, as Renal rushes out of the manor and grips Molers by the shoulders before throwing him onto the ground. The fury on Molers' face chills me. I have seen it before, too many times. He looks in my direction, but before he has time to register that it is me out after curfew, Renal rams his fist into Molers' face, blocking me from view, and I sprint into the bushes and crawl through the window while Renal's back still faces me, and before Molers can recover. Before I close the window, I glance back at the Renal as he towers over Molers, daring him to challenge him, to question his authority, and once again, I wonder if Renal is a marshal, sent here to ensure that the eastern sector remains in line and adheres to Arel's authority. I imagine the glare on Renal's face as he waits for Molers to make a move; it's a look I've seen once before when he stopped Molers from killing me the day I interfered when Molers struck Sheila. I continue watching the scene unfold before me, unable to tear my gaze away.

"You're dismissed," Renal says to Chase, without taking his eyes off Molers.

Chase scrambles to his feet and runs inside, glad to be away from the test of authority between two high-ranking arbiters.

"I gave you strict orders," Renal says to Molers as he kicks the shovel to him, daring him to do something, but Molers remains on the ground. "Since you seem to have all this extra time on your hands, you can finish up here."

Molers picks up the shovel and stands up, as the sun peeks over the building, illuminating the two as they stand in a mixture of sewage and grass. He always searched for a chance to flaunt his authority over others, but never challenged anyone when the odds were not in his favor, and right here, right now, they have abandoned him, and he knows it. The shovel strikes the ground as Molers scoops up creamy, black, sludge and dumps it in a wheelbarrow, but his face tells me that he will have his revenge. Renal notices it as well. He leans into Molers, so that no one can hear what he is about to say, and whispers into Molers' ear before stalking away.

As golden sunlight spills across the grass, I am reminded that my time is up. I need to get back to my room, and fast. Sheila smacks my arm, holding her slender, pale hand out, waiting for me to give her Amal's wristband. I do. I start to say something, to thank her for her bravery, but she stops me.

"I'll be fine."

After a quick hug, I race down the musty hallway of the cellar and up the stairs, not caring if I make noise, since I haven't much time to get back into my quarters before the other arbiters wake up and leave their rooms, while those returning from duty walk through the front door. Pipes bang as water turns on in the bathrooms, and I quicken my pace, hurrying through the door to the main floor, and taking a quick peek to make sure that no one spots me as I rush to the stairs leading to the second floor. I take them two at a time, my heart beating against my chest from the exertion and the anxiety that surrounds me, threatening to suffocate me in an effort to make me fail.

A door opens as I reach the top of the stairs and I duck back behind the wall, before the woman leaving her room can spot me. She rubs her eyes and drags herself to the bathroom, while her night shirt hangs off her shoulder, exposing the top part of her right breast, without bothering to stifle a yawn. Her grogginess plays in my favor. Once she disappears, I race for my door and do not wait for it to open all the way before ramming my way through and letting out the air that has been trapped in my lungs since Molers' confrontation with Renal. Safe in the confines of my room, I slump against the door as the sun fills my window, allowing me to view the wall that surrounds Arel, and my thoughts drift to the people I helped escape. What will become of them? I will never see them again, or know their fate, but I hope they find the peace they are looking for.

As the sun rises higher, a red-orange glow stretches across the top of the wall, lasting only for a split second, before it disappears, but it catches my gaze, and I stare out at it, as though seeing it for the first time, and knowing its true purpose, its true nature. The sun's warm rays fall upon my face as I study my enemy, hardening my resolve to help others escape its imprisonment, and the tyranny of those who built it.

Chapter 20

Discretion

My foot reaches the last carpeted—the brown color of the carpet has turned a darker shade, and it now seems to crunch underneath my weight, giving me a sickened feeling—step of the stairwell, settling on the cracked wooden edge of its surface, before allowing me to step down onto the main floor of the manor so that I may begin my day. My hand still rests on the railing, and the nicks that make up what once had been a smooth and polished surface that reflected the yellow light pouring in from the stained window, and its grimy edges. Lost in the moment, and forgetting where I am because of a lack of sleep, I imagine what this manor must have looked like, brand new and filled with arbiters for the first time; but, perhaps, it has not always been filled with arbiters, but served a different purpose before being reassigned.

I spot Sheila near the kitchen and hurry over to her, hoping that everything is all right, that she isn't in any sort of trouble because of me. None of the other arbiters seem to be paying any attention to me, which is just as well; I prefer to go unnoticed. I slip through the doors to the kitchen with its counters full of baskets of fresh fruit, and the musty smell of dirty dish water fills my nose, glad that the cooks are elsewhere, leaving Sheila and me alone.

"Is everything…" I begin.

"I'm fine." She hands me a plate with buttered toast, crisp apple slices, whose intoxicating smell causes my mouth to salivate, scrambled egg, and cooked ham. I look at the toast and its inviting texture, wondering where she has gotten it, since arbiters are not supposed to eat bread very often, and are denied it on most occasions. She must have read my mind because she laughs, saying, "Molers has toast snuck into to his room most nights. I borrowed some on a permanent basis."

Soft laughter escapes my mouth at her joke. "How did you get so good at sneaking things?" I ask.

Her face falls as unpleasant memories are drudged up, and my laughter dissipates at the somber note in her voice. "I had to, to survive."

"Not anymore," I tell her, placing a gentle hand on her shoulder. She shouldn't have to go to such lengths just to survive.

She smiles.

I take a bite of the toast, and finish it within seconds.

"Thank you."

Two arbiters stroll past the kitchen, and I know I need to get going, or we will be caught and punished, and Sheila's will be more severe than mine. I hug her, doing my best to protect her from this world, but it is insufficient, superficial at best, as we both know that there is little else I can do.

"Stay safe," I tell her.

"Do the same," she replies as I leave the kitchen with my plate of food.

Once in the dining room, I spot Amal, and his gaze is fixed on me, unnerving me, and I wonder how long he has been there, watching the door to the kitchen, waiting to see if I came out with anyone in particular. I stare at him, keeping my posture tall and proud, hoping that he doesn't see through it or the anxiety building within me. Before I have a chance to force myself to walk past him and find a chair at the table, Commander Vye's sharp voice breaks through my fears and snaps me back to attention.

"Noni," she says, causing all murmuring within the room to cease, "a word."

I hurry after her, clutching my plate close so that the food on it will not fall to the ground as my stomach gurgles at me, demanding that I feed it, and shove my way past Amal. Commander Vye and I reach the oval doorway underneath the stairwell, with me shoving the slice of ham in my mouth and swallowing it in two bites as I follow her into her office, noting the line of pens on the left side of the desk that still sit in a neat line, and the stack of reports on the other side seems to have grown. She sits in the chair behind her desk with her hands clasped before her, reminding me of my first day here and the terrible impression I had made, but something seems off; she seems worried, something I have never seen plague her before.

"Your duties for today have been suspended," Commander Vye says, while I finish chewing the apples.

What? Suspended? Has she discovered that I have been sneaking out of the manor at night? Worry that my exploits the night before and the people I smuggled outside of the city fills my mind as it races to come up with a legitimate excuse, or anything to mitigate the impending consequences of my indiscretions.

"Ma'am?" I say, doing my best to keep the inflection out of my voice so as not arouse suspicion.

"An old friend of yours is visiting the eastern sector and she has requested your presence. You are to meet her here." Commander Vye sends the location to me and it pops up on my wristband, and I recognize it as one of the cafés in the plaza.

An old friend? Faya? The last time I saw here was before I had been taken to visit the outposts, before Chase and I were forced to rely on each other for survival after our convoy was attacked. She had mentioned coming to the eastern sector for a visit; perhaps she has finally gotten the time off to come. I have no knowledge of how things are done in the business sector, but the one time I was there, they did not seem to be as strict as the eastern sector, nor do they need to be.

"You will report there immediately," Commander Vye tells me.

I salute her and turn for the door, but she stops me.

"One other thing," Commander Vye says, and her shoulders sag, a motion that would go unnoticed by most, but I notice it, "be careful."

Concern fills her voice, and it unsettles me. I have always known her to be proud and strong, but today, she seems vulnerable, worn, beaten, and I wonder what has been happening behind the scenes, the secrets that no one ever sees. It seems as though it has been ages since I have been in her presence and talked with her, even if it was just her issuing me orders, and my mind wanders back to the conversation between her and Molers that I overheard, before Tapiwa sent me to the mines. I haven't seen Renal much either. So much has happened in such a short period of time, but I feel as though I have aged ten years, and she looks to have aged 20.

"Commander," I say, keeping my voice low, "is everything all right?"

"You've, no doubt, noticed some changes around here."

Some, yes, but I never thought about it too much, until now. There is a different feeling in the air, one of anxiety and tension, so overwhelming that it drowns any who are trapped in it.

"I know the attack outside the tribunal…"

"It's not just that." Commander Vye's eyes flicker to the door, making certain that it is shut, as she lowers her voice even more, forcing me to strain my ears to make out her words. "There has been a series of unrests since you were sent to the mines."

More than one? There has always been a bit of rebellion, but never enough to cause such trepidation within my commander.

"There are rumors of a group of rebels whose sole intention is to bring down Arel and its society."

Sweat forms underneath the collar of my jacket. Sneaking people out of the city is an act of rebellion, and one that could be seen as trying to destroy Arel, and there has been a grumbling in the back of my mind that parts of Arel need to change, though I am always reminded of the cost.

"Sometimes change can be beneficial," I say, choosing my words with care.

Commander Vye raises her eyebrows at me.

"Being sent to the mines required me to change."

"How so?"

"I had to negotiate with others, not in words, but in actions."

"I am aware of your exploits in the mines: how you demanded better treatment for the workers, reprimanded Commandant Gant, and the rebellion that ensued there."

I cannot deny any of that. The entire mine was turned into a graveyard by the Arelian air fleet, and all because of my actions.

"The workers were starved and unable to meet the demands. Treating them better helped production go up. Commandant Gant did what he thought would bring him self-glorification and help him advance up in the ranks, not for the betterment of Arel. The uprising was the result of years of mistreatment by the hands of a man bent on furthering his own ends. I failed to consider that my actions might give them the courage to act upon their sentiments. It's just…"

I should stop myself. I have said too much, but the words spill out of my mouth before I can stop them, betraying me.

"…I am an arbiter, charged with protecting all citizens, and that included the ones at the mine. It turned into something I could not control."

"Most situations do. The world is a messy place, Noni. We have rules for a reason."

"Some of them seem a bit too strict," I mumble, but Commander Vye hears it and raps her fingers on the edge of her desk, stopping me.

Her eyes dart between me and the door before she jumps from her chair and hurries to it, opening it, making certain the hallway is empty. A single click pierces the tension I have caused when the door closes, and Commander Vye rounds on me.

"Expel such thoughts from you mind!"

She grips my shoulders, causing me to tip my plate up and spill the scrambled eggs onto the carpeted floor, and I try to take a step back, to get away from her, as a crazed, but frightened, look covers her face, but she stares right into my eyes, holding me in place with her hawk-like gaze. My reaction forces her to release me and calm herself as she places her hands by her side, straightening her shoulders, standing even more erect and looking like the Commander I know.

"I apologize, commander," I say, hoping that this will quell her sudden rage, but perhaps it wasn't anger at all, but something else.

A grim line settles on her face before she speaks. "There comes a time, Noni, when every arbiter realizes just how uncertain the world is, and they have to make a choice. Each choice has a consequence. Make sure it is one you can live with."

Commander Vye paces the room before going back to the chair behind her desk and settling down in it, while still maintaining her erect posture.

"What happened in the mines is in the past. Lieutenant Renal spoke very highly of you in his report and mentioned how Commandant Gant's rebellion helped lead to the uprising. He also mentioned that you are responsible for rescuing him from such insurrection."

I couldn't have done it without Trevors, but instead of opening my mouth, I ascertain that it is best if I let Commander Vye finish.

"Therefore," she continues, "it is best if you do not speak of it again. Once you have finished your visit, you may take the rest of the day for leisure activities. Just make sure you are back before curfew."

"Yes, commander," I say in a robotic tone.

"And as for the crematoriums, it is best you forget that they happened."

I understand. The aftermath of our actions there have not been felt, at least, not by me. We both overstepped our bounds that day. The council may decide that it is the normal happenings in such a place, as everyone there is considered expendable, or, they may decide that a stricter hand is needed to keep their arbiters in line.

"Understood," I say.

"Dismissed."

I salute her and reach for the door.

"And, Noni," Commander Vye says before I can open the door, "you'd do well to remember that you are not the only one who has changed since leaving the training facility."

I hurry out into the hallway, wondering what caused the entire exchange, but that isn't what bothers me most: her last words to me seem to be more of a warning—her way of protecting me. I spot Chase, hunkered behind a wall cabinet, waiting for me, and I start to head for him, but stop when Molers appears in the corridor. We lock eyes, and as though we are able to read the other's mind, we both turn and leave, going in opposite directions. Chase disappears into another room, while I hurry to the front door, noting how its yellowed glass has darkened even more, and slip outside, glad to be away from the oppressive atmosphere within the manor. I inhale as deep as I can, relishing the feeling of the warm sun on my face as my skin tingles beneath its rays, before heading down the driveway to the street. Faya is waiting for me in the plaza, and I have been ordered to go see her.

Chapter 21

An Old Friend

I reach the plaza in the eastern sector, somewhat comforted by its familiarity, as I step across the broken, discolored bricks that make up the square itself, as people dart back and forth in a hurry to get to where they need to be, afraid of lingering too long and attracting an arbiter's attention. The bell of the trolley echoes around me as it storms past, bouncing down the rails in an effort to get to its destination on time. Schedules must be kept. Someone bumps into me, dropping his bag, and I turn around to find a man scrambling to pick up the spilled cylindrical packages that roll across the blackened bricks, which seem to have been soaked with blood, and upon closer inspection, I can see that they have been—a concept that does not surprise me.

The man looks up at me as his glasses slip down his nose, threatening to fall off, as he reaches for a cylindrical package, more afraid of losing it than of angering me; though his wide eyes remain fixed on me as he waits to see what I will do for his indiscretion. I stare at him, mesmerized by his spectacles. It isn't often that one sees a person wearing glasses in Arel, as they are a sign of physical weakness and discouraged, unless the individual is of some value to the city. Without a word, I pick up one the cylindrical packages, wondering if they are maps or designs for a new building as I study the man's uniform. I hand it to him, and like I have experienced on many occasions, he hesitates to take it, wondering if I am toying with him, or testing him, and as he continues to debate whether he should fall for what he views as bait, I place the package in his bag, noting that the edges show some signs of wear as they start to fray, sending small bits of threads in various directions.

Once his packages have been recovered, I motion for him to go about his business, and he scurries away, thankful to be free of me. I watch him, not with pity or judgement, but with sadness. I do not want people to fear me just because of my uniform, I want them to understand that I am here to help them and protect them from danger, not abuse them, but Arel has made good people fear me.

Once the man has disappeared, I remember my purpose for being in the plaza, and glance around, wondering where Faya is. Perhaps I am early, which would be a minor miracle if it is true.

"Noni!"

No such luck.

I whip around and find Faya sitting at one of the outdoor cafés that we have—though I have never eaten here, having always preferred Sigal's, and finding my mouth lamenting the absence of his miracle entrées—with a man I have never seen before. Glad to see her, (How long has it been?) I rush over to her and we give each other a hug, while a few people passing by us give us a wide berth. Faya takes a seat, while I glance at the man with her.

"This is Joel," she says, with an elated smile on her face, and memories of the last time we had lunch together as she told me all about him come to mind. Coupling among arbiters is not allowed, but it still happens, and as I watch the way she lights up around him, I cannot blame her.

Joel stands up, showcasing his muscular shoulders and tall stature as he reaches out for my hand, and I shake his, putting as much pressure into it as possible, so that he does not think of me as weak.

"Good to meet you," I say to him before taking my seat.

"I've heard a lot about you." His deep, resonating voice tickles me, and I see why Faya is attracted to him: the perfect physique, the deep voice, and a genuine sense of propriety surrounds him; I detect no arrogance—something that plagues most citizens in Arel. Well, no more than usual. Nothing like what Molers displays.

"She has mentioned you as well," I say.

"All good things, I hope." Joel smiles a little, which makes Faya beam even more, and I can tell that she is having trouble not wrapping herself around him, but public appearances must be maintained because no one ever knows when someone will decide that your happiness is undeserved and seek to take it away.

"So," Faya says, "how have you been?"

"Okay," I tell her.

I don't know what to say. I cannot tell her about my excursions at night, nor can I divulge my feelings toward Chase, and how he spared me from a beating, not out of a sense of obligation that a servant has toward his master, but because he did not want me to suffer; and I have been unable to repay him.

"Just okay?" Faya looks at me over the rim of her glass of water with a doubtful expression.

"It's the eastern sector," I say, hoping that it eases her curiosity and stops her from trying to delve too much into my current life.

She rolls her eyes and agrees with me, for which I am pleased.

"I see what you mean," Joel says as he watches a couple of plebeians hurry across the street, jumping two steps back when an arbiter arrives, their ragged clothing trailing behind them in the breeze, with bits of thread falling off. "They definitely gave you a terrible assignment."

"Joel!" Worry crosses Faya's face when he says that, not because she disagrees with him, but because of what might happen if the wrong ears hear him.

"Everyone knows it's true," he defends himself.

Faya gives him a reprimanding expression, mixed with worry.

"I'm sorry," Joel says, placing a gentle hand on hers, but removing it the moment the waiter shows up with three plates, each with a steak, cooked to medium, roasted Brussels sprouts, and some sautéed leafy greens. We hold up our wrists, allowing him to scan our wristbands as he fills our glasses of water, and he gives us a curt nod before hurrying away.

"I didn't realize you guys had ordered already," I say.

"We didn't," Faya replies.

"They must have an arbiter special," Joel quips, and we all chuckle.

Arbiter special is a term used among arbiters to describe a place that only serves one dish to arbiters, instead of giving them a choice. Every eatery knows the dietary restrictions that arbiters have, and the punishment for deviating, not that it ever stopped Sigal, but some would allow us a few choices. This place is one that does not, not that it matters; I am famished and need to eat something.

As I chew on a piece of steak, my thoughts turn to Sheila, Gwen, and Chase. They could use some better nourishment than what plebeians are allowed, and the thought of wrapping my meat up strikes me, but dissipates quicker than it had arrived when I remember that I have company.

"Is something wrong with your food?" asks Faya.

"Wha—no, it's fine," I say. "I was remembering this place I and others went to that always served the best food."

"Anything would taste delicious after that training facility garbage," Faya mutters as a Brussels sprout rolls around in her mouth.

"True," I laugh, "but Sigal had a way of making the most basic food taste like the stuff served in the presidential palace."

"What happened to him?" Joel asks.

"He disappeared and his place has been closed down," I respond as I think back to the night I had helped Sigal and his family escape, even though it meant betraying Renal, a fact that still haunts me, since Renal has done nothing but protect me since I arrived here.

They chewed on their food in silence, knowing what I mean by "disappeared".

"It's probably just as well," Faya says, after taking a swig of her water. "We don't need people like that in Arel. Didn't you tell me once that it was popular among the arbiters here?"

"Yes."

"And none of them spotted anything odd?"

This line of questioning is a side of Faya I have never seen before. When we were at the training facility, she never struck me as someone who would be so callous about a person having been disposed of for going against Arel, and this newfound coldness unnerves me; though, maybe it isn't new; maybe I never noticed it before because I once thought just like her and such a notion fills me with guilt.

"Noni," she says, mistaking my internal conflict for feeling like I had let down all of Arel for not noticing Sigal's crimes, even though I had suspected but never said anything, "you cannot be blamed for what he did. You were new and hadn't been here that long. It is the others who are at fault. They should have known."

I manage a weak smile, but remain silent, fearing that I might give myself away and tell her about the night I hit Renal over the head with my baton before helping Sigal and his family escape Arel.

Faya continues talking, going on about the business district and the demands placed on her there, and how she had to put two economists in their place when they got into a public argument about the proper way in which Arel's economy should be handled, but I'm not listening. As she drones on and on, her voice becomes distant, mired by my own internal thoughts about everything that has happened to me since I had arrived in the eastern sector, as I shove one bite of food after another into my mouth, as though I am little more than a mindless drone, while my gaze remains fixed upon the people walking by, each with their own internal struggles, each with their own fears, and each pretending to be happy… just like me. I watch as a young plebeian girl hurries to a store, her hair covering her face the same way Gwen's covered hers the night I first met her, the night I first met Chase, as he shoved me down a flight of stairs to protect his sister. At the time, anger over my failure to stop two curfew violators had filled me, but now, guilt anguishes me as I think about what would have become of them if I had succeeded in detaining them.

"Noni? Noni!" Faya waves her hand in front of my face, and I realize that I have been holding my fork in the air as bits of sautéed leafy greens fell from it, almost like I am frozen in time. "Are you all right, Noni?"

"I'm sure she's fine," Joel steps in. "Probably just tired of hearing you go on about yourself."

Annoyed, Faya chucks a Brussels sprout at him before relinquishing. "Sorry. I have been dominating the conversation. Tell us about your exploits. About the eastern sector."

"There isn't much to tell." I eat the last of my lunch and place my empty fork back on the plate. "With the constant attacks on the wall, and the rise of terrorist attacks within the city, we are all on edge."

"I've no doubt."

"Is that why you volunteered for the trial of fears?" Faya asks.

I had almost forgotten about that. "No," I reply.

"Then why did you?"

I look at Faya, trying to decide how to form my words, when I settle on, "Molers happened."

"He's here?" says Faya with incredulity, while Joel has a different reaction.

"I'd heard that he had finally managed to get transferred here."

"What do you mean by finally?" I ask him. Everyone at the training facility knew that Molers had wanted a transfer to another sector, but I didn't know that he had been trying to get here all those years.

Joel leans in closer, keeping his voice low. "Word is, he has been vying for a position in the eastern sector for over ten years. I guess he got his wish."

"But why now?" I ask, confused as to why Molers would be allowed the assignment of his dreams, if one could call it that, now of all times.

"The increased unrest within Arel. It is believed that if the eastern sector, the most troublesome sector, can be controlled, it will send a powerful message to the other sectors."

And stop future riots, no doubt, but I don't voice my thoughts.

"And whomever can control the eastern sector will have their pick of assignments in Arel," Faya says. She had told me something similar when I was first assigned here. "But you received the Arelian Medal of Honor," Faya continues, pointing at me. "That would reflect favorably on your commander."

"Except," I say with dismay, "there have been a lot of riots lately, and that bombing would be a black mark on her record." If all our speculations are accurate, this explains not only why Molers is here, but the increased tension between him and Commander Vye. I do not know what Molers' final aspirations are, but, for now, they seem centered upon getting rid of my commander, and somehow, I feel responsible.

"None of this affects you," says Faya.

"It will if Molers is made commander here," I say.

A sly smile creeps across Faya's face as she nudges Joel's arm, and the thought that the two have held a secret from me permeates my brain.

"What's going on?" I ask.

"Tell her," Faya urges Joel.

"We wanted to wait until it is official, but there is the possibility that you won't have to be in this sector for much longer."

"What do you mean?" I ask, confused.

"Joel got that transfer to the executive district and..."

"And," continues Joel, "I have put in a good word for you. Faya told me about what you did for her in the gauntlet, and achieving the honor you did looks very good. Now, don't get your hopes too high. My influence is limited, but I like to think that I have my commander's ear, and it helps that President Tapiwa has taken an interest in you."

He knows about that? Does he also know about my mission to the mines?

My face must have betrayed me, because to assuage my misgivings, Joel says, "Much of what happens at the presidential palace gets gossiped about in the executive district."

My lips do not move. I know I must say something. I have to say something. They expect me to say something, and it would be rude to not show any appreciation for their efforts at helping me move up, but silence settles between us as a familiar shape steals my attention, and I recognize the person on the other side of the plaza, and disgust fills me the moment I do.

Amal. He approaches a girl—who looks to be no more than 11—wearing a blue uniform, the color for the water treatment and sewage departments, and one of the few who are looked upon with as much disdain as plebeians. She walks with a plebeian boy of about the same age, but instead of forcing the plebeian to walk behind her, she allows him to walk beside her. It is not unusual. This happens sometimes among the young, until they are trained to loathe the plebeians as much as Molers does. Amal sneaks up behind the two kids and grabs the plebeian boy by the shoulders, throwing him to the ground, before knocking the tablet out of the girl's hands, causing it to break into three pieces as it hits the pavement.

"Thank you," I say, but my mind is on Amal and his brutish behavior.

I jump from my seat and race across the pavement, knocking people out of my way, while a crowd gathers around Amal to see why he chose to pick on the two children. I knock the hat off one woman, apologizing for my actions, while tripping another by accident, in my efforts to get to Amal before he does irreparable harm.

The crowd around him grows, but a small sliver of space remains, allowing me to watch in horror as he raises his fist and punches the girl in the face. No one stops him. No one says anything. But I am not no one. I ram my way through the crowd, yelling at people to move out of my way. At first, a few challenge me, until they see my uniform and jump out of my way, not wanting to be on the receiving end of my anger. I shove the last of those between me and Amal out of my way, bursting onto the scene just in time to see Amal raise his baton, preparing to bring it down upon the girl in the blue uniform. She watches in fear, as tears stream down her dark face, and the curls from her ebony hair outline her terrified eyes.

My hand seizes Amal's wrist, and I wrench the baton away from him, striking him in the face before swooping down and ramming it into the back of his knees, causing him to fall backward. He glares back at me, cursing me with his eyes as he wishes me harm for stopping him, but I remain firm, towering over him with his baton in my hand, ready to strike him again and daring him to give me a reason, while the crowd backs away, unsure of what to make of this scene as two arbiters challenge each other.

"What is the meaning of this?" I demand, not caring that I am not Amal's superior officer. His attack on the two children is unwarranted, and he did something that even Arel frowns upon: he didn't just reprimand a citizen who is a minor, he intended to kill her without cause and without the authority of the ministry of justice.

"None of your business," spits Amal.

"Statute 72369 clearly states that no citizen is to be detained unless there is proof of a crime having been committed. Statute 72369A states that all minors who are detained are not to be physically harmed, but sent straight to the ministry of justice for detainment. You have violated both statutes."

It may seem odd to be quoting the law in the middle of a square, surrounded by a crowd of citizens and plebeians, but from the moment we can talk, we are taught the law, and expected to recite it word for word. Failure means death. Failure to uphold it means death. What Amal has done can get him sent straight to the crematoriums, and as we glare at one another, the small notion that something isn't right creeps into my mind, but before I let it grow into a full-fledged thought, he charges me.

Amal rams his head into my stomach and forces me onto my back, causing me to grunt as the wind is knocked out of me. He sits up, preparing to strike, but I kick him in the chest, forcing him off me, before jumping to my feet. Amal rises to his full height with murderous intent in his eyes. If he wanted an excuse to try and kill me, I have just given it to him.

He rushes me, and I step back, blocking his left fist with his baton, but as I bring the baton to block his right fist, he snatches it from my grip and punches me in the face with a counter swing. Stunned, I take two steps back as blood trickles from my nose, but I haven't time to regain my senses, as he runs for me, swinging his baton. In one swift action, I jump back, releasing my baton, and the two metal rods clang as they meet in midair. Seconds tick by as the ringing sound of our batons striking one another echoes around us in a morbid melody as we try to harm one another, with me backing up while Amal pushes forward. He feigns a swing, and I fall for it, cursing when he kicks me in the chest, causing me to stumble backward again. Thinking he has won, Amal swings his baton at me again, but I jump over it, somersaulting on the ground when I land, and twist myself around so that I can wrap my legs around his. He falls face first into the ground. I pounce on him, ramming my fist into the middle of his back. Fury overtakes me as my blood boils over his actions, and my fists develop a mind of their own, pounding his back as he tries in vain to escape my wrath, but I refuse to stop until...

A single gunshot rings out, silencing the entire plaza.

I crawl off Amal, and we both look up into the stern face of an arbiter I have only met once, the same one that Renal had introduced me to during my first day within the eastern sector, and all my anger dissipates, replaced by fear, as I look into the man's face, knowing why Renal had warned me to not be on the receiving end of his wrath.

"Explain yourselves!" he demands as three other arbiters walk up behind him.

"She attacked me without cause," Amal says.

I open my mouth to protest, but the senior arbiter before us silences us both. He walks up to Amal, bearing down upon him, and Amal shrinks underneath his gaze. Heat rises up, enveloping me in its anxiety, as the man moves over to me and looks me up and down.

"Speak," he says, pointing at me, and Amal is wise enough to not challenge him.

"I witnessed Arbiter Amal strike a citizen without cause"—I spot Faya's and Joel's faces and can only imagine what they think of my rash actions, and I wish they haven't had to witness my failure—"and continue to beat her until the point of death."

The senior arbiter glances behind me and notices the girl on the ground bruised and crying with the plebeian boy trying to help calm her. He walks over to them, and both Amal and I know better than to move, and in a gentler voice asks, "Is that what happened?"

"Yes," says the girl in a meek voice through her tears.

The arbiter points at someone within the crowd. "Take her to the medical center," he orders, and a man jumps from the crowd and helps the girl up, disappearing with her as she holds her face, while the plebeian boy follows behind, after having picked up the pieces of her tablet. My hands shake as the senior arbiter stalks back to us, but not as much as Amal does, knowing that he has made a terrible mistake.

"What reason"—the senior arbiter leans in close to Amal, but his words are heard by all—"did you have to harass that child?"

"She," begins Amal as he swallows a wad of spit, "stole a tablet."

His pathetic excuse stirs up murmurs among the crowd, but they stop the moment the senior arbiter straightens up.

"There have been no reports of a theft."

Sweat drips down Amal's face.

"I'll ask you again," says the senior arbiter, "what reason did you have to strike that child?"

"None, sir," says Amal.

"You understand the severity of your actions," says the man.

"Yes, sir," Amal replies.

The senior arbiter turns to me.

"Yes, sir," I say, knowing what is to come next.

"Clear the square!" yells the senior arbiter, his voice reverberating off the surrounding buildings.

One by one, people file out of the square, knowing better than to challenge a direct order from an arbiter.

"That also means you two," the senior arbiter says to Faya and Joel.

They walk away from the crowd, but Faya gives me a sympathetic look. I remain facing forward, but hope she knows that I appreciate her little bit of comfort, even though I am unable to tell her, but as I watch her leave with Joel, I spot a woman observing the proceedings with interest, her gaze fixed upon me, but before I have a chance to ponder it, arbiters seize my shoulders and drag me to an information booth, which also serves as a detainment box; protocol must be followed. One places their hand, with the wristband, on the screen and it scans it, bringing up their information. Next, my hand and wristband are scanned.

"State the reason for detainment," says an electronic voice.

The arbiter lists the infractions I am charged with: disturbing the peace, attacking a fellow officer, and insolence.

The detainment box opens and fear rises within me, choking me. I have always been the one placing people within the box, but now I am the one being detained. I get to be locked away in the darkness. The arbiter jerks me toward the box, not caring if I bump into it and end up with a bruised shoulder, and pushes me inside, and the door slides closed, sealing with a small bit of suction, encasing me in total darkness, and leaving me to my fate.

Chapter 22

Detainment

The floor drops out from beneath me, and I plunge downward, unable to see anything, except a blur of metal, as I fall faster and faster, until I believe that I will crash on the bottom and be nothing more than a flattened mess of flesh and liquefied bones, while air rushes past me from my feet to my head, forcing strands of my hair out to whip me in the face, stinging my eyes, as my bun wobbles and loses its hold. I crash into the side of the metal chute—or is it the bottom? —as it bends, forming a slide of sorts, as it carries me to my destination, despite my pathetic attempts to slow myself down by pressing my hands against the sides, doing my best to ignore the excruciating pain as my palm burns from the friction building between them and the metal chute. For a split second, I wonder how Amal is faring, until I slam into a metallic seat and come to an abrupt halt. Before I have time to catch my breath, a glass casing covers the transport I am in, reflecting the lights from the console, the only light in the dark tunnel, and seals me inside.

The transport speeds down the tunnel, slamming me into the back of the chair, allowing its edges to dig through my uniform and into my skin, but my mind remains focused on the twisting darkness before me as the car slips up the side of the tunnel. Realizing what is about to happen, I wrap my feet around the bottom of the seat and grip the arm rests with such force that I am afraid I will tear them away. The transport follows the track until it is upside down and blood rushes to my head, causing it to ache with tremendous pain as my pulse beats against my temple with each pump of my heart, which pumps faster and faster the longer I am forced to grip my seat for dear life in an effort to not hit head first into the glass covering. My arms tire and my feet loosen their grip as I continue to plunge, upside down, down the tunnel. This is planned. It has to be, as a way to weaken the detainee so that they will be more compliant when they reach the end.

Without warning, the track spins down the tunnel until the transport is right side up, but the sudden movement dazes me and my vision blackens as my equilibrium returns to normal, not that I can see much of anything in this tunnel. I see specks up ahead. They grow bigger and bigger, intensifying, until I realize that they are lights, and that I must be nearing the end of this horrific ride. I have never before thought about the ones I had sentenced to detainment and placed in the box, forcing them to endure this nightmare, but now, I pity them: some, others deserved their fate.

The car comes to an abrupt halt, forcing me to slam against the console and gasp as the air is knocked out of me, but before I have time to recover and gain my bearings, the glass shield recesses and hands seize me, yanking me out of the transport and throwing me onto the platform. I see no faces. Masks cover them. Of course, they do. This way, any who come through here will have no idea who the arbiters are that drag them away, making it impossible for retaliation later. It also adds to the intimidation, to the feeding of one's fear, but I refuse to give in to that fear.

One of the arbiters tries to lower a black, canvas bag over my head, but I ram the sole of my boot into his knee, relishing in the sound of it breaking as he doubles over in pain. I snatch the bag out of his hands, jump to my feet, and round on another, ramming the bag over her masked face, and pulling the cord so tight that she claws at her throat as she struggles for air, but I hold firm. As another rushes for me, I swing the woman by her neck, still holding onto the cords around her throat, placing her between me and my attacker. She grunts as she takes the impact, and I am forced to take three steps back, but before he can force me off the platform, I kick the woman in the chest with all my might, forcing both of them to fly away from me and crash onto the ground. Judging by the odd angle of the woman's head, and the stillness of her chest, I know that her neck is broken and that her troubles are over.

Furious at being forced into this place, even though my own actions brought me here, I stalk over to the arbiter on the ground as he struggles to get up, ready to end him, if need be, but before I reach him, before I can make my move, electrical shocks course through my body, as three cattle prods dig into my back, and I collapse, jerking with each jolt, unable to control my spasms. The arbiter on the ground stands up, pleased at my demise. He stalks over to me, and I sense the triumphant smile behind his mask as he raises his left foot and kicks me in the face.

Stunned, and still crippled from the jolts of electricity that have seized my muscles, I remain limp as two arbiters lift me up and a third places a bag over my head. They drag me from the platform and through a doorway—the tips of my boots smack into a bump as we are forced to step up—and into a tunnel, while my mind struggles to focus, choosing to concentrate on the stinging pain that ripples my body, while my muscles continue to spasm from the residue of electricity still flowing through me. A small tear in the bag allows in a little bit of light from the bulbs above me, and I crane my head in an effort to get a glimpse of my surroundings, but receive a fist in the face for my efforts. Seconds seem like hours as they carry me through the detainment facility, with their feet stomping the metallic floor with such force, that a series of endless echoes reverberate through the tunnel, surrounding us, and spelling out my doom. We stop. Three distinct beeps hit my ears, but my confused mind finds it difficult to process their meaning, until we move again, and I am dragged through another doorway—the tips of my boots get caught in another crack as the flooring changes—and the hands gripping me let go, allowing me to drop onto the floor before stomping away, not caring about what will become of me.

Still hurting from the jolts of electricity, I manage to pull the hood off my head and look around my cell, noting the camera in an obscure corner with its edges illuminated by the pale green light coming from two rods in one of the walls for me to see its presence. I snort, unsurprised by it; spying on people is common in Arel, and they will want to observe every move I make to assess how well I am taking my confinement. This must be what is done to every individual that is sent here.

I scrape my hands along the ground, feeling for anything of use, and my fingers brush against a pebble. I pick it up. After pulling on the cords attached to the bag, I determine that they are stretchy enough for what I want and fashion them into a sling. I hope whomever is monitoring the camera is watching. Taking my makeshift sling and pebble, I aim at the camera and release my shot, striking it, pleased when the lens cracks, but my pleasure is short-lived, as the weight of what I have done crushes me, causing me to lay on the ground and curl up into a ball as my eyes burn from the tears forming there, tears I have not cried in so long, that I have refused to allow to be free for fear of what would happen if I do, but I cannot stop them, just like I was unable to stop them the night the woman died because I tried to help her escape. Faces float in front of my mind's eye: familiar faces, as the tears pour forth, refusing to be stopped, refusing to be imprisoned, and I think about Chase, about Sheila, and about Gwen, and how I have let them all down. So, I remain curled on the floor, in a pool of crusted urine and feces, unable to stop crying, comforted only by the untouched dust on the floor as it coats my face and uniform.

A clang rings out, echoing off the rusted metal walls, as the latch is released and the door opens, letting in the tiniest sliver of light, but not enough for me to make out the faces of the arbiters that storm inside my cell and seize both my arms, hauling me to my knees before dragging me outside. A third snatches the mangled bag I had left discarded on the floor and rams it over my head, but not before I manage to bite him, tearing a piece of skin away from his wrist. I receive a baton in the stomach in response, causing me to double over. My captors drag me down a corridor, allowing the rough and uneven floor to tear a hole in my pants before scraping the skin away from my knees. Biting my lower lip to keep from releasing even the slightest moan, I clench my fists in an effort to take my mind off the stinging pain that grips my kneecaps. I'll not give these bastards the satisfaction of knowing that they caused me pain. Pain is weakness, and weakness is not allowed, not in this place.

The clomping of the boots beside me stop, and I am forced to sit on my bleeding knees and endure the pain they bring me, while the arbiters release my arms. Moist vapor from my mouth fills the bag, causing my face to sweat as droplets of moisture drip from the tip of my nose, settling into the canvas around my face, soaking it. Claustrophobia starts to overtake me as I am forced to remain in this forced isolation of not being allowed to see the faces of those who sit in judgement of me.

"Arbiter Noni," says a harsh, male voice, the voice of one of those charged with passing judgement over me, "you stand accused of assaulting one of your fellow arbiters."

I almost laugh, but catch myself. Such an act will get me executed, but it is ironic that I am being punished for challenging a fellow arbiter, when such challenges are encouraged, to a point. Though, when arbiters fight among themselves in front of civilians, it can prove problematic, and maybe even cause dissent among the public, or make them question the authority of the arbiters.

"How do you plead?" says the same voice.

"Not guilty, sir," I reply.

Silence follows for a moment. They must not have expected this answer. Perhaps all the others that have been brought here before me have plead guilty, knowing that you are always guilty in Arel, with no chance of proving your innocence, regardless of the truth. It is unclear as to why they insist on getting me to admit that I did something wrong, unless this is another test, another power play, performed to prove to me, and the rest of Arel, who is truly in charge.

Heavy boots move on my right as someone pulls out their baton. I listen and wait for him to get closer. At the training facility, each arbiter had to undergo a test of being blindfolded, and be able to defend themselves against an attack. Some excelled at it; others did not. I managed to get by, but right here, right now, will be a test of my skills. I prepare myself for what is coming. I listen to the thundering sounds of heavy-soled boots against a metallic floor, worn down from use, muffling the sounds. The snap of a baton being whipped out hits my ears, and I listen for the unmistakable sound of it slicing the air. I hear it. Just before the baton can strike me, I bring my arms up, forming a cross, blocking the attack, and snatch the baton from the arbiter before swiping it across the floor, catching him in the shins and knocking him off his feet. That lesson in the training facility has paid off.

Before I can make another move, two arbiters throw me to the floor, restrain me, and wrench the baton from my grasp.

"Enough!" yells the one sitting in judgement; his voice thunders off the rafters, but instead of dissipating with each echo, it grows stronger, imbuing me with fear, making me second guess my actions.

"Arbiter Noni," he begins again, "do you plead guilty—"

His voice cuts off. I strain my ears to listen to him, but his boom-
ing voice drops to the smallest whisper as he speaks with someone
else, someone whose presence I am not supposed to be aware of. I
try leaning forward, hoping to glean a few words, but a gruff hand
jerks me back into a kneeling position, refusing to allow me the
courtesy of receiving some sort of forewarning about my fate. The
arbiter in judgement clears his throat before speaking again, but before he does, the distinct sound of a monitor being turned off hits
my ears as he ends his transmission.

"Take her away."

What? Away? Away where?

Hands seize my shoulders, pulling me backwards as they obey
their orders, and drag me from the room. Bits of light spill through
the few loose threads of the bag over my head, but everyone moves so
fast, that I am unable to gather my bearings or even understand what
is about to be done with me. I am dumped on the floor, but before I
can turn over on my side and stand up, cold steel snaps around my
right wrist, locking into place, as the rattling of a chain clinks against
the floor before someone shoves their foot into my stomach, forcing me to roll over the edge of a drop off and plunge downward. My
stomach surges into my throat as I fall, expelling its contents the moment I crash into a barrier that gives way beneath me, but still slices
through my jacket and into my skin, drawing bits of blood. I rip the
bag off my head, tossing it aside and hoping to never see it again, and
look at my wrist and the archaic shackle that has been placed on it,
but that isn't what bothers me. On the other end of the chain is Amal.

"If you wish to survive this day," says the arbiter that has ordered
us down here, dropping a key that lands on a protruding edge of the
chute itself, something both Amal and I notice, "you will climb to
the top of this chute before it's sealed."

The low vibration of gears, metal on metal, moving a gigantic
door, in this case, a barrier sealing the chute off from the outside
world, rumbles around me.

"Failure means incineration."

We're in a garbage chute!

"Consider this a test of your will to serve Arel."

The arbiters above us disappear, leaving me alone with Amal and a possible future of being cremated, with him as my only companion.

My foot moves and something crunches underneath it, piercing the rumbling around me, as though it has managed to silence all extraneous noise so that its distinct note is the only thing I hear. An ominous feeling overtakes me as I look down at what I am standing on, knowing that I will not like it: bones—human bones, mixed with bits of burnt clothing that have somehow escaped the fury of the fire and create the surface I stand on, and every little movement breaks their brittle structure, reminding me of what I will become—what we all become—should I fail to escape this place. Bits of sweat drop from the tips of my hair as it escapes its bun and rolls down my back, leaving a streak on my uniform jacket, as more beads of sweat dot my skin in this stifling chute, threatening to suffocate me. Something isn't right. This is no ordinary garbage chute. This had to have been created for the sole purpose of watching people struggle to survive, only to meet a terrible end. A clanking noise surrounds Amal and me as rungs appear on the sides of the chute, beckoning us to climb up them, but the feeling that they are a trap gnaws at me.

Our eyes meet.

As one, we both move to opposite sides of the chute, desperate to cling to a rung, but we both are pulled backward and crash into the human remains—I wince as a single rib stabs me in the side—while the chain attaching us pulls taut, forcing us to an abrupt halt. Once again, we look at each other, knowing that we will have to put our differences aside and work together if we want to survive, but betrayal always lies just beneath the surface, and almost always rears its ugly head; a fact I am reminded of as we both eye the key poking out over the edge of its little ledge, calling to us. He points at a set of rungs that are side by side and beneath the key, and I follow after him, slipping on the mangled mass of skeletal remains as I try to hurry, while foreboding sounds weave their way around us, mocking us and our feeble attempt to escape their lair. We grip the rungs of a metallic ladder that seems to have formed from the chute itself, though the rungs seem to be somewhat rubberized, and for a moment, I marvel at the technology involved to create such a thing, before reminding myself of where I am.

The chain around our wrists dangles as we climb higher, clanking against the chute with each movement, mimicking a ticking sound that fills the air, almost like a timer, urging us to hurry up. The hair on my arms and neck stand up as though charged with electricity as a low buzzing that grows with intensity with each passing second builds, wafting over us, warning us of impending doom. Before I have time to register what it means, the rungs that I am climbing disappear, melting into the side of the chute, and I plunge downward, taking Amal with me, and we both crash into the skeletal remains below us, as a bolt of electricity stretches from the top of the chute and strikes the side to our left, releasing a tremendous popping sound and forcing us both to turn away as its intense heat singes our skin.

That's new.

For a moment, I watch as rungs appear and disappear on the sides of the chute, noting that there seems to be a pattern. Where one set disappears, another appears next to it. Another set of rungs appear next to us, and I drag Amal with me as I bolt to my feet and sprint for them. We jump on them, climbing upward as fast as we can, as the ticking sound starts again, counting down the seconds until the rungs disappear. My hands slip from the metal rungs as sweat coats them, and I try wiping them on the sides of my pants to dry them, but to no avail. I push my way upward, doing my best to not become entangled in the shackles connecting me to Amal as we inch our way upwards. The static builds around me again as the individual hairs on my body lift upward as the ticking stops.

I jump to my left, and Amal follows suit, as the rungs disappear and a bolt of electricity strikes the side of the chute above me, leaving a fresh burn mark that looks more like a splatter than a charred piece of metal plating, while hoping that my guess on where to go is correct. New rungs appear as gravity starts to take its hold, and I reach out to them, grasping them and holding tight, refusing to allow my sweaty palms to let go. Pain grips my chest as I smack into the rungs, but neither I, nor Amal, have time to catch our breath as the ticking sound begins again, reminding us that time is our enemy.

We both climb upward once again, while keeping a close eye on where the key is, and the covering that moves over the top of the chute, threatening to seal us inside forever. We take the rungs two at a time, ignoring the swinging chain between us as it smacks against the side of the chute, while the timer counts down. The ticking stops. Knowing what comes next, we look at each other, wondering which direction to go in, when Amal points to the right. I don't argue. As the rungs we are climbing vanish, we throw ourselves to the right and seize the new ones that materialize within the metal sides of the chute, while another electrical shock strikes the side of the chute, forcing us to duck in an effort to protect ourselves.

As I grip the rungs that have just formed, the skin on my hands stings as though thousands of pins have stabbed it, while the flesh burns, making it difficult to cling to the metal rungs as I climb. I glance at Amal and he is having the same difficulty. The bolts of electricity. With each strike, the handholds heat up and will soon be too hot to climb. The creeping covering above us taunts us while the key laughs at us, and anger rises within me, fueling my resolve, urging me onward. I pull at my jacket, tearing off pieces of fabric and wrap them around my hands to provide a barrier between my skin and the hot rungs of the ladder. We continue our trek upward, pausing as the familiar ticking sound ceases, while the electrified air around us builds.

New rungs appear and both Amal and I jump for them as another bolt of electricity slams into the sides of the chute, but my hand slips and I tumble downward, slamming into the side of the ladder, as Amal catches my hand, stopping me from plunging to my death. Before he has time to change his mind, even though I know that a sense of self-preservation stopped him from letting me fall, knowing that my weight would take him with me, I seize the rungs before me and wrap my arms around them. I look up to say something, but stop when I notice the key is not that far above us, and neither is the top of the chute. Amal sees it too. Knowing what the other has planned, we both climb as fast as we can, but my fall has given Amal an advantage. He reaches the tiny ledge with the ornate key and reaches for it, but as he grabs it with his shackled hand, I tug on the chain, forcing him to drop the key and snatch it out of the air as it falls past me. Before Amal has a chance to retaliate, I ram the key into the keyhole on the shackle around my wrist and twist, freeing myself from him.

The ticking stops.

Once again, the thin hairs on my skin stand on end as the static in the air builds around us, warning us of another strike. The rungs vanish as I jump to my right, while Amal flings himself to his left, and we both grab the new set of rungs that have appeared, our feet swinging to the side from the momentum of our movements, while another bolt of electricity strikes the area where we had been. That is too close. Without bothering to glance at him, I hurry up the makeshift ladder that has appeared, wishing that the material around my hands was thicker, as the smoldering heat within the chute itself burns into my skin, but I ignore the pain as I focus on the door closing above me, and the ever shrinking space in the top of the chute. I reach the top as the ticking resonates around me, urging me to move faster. Flinging myself over the edge of the chute's opening, I drag myself away from its peril and to safety, or what passes for safety in this dreadful place, and turn back around to watch as Amal flies over the rungs of the ladder, desperate to break free of this nightmare. He is only three feet below me.

The ticking stops for the last time.

Our eyes meet. For a moment, I consider allowing him to fall to his death, to be rid of this annoyance, this pain in my side that has burdened me since the day I arrived in the eastern sector, but as I do, the memory of me clinging to the side of a rock wall with Chase, and of a hand that appeared from nowhere to help us, slaps me in the face, reminding me that not every option involves allowing someone to die. Shamed by it, I hurl myself over the edge of the chute and seize the other end of the chain around Amal's wrist, stopping him from falling, and haul him upward, pulling him out of the chute as the cover seals shut and more electricity grips the chute's interior. For a moment, we sit side by side, breathing hard, but before either of us can react to our new circumstances, arbiters appear from behind and ram bags over our heads.

Once again, hands grip my shoulders, digging into them as they haul me to my feet and shove me through a corridor, forcing me to trip over the exposed edges of the uneven floor. My feet twist and turn, entangling themselves as I am shoved in several different directions, unable to catch my bearings or my breath, while boots stomp around me, chastising me for daring to uphold the law, for daring to protect an innocent person from the actions of a bully. My back slams into a wall, and a sharp edge stabs it, causing me to winc, though I am grateful that the bag over my head prevents my captors from seeing that they succeeded in causing me pain.

Steam hisses as it is released from a pipe, making me wonder where I am being taken, but the hands pushing me refuse to allow me to know, as they shove me around, not caring if I bump into obstacles or trip from the disorientation forced upon me. Just as the fear that I am being led to my execution settles in, fresh, cool air engulfs my hands, as doors open and the wind brushes past me in an effort to calm me, but before I can relish in its comfort, the hands gripping me throw me into a transport, not caring that my head bangs into the top of the vehicle as I am shoved inside.

The door seals shut. I feel the presence of someone sitting next to me, but cannot be sure. The only way to find out is to take the bag off my head, but I know that if I do, I risk being punished. The transport jerks into action as it speeds down a roadway, making sharp turns, and not caring if its passengers are thrown around. I try to position my head so that I can see through a worn spot in the material of the bag covering me, but every time I try, the transport jerks to the side, causing me to slam into its side. It picks up speed, jerking me backward, before coming to a sudden stop, flinging me forward into the seat in front of me. The door opens and more hands seize me by the arms, hauling me out of the transport, delighting in the fact that my feet are caught, causing me to fall to the ground.

My hands burn from the impact, but before I can lift myself up, the same hands grab me and jerk me to my feet, causing me to become dizzy for a moment as they shove me forward, growing frustrated as I stumble and almost trip again. Each time I start to fall, they jerk me upward. The sweltering air encasing my head makes it difficult to breathe, as more spittle and water vapor coats my face, causing me to gag. Just as my mind races from one dismal possibility to the next, the hands gripping me thrust me to the ground and my knees slam into hard metal with small, raised bumps covering it, causing instant pain to surge through them as the metal bumps dig into them. Someone rips the bag off my head, and I turn in time to see them do the same to Amal as he kneels on the ground beside me. Blinking in an effort to focus as I grapple with my changing situation, a stark figure towers over both of us, silhouetted by the railcar's lights behind him.

A railcar? We're on a platform, but it is empty, void of any activity, except for the arbiters surrounding us.

The arbiters encircling us lift Amal to his feet and drag him onto the railcar without waiting to be told, forcing him to sit in a seat near a window. My stomach jumps when I see him sitting there, while I am left on the platform, and I wonder if perhaps this is another test, another trick, or something much worse, but before my mind has a chance to mull through the worst-case scenarios, a voice speaks from behind me, the same voice as the man who had me thrown into the chute.

"You are lucky," he says in a mocking tone as he paces around me, until he stands in front of me, bearing down on me, making me feel smaller than a mouse, and wishing I was back in that chute, "to have the loyalty of friends."

What is he talking about?

"Someone has vouched for you, collaborating your story," the man continues, "so you are being released. However, you will still have a demerit placed on your record."

He walks away, leaving me to wonder what the hell the chute was all about, and why it is that I have the demerit and Amal gets nothing. I turn my head and start to open my mouth, but a harsh voice stops me cold, a voice I recognize and had never possessed such coldness before.

"Get in!"

Renal? Why is he here?

I look at the open door to the railcar and Amal sitting in a window, doing his best to not look at me, though the curiosity on his face is evident, despite his futile attempts to hide it. Ashamed and feeling vulnerable, I stand up, ignoring the wails of my knees at being forced to move while they still burn from the torture thrust upon them, and mosey over to the railcar, afraid to walk too fast or to make any sudden movements. Once aboard, I pick a seat away from Amal and stare out the window as Renal steps onto the car and the door closes with a slight hiss.

The railcar takes off, thrusting me backward into my seat, but I do not care. I have failed. Failed to stop Amal from abusing his authority. Failed to be the epitome of a good arbiter for Commander Vye's sake. Failed Faya. Failed Chase, Sheila, and Gwen. And I have failed Renal. I allowed my own sense of justice to get in the way, and here I am, on an empty railcar with Amal and Renal, heading back to the eastern sector in the middle of the night as a warning to others.

The moon breaks through the clouds and envelopes me with its pale rays of silver light. Perhaps it is trying to comfort me, or perhaps it is admonishing me for being so ignorant, in allowing my emotions to dictate my actions. I glance at Renal as he stands between Amal and me, facing forward and keeping his eyes fixed on the door in front of him, before turning back to the window to watch the spires of the executive district as the moon illuminates them and the specks of light that dot their majesty, a true testament to the might of Arel. The shuttle swings upward, shifting my center of gravity, but I go limp, not fighting it, and instead, allow it to push me where it wills, until we are high up and pass over the tops of buildings.

Despite my empty feelings, I cannot help but marvel at the purplish hue of the buildings as the moon graces them with its ethereal glow. A few stars poke through the clouds, curious as to the happenings of the world below them, and the railcar pivots downward, and I brace my knees against the seat in front of me to hold myself in place as the smooth glass buildings passing by are replaced with roofs missing tiles, beams hanging in a precarious fashion, broken windows, and decaying brick.

The railcar comes to a stop, and neither Amal, nor I, wait to be told to get off. We follow Renal onto the empty platform—its eerie silence unnerves me—and to a waiting transport, crawling into the back seat, while Renal sits in the front. The driver says nothing as he puts the vehicle in gear and we speed off, heading toward the manor, and I watch as it grows larger in the windshield, wondering what awaits me when I arrive. The transport stops in front of the door, and a small smirk crosses my face as I look at the yellowed pane of glass covering it, preventing anyone from being able to see inside, remembering my first day here. I wonder if Commander Vye knew then how much of a burden I would be to her.

Renal gets out of the transport, and Amal and I do the same.

"Go to your quarters," he says to us.

Amal wants to argue—I see it on his face—but decides against it, knowing that he is already in enough trouble and not wanting to be on the receiving end of Renal's anger. He goes inside and disappears, but before I can follow, Renal stops me.

"Noni, a moment."

I hang back, working up the courage to look into his eyes.

"Caution is your friend," he says to me in a cryptic sort of way, and in a gentler tone than what he had used earlier.

"Sir?" I say.

Renal drops something into my hand. "One day, your luck will run out."

He walks off, leaving me alone outside the manor. Confused about his warning, I look at what he had placed into my hand and gasp when I see the thin metal wire I had fashioned into a wristband on one of the nights I had snuck out after curfew: a warning in and of itself.

Not wanting to get caught outside, I rush inside and up the stairs to the second floor, wasting no time in going to my room, where I find Chase. He covers his mouth before I can speak, warning me to stay quiet, and I shut the door, running to him.

"Are you all right," he whispers to me, examining me.

"I'm fine," I tell him.

"What were you thinking sneaking out last night and today..."

I place a finger over his lips to calm him, touched by the concern in his voice, and knowing that I owe him an explanation. After everything we have been through, the least I can do is let him in on my secret. I sit down on the bed, and he does the same.

"I have something I need to tell you," I say.

Chase looks at me with gentle eyes, worried about what I am going to say, or perhaps more concerned about what I won't tell him. His hand reaches up and touches my chin, and I cringe from the pressure, realizing for the first time that I am missing a patch of skin there. The intensity of the chute, and my desperate attempts to get free, must have prevented me from noticing it and the bit of blood that dots it. He takes his shirt off, unable to find any other sort of cloth, and knowing the importance of keeping the uniforms in my closet free of stains and contamination, he pours water from the pitcher onto it before holding it to my face and dabbing the blood and dirt away from the scrape on my chin. I pull back as it stings, but stop myself, reminding myself that the feeling of pain is weakness.

"What did they do to you?" he asks, as he cleans my chin, being careful not to cause too much discomfort. I think back to that night in the cave, when I had tended to his injuries and stayed with him to make sure he had made it through the night. It wasn't that long ago, but so much has happened, that it seems like a lifetime ago.

Words form in my throat, choking me, forcing their way out despite my desperate attempt to keep them confined, so that I could continue to have the illusion of safety, but in Arel, safety is a figment of one's imagination. No one is safe in Arel.

"They gave me a test of my commitment to Arel."

Chase lowers his hand with his crumpled shirt in it.

"They threw me into a garbage chute, and I had to climb my way out before burning to death."

"Animals," Chase spits.

"I have been," I say, keeping my voice low so that no one outside the room can hear me, "helping people leave the city."

"What?"

I place my hand over his mouth to stop him from saying anything else, for fear that he might be overheard.

"It started the night of the bombings," I tell him. "Sigal—you know him?"

Chase nods.

"Renal had caught them trying to leave. He never saw me come up from behind, and I knocked him out. After that, I helped Sigal and his family get past the wall. And then, during the riot, I stumbled upon this pregnant woman."

"But the sterilization in the water…"

"I know. But somehow, she was, and she had a bag with her. I knew, right then, that she was not a part of the riot, but was trying to get out before her baby was born and taken from her. So, I hid her, and went back to get her that night. Everything had gone so well, until after she had gotten outside of the wall, and"—tears form in my eyes and my throat clenches in an attempt to stop them, but they refuse to be stopped—"she stepped on a landmine."

Chase holds me close, wrapping his muscular arm around me, comforting me as I relive my failure, and images of the woman's body fill my mind, tormenting me, refusing to let me be free of my guilt.

"She is dead because of me."

For the first time, in a long time, I cry without fear of repercussions, or of appearing weak. Tears stream down my face, stinging my skin as they edge their way down past my chin and drip onto my chest. The more I try to control myself, the more the tears force their way out, refusing to let me rest. In an effort to stop this outpour of emotion, I wipe my face with the back of my hands, doing my best to stop the tears, but Chase grabs my hands and force them away from my face as he stares into my eyes, his soft expression soothing me and forcing me to calm down.

"It's okay to cry," he says.

"I am an arbiter. I am not supposed to show weakness."

He pulls me close to him, allowing me to feel his strength and his calmness. I place my ear on his chest and listen to the air as he breathes in and lets it out, remembering the night I had done the same to make sure that he was alive after he had spared me from the wrath of Commandant Gant.

"You're not weak, Noni," he says to me as he holds onto me. "You are the reason we survived the wilderness. Your resourcefulness, your fortitude are why we are here. It is not weakness to feel shame, or to cry when things get to be too much to bear. It is human."

"But…"

"You are the strongest person I have met, next to Gwen, of course."

I chuckle at that last statement.

"So, you do smile," he says to me.

"Gwen despises me," I say. "And she should."

"She doesn't."

"But I am the reason you were taken from her."

"No, you are the reason I am reunited with her."

More tears spill onto Chase's bare chest as he continues to hold me close in a comforting hug, letting me know that he is here for me.

"Don't worry. I will help you carry your secrets," he says.

I lift my head and look at him, unsure of what to say.

"You're not alone, Noni. You don't need to do any of this alone."

"I have to," I say. "I don't want to endanger any of you."

Chase cups my cheeks with his hands, as he brings his face close to me and his warm forehead touches mine.

"This is my choice, and I choose to be here for you. If this is what you want to do, if you are going to continue helping people leave the city, then I am going to be with you, by your side."

I manage a weak smile, unsure of what to say. I have never had anyone willing to risk their life for me, or willing to help me break the law, knowing full well what the punishment is if we are caught, but Chase is; and the resolve in his voice gives me strength.

"Now, tell me about last night."

I swallow a lump in my throat, doing my best to moisten my mouth before I speak.

"Last night, I helped a group escape the crematorium and get outside the wall. And they did. They made it to the woods beyond the grassy field. But I wasn't alone this time."

"What do you mean? Who helped you?"

"A man who has every reason to hate me."

"No, he doesn't."

"What do you say that?"

"I'm a plebeian. I have more reason than any to despise arbiters, and I don't hate you."

I snuggle into his embrace and he kisses the top of my head, but before I can fall asleep, Sheila bursts into my room, her face filled with worry and fear, and I jump up, forgetting all that has happened to me and only caring about what troubles her.

"It's Commander Vye," she says, her voice squeaking.

"What's wrong?" I ask, my voice taking on the arbiter tone.

"She's… she's acting strange."

"Where is she?"

"Her office."

I glance at Chase, who motions for me to go, and run out of my room, racing down the hall and to the stairs, while still trying to not make any noise. I reach Commander Vye's office within a minute and stop once I open the door and see her slumped on her desk with an open bottle in her left hand. The once neat stack of reports on her desk lay strewn all over the room, forming mishappen piles in every crevice; one even has the print of a boot on it. She raises her head and looks at me with an unfocused gaze as I shut the door and pick up the papers, shoving them together and placing them in an even stack on her desk, in the same corner they had been in on my first day here, and pause for a moment when I notice a report with my name on it, and my curiosity urges me to pick it up and read it, but I'm stopped by the solemnness that has taken possession of my commander's once strong and curt voice.

"You needn't bother," she says, her words slurred.

I ignore her.

"I see you survived the detention center. I don't know if I should congratulate you, or offer you my condolences."

Puzzled, I stare at her for a moment, unsure of what to make of her words. There is no malice in them, no mocking, no condescending undertone, just unabashed honesty. I reach for the glass bottle in her hand. She jerks it back, but my firm grip stops her unsteady one, and I rip it free of her grasp, not caring if I anger her.

"Take it, then," she says as she sits up and leans back in her chair. "You're going to need one."

I place the opening of the bottle underneath my nose and sniff, wrinkling it as the aroma of alcohol fills my nostrils. Drinking among arbiters is forbidden in Arel, but that doesn't stop a few from sneaking the occasional one in.

"Go on. Take a swig."

I scrunch my eyebrows together, uncertain as to why my commander is ordering me to disobey the arbiter code of conduct, but decide that I have already committed several infractions; so many, that it is a wonder I am still alive. What's one more? I place my dry lips over the rim of the bottle, ignoring the thin film of saliva that already coats it, and tip it up, taking a mouthful, wincing as its amber liquid burns my throat and warms my chest on the way down, wondering why anyone would want to drink this.

"First drink, huh?" Commander Vye laughs.

I walk over to the window, open it, and dump the contents of the bottle onto the bushes outside, before closing the window and tossing the bottle into the open drawer of her desk. Commander Vye smiles as though she had expected me to do that.

"He wants my job," she says, and I stand there, listening to her as she talks, seeing a side of her I would never have guessed existed, a vulnerability, a weakness. "He won't stop until he has it, and with the riots and recent attacks within the city by a group of terrorists, it won't be long until he gets his wish."

"Attacks?" I ask. I know of two: one on the night I helped Sigal escape, and another on the day of my questioning before the tribunal.

"While you were gone, there were at least two. Terrible ones. So, many citizens dead. The bodies—if you can call them that— mangled and spread all across the city with pieces scattered among the pavement and entrails dangling from the eaves of the nearest buildings. But that isn't what bothers me most. It's the silence that follows. The awful, deadened silence of nothing left alive." Commander's Vye's gaze, sharp and hawk-like on so many occasions, focuses on the door to the hallway, as though she doesn't see it at all, just the aftermath of a bomb's wrath. "The council believes that they originated in the eastern sector," she finishes.

If that is the case, then Commander Vye's days are numbered, which explains her slippage and indulgence in a forbidden vice. For the first time in the year that I have known her, I pity her. She had seemed so strong, confident, as though nothing would ever strike her down, but, on this night, alone in this room, she seems wounded, but instead of being visible, her wounds are attached to her soul.

"Who wants your job?" I ask, already guessing the answer.

"Molers," she hisses. "You know the saying. The one who can control the eastern sector can govern all of Arel."

If there is one thing Molers craves above all else, it's power. He more than craves it. It's an obsession.

"I thought I was cursed when I was first assigned here, much like you did. Don't deny it," she says when I start to protest. "I saw it on your face the moment you walked through that door."

I keep my mouth shut and say nothing as my commander rambles on, but it seems more like she is confiding in me, instead of babbling nonsense.

"They allow the commanders of every region to watch the gauntlet, if they so choose. I went every year as recruit after recruit battle their way through, hoping to make it to the end, searching for someone strong enough to withstand this place, but even more so, someone I can trust. You were the first recruit I noticed. While the others thought of themselves, you went back to help a fellow recruit. You're an enigma, Noni. Most like you are sent to the crematoriums and last only six months, but you managed to finish your training, and passed the gauntlet, all without allowing your intricacies to be noticed. It isn't often, but sometimes the commander of a region can request that a particular recruit be assigned to them."

She requested that I be assigned here? Everything I have gone through, is because of her?

"Why?" I whispered, without realizing it.

"I told you once, that I see a lot of myself in you. The eastern sector is the first line of defense for Arel. If it falls, the entire city falls, and so do the people within it. Prestige isn't found in the halls of the presidential palace, but in what you do, in how you conduct yourself, and in the choices you make. Arel needs someone who will defend her, defend her people."

"But Arel is flawed," I say, knowing the risk I take for voicing such a sentiment.

"Every place is flawed. It is up to you to choose how you deal with those flaws. If I fail here as commander of the eastern region, a more stringent policy will be implemented, and a new commander, more strict, more unforgiving, and harsher than me will be assigned here, and who do you think will suffer for it?"

As Commander Vye speaks, I start to understand why she insists on staying here. This isn't a job to her, but something more; she believes that her presence here helps the people of Arel more than if she were somewhere else. Though she has never shown mercy to me, I wonder how many times she has shown it when I wasn't around. Has she chosen the lesser of punishments in order to give someone a second chance, much like what I have done? How many arbiters have done the same, conflicted between upholding the laws of Arel no matter the cost, and doing what they knew to be right?

"Don't be like me," Commander Vye says, her voice so soft that I almost don't hear her.

It seems strange for her to tell me such a thing, and not knowing what else to do, I look at her and notice her haggard appearance for the first time, with a few bags under her eyes, lines around her mouth, as though she has aged 20 years in one day, and is worn and tired, and the sense that much has happened in my absence, and despite her efforts to keep others from seeing its effect on her, it rears its ugly head anyway.

"Don't you think it strange that you were taken to the detention center for challenging a fellow arbiter and not for what happened at the crematoriums?"

Once she mentioned it, my mind goes back to the crematoriums and how Commander Vye not only challenged Commander Aeron, but killed her as well. There have been no inquiries, no summons to the tribunal—nothing.

"Why do you think we haven't heard from them?" I ask.

"There could be a variety of reasons," replies Commander Vye. "None of them good."

"May I ask you a question?"

Commander Vye waves her hand, and I take it as a sign of approval.

"Did you know Commander Aeron personally?"

Commander Vye's lips form a thin line, answering my question, but just when I think that she is not going to speak, she opens her mouth and stilted words spill from it.

"Soon after my assignment to the eastern sector, when I was about your age, I was sent to the outposts, just like you, to see how Arel operated outside of the city. Commander Aeron ran one of those outposts. The smell of death surrounded her, and to this day, I cannot get it out of my nose. That night, I awoke to a commotion. I went outside to see what it was... and she had my commander chained to two transports, carving out entire chunks of his flesh from his body, feeding it to the two wild dogs she kept as pets. I still hear his screams, and they will haunt me until the day I die. Being young and stupid, I demanded to know why my commander was being tortured, and demanded that she stop. Aeron knocked me down and placed her foot on my head, pressing against it. I thought I would die that day, but she released me at the last minute, lifting me up and placing her knife in my hand, telling me that my commander was a traitor to Arel and that to prove my loyalty, I had to carve him up like an animal for slaughter.

"My commander was innocent of the crimes she accused him of. I saw it in his face and the faces of those under her command. They were too afraid to stand up to her. I refused. I tried to stab her with the knife, but she was ready for me and made sure to leave her mark." Commander Vye lifts her shirt and shows me a mark on the right side of her abdomen where someone had stabbed her a long time ago. "She gave the order for the transports to drive away, ripping my commander in half, and covering me in his blood.

"When Arel learned of her actions, they recalled her and placed her in the crematoriums. I later found out that my commander had slighted her at supper, so she decided to teach him a lesson. I made sure that bitch got what she deserved."

Commander Vye watched her commander die, over something so trivial? I have no idea what I would do if I ever saw her die. I can't even…

Commander Vye slumps over the table, exhaustion taking its hold on her, and I rush to her side, helping her up, knowing that I need to get her to bed before anyone finds her like this. She protests at first, but stops the moment I fling her arm over my shoulder and guide her to the door. The hallway is empty as we head for the staircase and make our way up, making certain to not step on the one creaky step. Darkness swarms around us as the hall lights shut off, leaving us to fend for ourselves, but I refuse to leave her in the hallway, to be the perfect victim for Molers to sink his teeth into.

Her room is at the end of the corridor, and I help her down there, hushing her when she starts to speak, knowing what the consequences will be if she is seen in such a state. Relief showers over me when the door to her room—coated in grime and fogged just like the others—slides open, allowing us entrance, and I place her on the cot, tucking the pillow under her head. Her eyelids flutter, telling me that she is on the verge of passing out. Before I am able to turn and leave, she grabs my arm and pulls me in close.

"Don't trust anyone," she tells me, "except Renal."

Her grip loosens when she falls asleep, leaving me to wonder about the meaning behind her cryptic message. It seems odd that she would tell me not to trust anyone, though it could be the alcohol talking, but my mind dismisses that the moment I think it.

I leave Commander Vye alone, hoping that she will sleep off the amount of alcohol she has drunk and that she will be more like her old self in the morning. When I enter the corridor, the sound of a door closing catches my attention, and I turn toward the sound, unable to learn where it originates from, but the uneasy feeling that someone else in this manor is aware of Commander Vye's vulnerability fills me. Not wanting to be caught out of bed, I hurry back to my room, where Chase waits for me, and fall asleep the moment I lay down, with him holding onto me, afraid to let me go.

Chapter 23

Sickening Silence

The last bobby pin slips into my dark hair, securing the final strand into place. Taking a step back, I look into the mirror at my walnut colored face, and the slight blemish that is still there from where I received a burn from my time in the detention center and the chute that they had put me in as a test of my loyalty. Two weeks have passed since that incident, though it seems more like two years, since whenever I step outside my room, wandering eyes always stare at me, only to dart away the moment I glance in their direction, but they are the least of my worries: Amal has kept a close watch on me. Why, I do not know, but I guess that he has decided that I am a threat, and that he is going to deal with that threat the only way that is proper in Arel: by eliminating it.

Worried eyes stare back at me as I study my reflection in the mirror, a stark contrast to the confidence that my uniform instilled in me on most occasions. I reach up and touch the remnants of the burn on my face and scrape off the last bit of the scab with the tip of my nail, flicking it into the air and watching as it swirls downward, landing on my right foot—a speck tarnishing the pristine, black polish of my boot. A dish on my desk with a spoon next to it captures my attention. Turning, I pick it up and examine the quinoa mush with strawberries mixed in. Sheila must have snuck in here and left it for me before I woke up, since I chose to sleep most of the day in preparation for my shift, so that I would not have to eat in the dining room with Molers. I scoop some of the mushy mixture into my mouth and chew as I try not to think about the next few hours. I got stuck with night rotation—with Molers. Unnatural heat rises around me, surrounding me, as the dread of spending the next 12 hours with Molers overtakes me. I finish the last bite of my meal and place the dish and the spoon back on the desk, making sure that the spoon is even with the edge, before summoning my courage to face the unavoidable.

My door slides open, allowing me to leave, and I step into the familiar hallway with its peeling, speckled wallpaper, it's once white shade having darkened from time and the buildup of grime, and stalk toward the stairs that descend to the main floor, taking each step with purpose, determined to face the night's threats. Once I reach the bottom, I glance around for Sheila, Gwen, or Chase, desiring to assure myself that they are safe for the moment, but can find no sign of them, until a wisp of blonde hair dances from behind the staircase, pushing a broom, much like Sheila had my first day here. It's Gwen. She looks up at me and manages a small smile, but darts away the moment Commander Vye appears.

"Noni, a word."

Commander Vye's voice commands obedience, and I follow her to her office, remembering the night I had chanced upon her after she had indulged in a forbidden vice. I haven't seen much of her since, and suspect that she has been avoiding me, or watching me to see if I intend to turn her in. I could have, and any other arbiter might have. Commanding officers are not supposed to drink, though everyone knows that some do, but if caught, the punishment is swift and severe, and I would have been well rewarded for snuffing out a weak link in the strength and might of Arel; but I have no desire to be remembered for such a thing, for being a snitch. I do not wish my commander harm. I sympathize with her and now understand the weight she bears. I do not want to add to it.

Once I step into her office, she shuts the door behind me, before stepping around the room and taking her place behind her desk. The wild, disarrayed reports that had littered the floor that night sit in tidy stacks on her desk—read and to be read—though I cannot find the one that had my name on it. She must have hidden it. Disappointment rises within me at the thought, not that I blame her for doing so; but I do want to read what it said.

"Two weeks ago, you may have witnessed something…"

Her words are cautious, as though she is gauging my reaction more than struggling to find the right words, to discern my loyalty to her. We both know that all I have to do is go to any of the other arbiters here and mention that she has violated Arelian law, give details of the infraction, and she will disappear like so many, but I do not want that, and having that sort of power over her sickens me.

"…and I want you to know…"

"What I saw," I say, interrupting her and hoping to put her anxiety at ease, "was my commander sacrificing much needed rest to do her duty for Arel, and reminding me of my own duties as well."

Commander Vye's hardened face stares back at me, but despite the façade she exhibits, relief floods her eyes, and my mind.

"You be careful out there tonight," she says in a low voice, with a note of caring that I have not heard before. "Do as Molers tells you. Do not give him a reason to report anything negative about you."

The warning in her voice unnerves me. The gnawing feeling that she had tried to prevent me from having to go on patrol with him, but was unable to, fills me with dread.

"Yes, ma'am," I say.

"Watch yourself," she says to me in a lower voice. "Dismissed."

I open my mouth to ask her about her warning, about why she is giving it to me, but think better of it, and leave her office as ordered. Taking a deep breath, I walk to the entrance, and the yellowed door slides open, allowing the last rays of the sun's light to enter the building as I step outside, and find Molers tapping his foot with impatience.

"Your shift started five minutes ago," he says to me, as a way of trying to instill fear into me, but I ignore him and continue down the driveway to the gate, and into the street as a trolley races past, allowing the long shadows of a building to flicker on it as it roars down the street to its destination.

Curfew will be soon. Molers catches up to me, but I continue to ignore his small outburst of frustration, refusing to allow him to dictate how this night will go. I make my way to the plaza, passing under the moving walkways, and the hum of the conveyor belts working nonstop fills my ears as I near them, only to fade away as I continue on, to be replaced by the bustling, ordered chaos of the square. The crowds are not as thick as they would have been earlier in the day. The lower the sun sinks in the sky, and the longer the shadows of the buildings become, the more people hurry inside, knowing that curfew will be soon, and what the consequence is for being caught outside once it passes. I check the time on my wristband. There is still a couple of hours left, but I am just as pleased to see people abiding by the curfew law. I don't feel like arresting anyone today and sending them to the detention center, where they may face far worse than I did.

Molers grabs my shoulder and whirls me around to face him, not caring about the odd glances from the people around us.

"You don't have to like being on patrol with me," he growls, placing his face so close to mine that our noses almost touch, "but you will respect me. Understand?"

His fingers dig into my shoulder, pinching a nerve and causing it to burn, but I refuse to allow him the satisfaction of knowing that he has hurt me.

"Yes, sir," I say, keeping my voice even.

Before he can respond, a shop owner rushes out of his store, yelling, "Thief!"

We both look over and see a man in brown overalls and a long-sleeved, brown shirt, indicating that he is one of the Arelian maintenance crew (people responsible for fixing power lines and water lines), running through the square, clutching something in his hand. Molers lets go of my shoulder and motions for me to chase after the man. I sprint across the square, shoving people out of my way, though most jump to the side on their own, not wanting to get caught up in arbiter business, as I hurry after the thief. A woman screams as the man grabs her and throws her at me, but I catch her before continuing after him. He darts down a side street.

"Stop!" I yell at him, but he continues to run away.

My feet pound the pavement as I hurry after the man, ignoring the pain in my side from the exertion, but he continues to outpace me and darts down another side street, knocking over a cart full of apples. I jump over the cart, but my foot lands on an apple, causing me to lose my balance and fall to the ground, but I ignore the stinging pain of the hard pavement digging into my skin, and grab an apple, throwing it at the man, hitting him in his calf. For a moment, he stumbles, and it appears that he might fall, but he manages to regain his balance and continue on. I scramble to my feet and hurry after him, stretching my legs as much as I can to make up the distance. Squinting, I do my best to keep my eyes on the thief as he blends in with the ever-darkening part of the city as the buildings block every part of the sun.

He heads for the trolley tracks, and its whistle reaches my ears, warning us of its approach. Dread fills me as he races for the rails while the trolley draws nearer, playing a dangerous game of chicken. With each passing second, I watch as the two continue on a collision course, and hold my breath as the man jumps the tracks right before the trolley rushes past. I stop. Heaving, I wait for the trolley to roar past, allowing me passage across the tracks. Once it's gone,

I scan the crowd of people beyond for the thief, but the darkened area around me makes spotting him difficult, except I see a man in brown overalls. Taking a chance that he is my thief, I jump over the tracks and rush for him. He turns around and sees me. The man takes off. Once again, I shove my way through people as they head home, trying to catch the man before he gets away. I do not need another failure on my record.

The thief veers left, taking another side street. Knowing that I will never catch him like this, I pause, scanning the buildings, and spot a door that leads to a small eatery. I run for it, bursting through the door, and ignoring the man asking if he can seat me, as I charge past tables where diners finish up their meals and prepare to leave. A tray clatters to the tile floor as dishes crash around it, splattering food all over the nearby tables and chairs, and the waitress glowers at me as she cleans it up, but I don't have time to apologize for making her drop her dishes. I rush through the dining area and into the kitchen, looking for the back exit. Found it.

As dishwashers and cooks glance in my direction, I hurry past them, ignoring them, while they turn back to their work, not wanting to get involved in my reasons for disturbing their workday. I slam into the exit door, forcing it open as the thief races by. Quickening my pace, I charge after him, moving my feet as fast as I can, until I am close enough to him that I jump on him, tackling him, and taking him to the ground. He tries to get away, but I place my left knee in the middle of his back and wrench his arms behind him, forcing him to drop what is in his hand and it clatters on the pavement, rolling away, until it nestles into the concrete foundation of the building next to us.

"Please," begs the man, "let me go. I was told not to come back without it!"

"You are being detained for stealing," I say, ignoring his pleas.

"Please," the man continues, "my supervisor told me it would be my head if I failed to get it, but didn't give me the credits to buy it."

Before I can bind his hands, a single gunshot rings out, echoing off the sides of the tall buildings, and the man goes limp, while a hole appears in his head and blood splatters onto my uniform jacket. Stunned, I let go of him and turn in the direction of the sound. Molers approaches from my right and holsters his pistol. As I stare at the lifeless body in front of me, I spot the item the man had stolen and pick it up. It is just a copper fitting for a pipe. That's it. This is what the man died for. Enraged, I throw the copper fitting away and jump to my feet.

"Are you crazy!" I yell at Molers, not caring about the consequences afterward. "The man was just a thief. According to statute 2626, all thieves are to be remanded to the detention center where—"

"There have been a few changes since you've been gone!"

Molers' voice echoes around me in the alley, and anyone passing by on the street continues on, ignoring the exchange, not that I blame them.

"But you wouldn't know any of that, would you," says Molers, "since you were so busy being President Tapiwa's emissary. To deal with the terror threats, arbiters have the authority to deal with violators with any means they deem necessary."

What? This goes against the law that I am sworn to uphold—that we are all sworn to uphold. The man hadn't harmed anyone. He just stole something, and if it wasn't his third offense, he could have been reeducated, and... My stomach churns as I realize that the thoughts in my head are no better than the ultimate solution Molers had decided on. Maybe killing the man was more merciful than sending him to a reeducation center, but what is the point of the law, if we can just decide how it is to be executed? Confusion mixed with anger roil through me, filling me, until it boils over, causing me to not think about my next set of actions.

"You could have struck me," I say, my voice a low growl.

"If I wanted you dead, you would be."

"Then perhaps you should have."

Molers whips out his pistol and points it at my forehead, saying, "I can right now, if you'd like."

Refusing to flinch or show any ounce of fear, I stare into his cold eyes, remembering all the pain he had put me through while I was in the training facility, and this is no different. It's just another mind game of his.

"Do it," I say, stepping forward so that the cold end of the barrel presses into my sweaty forehead.

He smirks, entertained by my boldness and puts his pistol back in its holster.

"This way," he says, turning around and walking away, while speaking into his wristband to report the dead body next to me. A cleanup crew will be here soon to cart it away.

Knowing that I will not get away with disobeying him again, I follow after him, clinching my fists as I do, and drawing blood as my nails dig into my palms.

"It's time you learn that everyone in Arel has their place," Molers says as he leads me to a disreputable part of the eastern sector, one that Commander Vye forbade her arbiters to go to, "and you will either learn yours, or be assigned other duties."

Molers marches through the streets of the eastern sector, and I dare not disobey him, knowing what can happen to me if I refuse. His quick pace proves difficult to keep up with, and I find myself somewhat surprised, considering that he is at least 40 years my senior. The streets turn narrower, with more cracks in the pavement, and in some areas, entire chunks of concrete are missing, leaving sinking holes in their place to capture unsuspecting people who are unaware of their existence.

The deeper we go into the heart of the eastern sector, an area I never had the courage to venture into, the darker it becomes, as the sun's rays cannot reach between the tightknit buildings that are squished together, forming a prison of decaying brick that crumbles away from its place, yet refuses to allow its structure to wither into nothingness. Despite the eldritch nature of these tucked away roads, no graffiti, no trash, no rats plague this area, unsettling my nerves as the ominous feeling of being led into the deepest chasms of a sickening horror, so evil, so diabolical that even hell itself repudiates it, for the vomitous thing that it is. My heart skips every other beat as Molers leads me deeper into a tangled web of malevolence that many in Arel pretend does not exist, though all make use of its offerings.

He stops in front of a wooden door, which does not belong in a city full of automatic entrances and constructions made of steel and glass, yet here it is, an ode to times past, or a reminder that some things never change, no matter how hidden society pretends it to be. But it isn't just the door that is odd. It's the darkened color that stands out among the white brick, not stark white, but gray, soiled by dust and debris, and the sinister happenings that my intuition tells me takes place behind such an innocuous setting. No windows, no signs, just a black door with a curved handled, nestled between bricks of false purity.

Molers raps on the door, and a solid, yet somewhat hollow, sound fills the area around me, causing a chilled sensation to work its way up my spine until perspiration overtakes me, making my uniform stick to my skin like an uncomfortable second skin that needs to be shed. The idea that he has been here before and made use of the diabolical offerings behind that door swarms over me, warning me that I will not like what I find, and that this is a test—not Arel's, but his.

The door opens, with no sounds, not even the slightest bit of a squeak from the hinges, telling me that they are oiled each day. A face, paler than most of the dark-skinned in Arel, telling me that this man never sees sunlight, peeks out from behind the barrier. His yellowed eyes take in Molers and me, and without a single word, he opens the door wider, allowing us passage into an underbelly of filth. I refuse to move, but Molers' iniquitous glare forces me to do as I am told, without question; so I walk through the dark hole in a structure of fraudulent piety, and disappear behind the barrier that seals me inside.

Seconds pass as my eyes adjust to the darker atmosphere, and the horrors within. Lamps are dispersed throughout the main room, illuminating couches and benches covered in silks and pillows and adorned with—children! Dark-skinned, fair-skinned, or in between, children of every age, ranging from four years old to 16, sit poised—clad in such scant clothing that they might as well have been naked—and line the room, all of them staring at me with hollow eyes, devoid of emotion, having had their innocence, their humanity, ripped away from them just so they could provide entertainment to the sickness of Arel's citizenry.

Behind them all stand shapes, stiff, unmoving, doing their best to pretend that they do not exist, but as I study them and force my eyes to focus on them, to see through the shadows they hide behind, I realize that they are older, yet still under 30: men and women, dressed in the same see-through material so as to showcase what they have to offer, and with the same eyes devoid of any emotion, of any sign of life. Behind them are armed guards, each in a black uniform, similar to an arbiter's, but unlike an arbiter's, their chests bear triangles and circles woven together, forming a never-ending web of sickness, and each holds a baton, ready to strike should anyone in the room dare disobey.

Heavy boots stomp across the breezeway as a man exits a room, leaving its door open, and stomps down the stairs that are tucked away on the left side of the room. I almost don't see them as the long shadows of the lamp cover them. Each thump rings in my ears, and I turn, watching as an arbiter, male, and older than me, descends, straightening his jacket, and zipping his pants closed as he reaches the bottom step. He strolls past me, pausing for a moment to look at me, not appreciating my censorious scowl, as the knowledge of what he has done in that room contaminates my mind, and I commit his face to memory before he leaves. I've never seen him before, but Arel isn't that big of a city.

"Master Arbiter," says a deep voice, somewhat scrappy, as though its owner had the misfortune of breathing in mustard gas for long periods of time at some point in his life, and a man jumps out of whatever hiding hole he was in, and stands in front of us, "I didn't expect to see you here so soon."

So soon? The fact that Molers not only knows of this place, but frequents it as well, does not surprise me.

"I brought a guest," Molers says, pointing at me. "I thought it best that she learn what happens to those deemed to have other qualities when they prove too troublesome."

The man, whom I assume runs this place, turns toward me, his soiled shirt twisting around his protruding belly as he does, show-casing the tears in it, giving me the impression that he cannot be bothered to put on clothes with no rips or holes in them, much less ones that are clean.

"You have come to the right place, if you are looking to have cer-tain needs fulfilled. We serve everyone," he boasts, "from arbiters to the average Arelian, from the presidential manor to the council. I don't mean to brag, but I do think we offer better merchandise than some of the other houses in Arel. I always make sure to have a fresh supply."

Other houses? There is more than one place like this?

"Do you have any preferences?" he asks me.

I remain silent, thinking of what I could do to him if left alone with him.

"Come now," he prods, "you must have some idea of what you like."

He waves two children over—they look to be around 12—a boy and a girl, and forces them to stand in front of me, their sheer clothing allowing me to see something I wish to erase from my mind; but for the first time, I notice the brand on their right cheeks: a triangle and circle woven together. They keep their eyes focused on the floor, on their grubby little feet, as their bare toes curl un-derneath them; each of them aware of what awaits them should I choose either of them.

The proprietor of this filthy establishment steps behind them, placing his gnarled hands underneath the pointed chin of the girl, digging his yellowed, mishappen nails into her skin, forcing it into the light.

"Do you prefer something delicate and soft?" he asks, moving on to the boy, rubbing his black hand down the child's side, making my stomach churn in multiple directions as the desire to vomit, as well as rip the man's face off, rises within me, as I imagine myself breaking every bone in his rotund body.

"Or"—the man sends the two children away and strolls over to a five-year-old boy, whose wide eyes fill with terror, lifting him from his seat and dragging him in front of me—"do you prefer something a little younger, more untested?"

My fists clench, but before I can follow through on my desire to beat this man to a pulp, Molers places his muscular hand on the back of my neck, squeezing just enough to let me know what he will do, should I act upon impulse.

"You might want to rethink that decision," he whispers into my ear, as his moist breath coats it.

I unclench my fists.

"You'll have to forgive her," Molers says. "This is her first time."

"Ah, yes…well," replies the proprietor, "perhaps you should look around. I have some stock in the rooms upstairs too, should you find nothing here." He hurries away, giddy and excited at having a new customer.

With his hand still on the back of my neck, Molers steers me toward the main part of the room. "I suggest," he says, "that you make good use of this, and remember, the crematoriums, the fields, and the mines are not the only places undesirables can find themselves."

He snatches a male, who looks to be 15, and pulls him over to me.

"State where you were before you ended up here," Molers demands of him.

"The training facility," says the boy in a small voice.

"What training facility?"

"The Martial Diplomatic Corps."

Molers shoves him back to his place next to a couch, before pushing me into the middle of the room.

Words are not needed to tell me what is expected of me. I know what I am supposed to do, and that I cannot win this battle. My boots send up hollow taps as I pace the perimeter of the room, with my arms behind my back, doing my best to play the part that is expected of me, while swallowing down the bile that creeps into my throat. As I move closer to the ones with batons, I spot the same brand on their right cheeks: the triangle with a circle woven together. Were they forced to work here as sex slaves, before being allowed to be an enforcer?

The sickening thought that they would volunteer to force others into this life strikes me, before I remind myself that I am no better. I am an arbiter. Bred to be one. Trained to be one since infancy. And I uphold the laws of Arel, including the more sinister ones. Why should I expect the enforcers here to be any different? If they were brought here at a young age, forced to allow others to touch them in reprehensible ways, how can I blame them for taking the only way out of such a life, when they know no other way? Yet, I can blame them. They know better than anyone the cost of being here, just as I blame any arbiter who abuses their power for their own gain.

A young girl quivers in her sheer gown, doing her best to not cry, but a few tears escape her eyes as a puddle of urine forms beneath her. In an instant, one of the enforcers steps forward, ready to punish the girl, but I stand between them, ready to stop the admonishment that is to be dealt to her. The enforcer studies me for a moment before stepping back into the shadows, deciding it best to not test me.

"Clean her up," I say to another sitting next to the girl, and after she receives an approving nod form the proprietor, she takes the girl who had soiled herself away from the main area and to the bathroom.

Once they are gone, I wander to the stairs and go to the second floor. No one stops me. Perhaps the proprietor figures that I am interested in seeing all that he has to offer before making a decision. In reality, I just want out of here, away from this putrid stench of depravity, this black hole of misery, and the feeling that I will never be clean again. Once at the top of the stairs, someone knocks on the door. I turn. The same man who had let Molers and me inside allows a woman dressed in a blue silk shirt that drapes over silk pants of burgundy orange inside. She smiles and laughs with the proprietor about needing some relaxation from the grueling duties she has had to perform the last few days. As she talks, her curls bob from the motion of her head, breaking free from the multi-colored scarf tied around her scalp.

It takes a few moments, but as she and the proprietor chat, I realize that the expensive dress and her mannerisms indicate that she is a member of the Arelian council. It is rare for someone of such background to come to the eastern sector, which means the proprietor had told me the truth about the people he services, and that she must have used a private transport to come here in secrecy. I watch as she stalks to a young boy and motions for him to follow her. Before she reaches the stairs, I slip into a room, the very room that the arbiter from earlier had been in when I first arrived, and shut the door.

Gurgled breathing, as though someone is trying to breathe through a straw just under the surface of water pulls me from the door, and I whirl around, finding a bloody mound on the bed. As the gurgled breathing continues, I approach it, my face scrunching up in horror as I realize that the bloody mound is a nine-year-old kid having been beaten to the verge of death. His jaw hangs at an odd angle, while his chest remains very still, unable to expand with each desperate attempt at a breath.

I sit on the bed next to him as the blood pooling on the sheets seep into my pants, matching the blood stains on my jacket, looking for a place to go, unsure of what to do, as he stares at me in fear with his one good eye. I want to tell him that it will be okay, that no harm will come to him, but I can't when the truth is the opposite. No medical center will take him. He has been deemed expendable. Memories of the woman Commandant Paq had beaten and how I relieved her of her suffering flood my mind, only to mingle with those of the girl from the inquiry that I was forced to execute in order to prove my loyalty, but she, too, had been beaten. I saw the same look in both of their eyes that I see in this kid's. He knows he is dying. He cannot tell me, but he doesn't need to. A sickening feeling envelops me as two choices are presented to me: relieve his suffering, or leave him here to die an agonizing death. His end will be the same, either way.

Grinding my teeth, and hardening my resolve, forcing myself to do the only merciful thing I can think of, I place the heel of my palm on his throat. It slips from the blood coating it, but I do not let that stop me from doing what must be done. I press down.

His one eye widens with fear, while the other remains sealed shut.

"It's okay," I say to him in a soft voice. "Just close your eyes. Death is not to be feared. Just go to sleep." My voice chokes in the end, and I swallow a lump that has formed, doing my best to remain strong.

He closes his only eye as I press harder on his throat, cutting off his air, until he no longer moves. Unable to move myself, as grief over the loss of someone so young, so defenseless, overwhelms me, I remain seated in the pool of blood, not caring if I am forced to throw this uniform away later.

Just then, the door opens and the same woman from before pops her head in. I glare at her, but before I can scream at her to leave, she gives me a whimsical smile, and steps out, shutting the door behind her. Pulled from my stupor, I place a blanket over the boy's face, bending down to his ear to whisper, "I'm sorry."

Jumping from the bed, I hurry to the door and open it with care, not wanting to make a sound, and peek into the hallway in time to see the woman disappear into another room with a boy about the same age as the one whose suffering I just ended. I creep down the hallway, not allowing my boots to make a sound on the hard wood, hoping that it doesn't creak from my movements, and pause at the door the woman disappeared behind. I grasp the knob, its cold exterior cooling the sweat coating my palm, and twist it, mimicking a snail with my movements. Once the latch clicks free, I ease the door open, making no sound. The woman stands in front of a dresser with a mirror attached to it with her silk blouse unbuttoned, revealing her breasts, while rearranging her hair, ignoring the boy seated on the bed with his head bowed low.

One step at a time, I sneak up behind the woman. She never sees me, nor does she hear me. With one swift motion, I grab the back of her head and slam her face into the mirror, breaking it, and allow her unconscious form to slump over the dresser with the bits of broken glass that now lay scattered across it, not caring if its sharp edges slice her. The boy stares at me with frightened eyes, but he never screams.

"Is there a way out of here?" I demand. There is no time to waste. I cannot save all of them, but I might be able to get him out of here.

He doesn't respond.

"Is there any way out of here besides the front door?" I say again.

"The gar… garbage chute."

"Where is it?"

He points to the door.

"Do you wish to leave this place?" I ask.

He nods.

"Arbiter Noni!" Molers' voice echoes through the building, resonating off the walls, and filling me with dread. He has grown tired of waiting for me.

I grab the boy and drag him to the door and into the hallway.

"Where?" I ask him.

He points to a slim, metal handle sticking out of the wall. Of course, they would have tucked it away, but it is convenient for my purposes.

"Do you know where it leads?" I ask.

"To the dumpsters outside."

"Don't make a sound," I tell him.

Straight to the dumpsters. Makes sense. This way, no one leaves this place, and they have every one so scared that no one would dare try to escape, not to mention the penalty for doing so. I carry him to the garbage chute as Molers yells for me again, open it up, and dump the boy inside before closing it behind him. With no time to hope for the best or think about how things can go wrong in an instant, I march down the corridor, as Molers yells my name for a third time. I tromp down the stairs, ignoring his irate face and the threats spewing from his mouth as I pass him, heading for the door. The man who had allowed us entrance, tries to stop me, but I toss him into Molers, not daring to stop, open the door, and slam it shut behind me as I step outside into the twilight.

Once free of that suffocating place of desecration, I run down the street and hide before Molers steps outside. He looks around, but I remain crouched, willing him to go away. Relief floods over me as he runs in the opposite direction. I step out of my place of hiding and circle the alleyway, searching for a dumpster, growing anxious for every minute that passes, and the nauseating thought of having failed percolates in my brain, growing stronger with each second, but dissipates the moment I spot it. I race for the dumpster and fling open its top, revealing the boy inside, and help him out. With no time to waste, I hold him close as I dart through the narrow street, glad that it is devoid of people; they are all heading home by now, not that anyone was here when Molers and I first came through. I need someplace to hide him. But where?

Panic rises within me as my frantic search turns up nothing and the ever-growing possibility of being captured turns into a reality. A flapping sound reaches me. Following the noise, I dart around another corner and find black tape stretches across the door to a residence: arbiter tape, left there after a raid had been performed. When the raid took place, I cannot say, nor does it matter. No new residents have been assigned there, yet, and no one will dare enter a place that has been searched by arbiters, meaning that I have found a safe place to hide the boy, for the moment at least.

I carry him over to the door, and glance around for any prying eyes, but am not surprised when I find nothing. No one ever strays near a place that has been the site of a raid. The punishment for doing so is severe. I test the door. It opens. Relieved, I put the boy down and tell him to go inside, but he refuses to budge.

"I need you to go in there. Don't make a sound. I will send someone for you tonight. His name is Chase. You can trust him."

The boy's worried and frightened eyes stare into mine.

"Go!"

He ducks under the tape and slips inside. I hope he remains undiscovered.

Knowing that I cannot stay here, and I will need to face Molers at some point, I leave the marked-off residence and navigate my way back to the main part of the eastern sector, hoping that the boy stays where he is. I run through the maze of narrow streets and alleyways as I head back to the plaza, hoping to get here before Molers does. Darkness creeps around me, warning me that the sun has set, and curfew will be soon; all citizens and plebeians are expected to be inside an hour after sunset. Familiar sounds reach my ears, and relief hits me as the trolley speeds past, ringing its bell as it carries its passengers to their destination.

A plebeian almost bumps into me, but veers to the side just in time to miss me, as she hurries away with her arms full of packages, while a bulging red bag slams against her hip as she runs off. I am almost to the plaza, and some semblance of normalcy to wash away the stain of decrepitness that Molers forced onto me. As I watch the girl, wondering why she is in such a hurry, besides the impending approach of curfew, and who her master is, a broad shoulder rams into me, almost knocking me over as the man it belongs to stalks away, without bothering to give me so much as a side glance or even an abrupt apology. My eyes stay fixed on him as I consider his behavior to be odd. Most people do anything they can to avoid bumping into an arbiter, but this man acts as though he never saw me, as though his mind is focused on something else.

I follow after him, dodging a group of people as they hurry down the street in an effort to get home, lest they be caught out after curfew, and their sandaled feet flop on the pavement in a mish-mashed tune that sounds as though they are stomping on potatoes in an ill-conceived attempt to mash them. Rushing through the streets, I push person after person out of my way, though most jump back, glad to that I am not interested in them, as I keep my eyes on the mysterious man, and the bulging, padded jacket he holds closed, but the bulge hidden underneath, does not match his slender physique; it is unnatural, as though it does not belong. He turns his head from side to side, allowing me to see the scared expression on his face, but the foreboding sense that his fear is not for himself fills me. He hikes up a stairwell leading to a moving walkway.

Running, I speed for the causeway knowing that I cannot lose him and afraid of what will happen if he escapes me. A woman gasps as I ram into her, but she keeps her insults to herself, as I take the stairs two at a time, while keeping my eyes on the man as he moves down the walkway, too impatient to just allow it to carry him to his destination, and as he bumps into person after person, unaware that he is not the only one on the causeway, the sinking feeling that something is amiss grows deeper, forming a chasm so deep within me that I cannot escape. My boot thumps on the metal grate of the final step as I push myself onto the platform before jumping onto the walkway. For a moment, I fear I will lose my balance as the conveyor belt jerks me to the side, but I grow accustomed to its motion within seconds. He is ahead of me, but doesn't seem to have noticed my interest in him.

A huge crackle, followed by a deafening monotone, spew from

the loudspeakers surrounding us, warning everyone that curfew is near. "Curfew will be in sixty minutes," says a robotic voice, masquerading as feminine, as though that is supposed to put people at ease.

I worm my way through the few that are on the moving walkway, while some jump off and hurry for the stairs in a desperate attempt to get home, being careful to not cause too much of a ruckus and alert the man to my presence. The gears of the causeway squeal, forcing the conveyor belt to cart me onward. I spot another arbiter directing people, urging them to hurry home, and I yell at him, knowing that I might need help, but my voice is drowned by the bustle of those around me, and he is out of earshot within seconds. Quickening my pace, I hurry for the man, as each step seems to make me bounce just a little as the rubber soles of my boots meet the ribbed, rubber surface of the walkway, while the feeling of dread urges me onward. Two people step onto the walkway in front of me, but I shove them out of my way, not caring if they say anything, as the man moves further ahead of me, shrinking in the distance as though mocking my efforts. I need to catch him. I need to… What are they doing here?

For a brief moment, I allow myself to do the one thing arbiters are not supposed to do when fulfilling their duties: I become distracted. Underneath a lighted sign, reminding all Arelians to do their duty for Arel because we are all one and are all in this together, are Mandi and Natalie tucked away in its shadow, and they seem to be having a heated argument before Mandi stalks away, slipping into a crowd and disappearing, leaving Natalie to do the same. An unending barrage of questions about why they are here, and the notion that this is not the first time I have seen them meet in a secretive manner, while pretending that their rendezvous is nothing more than innocence, fills me. Lost in my own musings of what I just saw, I forget about the man, until I look ahead and find that he has gone.

Dammit!

Panicked, I scold myself for allowing him to get away. I need to find him. If something happens because of my negligence, I will turn myself in to the detention center, as the blood of others will be on my hands. I do not know how I am certain of this; I just am. I rush to the railing of the moving walkway, and search the causeways above and below me, scanning them, searching for the man in the bulging coat that does not fit him as my failure taunts me, reminding me that this will be another to add to the list, but all I find is an assortment of uniforms, each a certain color, signifying their station, mixed in a sea of others not chosen to serve the way I was, but allowed to have a semblance of normalcy—so long as they obey Arel—as they parade around in their ostentatious, tie-dyed outfits. Second by second, the people on the walkways grow thinner, while anxiety brews within me, intensifying as the man remains elusive, until…

There he is!

I spot him stepping off a walkway above me and heading for the railcar platform. I need to get up there, but if I wait until I have reached the stairwell that borders this walkway, I'll lose him again. Frantic, I look all around, searching for a shortcut, and settle upon one: a pole, stretching from the overhang that covers the walkways to the street below. This is my only chance. Bracing myself, and judging the distance between me and the fast approaching pole, I race down the causeway, allowing its movement to give my speed an added boost, before jumping onto the railing and leaping to the pole, amidst a few screams as onlookers watch my death-defying stunt.

My hands grasp the warm metal post, squeaking as my sweaty palms threaten to be my undoing, but I cling to the pole, refusing to let go, and wrap my legs around it, letting them support my weight. Inch by inch, I climb upward, pushing with my legs and pulling with my arms, while my jacket bunches around me, digging into my armpits and elbows, scolding me for being so reckless. I ignore it, ignore everything and everyone around me, as I push myself to the moving walkway above me, concentrating on the overhang towering over me, reminding myself of my goal. An eternity passes before me, ticking the seconds away, as I ease my way upward. I'm almost there. Just a little further.

With one final push, I am level with the walkway. My heart pounds in my ears as I take a deep breath to calm my nerves and let go, pushing with all my might, leaping from the pole to the causeway. I slam into the railing, but cling to its smooth surface, my muscles burning as I pull myself over it, until I am able to swing my feet over it and onto the conveyor belt, landing with a thump, while the sudden sensation of moving causes my stomach to leap into my throat, before I refocus my attention. I look where the man has disappeared and race down the walkway, glad that only one or two people are on it, as I hurry for where I last saw him, knowing where he is headed. I plow through the exit for the walkway and charge down the platform to the stairs leading to the railcars, ignoring any who get in my way, as I race past them, and stomp up the stairs, shoving everyone out of my way with such force that some almost topple over the railing. Like a madman, I weave between people, almost tripping over one or two, as I make my way upward, until I burst onto the railcar platform and the crowds forcing their way onto the last shuttle.

"Curfew will be in fifty minutes," says the loudspeaker, but I ignore it as I scan the crowd, searching for my target,

People brush past me, sprinting for the edge of the platform, wanting to be the first on the approaching shuttle as its whine draws near. Dammit, where is he? I move around, edging my way into the gathering crowd, knowing he is here, as I glance from one individual to the next, hoping that the next one I spot will be him. He could not have gone far.

I see him.

Near the edge of the platform, the man stands with his hands gripping his oversized coat, as he summons the resolve to do what he has planned. Another man stands in front of me. I grab him and throw him to the side as I squeeze through the tightknit crowd, forcing my way to the man. He opens his coat, revealing a vest of explosives with a symbol painted on it (the Arelian insignia with a line through it) as he stretches out his arms and raises his right hand with a trigger in it. Realizing that their lives are in jeopardy, people scream and run away in a desperate attempt to put as much distance between the bomber and themselves, while I charge for him.

Ignoring the screams, ignoring the chaos, I race for him and plow into him, knocking him to the ground as the trigger shoots from his hand and skips across the platform before rolling over the side and onto the tracks. The man struggles to get away, but I pin him to the ground, noticing the wires on his vest. Fearful that it can still detonate, I reach for the wires, knowing that this could be my last act, and rip them out. The man screams in frustrations and flings an elbow at me, but I block it, and throw him onto his stomach, straddling him so that he cannot get up.

"Who are you working for?" I demand as I grip his hands and pin them behind him.

Before he can answer, movement catches my attention as more arbiters move in to subdue the man, distracting me just enough for him to roll on his side, tossing me off him. Stunned, I shake my head to clear it as he scrambles to his feet and reach for him, but I am too late. The whine of the railcar fills the platform and pounds against my ears, suffocating me as it races forward, desperate to stay on schedule.

"No!" I scream as the man in the vest jumps from the platform and into the path of the shuttle.

Bits of his flesh smack into me as he is sprayed in every direction from the impact, turning him into nothing more than a terrible memory, while I am left on my knees on the platform, wondering if I should feel relief, or shame.

Chapter 24

Still Not Over

Commander Vye stands next to me, while I stand at attention in her office, reading my demeanor, my every movement, trying to discern if I have hidden anything from her while I recount the events of the past few hours.

"Are you sure that is everything?"

"Yes, ma'am," I say in a stoic voice, burying my emotions and refusing to allow them to escape, fearing that I may betray the young life that depends on me now.

"And just why were you at such a disreputable place, knowing full well that it is forbidden?" she asks me, her sharp voice slicing through me as though I am nothing more than softened butter.

"Master Arbiter Molers commanded me to," I reply, refusing to flick my eyes in Molers' direction as he stands at attention in the room with me, knowing full well that, for the moment, he is not the one in charge and must submit to Commander Vye's interrogation, but I feel his eyes burning holes into my skull for having reported that he forced me to go to a house of pedophilia. I hope he burns for his crime.

"And?" prods Commander Vye, rounding on Molers, "where were you when the suicide bomber was spotted?"

"Arbiter Noni ran away," answers Molers, "and I had no knowledge that she was in pursuit of a suspect."

"Perhaps you would have been if you hadn't been piddling your time away at a house full of child prostitutes!" roars Commander Vye. "You know that all my arbiters are forbidden to go there and you just demonstrated why!"

Ringing silence fills the temporary void as Commander Vye regains control over her anger.

"Noni, you are dismissed."

Not wanting to be there any longer than necessary, I salute and leave, glad to be out of there, but now is not the time to rejoice in such a small victory; there is still the matter of the boy, but I know that I will not be able to get him out of the city, yet he cannot stay where he is. I need help, and there is only one person I can think of who will be able to do what I need done, but the thought of risking his life for a situation I created sickens me, but if I don't, someone far more innocent will die. The empty hallway gives me courage to do what I must. I creep down the corridor, almost tripping over the strings of a rug that has begun to unravel, a form of its revenge for not being maintained, and head for the door leading down to the plebeian quarters. Though the barrenness of the hallway unnerves me, I assume it is because some are on duty, while others are avoiding being caught eavesdropping, lest they also suffer Commander Vye's wrath, not that I blame them. I find the rotted door and grip the handle, prying it open, hoping that Chase is down there and not on some other task.

The stale air of the basement attacks my lungs, causing me to cough as I grip the rail, while flecks of the peeling polish flick off and coat my hand as it slides down it in an effort to balance me while I step on each of the bent, wooden steps that wobble beneath me, giving me the sensation of floating as I descend into the unknown depths below. A small splash sounds as I reach the bottom. Musty light greets me as I look up and watch the balls of dust hang in the air, forming a thin curtain of pollution that my lungs detest inhaling, but I ignore their protests as I hurry to the end of the first corridor and past the swaying cobwebs hanging from the bare walls with strips of wood missing, having fallen away from rot.

I turn the corner, heading down the other corridor, like I did the first night I had snuck down here, leaving prints in the layer of dirt on the concrete floor—it looks as though it has not seen a broom in years—and charge past the swinging manual doors as I head for one particular one. I burst through it. Chase sits on the bed with Gwen, combing her hair for her as she fiddles with the tattered blanket that has brown stains on it; I hope they are not the remains of someone's blood. They both stop what they are doing and stare at me with wide eyes, each asking a question, but not daring to speak it.

"I need your help," I say.

Chase stands up and pulls me inside, after looking up and down the hallway, assuring himself that no one has witnessed my presence down here.

"Tell me," he says.

"There is this boy," I begin, keeping my voice low so that prying ears will not hear me as I tell him about the house of pedophilia and the child I had helped escape from there, but now have no place to take him so that he can be free from ever having to satisfy another's perverted needs. "After what has happened today, I cannot sneak out without attracting attention."

"I'll go," Chase says, without me having to ask.

I tell him where the boy is hidden before telling him about Luther.

"Are you sure you can find it?"

"I know my way around these streets."

"Just be careful."

"Are you sure he will help?" Chase asks me.

"He pretends he doesn't care, but something tells me that he does," I reply.

Without another word, Chase puts on his shoes and grabs a sweater before rubbing dirt on his face, but before he leaves, he squats down, putting himself at Gwen's level and looks her in the eyes as he touches his forehead to hers, trying to ease her fears.

"I'll be back," he says. "That's a promise."

She wraps her thin arms around him and squeezes, not wanting to let him go, but releases him when he stands up.

He looks at me and says, "You should go back upstairs before they notice you're missing."

I nod in agreement. Just as he steps out the door, I grab his arm, trying to ignore the sinking feeling in my stomach, afraid that I am sending him to his death.

"Come back to me."

"Always." He disappears, heading for the window that we had used the night he took me to see how plebeians are treated in Arel.

Gwen looks at me with those wide eyes, and I remember the night I had first seen her when she tried to get medicine for her mistress, but her mistress died anyway. The worried expression on her face gnaws at me, and I do not know what to do other than to hold her for a moment; so I walk over to her, sitting on the cot next to her, and place an arm around her, comforting her the best I can, hoping that my embrace alleviates some of her fears. No words pass between us. There is nothing I can say that will eradicate her fears. All we can do is wait and hope.

"I have to go," I whisper to her. It's true. I cannot stay here, not tonight.

She nods and I wipe a stray tear from her eye, helping her to lie down as I tuck the blanket around her before leaving and running for the stairs that will take me back to the main floor.

My lungs thank me as I step through the door, crossing the threshold from the basement to the main floor of the manor, thankful to have cleaner air to breathe, if one could say such a thing, as the air has smelled foul to me these past few weeks. I close the door to the basement and hurry to the stairs leading to the second floor, but pause when I notice a commotion, followed by an unusual silence, as though everyone is in a hurry to be somewhere, frightened of the consequences of disobedience. Grasping the rounded curve of the railing and ignoring the few splinters that try to dig into my hand, I look around, watching as the arbiters that live here with me hurry outside to the green atrium, wondering what is happening, and what I have missed in my short absence.

One of the arbiters stops in front of me, giving me a pondering glance.

"What are you doing?" he says to me. "We have been ordered onto the green."

What? Why?

Knowing better than to ask questions—this is not the time to be inquisitive—I tuck the few stray strands of my black hair behind me ear and straighten my jacket, smoothing out the wrinkles as best I can, before running for the back door that leads to the giant quad where the exercise equipment is, not wanting to be the last one there. This could be a surprise inspection, a visit from a councilmember, or some sort of hazing of a new member to our ranks. Untold possibilities run through my mind, but I haven't time to think about them.

When I reach the quad, I pause, spotting two poles, spaced an even length apart, and my stomach sinks as I remember the day I was brought out here to receive my punishment for failing to carry out my duties as an arbiter. Not wanting to be forced to stand between them again, I fall in line with the other arbiters as they form two lines, one on each side of the poles, standing erect and facing forward, refusing to show an ounce of pity toward the offender. Commander Vye stands between the two poles, staring out at those under her command, her hawk-like gaze missing nothing as she watches from her perch, with a stoic look on her face, causing me to quiver as I take my place in line, glad that I am not the one being punished. A soft roll of thunder echoes above us as clouds move in, blocking out the stars and making the night sky appear darker than it is, adding to the foreboding atmosphere that has overtaken us.

"Bring him forth!" says Commander Vye, her hardened voice ensnaring us in its vicelike grip, causing a chill to coarse through me, making me shiver, despite the warmth in the air.

I move my eyes so that I can see who has earned this sort of admonishment and almost gasp when I see Molers marching to the front between Renal and another arbiter, his head held high in defiance of Commander Vye's attempts to humiliate him. With each step he takes, thunder rumbles, growing closer, warning us of a storm that none shall escape. Memories of my own lashing flood my mind, but I push them away, willing myself to remain focused and to not give in to their terror. He stops between the poles and allows arbiters to tie each arm to one and rip his shirt off, exposing his back, and the marks that already litter it, forming crisscross patterns from previous punishments. For a brief moment, I feel sorry for him, realizing that, like most arbiters in Arel, he has received his share of chastisement, and bear the scars of such harshness, just like me, but that pity ceases the moment I see the smile on his face, as though he is enjoying this moment, relishing its teachings and how it helps one build strength.

"Arbiter Noni!"

Commander Vye's voice stabs me, jerking me from my internal conflict. Unsure of the reason for my name being called, I step out of the line of arbiters and face her. She motions for me to approach. I do, all the while, my heart jumping around in my chest, desperate to break free and to run away from this moment, not wanting to be a part of it, but knowing that there is no escape. More thunder rumbles overhead, and I feel its vibrations in my chest as I inhale, until I am in front of my commander. She stares at me, her cold eyes making me feel like an ant underneath a boot, knowing that its end is near, and I wish I could run away. She hands me a whip as a crack of thunder reverberates above us. My hand shaking, I reach for it, not wanting to take it, unsure of her reasons for forcing me into this situation. The moment I grasp the smooth leather, a great weight forces my hand to drop downward, pinning me to the ground as the remainder of the whip smacks into the grass with its metal tips clinking against one another.

"Master Arbiter Molers," says Commander Vye, her cold voice ringing out, mixing in with the growing thunder above us, "you have been found negligent in your duties, having allowed a terrorist to almost commit irreparable harm to the citizens of Arel. For such an act, you have been sentenced to twenty lashes."

"I'll wear them with pride," Molers says, loud enough for everyone present to hear him.

Commander Vye steps back and looks at me as I continue to hold the whip in my hand. I know what is expected of me, what is always expected of me: to obey, to show my commitment to Arel. Minacious grumbling moves above me, filling the clouds with its sounds as though it is a harbinger of what is to come. Commander Vye clears her throat as a silent warning to me. Squeezing the handle of the lash, I step behind Molers as small flashes of lightning illuminate his muscular frame, and swing my arm backward, preparing to strike. In one swift motion, I bring my arm up overhead, swinging it as hard as I can, and strike Molers' already scarred back as a streak of lightning stretches across the night sky, lighting the entire quad, followed by an ear-splitting crack of thunder that rattles the glass in the windows on the manor.

"One!" Commander Vye counts.

A drop of rain strikes my boot as I swing my arm back before snapping the whip again, wrapping it around his shoulders, and I watch as the metal bits on the end rip into his skin, tearing bits of it away, spraying droplets of blood. Again, Commander Vye counts the number Molers has received. As I fling the lash at him again and again, thinking of how he had tried to choke the life out of me, of all the horrors he had put me through while at the training facility, of the man he had executed in cold blood, and of the place he had taken me to earlier, filled with children too young to understand what was being done for them, but old enough to know that their lives were forever changed. The more I focus on what he has done, the harder I snap the whip, willing it to massacre him, to tear into him, and to cause as much pain as possible so that he will feel what I feel, understand what he has done. With each strike, lightening fills the sky above us, demonstrating its displeasure and its fury. I ignore it. Again, I bring the lash down upon him, not flinching as it digs into his skin, leaving a gorge where smooth flesh had once been. Again, and again, I strike him with the whip, losing myself to its power, and the dangers it holds until...

Lightning stretches from the sky and strikes the wall surrounding Arel, sending sparks and debris in every direction, warning me of my slippage into depravity, of what I risk turning into. I stop, allowing my arm to go limp by my side as the lash snakes around me, forming a leathery coil with metallic teeth, ready for its next victim. I am becoming Molers. While I stand underneath the stormy sky, ashamed of the pleasure I took in torturing him, Molers laughs, not a whimper or a soft chortle, but a baleful laugh, deep from within, as though he senses my shame and knows that once again, he has won.

"Noni," says Commander Vye, "there is still one more to go."

Setting my mouth in a firm line, as I grip the whip once more, feeling the raised nobs of the handle press into my skin, I swing my arm back, and bring it forward, allowing the lash to sail through the air and find its mark, delivering the final count of Molers' punishment. Once it hits its mark, I hold the whip out and drop it, allowing it to land in the grass with a plunk, before turning and taking my place back in formation with the other arbiters, feeling Commander Vye's gaze upon me the entire time. She motions for a couple of arbiters to come forward and take Molers down. They hasten to do so and carry him away from the quad and into the manor.

"Dismissed!" yells Commander Vye.

Following orders, the two lines of arbiters break up as everyone files back inside, but without me: I remain rooted to the ground underneath the grumbling thunder and flashes of lightening, and for reasons I do not understand, no one says anything, not even my commander, but instead, they leave me with a turmoil of thoughts and emotions that I do not understand for company.

Wind whips around me, as I remain outside, not caring about the storm raging around me. I felt pleasure while inflicting pain on my former instructor. I wanted revenge. I did as I was told. I didn't question it. Is this who I am? A robot, a drone, programmed to follow orders until my dying day? I think of the people I have helped escape Arel, of how I had helped Luther when his home was searched, and of the boy Chase is with now. No. I am so much more. I am Noni. Molers will get what he deserves someday, but not tied up; it will be a fair fight when it happens.

Footsteps sound behind me, causing me to whip around, ready to defend myself from whomever had decided to sneak up behind me, but I put my hands down the moment I see who it is.

"You should go inside," says Renal.

"I know," I reply in a low voice.

"Commander Vye never should have made you do that."

"Why did she?"

"I don't know, but I'm sure she had her reasons."

A thought plagues my mind, and I do not want to think the worst of Renal, but he has been here longer than me, and I need to know.

"Did you..." I begin, allowing my voice to trail off before starting over. "Did you know about that place? A house of pleasure provided by the young?"

"Yes."

Surprised by his answer, I glare at him as ill thoughts roam through my mind and my perception of him changes.

"How..." I begin, but he cuts me off.

"Such places are all over Arel. Each sector has one or two, providing services for the despicable, allowed by the council and the presidents."

A part of me cannot believe what I am hearing, but another part knows it to be true. A stain, buried deep beneath shiny glass and steel for none but the partakers to know about, or those unfortunate enough to discover the truth.

"That place deserves to burn," says Renal, but, judging by the way he says it, I don't think he meant for me to hear it.

I remain silent, unsure of what to say.

"You never should have been sent on patrol with him," Renal continues, referring to Molers. "You need to watch your back around him."

"Sir?" I say, wondering where all this is coming from.

"Don't you think it is strange, that the only punishment he received for allowing a suicide bomber to almost take out an entire railcar platform is twenty lashes, while you were sent to the detention center for stopping another arbiter from abusing their power? And don't you think it is equally strange that you have received no commendation for stopping the bomber?"

I hadn't thought about it, but Renal is correct. Many arbiters receive far worse punishments for the most minor of infractions, but not Molers. Things have been amiss ever since Molers was assigned to the eastern sector.

"Watch yourself, Noni." Renal gets up and heads for the back door leading into the manor, motioning for me to follow. As I take a step toward him, I notice movement out of the corner of my eye and glance at it, thrilled to see Chase standing behind some bushes, but manage to keep my face unreadable, in case I alert Renal to his presence. Chase and I look into each other's eyes and somehow, I do not know how, but somehow, I know that he succeeded in getting the boy to safety, and in coming back to me.

Chapter 25

An Invitation

The massive wall stretches outside my window, texturizing the reflection of my walnut-colored face in the glass, as I stare out at its ever-present reminder of how we are all locked inside the city, never allowed to leave. I understand the need to keep the barbarians from being able to invade us, and they have been silent of late, making me wonder what is happening that no one within Arel knows about, or if they are planning something. I fear the latter.

The reflection of my brown eyes in the glass is level with the top of the wall, as dark, miniscule shapes trace back and forth along the top, making me believe, just for a moment, that I can see over it and the field of grass beyond before it melts into the tangled mesh of trees as vines and branches twist around one another, forming an impenetrable wall itself, as though it wants to separate the wild from civilization. My eyes trace the line of the wall as it stretches around Arel, curving just so, in order to form the perfect barrier, preventing anything from getting in, but its primary function is to stop anyone from leaving. Opposing feelings battle one another as I observe the magnificent structure, each trying to triumph over the other, and as they tear my mind apart, a soft knock sounds on my door.

I say nothing as my mind dwells upon the night Molers received a flogging for disobedience, for forcing me to go to that despicable place full of children who are nothing more than objects meant to appease the desires of certain members of Arelian society. My face flushes with anger at the thought of that place, and though it has been three weeks, I still smell the musty odor of the mildew that seeped into the porous bricks of its walls and the wooden stench of the lumber beams that had warped from the humid air and never dried out. Renal's sentiments that that horrid place should burn mirror my own; I just wish I could do it without consequence. But if it did burn down, what would become of its residents? The knowledge that they would be sent to another place just like it tears away at me.

You can't save them all.

Luther's voice plays in my mind, reminding me of the sad truth of my world: I can't save them all.

The soft knock sounds again, more forceful than before, jolting me from my sullen reverie, as, once again, I grapple with the reality of my world.

"Enter," I say in a flat tone, devoid of any emotion or warmth.

Sheila stands in the doorway when it slides open, and I turn away from the window as pangs of guilt gnaw at me for being so cold toward her.

"Sheila," I say, "is anything wrong?"

"No, mistress," she says.

"You don't need to call me that," I tell her.

A door down the hall slides shut and Amal strolls past, glancing at me for a moment, but my eyes narrow as I stare back at him, daring him to try something, and wishing he would, just so I would have an excuse to beat my fists into someone in a vain attempt to alleviate my anger. As he waltzes past, his sleeve rises up on his arm just enough to expose his wrist, and the missing band. Once again, he has forgotten to wear his wristband. I wonder how he manages to get away with such an infraction, but the more I think about it, the more I remember that I have not seen him eat at any of the eateries in the eastern sector. He only eats at the manor. Maybe I should report him, just to put another mark on his record and earn favor with the powers that be, and perhaps get the mark on mine removed, or changed to a less severe one.

No. I have a better plan.

"There is a message for you," says Sheila, ripping me from my never ending thoughts, once again.

A message? From whom?

"Thank you," I tell her, and she steps back into the hallway, knowing that the message for me is private.

I take two steps from the window to the wall monitor and turn it on, taking a step back when I see Faya's face appear, filling it from edge to edge, having not expected her to call me, nor have I thought about her since the day I had been taken to detainment.

"Noni!"

"Faya," I say with surprise. "Is everything okay?"

"I'm worried about you."

"I'm fine," I say, trying to relieve her fears, and wondering why she hadn't called me earlier if she is this concerned about my well-being, before scolding myself that arbiters are discouraged from having friendships, and her very call puts her at risk, unless she can make it seem like an official communication.

She glances around before leaning in closer to the monitor on her end, lowering her voice.

"Noni, what were you thinking? Attacking another arbiter like that!"

"He was going to kill someone," I reply, aghast that she would even ask me such a question.

"You should have let him," Faya says.

I cannot believe my ears. Never has Faya told me to leave another to their fate, to die a senseless death. I have never left her to hers in all the times her life was in danger while we were recruits.

"We are tasked with upholding the law, and the law states that arbiters are not to attack citizens of Arel without just cause. They must have—"

"Noni, we aren't at the training facility anymore! Your idealistic ways worked there, but here in Arel—you need to keep your head down."

"But we all swore an oath to protect Arel and uphold its laws."

I sound like little more than a first-year recruit that has just learned to speak, but the last bit gnaws at me, chastising me, reminding me that I had been breaking one of Arel's most sacred laws by helping people escape the city and her long arm of tyranny. In a way, I am as bad as Amal and some other arbiters, choosing which laws I will uphold and which ones I won't, but I fail to see how stopping a man from beating a girl to death is equatable to helping people leave who chose to leave.

"Don't be so naïve."

Faya's words strike me, stabbing me where it hurts most, and memories of all the times I had helped her, of all the times I had sacrificed for her, flood my mind as her words cut deeper than any knife ever could.

"I shouldn't even be talking to you."

"What are you saying?" I ask, confused.

"You were sent to detainment. You have a black mark on your record. Talking to you could be putting myself in jeopardy."

"So..."

"You put Joel in a terrible position!"

This explains the call. I never considered the position I would put her and Joel in when I stopped Amal, and she is worried about him, about how my actions will reflect on him, since he had put a good word in for me with the palace guards.

"I'm sorry," I say in a low voice. "I never meant..."

"You never do, but you never think about the consequences of your actions either."

This new side of Faya unnerves me, and a strong desire to end the call propels me to raise my hand and tap the button on the screen, but I pause for a moment, rethinking my actions and how it will look. But this... this is not the Faya I remember.

"Noni, please, be careful. Don't do anything stupid. Don't do anything dangerous."

Her face says that she is concerned for my welfare, but her voice betrays her, revealing the fact that she is more concerned about how my actions may reflect upon her, which cuts through me, considering we were friends while at the training facility. A part of me always knew that we might go our separate ways after being commissioned, but I had hoped... Faya, is right; I am naïve.

As I stare at her on the wall monitor, with a wroth expression poking through the façade of concern, an anger rises up within me, threatening, once again, to overtake me, as I realize that Faya called me more for her own benefit instead of mine, and before I can stop it, my mouth speaks the words on the forefront of my mind.

"Dangerous for whom? Me? Or you?"

Faya is taken aback by the harshness in my voice, and I regret saying those words the moment they leave my mouth. Tact was never my strong suit, and now more than ever, I need to practice it.

Faya chews her lower lip, a slight nibble, as she gathers her thoughts and considers her next move.

"I don't want anything happening to you. You're the only friend I have."

My face softens as I rethink my previous words to her and change direction. I do not want the call to end on bad terms, and I cannot blame her for being worried about how my actions might reflect upon her and Joel.

"Thank you," I say, in a humble voice, "for backing me up when questioned about what had happened."

"I never collaborated your story."

My eyes widen when Faya says this. When I was released from detainment, I was told that someone had confirmed my version of events, and I just assumed that Faya had been the one person who had done so. If it wasn't her, then who did?

"What do you mean?" I ask her.

A single curl from Faya's wiry hair falls in front of her face, as though to help her next words punch me in the gut.

"When questioned about your actions, I told them the truth: that you had run from the table and attacked another arbiter unprovoked, and that I never saw him strike anyone."

Words leave me when she says this, and I do not know what to think. Faya had been my friend since we were in our fourth year at the training facility. All recruits had been gathered into a room and were expected to not speak, to not move, to do nothing but sit still in such a way that it put a statue to shame. Any who failed were carried away kicking and screaming and were never seen again. Faya had trouble not fidgeting, like most toddlers, but obedience is demanded of us since the day of our birth. She kept shifting her feet, and at one point, her foot got caught in the cracks between the mosaic (a geometrical pattern formed from the Arelian insignia: gray upon black) tiles of the floor and she tripped, almost falling over, but I caught her. Even at four years of age, I prevented her from going to the crematorium. From that day forward, we have been friends, but now, I question whether she knows me at all, since she chose to believe the worse about me.

"I have to go," she says and switches her monitor off, thus ending the call, and leaving me in my room, surrounded by shadows and floating bits of dust, as the morning sun focuses its yellow rays upon me and my sudden solitude.

Faya left me to my fate in the detention center.

Numb, I step to my closet and pull out a clean jacket that had been pressed the day before, allowing my automatic movements to take over as I put it on and smooth out any creases, while my mind dwells upon my conversation with Faya and the ambivalence, laced with anger, she displayed toward me. Still trapped in a mental fog, I leave my room, allowing my feet to lead me down the stairs and to the main floor, since they know the way, still not believing that Faya had treated me in such a cold manner, but before I can dwell on it further, a man in an arbiter uniform, but with white stripes stretching from the cuffs of his sleeves up to his shoulders, stands in the hallway, staring right at me, as though he expected me to appear at this exact moment.

"Arbiter Noni?" he says to me in a brusque manner.

"Yes," I reply, trying to sound unconcerned and not as though my mind had been somewhere else.

The man hands me an ivory envelope with gold ribbon pressed into its edges. No writing stains it, piquing my curiosity. I open it with care, not wanting to tear the flawless envelope, and pull out a card with the Arelian emblem forming slight indentions in it as fancy script stretches across it.

> Arbiter Noni is hereby requested to appear at the presidential palace.
>
> Signed,
> President Tapiwa

I have been invited to the presidential palace?

The man stretches his right arm out, pointing at the entrance. No other arbiters are around, having made themselves scarce, no doubt the moment this man arrived. A quick glance around proves that even Commander Vye is nowhere to be found. Perhaps she is under strict orders to not interfere in this matter.

"Shall we?" the man says, though I have the feeling that his politeness is more courtesy than anything else.

Knowing that I have little choice, and apprehensive about

why Tapiwa has summoned me, I hand the invitation back to the man and head for the door, well aware that refusing a presidential summons can be fatal. I nod my head and walk outside into the bright sunlight, squinting as my eyes adjust, and head for the presidential transport with its flags on full display, exhibiting pride in its function. A plebian holds a door open for me as his burgundy shirt moves in the breeze, held in place by the white pants, with embroidered burgundy and gold circles stretching from the hem to the waistband. There is nothing for me to do, except to get in the transport, but the desire to run away fills me as the fear of what awaits me settles in, considering that there is no logical reason for Tapiwa to summon someone who has been to detainment, unless this is another test. I crawl inside the transport, without bothering to acknowledge the plebeian's presence, as is expected of me, and scoot over to the far left seat, almost stopping when I notice Kaleb next to a tinted window that allows one to see out, but no passerby to see in, as the man in uniform climbs inside next to me.

Within moments, we are off, with the vehicle bouncing down the uneven roads of the eastern sector, only to level out the moment we enter the northern sector, and once again, I am struck with awe at how smooth the road is compared to the sector I am assigned to, and I wonder as to why it is always left to suffer neglect and ambivalence. It can't just be because the eastern sector experiences the brunt of the barbarian attacks. Maybe it is because those who do not live there give it no thought because they never had to. Their pristine buildings are never touched by the world's cruelty. Spires stretch up my window as we worm our way to the executive district, each building morphing into a more resplendent one than the last as colored, tempered glass reflecting more colored, tempered glass, forming a sea of vibrant pastels mixed with earthy tones radiating their splendor and importance on any passing by underneath, and managing to break through the dark tint of the glass, forming a bold display of art on the white leather seats, causing me to notice, for the first time, that the emerald and gold embroidery has been replaced with lavender and silver forming a cylindrical pattern, instead of the horseshoe from before. My boots bunch up the edges of the maroon shag run on the floor. What happened to the purple one?

"Hungry?" asks Kaleb as he holds out a plate with cherry tarts and candied cucumbers, while the mirrored interior makes it look as though six of him are urging me to indulge in a treat.

My mouth waters as I glance at the plate, wanting to eat everything on it, since I had no chance to eat breakfast, but the feeling that this is another test prevents me from reaching for it.

"Arbiters are not allowed to eat such things," I say in a robotic tone, doing my best to not give away my desire to snatch the tray out of his hands. "Proper nutrition and physical fitness must be maintained at all times."

"It's just us here," urges Kaleb, pretending that the uniformed man is not with us.

I glance at the mirrors and the divider between the front and the back, knowing that the driver and plebeian are up there, before looking at the man in uniform, knowing full well that it is not just the two of us. Whatever I do and say, he will report back to his masters; there is no doubt of that.

"I'm fine, thank you," I reply. "If you have some water, that would be much appreciated."

Smiling, Kaleb puts the tray of treats away, much to the dismay of my mouth and stomach, and opens a door underneath the seat, revealing a refrigerated compartment, and pulls out a golden cup with a copper lid and hands it to me. The cool exterior chills my hand as I take it, removing the lid and taking a sip, to the relief of my parched throat.

"Thank you," I say, trying to remain polite, knowing that every word I utter, every move I make, will be reported back to his superiors.

"Perhaps an apple," Kaleb holds out a green apple, its shiny exterior reflects my face back at me, and grins, even though he should not be aware that I have not had a chance to eat, despite the fact that my grumbling stomach does a good job of giving me away.

Apples are allowed for arbiters, as they are nutritious, so, I take it, and sink my teeth into it, doing my best not to allow the juices to slide down my chin and onto my uniform, and chew with dignity, not wanting to show him how hungry I am.

The transport stops at the copper gates with the Arelian insignia in its center, signifying that we have reached the executive district. Kaleb rolls down a window as two guards approach, pointing their weapons at us.

"State your business," demands one, reminding me of my previous times here.

Kaleb bows his head, allowing the tattoo on the back of his neck to be scanned, and says, "I am Kaleb and I am here with Arbiter Noni, by president Tapiwa's invitation."

Invitation. He means orders, of course, but we never speak of such things as being orders. The illusion of choice is pervasive in Arel. As the guard looks in my direction, his shiny helmet allowing me to see my face with perfection, I bow my head to allow my tattoo to be scanned, before remembering that they never search those with personal invites by the presidents.

"You may pass," the guard says, waving us through, and the giant, copper gates open before us, allowing us entrance as the presidential transport eases its way up the driveway and to the immaculate building before us with its marble steps drawing all eyes to its 20-foot high, copper-lined steel doors, and the silver Arelian insignia in is center, as hexagonal columns form a circle around us, surrounding us in their pristine glory. Even though I have been here twice before, the scene still takes my breath away. The transport stops in front of the marble steps, and before I can move, the plebeian jumps out and opens the door for Kaleb and me, while the man in uniform remains seated. As I get out, I continue to marvel at the palace exterior and place the apple core and empty water container in the plebeian's hand, as is expected, since there is no obvious place to dispose of them.

"Come. Come," says Kaleb, trotting up the steps and motioning me to follow him, afraid of being tardy; I'm sure that Tapiwa gave him a timetable of when she wanted me here.

I follow him up the marble steps, admiring the way the brown swirls within the ivory curl around it, accentuating its pristineness, until we reach the top and pass beneath the copper-lined archway and into the domed area. Just like before, I arch my head backwards so that I can admire the paintings of the dome itself—it is a remarkable piece of construction—and notice something I had missed before: engravings of maple leaves fill the underside of the archway, brought to life by the reflection of the sunlight bouncing off the marble steps and hitting it just right. After several moments of silence, with me standing poised beneath the dome, looking straight up, my neck starts to ache from the sudden strain, and I bring my head down so that I am looking straight ahead, once again, and find Kaleb watching me with an amused grin, pleased that I still admire one of Arel's finest pieces of artwork and construction.

"It is magnificent, isn't it?" he says.

"Yes, sir," I reply.

If he had expected me to say anything more, he doesn't show it, but I'm sure he's used to arbiters being people of few words. We are not expected to talk, but to enforce the law.

"We mustn't keep President Tapiwa waiting."

He shuffles through the domed area to the main foyer, his feet making quick, little steps, while my long strides have little difficulty keeping up. He pauses in front of a grand marble staircase, and being unable to contain myself, I reach up to touch the cool railing, admiring its smooth exterior and how it feels like velvet in my hands. Lala palm, that is what Kaleb had told me when I first found myself enamored with its exquisiteness, and again, he smiles at me, amused by my reaction at being in such an immaculate place.

"Kaleb," says a voice, and it sends soft echoes around the room, before fading into the distance, "there you are."

President Tapiwa stands at the top of the stairs with her brother, Kumi. She descends the staircase, while Kumi stays behind her, in an elegant fashion as her wavy skirt and sleeves make her appear to be floating toward me as though she is some being from the heavens who has deigned to visit a mere mortal.

"Hello, Noni," she greets me. "I'm glad you accepted my invitation."

"You honor me by sending it," I say, going along with the niceties; we all know that refusing a presidential summons is never acceptable, and what the consequences are for doing so.

Her rouged lips curl upwards, showcasing her pearly teeth. "I would have asked you here sooner, but there has been so much going on."

I remain silent, knowing that speaking will add nothing, nor am I expected to speak, since no question was asked.

"Wouldn't you agree?" asks Kumi, forcing my hand.

"Such is the nature of your service," I reply, keeping my words neutral, to which he seems pleased.

Tapiwa holds her hand out, and the silver ring on her finger gleams in the ambient light of the room, adding an elegant flare to the purple stone recessed within its metal coil, and a plebeian appears from nowhere—I should have seen him, and am certain my failure to do so has not gone unnoticed—holding a tray with two crystalline glasses filled with a rosy liquid. She takes one and holds it to the plebeian who takes a sip, before bringing it to her plump lips and ingesting a third of the glass' contents, her flared sleeves swaying from side to side as she does so, allowing me to get a better glimpse of the embroidered, swirling pattern of chaotic lines in a lighter shade of green than the color of the material itself. Its shine must be either silk or satin, two things I have never worn, nor will I ever wear them: they are reserved for the most privileged in Arel.

Just as she starts to replace the glass on the tray, a glint of steel flashes as the plebeian reveals a knife. I pounce on him, relying on instinct, and shove him away from both presidents—Tapiwa's glass falls to the ground with a plink, dumping rosy liquid all over the amber-colored tile—until he slams into the wall, grunting in pain, but before he can make his next move, I grip the knife by its hilt and rip it away from his grasp, and plunge its blade into the man's chest. His eyes widen in horror, causing me to release the knife and take a step back. This isn't the look of a man bent on assassinating either of the presidents, and accepting his inevitable demise in return. This is the look of a man who never thought he would die like this, as though...

This entire incident was a setup, another test to prove my loyalty.

Shaking, I pull my hands away from the plebeian, allowing his body to crumple to the floor as red blood oozes from the mortal blow I have dealt him, and pools on the mirror-like floor, coating the diamonds embedded within each tile with its crimson color. I glance at my fingers and the blood that stains them, blending in with my skin tone, while my own blood boils from the knowledge that I have been used.

Both Tapiwa and Kumi stand erect in the room, pretending to be shocked by the incident, but their eyes give them away; they had planned this, of that I have no doubt.

"Arel owes you a debt of gratitude," says Tapiwa, "for saving our lives."

"At the risk of sounding bold," I say, trying to keep my rage under control and my voice calm, "neither of you were in any real danger."

I glance around, realizing for the first time that no guards are present, like they should be, confirming that the entire incident with the plebeian had been planned for their benefit. The only other person in the room is Kaleb, who now stands with his back pressed into a wall, hoping that no one sees him or the dark expression on his face, and the way he has made himself scarce the moment danger presented itself. I should notice this oddity, but I allow myself to be distracted by the grandeur of the palace, and by Tapiwa's and Kumi's lack of reaction, and pass his actions off as those of one who is not used to experiencing such dangers.

"Where are your guards?" I demand. "Why are they not here? Such a dereliction in duty should be punished."

"And it shall," says Kumi in a nonchalant voice, confirming for a third time that my suspicions are correct. The guards are absent because they were told to be somewhere else.

I glance at the body on the floor and the horror-struck eyes staring back at me, fighting the urge to close them, to show some semblance of decency, knowing what will happen if I display any ounce of mercy for a plebeian, and one who appeared to have tried to commit murder, even if it was a ruse. I can do nothing for him now, except pity him.

"Kaleb," says Kumi, breaking the silence surrounding us, "we have matters to attend."

"Yes, yes," says Kaleb, returning to his usual flighty mannerism, as he rushes after Kumi, and they disappear down the corridor and into another room, leaving me alone with Tapiwa.

"Please," she says to me, "walk with me."

Tapiwa struts down the hall in the opposite direction Kumi and Kaleb had gone in, and I take my place by her side, as asked, knowing that I cannot change what has happened, and that I must stay in control of my reeling emotions as I wipe the innocent man's blood on my pants in a vain attempt to clean my fingers. We move from the foyer and it's bright interior as sunlight pours in through skylights, illuminating the most intricate detail of the wallpaper—the pattern of raised fists coating the walls is unmistakable, even if it is pale silver on white—as it tucks itself underneath the Lala palm molding that marks the beginning of the ceiling and the pinpricks of lights nestle in it, forming stars, and I imagine what it will be like to look at such a sight when it is nighttime.

Her coral shoes clack on the tiles with each step she takes as we move further away from the entrance and into a long corridor that looks more like a tunnel to an unending cave as the light fades behind us and long shadows consume us, but before we are overtaken, lights appear on the floor, forming a pale, bluish line where Tapiwa's feet touch the tiles, illuminating our path, letting us know that we are not alone, but as each light appears, a chill grips me, growing stronger the deeper we go into the tunnel.

"I've been told that you are interested in joining the palace guard," Tapiwa says, her voice echoes around me, letting me know that there is no escape.

Slight movement forces me to snap my attention to a dark spot within the never-ending hallway, and for just a moment, I make out the faint outline of a man, poised and ready to strike should I make a wrong move. I should have known that there would be guards spaced at certain intervals within the presidential palace, even if I could not see them. Tapiwa and Kumi would never leave themselves that exposed.

"Yes," I say, when I realize that I have been silent for too long after being asked a question.

"And you believe yourself to be worthy?"

This has to be a test. I decide to gamble on the side of humility. Anyone thought of as too ambitious in Arel sometimes disappear, depending on where their ambitions lie.

"No, ma'am. Only the strongest, the fittest, and the worthiest are allowed to protect Arel's most valued treasures."

Tapiwa stops in front of a black steel door; I never even saw it and would have run into it if she hadn't alerted me to its presence. Even in the darkness, her pearled teeth glow, allowing me to see the diamonds within them.

"You may be more worthy than you think."

She places her hand on the door and it melts away, allowing us to enter. Synchronized shouts pierce my ears as I step into light that seems brighter than the sun and find myself on a balcony, over-looking a courtyard with arbiters in skintight, red uniforms with black stripes running down their sides, stretching from their necks to their feet. They move as one unit, attacking the air with batons, stepping in unison and releasing a chant with each strike.

"Strength in…" yells a man from above us.

"…our kind!" shout the arbiters, or I should say palace guards, as one.

"Strength in…"

"…numbers!"

"Strength over…"

"…weakness!"

"Weakness is…"

"…failure!"

"Failure is…"

"…death!"

I place my hands on the rail, marveling at how it feels warm to the touch, as if raised bumps brush against my skin, digging into it, letting me know that this is not a place I want to falter in.

"I knew there was something different about you the night of the ceremony," Tapiwa says, walking along the balcony, and I follow her. "That is why I sent you to the mines and the agricultural sector."

I remain impassive when she glances in my direction to see if her praise has had any effect on me as I do not want her to believe that her words mean anything to me. I am an arbiter. Praise is appreciated, but not desired; at least, that is supposed to be part of our code of honor, but everyone knows that there are those who do not follow it. Her lips part, showcasing the pearls she has for teeth, but I am unable to decipher if she is pleased, or not, but I hope for the former. Her shoes clack on the charcoal floor as my boots clomp on it in tune to her steps as I follow her along the balcony to a set of stairs that appear out of nowhere, having blended in with the lighted walls above and stretching all the way down to the amber floor below with its blackened patterns of Arel's insignia woven together, forming what appears to be a mesh carpet on tile. She steps on the first step and pauses for a second, causing me to halt as well, as I wonder what is going through her mind, but I know better than to ask, though I can swear that she looks at the instructor on the bottom floor before continuing, with me in tow.

The instructor yells an animalistic sound—I cannot make out any discernable words—and those around him hurry to the edge of the square floor, forming a perimeter as his bass voice echoes around me, causing the hairs on the back of my neck to stand on end as an uneasy feeling overtakes me. Heat rises underneath my collar as Tapiwa leads me downward. The moment my foot touches the amber tile, the lights go out, plunging me into darkness, as strong hands seize me around the waist and chuck me to the side, as though I am nothing more than a toy. My palms scrape against the smooth tile with a small screeching sound, and a burning pain overwhelms them as I grapple with what has just happened and realize that this is nothing more than one gigantic test.

I am sick and tired of these tests!

The same hands flip me over on my back as someone straddles me and wraps their fingers around my throat, squeezing with all their might, forcing me to gasp for air, while being unable to give my lungs what they desire most. Unable to see my opponent, I flop around like a maniac, pulling at the arms, forgetting my training like a six-year recruit, until, out of desperation, I thrust my hand upward with my fingers out and hit something. The weight on me shifts enough for me to whip myself to the side and throw the person off me. As I try to get to my feet, fumbling in the darkness, unable to see anything, the same hands seize my jacket and yank me back onto the tile with a grunt. My head slams into the floor, stunning me, but I haven't time to dwell on it, as an arm wraps around my throat and squeezes.

Again, I find myself wanting to panic as my ability to breathe is impaired. I throw my hand back, hoping to catch my opponent in the eye, but he is ready for me, and wrenches it behind my back with his free hand, twisting my shoulder until it screams at me for release. The arm around my throat tightens. I go limp, allowing myself to hang in midair, supported only by the arm around my throat, hoping that it fools my opponent. His arm loosens. Not wanting to jeopardize my only chance for escape, I remain limp, hanging on his arm the way a towel hangs on its rack, until he loosens his grip enough for me to make my move.

I drop to the floor, twisting so that I land on my back, and kick my feet out in the direction that I believe his knees to be. A strangled cry of pain tells me that I struck something, but I haven't time to rejoice. Before he can retaliate, I roll to the side, jump to my feet, and ram my whole body into the general direction I remember my opponent being in, losing my balance as I hit his side and not the middle of his back, but he is ready for me. He grabs me by the waist, lifting me into the air and slams me into the tile floor, but I grip his hand, bring my legs up, wrapping them around his arm, and twist, forcing him onto the ground, causing him to let go. Once released, I scramble to my feet and run away, unsure of how to fight an opponent I cannot see, but seems to be able to see me just fine. I look all around, but all I see is darkness. Panicked, I scramble around, hoping to remain free of my attacker, unsure of what to do. I just...

Mandi's voice echoes through my head—well, not her voice so much, as a memory from a time when I was still a recruit and she had gathered my class into an arena, of sorts, to teach us how to fight when impaired, in this case, when we can't see.

"When in battle, your opponent will do what he can to stop you, to make it where you cannot fight. One of the best ways to achieve that end is to impair your ability to see. Just like you have been taught to fling dirt into your opponent's eyes, so has he," Mandi's strong voice fills my mind, reminding me of her lesson from long ago, one of the few she gave us, and in which Molers was absent.

I allow the memory to settle over me, hoping for a bit of wisdom, as images of my former recruits from the training facility fill my mind, forcing me back to the time we had all gathered outside in the courtyard, forming a circle. Mandi had positioned herself in the center, while we all stood at attention in our crisp black uniforms, keeping our eyes on her.

"In the moment of chaos, when you are fighting for your life, you need to learn to keep your wits. This exercise will teach you what to do, should you find yourself unable to see them. Any who fail will not move on to the next exercise."

She waved one of the recruits over and two other instructors placed a bag over his head, while another kicked him in the back, forcing him to crash into the concrete ground. I remember watching as the recruit tried to gain his bearings and fight off his attacker, but each time he tried to stand, his was knocked back onto the ground.

"Block the attack!" Mandi yelled, her voice echoing off the buildings. "Use your other senses. You cannot always rely on just one!"

Once again, the recruit tried to block, but received a kick in the chest, causing him to fly backward until he slammed into the pavement and his head hit the unrelenting surface with a sickening crunch, followed by blood pooling around him. Even then, I thought I noticed a flicker of anger from Mandi, not at the recruit, but at her fellow instructor, but it disappeared within milliseconds. One after one, recruits were called to the center. Some managed to block an attack, allowing them to continue at the training facility, while others did not, and I remember watching them being dragged away, screaming for mercy, only to never be seen again.

"Noni!"

It was my turn.

I walked to the center of the circle and stood in front of Mandi, as her hardened face vanished the moment someone rammed a black bag over my head and tied it tight around my neck, making it difficult to breathe. I had brought my hands up to loosen the straps, but someone smacked them away and shoved me forward where I was greeted by a punch to the face. Dazed, and unable to breathe through the thick, coarse material that scratched my skin, I fumbled on the concrete, crawling on all fours, as I tried to remember where

I was, as the swift succession of movements hit my ears before something else rammed into my back, forcing me onto my stomach. Another kick flipped me over onto my back.

"Stop stumbling around like an idiot!" yelled Mandi at me. "You have four other senses! Use them! What do you hear? What can you feel? What do you taste? Think!"

I rolled around on the ground as crippling pain gripped my back, as a soft thump on the concrete stones of the courtyard hit my ears, alerting me to danger, and I folded my arms in front of me, blocking the attack, allowing me to continue as a recruit.

The memory of Mandi's instruction dissipates as I snap back to my present situation, while the soft whistle of a fist flying through the air toward me strikes my ears, and I duck to the side, as knuckles graze my cheek, causing my to trip and fall over, but before I hit the floor, hands push me away, forcing me into the center of the circle they form around me. My feet flop on the tiles, making too much noise, as I stumble to the other side, only to be greeted by another wall of hands shoving me back into the center of the room. I use this information to form a mental picture of the room, while figuring out where to place my opponent, when the soft padding of feet catch my attention. Of course! He is barefoot, just like the others in the room, which is why I failed to hear him moving around. I step to my left and pause, straining my ears to pick up any measure of audible sounds when I hear it, a soft clap on the tile from a bare foot setting itself down with care, doing its best to make no sound. I take a step back and the same hushed sound follows suit.

Gotcha!

Taking another step back, I kneel down with one knee touching the floor, while my other leg stands ready to propel me upward at a moment's notice and wait, hoping my opponent believes my ruse as I pretend to be giving up. The soft pads of bare soles on tile creep up behind me, drawing closer and closer, as I remain still, listening to my opponent as his steps quicken from confidence, and the false knowledge that I am no longer a threat. As he steps behind me, I jump to my feet and twist around, thrusting my arm out and ramming the heel of my hand into his chest, forcing him backwards, but before he can recover from my surprise, I kick my foot out, catching his ankle, and he topples over, crashing onto his back. Though I still cannot see him in this pitch blackness, I run to where I heard him fall, preparing to strike, but before I can, the lights turn on, illuminating every crevice of the walls and the floor, blinding me for a moment or two as my eyes adjust to the brightness, forcing me to stop cold in my tracks. After blinking several times, I notice that my opponent's eyes are blue, the same unnatural blue that Grelyn's are, meaning that he can see in the dark.

A quick scan around the room reveals more unnatural blue eyes mixed in with the standard brown of Arel. Grelyn isn't the only one? But it isn't the eyes that capture my attention, but the vacant expressions, as though no individual mind exists behind those faces; they are one, a collective, with one goal, and dissent is not tolerated—such is the nature of Arel—and their collective stares frost my bones, unnerving me as the desire to run and break free builds to an overwhelming furor. The instructor in the room makes a sound with his throat, and my opponent springs to his feet and takes his place with the other palace guards, while I remain in the center of the room, unsure of what to do as Tapiwa and the instructor approach me.

"She shows some promise," the instructor says to Tapiwa. He grabs my arm and looks it up and down. "A bit scrawny. She could use more muscle."

I jerk my arm back, insulted by his insinuation that I am not fit to do my duty as an arbiter.

"That can be remedied," replies Tapiwa.

The instructor grabs my face and lifts it toward him so that he can examine me further as he and Tapiwa continue to talk about me as though I am nothing more than a commodity, even though, that is all we are in Arel: people whose purpose is determined by

Arel itself, as we are all nothing more than possessions to be used and disposed of at will.

"I may be able to do something with her. She has some resourcefulness. Now, if she were to get the surgery…"

I know what surgery he refers to; it is the same one that Grelyn got, which allows her to see in the dark, but I want none of it.

"No, sir," I say, cutting him off, and earning a disapproving glare from Tapiwa, warning me of how close I am to stepping out of bounds. "I do not wish to have the surgery."

"That is your choice," says the instructor, "but it may be prudent to agree to it."

"I must decline. The risks outweigh the benefits, and if it doesn't take, then I will be of no use to Arel. And, as you can see," I say, inclining my head toward my opponent from earlier, mindful that my forwardness may be putting me in jeopardy, "I do not need it."

The instructor turns toward Tapiwa and says, "As you know, I do not need another guard. However, I will keep your recommendation in mind, Madam President."

"That is all I am asking," Tapiwa replies with a smile that could curdle milk.

She turns and heads for the stairs without a word, and I follow after her, not waiting to be told to do so, while the instructor barks orders at the others in the room, and they continue their exercises, surrounding us with their shouts of commitment. As we leave the room, doubts weigh my mind down. Being called to be a palace guard is a great honor, but at what price?

My gaze moves to a darkened spot on the balcony where Kaleb stands in the shadows, unnoticed by all (wasn't he with Kumi?), but more menacing, as though the man I met before was nothing more than a façade.

Chapter 26

Strings Pulled

The whine of a railcar fills my ears as its shadow passes over me, creating an uneven stripe on my uniform for a moment before gliding over the platform I stand on, as though it is waving to the people bustling by in their frantic attempts to catch the next transport to their destination, while my mind ponders the events at the presidential palace. After leaving the room full of palace guards, Tapiwa told me to leave, and Kaleb saw me to the exit, but he seemed different, after which, I made my way here, where I now watch those around me while waiting for a railcar. Plebeians follow their masters without question, carrying bundles, or nothing at all, holding their heads down, making certain to stay in their rightful place, or so we have been programmed to believe. My mind wanders to Chase and all the times he helped me, and to Sheila and how she saved me from a severe punishment that would have led to my death. Why are they treated as inferiors whose worth is less than a piece of garbage? How did Arel come to be? I know the official story; it is taught to every child of Arel, and any who question it disappears, and all memory of their existence erased, and so people accept what they are told, lest they cease to be a memory themselves.

A man walks to the edge of the platform so that he can be the first on the railcar when it arrives, with his plebeian right behind him, carrying a satchel and clutching it close, as though she doesn't want anyone getting too close to it. When the man stops, she bumps into him by accident, and in a reflexive manner, he turns and raises his fist to strike her, but stops the moment I stroll between them, turn, and face him.

"It there a problem?" I ask.

"No, ma'am," he responds, and the plebeian hunkers even lower.

Sweat forms on his brow, and though it is a bit warm, it isn't that warm.

"You're sweating," I say.

"The sun," he says, "it is warm."

My arbiter senses go on full alert. The man is hiding something; his evasiveness gives it away, and now, I want to know what it is. The plebeian bumps my arm, and her frightened eyes look into mine as she shifts the leather satchel on her, but it is not me she is frightened of, but something else. I snatch the bag out of her hands and open it, revealing architectural drawings of an education center, something that this man should not have; his light gray uniform gives it away.

"Why do you have these?" I demand, holding them up.

"I... I..."

"You are no engineer, nor are you an architect. You should not have these, which means you stole them."

"You bitch!" The man lunges past me and reaches for the plebeian, while I seize him, trying to rip him away from her, but in the struggle, she flies over the edge of the platform and her head smashes into one of the rails, and she lays still. The man pushes against me and tries to run, but I tackle him and pin him to the ground, and before he can get up, I seize my baton and smack him in the side of the head with it, rendering him unconscious.

The whine of an approaching railcar reaches my ears and a few leaves on the platform lift off the ground and circle around one another as a suction is formed while the wind kicks up from the fast-approaching transport. The woman! She's still on the rails! I jump off the man and race to the edge of the platform, leaping to the rails and landing next to the plebeian. Her still body and the blood around her head causes my heart to sink as death hovers over her, warning me that it will take me as well, if I remain. I reach for her, lifting her up, but her head rolls to the side and her eyes flicker open before closing, making her ashen face look more like a corpse than a once living human being. I try to lift her up, despite the wind whipping around me as the train approaches and rounds a corner with its nose pointed in my direction. Her body refuses to budge. I lift her again, but the realization that I cannot save us both settles in, and I must choose: death, or saving myself.

The whine roars to a deafening screech as the railcar approaches and people gather around in the platform to watch my demise, and with one last glance at the woman, I realize that she is dead, so I jump to the platform's edge and lift myself up as my heart pounds faster with each passing second, while the knowledge that I am about to be torn to pieces grips me. I have seconds. Strands of hair whip my face as I force my arms to lift me to safety, but the dread of being too late fills me, and like anyone who knows their death is imminent, I face the oncoming railcar with acceptance.

Hands seize my shoulders and haul me onto the platform just before the railcar soars past and screeches to a halt. Eyes watch me as I rise to my feet and brush my uniform off before standing at attention in front of the arbiter that rescued me. I have never seen him before, meaning that he is not from the eastern sector.

"What is the meaning of your actions?" demands the arbiter that saved me.

"That man"—I point at the man I had knocked unconscious as he starts to wake up and move—"has the architectural plans to an education center, but he is no architect."

Two more arbiters appear and one puts a foot on the man's back, pinning him to the ground.

"In that bag," I add, pointing at the satchel.

The arbiter questioning me grabs the satchel and pulls out the blueprints before switching his focus to the man.

"You know the penalty for being in possession of these?"

Fear grips the man's face.

"Take him away," says the arbiter, before turning back to me. "And the plebeian? Why risk your life for hers?"

"I thought she might have more evidence of his disloyalty to Arel," I reply.

"You are young. Last year's?" he asks, referring to when I received my commission.

"Yes, sir."

"In the future, all you need is one piece of evidence."

"Yes, sir."

"Report back to your commander."

"Yes, sir." I salute the commanding arbiter and turn to walk away, but before I do, I spot something on the back of the satchel as another carries it away. At any other moment, the darkened spot on the leather would appear to be nothing more than a smudge, a stain from greasy fingers, or from being set on a grime infested surface, but the more I study it, the more I realize that it is not a stain at all, but something that has been put there on purpose, but only those who knew to look for it would have seen it; it is the same symbol I have seen countless times since the bombings: the insignia of Arel with a slash through it.

"Sir," I say, pointing at the satchel, "there's a…"

"You're dismissed, arbiter," the commanding arbiter snaps at me.

I start to say something, to prove that I am not just uttering useless words, but receive a reprimanding glare from the arbiter in charge, and decide to do as ordered and leave.

The doors to the railcar ding, warning everyone present of

its impending departure, and I hurry onto it, jumping onto the rail transport—a couple moves out of my way, allowing me some space—as the doors hiss shut behind me, enclosing me in its transparent tube as it takes off, jerking me backward, but I reach up and grab one of the handholds dangling from the ceiling. The railcar bounces upward, following the rail as it navigates its way through Arel and to the eastern sector, causing me to lean back and the muscles in my arm to tighten as I hang onto the handhold.

Stray eyes watch me—I feel them—while pretending that they are more interested in the amber building we pass, and the honey incandescence of the afternoon sunlight as its harsh glare reflects off the side of the building, being softened by the amber coloring and forced to cast a warmer glow on the people passing below. For a moment, the railcar pauses, almost as though it teeters on a precipice, deciding if it wants to take the plunge before rushing downward, forcing me to lean forward, as the muscles in my arm tighten again to keep me rooted in place. I allow my body to be carried by the motions of the transport before straightening myself up, remembering to maintain my erect posture and to not allow anyone to see any sign of weakness, knowing that those present always keep a tentative gaze on any arbiter they come across.

The railcar dips below an archway, and I look up at it, remembering my first day as a commissioned arbiter and the excitement I had then, only to be replaced by reality, though my desire to help the people of Arel and to protect them never wavered, just the misconception that Arel was perfect had. As we pass underneath the archway and its engraved depictions of a people once enslaved and set free by our presidents—the image of the saviors always changes to match the current president, or in this case, presidents, of Arel—with their resolute faces staring back at any who glance upon them, providing us courage in a time of fear, bright white paint catches my attention, and that of everyone aboard the railcar. The glossy white symbol stands out among the bronze archway as though screaming for attention, which it received, but whether it is favorable or not remains to be seen; but it is not the fact that another of Arel's pieces of art has been defaced that stuns me, as it is the symbol marking it that worries me. Once again, the insignia of Arel with a slash through it stares back at me, taunting me, and filling me with dread.

Crackling fills the railcar as the speakers come to life and dancing fuzz fills the screens that permeate the transport car. Most days, they are never used, but are meant only for emergency broadcasts from the presidents, but by the static greeting my ears, something tells me that this is not such a message.

"Rise up, brothers and sisters! You see the arbiter before you. She is part of the system of oppression that enslaves you all. Think of what they have done to you. How they have made you suffer. Join the revolution! Destroy the system!"

The voice cuts out and ends with a variation of the arbiter salute, except that the fist faces outward and is painted red. A multitude of questions pummel my brain as I wonder who is behind this and how he broke into the Arelian communication system, but as silence swarms around me, and the air stills, unease fills me.

Glancing around at the faces around me, I can tell that they all saw the symbol and heard the message, and as murmurs rise through the crowd on the transport car, I know that I must get off as a mixture of fear and rebellion swarms through the car I am in, and most eyes turn toward me, the lone arbiter. Hairs on my legs and arms stick up, rubbing against the material of my uniform, as I observe the faces in the car, knowing what thoughts go through their minds.

I press my wristband, sending out a signal for help, but am uncertain if I will make it until the next stop. The moment my finger leaves my wristband, someone charges me, his heeled shoes thudding on the metal floor of the shuttle car, and I jump onto a seat, dodging out of the way of his attack, only to land on another who shoves me to the floor. Pinned between the seats and the cold floor of the railcar, feet kick me with such force that no amount of effort on my part to block the attack protects me. Squirming, I wriggle my way free, crawl underneath one of the seats, and jump up, but a series of hands seize my arms and chest, holding me still, just as another jumps over the back of a seat straight for me. I lift my feet, shoving them into the man's chest, and he flies backward into a pole, while forcing the ones holding me to support my weight, causing them to lose their own footing, and we crash onto the floor, rolling over seats, until an armrest slams into my stomach.

I haven't time to catch my breath. A hand grabs the bun in my hair, jerking my head back, but I twist around, drop to my knees, and punch her in the stomach. She takes two steps back, but before she can regain her footing, I ram the heel of my hand into her nose, feeling the blood squirt from it as she drops unconscious. Someone kicks me in the side, but I ignore the pain and whirl around, swinging my fist, catching another in the cheek, while ramming my elbow backward, jabbing it in the stomach of another.

Clutching my side, I stumble down the aisle, trying to get away from these people, but there is nowhere to escape. Never before have people ever had any courage to fight an arbiter, having been forced into submission for so long, but the recent terror attacks have changed all that. More come at me. I lurch to the side, landing on some seats, and jump over them to another set of seats, swinging my feet out and catching a couple in the head, before landing on the floor again, as I try to make my way to the door, but there are too many. More hands seize me, ripping me off my feet, dragging me back, as a series of fists and feet fly for me, taking their anger out on me, and despite my struggling, their grip on me holds firm.

The railcar approaches a curve, and for a moment, I notice that it is approaching too fast, and we all tip to the side as the shuttle car nears the bend in the track, but the hands never release me. The car shakes. All movement stops as everyone within the railcar realizes that something is not right, and their own sense of impending danger takes over.

Before anyone moves, a roar rips through the shuttle car as the track explodes, and bits of metal and wood burst through the windows, ripping through any unlucky enough to be in its way, before jettisoning out the other side. Glass flies around me, pummeling me with its razor edges as I cover my face, while the railcar falls over the side. Gravity takes its hold and the car plummets downward with me in it, throwing unfortunate victims from its protective hold, only to stop with a sudden jerk as the rest of the train remains on the track and maintains its hold, while seats fly past me as I plunge downward, before my hand manages to grasp a metal pole and hold tight, stopping me from falling through the now open windows. Static fills the screens in the car as a slow creaking noise grows by the second, warning everyone that time is against them.

Below me is a man gripping the bottom feet of a seat, as his feet struggle to find their footing on the smooth floor of the railcar. Even though he is one of the ones that attacked me, I am still an arbiter; it is still my job to protect the citizens of Arel. I lower my right hand, while clinging to the pole with my left.

"Take it!" I yell at him as his dark eyes meet mine, but pure hatred fill them.

"Burn in hell!" He lets go and falls through the now glassless windows, landing on the streets below with a sickening crunch.

Another loses her grip on the back of a seat and screams on the way down. Once again, my stomach churns when she slams onto the pavement.

The dangling shuttle car lurches as the bolts securing it to the other cars still rooted on the track start to slip free. I look around for any survivors, but my hopes dissipate as I realize that I am alone in a tube of death. Knowing that I have two choices, death or life, I haul myself up onto the pole until I straddle it and reach for the a row of seats, jumping as the railcar lurches again, but my hand slips, and fear fills my frantic movements as I scramble to grab hold of anything until my fingers wrap around the back edge of a seat, stopping me from plummeting to my demise. Taking slow, deep breaths to calm my heart rate, I look up at the door and my only way out.

Resolved to not die today, I force my arms to lift me up, and I bring my feet up, placing them on the back of the seats, using what strength I have to push myself upward, until I can grab the back of another set of seats. Wires dangle around me, sending out sparks that singe my face, but I ignore the stinging, burning pain as my arms strain from the effort of climbing, but failure is not an option. My sweaty hands slip again, but I push myself upward with my legs and catch the back of the set of seats above me. Crackle, hiss, pop—that is all I hear as a creaking noise swirls around me, filling my chest with its ominous sound and its promise of certain death should I fail, but as my mind wanders to what might happen, I force it to think of Chase, Sheila, and Gwen. I force it to think of Renal and Commander Vye. I force it to think of what matters and how I refuse to be carted away as nothing more than a piece of refuse, and the knowledge of what will happen to them if I abandon them fuels my efforts, driving me onward as I climb seat over seat, inching my way to the sealed door above me.

I reach the last of the seats and see a pole above me, which will get me close enough to press the button, unsealing the doors, but I'll have to jump. Sweat drips from my ears, down the back of my head, soaking my hair as I gauge the distance and climb onto the seats, pressing the flats of my feet into the backs and bracing myself for one final leap to safety. As I prepare myself, a mixture of thunder and metallic creaks mix together, deafening me as it surrounds me, warning me of what is to come next, but I stop as the soft whimper of a young woman reaches my ears. Nestled in the same rows of seats I crouch upon, cradled by them as though they attempted to protect her from danger, is a woman who appears to be no older than me, sitting frozen to her spot, unable to move.

Was she one of the ones who attacked me?

I shake the question from my mind. It doesn't matter. All that matters is that she is in danger, and I am here to help her, as is my sworn duty, my oath, and the one thing I believe that arbiters are to do above all else: protect the people of Arel from outside and inside threats. If I save myself and let her die, I will be no better than the ones who had tried to kill me moments before the explosion on the tracks. I reach my hand out to her as the car drops, warning me that I need to get out of here.

"Take my hand!"

She shakes her head in fear, and I know that I must be quite the sight with the fresh bruises on my face, but I need her to trust me.

"Take it!" I yell, but she hugs her knees even closer, burying her face in them, having never faced death before, while death seems to be my constant companion.

Realizing that harsh words will not convince her to trust me, I lower my voice, talking to her like I would when talking to Sheila or Gwen.

"Look," I say, keeping my voice calm and low, "I know you're scared. I'm scared too. But I need you to trust me."

"I tried to kill you," she whispers, not believing that I would risk my life for hers.

"I know," I say.

The railcar lurches again as more wires release a loud zap, sending more sparks in every direction, showering her black curls and cheeks with orange flares, reminding me of embers around a flame.

"I don't know why I did. I was just so angry," she rambles, "and that voice said to do it, and…"

As I listen to her words spill out of her mouth, I realize that, like so many in Arel, she was assigned a job, her station in life decided for her, as was mine, and that no one bothered to ask her what she wanted, nor has anyone ever asked me the same; and so enters the puppet master, offering a false sense of choice, while pulling everyone's strings to achieve a master goal.

I look the woman in the eyes, keeping my voice calm, but firm, and ask, "What do you want?"

"To make my own choices," she says.

"Then make one now." I hold my hand out to her again.

She studies it for a moment, looks into my eyes, and seizes it. I grip it tight and together we jump from the row of seats to the pole above us and clutch it, while the clanging of the bolt popping free surrounds us, piercing my ears and forcing me to move fast. My hand rams into the button for the doors and they hiss open, allowing bright sunlight to wash over us, and causing me to blink as my eyes adjust, but I haven't time. The railcar falls away from the track as the last set of bolts pop free. I haul myself upward, placing my feet on the pole, while stretching my hand upward through the door, and lift myself up onto the side of the railcar. Once stable, I reach down for the woman, who looks at me with wide eyes, but she takes my hand, and I heave her upward, until she stands beside me on the dangling railcar.

It falls beneath our feet as we jump for the rails above us, and as we haul ourselves onto the track, the shuttle car breaks free of the ones holding it and plummets to the ground below, smashing into a multitude of pieces as people scurry out of the way and a flurry of screams reach us before fires consumes what is left of the car itself. Desperate to get out of here, I look around and spot the platform, but we need to run for it.

"Go!" I yell at her as I jump to my feet and take off.

She is right behind me. Together, we sprint for the platform, not wanting to stay on the track in case another train comes, our breaths coming in short, ragged gasps as we charge down to the platform. Almost there. I pick up my pace, forcing her to pick up hers, and leap for the side of the platform, clinging to it the moment I touch it. She does the same. I lift myself up, turn, and grab her by the shoulders, yanking her onto the platform and to safety, but before either of us can relax, armed arbiters appear from all around, yelling at her to remain on the ground, while others drag me away from her.

"Stop! Stop!" I scream at them, forcing those holding onto me to let go. "She helped me!"

An arbiter approaches me and speaks to me several times before I understand the words he says to me.

"Are you injured?" he says to me a third time.

"No… no, I'm fine." I reply. "Because of her, I am fine." I point at the woman. I have no desire to see her punished, even if she did join the others on the railcar in attacking me, but the other arbiters refuse to let her go as they shove her to the edge of the platform while clearing the gathered crowd away, and my mind races as it tries to grapple with the fast pace of events, not understanding why no one is listening to me.

"For participating in an insurrection and an attack on an arbiter," says the arbiter that had asked me if I had any injuries to the woman on the platform, "you are to be hereby executed without trial."

"No!" I scream. "She helped me! She—"

"It's okay," the woman says to me, standing proud and accepting her fate, and she looks right into my eyes, all the fear I had seen earlier gone. "You have given me hope."

An arbiter pulls out his sidearm and shoots her in the head, allowing her body to fall to the tracks below.

Enraged, I start to run for her, but another set of strong hands seize me around the arms, jerking me backwards off my feet, and dragging me away from the platform and to a secluded area, while a familiar voice warns me to calm down. I can't. I refuse to. There was no reason to murder that woman. I don't think she believed in the voice on the train, but that whoever had orchestrated it had used the desperation and the fear of those on the shuttlecraft to do its dirty work. The hands whirl me around and slam my back into an exterior wall, and I stop struggling when bits of brick poke me through my uniform jacket and, for the first time, I recognize Renal's voice.

"Calm yourself!" he hisses at me, and I stop struggling.

"What are you doing here?" I ask, confused. I don't think I made it to the eastern sector, but I am so turned around right now that I have no idea where I am within the city.

"I need you to get a hold of yourself," Renal says, ignoring my question.

"But they killed her," I say, and for the first time I lose my composure in front of him, and tears escape my eyes as a wall of emotions I have tried to keep suppressed burst forth, refusing to be imprisoned any longer. "It wasn't her. It wasn't all her. It was the voice, and something he said that caused everyone to—"

"What voice?"

"There was a voice over the loud speaker and it told them to rise up and revolt."

Renal mulls over my words, and I sense that he knows something, something that he is not telling me.

"What is happening? We are arbiters. We are supposed to protect Arel. Lawbreakers go to the detention center. They aren't to be executed in the public like this. They're..."

"What do you think happens to the people you send to the detention center, Noni?"

I stop speaking. I never thought about it. The detention center is where people are to be tried for the crimes they commit, but now... now I am not so sure.

"A lot has happened since we were sent outside the wall. Much of the rules have changed. You need to keep it together, and stay in control of yourself."

Renal's gaze holds mine, and I am unable to turn away.

"Can you do that?"

I nod my head.

"I'm taking you back to the manor."

Renal releases me and starts to walk off, but I stop him.

"Are we not supposed to protect the innocent?" I ask him, still holding on to the idealized vision of what being an arbiter means.

"I protect the ones I can."

He stalks off, and I know better than to wait for an order to follow to be issued, so I hurry after him, wiping the tears from my face, and doing my best to keep an impassive expression on it. As we turn a corner, I glance back at the platform, spotting the place where the woman once stood, promising my rage that its time will come, but that now is not it.

Chapter 27

Answers

A slow drip plops over and over into an overflowing bucket of murky water as Chase and I creep through the alley and to Luther's door as our shoes release splashy plops on the broken pavement the closer we get, doing our best to be quiet, but not succeeding. After the events of today, after the voice on the railcar that caused people to attack me, I need answers. There are too many questions and the only person I can think of who might have what I need is Luther, though I know he will be less than thrilled to see me; but something tells me that I can trust him more than anyone else at the moment.

We reach the hole in the fence, and I motion for Chase to go through first. He does, and he holds the loose board up for me to crawl through, while looking around for prying eyes, nosy busybodies looking to garner favor with the arbiters by informing on anyone who is out after curfew. Chase had insisted on coming with me when he caught me trying to sneak out on my own again, so I relented. Too many times in the past I had gone out on my own, but this time… this time I accepted his help.

We reach the small open courtyard, if you want to call it that, and the two doors, both dark, both rotting, both reminding me of how there is no turning back. Chase glances at me, but I point at Luther's door in answer to his unspoken question and he goes first, being careful to not make any noise as he steps on the stairs leading to the door. Giving him a nervous smile, I rap on the door, soft, but loud enough to gain the attention of anyone inside, hoping that he answers it. Nothing. Afraid that he might not be asleep, or worse, ignoring me, I knock a little louder, but not too loud so as not to attract unwanted attention.

"Luther!" I hiss at the door while trying to keep my voice low. "It's me!"

Seconds later, the door opens a crack and the brown iris of an eye peeks through it, followed by a disappointed voice.

"I should have known."

He opens the door wide enough for Chase and me to squeeze through before locking it shut.

"Make sure those drapes are pulled tight."

Chase and I run to the windows, double checking the drapes, and their three extra thick layers of material—perfect for not letting any light escape—cover every inch of the glass so that no one will know that someone is up at a time when most are asleep. It is not uncommon for a passing arbiter to burst into the home of someone whose light is still on so late at night.

Once done, we meet back in the main room where Luther awaits us.

"I see you brought a friend," he says, looking at Chase as I pull the hood covering my head off and pretending that he's never seen him before. "A plebeian. How interesting."

"Why's that?" asks Chase.

"Or, perhaps, he is just a means to an end. Someone to distract any arbiters that might catch you out after hours." Luther raises his hand to backhand Chase, and I stop him, gripping his wrist so tight that his fingers begin to turn purple, but instead of showing fear, Luther grins.

"So, not a means to an end after all," he muses. "Why are you here?" he says to me.

The soft pads of little feet touch the stairs up above, and we all look up at the boy I had Chase bring here, at what seems like a long time now. He looks healthy and cared for, even if he still doesn't seem to be speaking.

"Go back to bed, boy," Luther says in a stern, but gentle voice.

"Doesn't he have a name?" asks Chase.

"He won't tell me his name," replies Luther.

"He's okay though?" I ask, having not seen him since the day I took him out of that wretched place.

"I know you didn't come here to talk about the boy, but, yes, he's fine."

"I was hoping you could help me answer a few questions," I say, looking around at some of the stacks of books, real books with actual pages, not the simulated ones like what the manor has, though he doesn't seem to have as many as before, telling me that the raid on his place has forced him to be more cautious.

"Why would I answer your questions? I'm not here to be used whenever you have need of me."

"Why did you help me the day of the terror attack?" I demand, answering his question with a question.

Luther extends his arm, inviting me to sit at a table with papers and books covering its rusted turquoise surface and the geometric designs decorating it.

"So, what would you like to know?"

"Why is Arel the way it is?"

Luther snorts and a few droplets of spittle escape his lips as he tries not to laugh too hard.

"That's a broad question. What makes you think I know the answer? I may be older than you, but I'm not that old."

I look around at all the books. "I know none of these are on the approved reading list."

"You have me there. The truth is, I only know what I have managed to glean from these books."

"And?"

Luther leans back in his chair, clasping his hands together as his intelligent gaze settles on me, sizing me up and deciding whether I am worthy of such knowledge.

"There was a time when people of different backgrounds lived in relative peace together. They had massive cities with towering buildings of glass, much like what Arel has, modes of transportation, and various businesses all trying convince you to be their loyal customer. It wasn't perfect—no society is—but they had this ideal that they strove for: the idea that all people possess certain rights that cannot be taken away no matter the circumstance."

"So, what happened?"

"What always happens to a peaceful society: war and division destroyed it. It could have been a multitude of things culminating together. A viral outbreak, forcing people to be locked in their homes, brewing discontent, and opportunists using a crisis to their advantage, stirring the pot until civil unrest reigns supreme—puppet masters, if you will, pulling everyone's strings, manipulating them, until they were able to gain power."

"What do you mean?" I think back to the railcar and how that voice managed to get otherwise peaceful people to do its bidding.

"It started as an idea, like most things, and grew into a plague. Some thought that because one group of people had wronged another in the past, their descendants were forever branded sinners and would never be able to atone for the misdeeds of their ancestors, while the ones who were descended from the people who had been mistreated were forever owed atonement. Those seeking power feasted off this discontent and fueled it, until it grew to the point where riots broke out, innocent people were killed, and the very history of the country they lived in was no longer acceptable, as it was deemed too oppressive, too divisive, and not worthy of remembrance."

"But maybe that was a good thing," I say. "If they were being oppressed, why was it wrong for them stand up to it?"

"But were they oppressed?" Luther asks me.

I don't say anything. I have no idea what happened in the past, other than what I was told at the training facility, and any who questioned the accepted narrative was chastised until they stopped questioning it and accepted it, or they just disappeared.

"You tell me what happened," says Luther.

Unsure of where he is going with this, I recite the accepted history of Arel. "There was a time when the fair-skinned had enslaved the dark-skinned, but the dark-skinned rebelled and rose up against their oppressor, bringing about true equality and freedom."

"And who are the slaves now?" asks Luther.

I say nothing as I look at Chase.

"Freedom from what? Choices?"

"But we all have jobs," I say.

"Jobs none of us get to choose. Did you choose to be an arbiter? You were ripped from your mother's arms upon your birth and taken to the training facility, just like I was taken to be an engineer. None of us chose our stations in life. That was chosen for us, and if any dare to change it, they are executed. Don't you see? There was a time when the two got along, for the most part, and accepted each other as human beings, but there are always those who desire power and wealth above all else, and they knew that if they could turn people against each other, they could create their own society where they are in charge.

"And so they did. They turned rich and poor against one another, light and dark against one another, religious and atheist against one another, until the mob reigned supreme, and there was so much chaos that the puppet masters swooped in, promising order, and out of desperation, the people accepted it, without questioning the sort of order that was being mandated. If you stood against it, you were attacked, called unfeeling, a tyrant—anything, until you accepted the new order."

"But were they right?" I ask.

"Excuse me?" says Luther.

"Did the one group mistreat the other? Perhaps they should pay for the wrongs they committed."

"Even after several generations have passed?"

"Well," I say, repeating what I have always been taught, "it's inherent. Such wrongs surpass generations and can be felt for years to come; perhaps they should atone for it."

Luther presses his lips together for a moment, before speaking to Chase. "Will you go into the kitchen and grab me some water? My throat is a little dry."

Chase glances at both of us before standing up and walking to the kitchen, pointing at a door and going through it when Luther nods his head. Once alone, Luther looks at me, and in a flurry of movement, snatches a book off the table and strikes me in the face, catching me unaware, and knocking me to the floor, and before I can stand up, he places a chair over me, pinning me.

"You are an arbiter!" he yells, showing a fury I have never seen on him before. "Arbiters took my daughter and murdered her! Arbiters murdered my wife! They invaded my home in the middle of the night and destroyed my property because they thought I had contraband items! They have taken everything from me! Perhaps I should kill you for justice—for retribution! After all, all arbiters are mindless drones doing as they are told. Their evil is inherent, their lust for power is in their DNA, it's a part of who they are, and you are part of that system. Unfeeling. Unemotional. Uncaring. So, perhaps, I should kill you and take my revenge."

"But…" I say, pressing my palms against the chair in an effort to get it off my neck, "I had nothing to do with that. I warned you about the raid. I've tried to stop the abuses. I…"

"Oh," Luther releases some of the pressure from my neck, "so, now individual action is more important than collective guilt and punishment. It's no fun being thought of as evil just because a few people around you have made terrible decisions."

My feet kick as I beg to be released, while Chase appears in the doorway of the kitchen, desperate to find out what the commotion is all about, but before he can react, Luther pulls the chair off me, releasing me, and I sit up, coughing and spitting up some mucus.

Luther places the chair back by the table. "You are no more guilty of what another arbiter does, than he"—he points as Chase—"is guilty of what his ancestors did to yours. But instead of learning from the past, instead of learning to forgive, your ancestors chose to destroy his and set up a new society, and we are living in the end result: a place where if you dare speak out, if you dare go against anything Arel says, you disappear as though you never existed. This is the justice your ancestors achieved, or I should say injustice, because no revolution, no amount of change built upon anger and envy ever brings about anything good. It just breeds more anger, more hatred, and more division, while forcing everyone to conform to a set of rigid standards from which there is no deviance. Comply or die, that is the true motto of Arel, the motto of those who established Arel in the name of inclusivity and freedom."

"But, promising liberty just to gain control seems counterproductive," I say.

"If you live long enough, you will learn that tyranny always uses the promise of liberty and justice to sink its claws into you, but it also gets you to do its bidding by sowing seeds of discontent, discord, and envy. This person has more than you. That means you are oppressed and he is privileged. That sort of thinking will destroy you, but puppet masters are very good at using envy and division as a way of manipulating people."

I pick myself off the floor and sit back in a chair.

"You have a strange way of making your point."

"And you have a way of being hard-headed," replies Luther.

"But I don't understand," Chase says, placing a glass of water on the table, "if the people who lived back then were the freest in the world, why did they give it away?"

Luther laughs. "Freedom once gained is easily lost. It is not difficult to convince people that they have been wronged, nor is it difficult to work them up into a mob, and once the mob's usefulness has been used up, it is disposed of. Master manipulators have been doing this for ages: tap into some sort of grievance that people have; use it to make them envious and hateful toward others; let them create a mob, use the mob to tear down the society they want to control; then, step in as though they are the people's savior, and once put in power, dispose of the mob. This is as old as the world itself. Of course, once their ends are achieved, they have to keep the population itself under control."

"What do you mean?" I ask.

"Have you ever wondered about the yearly vaccines and how a certain number always fall ill and die while others are just fine? The number that dies always matches the same number we are told will ruin us if the population is not kept in check. Resources are limited, you know."

Luther says that last part with sarcasm.

"But…" I begin.

"Some of the vials are just the vaccine, while others hide something else: a form of population control," finishes Luther.

"So," begins Chase, "the people who lived here first just allowed themselves to be manipulated?"

"If you want to put it in simple terms," replies Luther, "yes. Divide and conquer has always been a useful strategy in war."

He's not wrong. At the training facility, we were taught how a divided enemy cannot resist being overrun because they are too preoccupied with fighting amongst themselves. Or as Molers put it once: let your enemy destroy himself before you eliminate what is left. Strategy. It always comes down to strategy.

"They allowed themselves to be divided, but there seems to be more to this story," I say.

Luther grins. "How perceptive of you. Yes, there is more. There is always more. Dividing people based on physical appearance, wealth, and sex is superficial and will only work for so long, requiring the addition of two remaining ingredients: fear and anger. Fear and anger are powerful emotions and excellent manipulators. Once a people are divided into separate groups, each hating the other, they need to be kept separate before they realize that they are not so different after all. So, enters fear and anger. There was an event that happened, whether planned or happy circumstance is unknown, but those who desired control seized it and used it to their advantage.

"A virus appeared, like they always do from time to time, and it spread quickly, causing people to fall ill and die. The exploiters seized the opportunity. First, their media spent everyday talking about how the virus is deadly and what people should do to avoid it, causing people to panic. Then, enters the politicians, the bureaucrats, and anyone who has an agenda; they used that panic to implement rules and mandates, banning social gatherings of any kind, closing down businesses, and imposing the use of face coverings and gloves so that no one could see the faces of those around them, and so they would be detached from the world around them."

"Gloves?" I say, confused.

"Touch," replies Luther, "is one of our most important senses. It allows us to feel the world around us and to connect with one another. It is used between mother and child to form a bond. Why do you think all newborns are taken from the breeders the moment they draw their first breath?"

"Why would anyone do all of this?" asks Chase.

Luther leans back in his chair, and the back legs creak as the front ones lift into the air.

"Humanity is a weakness. Love is a weakness. Empathy is a weakness. These are not people that you see, but resources, entities meant to serve and function as deemed necessary by society. Once their usefulness is used up, remove them the way you would remove a diseased limb," I say, repeating a lesson taught to me while at the training facility, stopping when I realize the words I have spoken.

"There is your answer," Luther says to Chase, allowing the front legs of the chair to thud on the carpet. "If you can remove the idea that we are human, make people forget they are talking to another person, you can prevent people from connecting with one another and finding commonalities for which to form a bond. Fear of death. Fear of falling ill. That is what was driven into people's minds, until that fear turned into anger toward any who did not comply with the new rules, thus dividing them even further, and when the time was right, another event happened, and reports about its injustice bombarded the people, until they were so filled with rage that they decided to act, but not against those who manipulated them, but against each other. And as the people destroyed one another in the streets, until chaos reigned, the puppet masters steered that chaos, until the mob destroyed those who refused to obey the new dictates. They weren't hard to find. Once they were destroyed, the mob was steered in the direction of those who were too afraid to take a stand, but chose to cower in their homes, hoping that things would magically improve, forcing them to hunker even further, until they begged for the madness to stop, until they were broken and had no will of their own.

"And, so, enters a savior," continues Luther. "A man promising to end the chaos, but only if the people put him in charge and vow to accept the new normal, knowing full well that, tired as they are from all the mayhem, they will do as he wishes just to have some semblance of peace, but they will never get it. And the life that they had before becomes forgotten to the point where it cannot even be called a distant memory."

"So, people were just manipulated into destroying themselves?" asks Chase with doubt.

"Is it that hard to believe?" asks Luther. "You are manipulated every minute of every day. Do you dare look a citizen in the eyes?

Do you dare speak up for yourself? Whenever there are grumblings of discontent, does something always seem to happen to put the people in a state of fear? Do you find yourself pondering thoughts that you never knew you had?"

"What happened next?" I ask.

"What always happens when there is complete chaos. War in the streets turned into a war in the countryside until it swept over the entire nation. Once everything had been reduced to rubble, the power hungry gathered the survivors and promised peace and prosperity, so long as you played by their rules. All the people had to do was destroy the mob that was used to initiate the chaos in the first place. In the end, the survivors divided themselves into small city-like states, trusting no one and despising any who were not like them, and from what I can gather, it was at this time that Arel was officially formed. Our first president of Arel saw an opportunity and took it, convincing people to follow him. He set about a series of laws that were to right the wrongs imposed upon certain people, and you are living in the culmination of all that has happened before."

Silence ensues after Luther finishes speaking, while I ponder all that he has said. A mob? That is what met me on the shuttle car.

"A puppeteer," I murmur to myself. "That explains the railcar."

"Railcar?" Luther looks at me with inquisitive eyes.

I look at both him and Chase. Chase knew there had been an incident, but I didn't tell him everything, and I should have.

"I was on a shuttle car on my way back to the eastern sector when a voice broke over the intercom and said something about how arbiters have abused their authority. I don't remember the exact words, but what he said turned the people on the car against me."

"They attacked you?" asked Luther.

"Yes. But there was also an explosive device on the track and it blew the car off the rails. I managed to get away, and only me. Arbiters executed anyone else who managed to escape as well. And… I've been seeing this symbol everywhere I go."

I draw it on the table, tracing it with my index finger, and Luther's eyebrows scrunch together in concentration as he rubs his chin with his left hand, deep in thought. The feeling that he knows this symbol washes over me; so, I prod him.

"Do you know it?"

"You need to practice extra caution, Noni," he says, evading my question.

"You say that like you care about me. The abrasive individual who has no love for anything Arelian, now shows compassion to an arbiter."

"Don't get too used to it," says Luther. "There are forces at play here; this you know, but they do not come from Arel."

"But why turn people against her?" demands Chase.

"A test," says Luther. "There are cameras on those railcars. If someone was able to temporarily hack into the intercom system, they would have had access to the cameras, seen you"—he points at me—"alone, among citizens, and decided to see if he could convince them to do something they would not do under normal circumstances. And it worked."

There is something Luther is not telling me. Those eyes reveal a network of thoughts, questions, and considerations all firing through his intelligent mind, but unwilling to tell me for some reason or another.

"What..." I begin.

"I think it is time for you both to go."

"But..."

He cuts me off again. "We can't have either of you be discovered out past curfew." He hurries to the door and motions for us to follow.

"I need to know if there are more tunnels," I say.

Luther stops. "You planning to sneak more people out of the city?"

"Maybe," I say. "I don't know, it's just..."

"It's time for you to leave."

Knowing that I will get no more information from him, I turn the knob on the door and stop.

"You say that puppeteers helped orchestrate the creation of Arel."

"It seems so. During times of peace, people will not willingly fight amongst themselves. So, conflict must be created."

"So, is everyone a manipulator?"

"A manipulator preys upon your emotions, most notably anger, hopelessness, the feeling of being inadequate, and the desire to belong to something. A liberator plays to your ability to reason and does not fear you as an individual. When it comes to deciding how far you will go to achieve something, you have to decide where you will draw the line."

Before I have time to respond, Luther opens the door and shoves both Chase and me outside in his usual unceremonious way, leaving us in the darkness.

"Well, that went well," Chase quips. "Did you find out what you were looking for?"

"I don't know," I say. "It sounds like certain events happened which created Arel, and now, the same thing is happening all over again, forcing us to..."

"Trade one master for another," Chase finishes.

"While giving us the illusion of choice."

I hold him close before leaving back through the hole in the fence and navigating our way back to the manor, hoping to get us back before anyone notices our absence, unable to get the staticky voice from the train out of my head. It toyed with me, used me and the others to achieve some sort of end—what, I do not know—but because of him, people are dead, and I will see the face of that woman for the rest of my days.

I think of Mandi and how she has met with Natalie in secret. Is she a part of this? Does she know something? She must, and I intend to find out what.

Chapter 28

A Plan

The pillow curves around my head as I open my eyes to another dreary day of rain and clouds, gray and emotionless, like the life of an arbiter, like my life. I roll onto my back and glance at the only closet in the room and almost jump when I spot Chase seated on the floor, watching me with those gray eyes of his, but unlike the outside world, his eyes are full of compassion, mercy, and something else... love?

I do not know love. Love is not permitted in Arel, and forbidden to all arbiters. We are the strong, the powerful, the ones who are worthy of being in Arel and having what it offers, though I have been wondering what that is of late. Forced compliance, death if we fail, no thoughts of our own—all must adhere to the mandates of Arel or perish. Individuality is considered a stain upon the purity of Arel and is stamped out wherever it arises. And love? Love is weakness and weakness is death. But can love be a strength? I shake my head. Such a notion is contrary to Arel's teachings and therefore, forbidden, just like everything else.

"I didn't mean to startle you," Chase says in a soft, warm voice.

"What are you doing here?" I ask, afraid that he might be neglecting his duties and will pay an immense price for it. "How's Gwen? Is something wrong?"

An uncomfortable heat courses through me at the thought that he might lose his sister, the one person he has spent his life protecting and who means more to him than the world.

"She's fine. She and Sheila are on laundry detail."

My shoulders slump, as though a great weight has been lifted off them for the first time, relieved that they are both okay.

Chase gets up and sits on the edge of my bed with me, wrapping a strong, muscular arm around me, and I bury myself into his embrace, feeling the smoothness of his skin, wishing that we could stay like this, that such a thing was allowed. Memories of people flash through my mind as their faces come into view only to be replaced by another, before landing on the woman that was executed yesterday.

"What's wrong?" Chase asks, noticing the change in my demeanor.

"People keep dying," I say. "I try to help them, and they die anyway. It's as though I am a curse; from the moment I touch them, they are doomed to the fate that awaits us all."

"Shh…," he says, holding me closer. "You can't think like that."

"But it's true," I say.

He wipes a tear that has settled on my cheek, and the rough edges of his calloused and dry skin scrap my soft cheek, but the gentleness of his actions outweighs the scabrousness of his finger.

"Arel makes slaves of us all. It eats away at us, until we have no humanity left, but you have managed to keep yours. I never saw it before, not until the wilds when you could have killed that barbarian who helped us, but you didn't."

"But that woman… I wasn't able to stop her from being executed."

"You can't save everyone. All you can do is help the ones you can to the best of your ability, and let nature takes its course. Most people will run into someone and not give that person a second thought, especially when it is a plebeian, but you... you do think about them, you concern yourself with them, even if they are a plebeian, despite the risks."

"I feel so alone," I whisper.

"You're never alone," Chase hugs me tighter. "I'll follow you anywhere."

I allow Chase to hold onto me, not caring that I do have to be on duty within an hour. What did I do to deserve his loyalty, his trust?

"When Mandi brought Gwen and I here, I never thought it would change my life. But I am glad she did."

Mandi. Mandi meets with Natalie a lot, and always in secret. During the banquet, Mandi seemed upset over the way Molers treated that plebeian girl, not the sort of anger at having a momentous occasion interrupted, but genuine disgust toward the treatment of another human being. When I was at the medical center and tried to steal the medication for Gwen, someone put it in my pants' pocket with instructions on how to administer it. Was it Natalie who did it? Either way, she and Mandi are up to something, something they do not want others to find out about. What are they up to?

"Mandi," I repeat in a soft whisper, but Chase loosens his hold on me, allowing me to sit up straight and look him in the eyes. "When I stopped that suicide bomber, I saw Mandi and Natalie meeting and acting as though they didn't want anyone to notice what they were up to, and it wasn't the first time. Why did she bring you and Gwen here? Did she know your former mistress personally?"

"No," answers Chase, "I don't believe so. When my mistress died, there was talk from the others about how Gwen had certain qualities that some find pleasing. She was..."

Chase's voice trails off as though he wants nothing more but to forget that time, but I urge him to continue.

"What?" I prod.

"There are rumors that there are these places some children are sent to entertain certain members of Arelian society…"

The brothels. Anger rises within me at the thought that Gwen was to be sent there, and the fact that they even exist to begin with, and the desire to burn it to the ground intensifies, threatening to possess me.

"…and I couldn't let that happen. So, I snuck us out that night. I didn't know where we would go. I just knew that I needed to get her away from there and keep her safe. Our absence was noticed, and we were being chased by arbiters when we ran into Mandi. I was afraid she was going to turn us in. She could have, but she didn't. She told the arbiters that she was taking us to our new assignment, and apologized for not letting anyone know. I was surprised that they believed her."

"She outranks them. Questioning an outranking officer is forbidden and the punishment severe."

"Soon after, we were brought here. I don't know why."

"This might have been the only place at the time that could take in two more plebeians, and Commander Vye probably wasn't in a position to argue."

Mandi. What is she up to? A few moments of silence pass between us before I break it.

"I need to get a message to Mandi and Natalie."

Chase looks me in the eyes. "For what?"

"I keep seeing them together, but in secret. I want to know what they are up to, but…"

"Stay here." Chase gets up and heads for the door.

"Where are you going?"

"Just trust me," he says in a soft voice.

I nod. I have no reason not to trust him. Too many times he could have left me for dead, but chose not to.

"Write a message to her. Something that will get her to meet with you. Have it ready by the time I get back."

The door opens and Chase peeks out into the hallway, making

sure no one is there, before slipping out. I'm not sure what he is up to, but I decide to trust him. He's earned that much, and so much more.

I rip open the drawer to my desk, searching for paper, something that is difficult to find in Arel, since almost all communications are electronic, but digital communications can be traced, and I need something that is untraceable. Nothing. Frustrated, I search my sparse room—just a cot next to the wall, a desk under the window, a single chair that makes rocks seem comfortable to sit on, and the closet—but find nothing. I need something. Anything. I don't know what to do, but…

Something skitters across the floor when my foot touches it. I pick it up, examining it, realizing that it is a piece of charcoal. How did it get up here? My boots. Where else? Sometimes, sticks, mud, rocks, and I guess even bits of charcoal, get caught in the ridges of the soles of my boots and get tracked inside, for which, I am very thankful right the moment. But, now, I need something… A speck of white catches my eye. I'm not sure why it didn't earlier, because it sticks out worse than a sore thumb amongst the dark-colored floor and grimy walls that are more gray now than white, but perhaps it is the lone ray of gold sunlight poking through the window and caressing the speck of white that makes me notice it, almost as though it was planned. I pick it up, realizing that it is a towel, one I had dumped in the far corner of the room earlier, having been too tired to fold it and put it out to be taken to the laundry. It is perfect.

I rip the towel in half and use the bit of charcoal to pen a message to both Natalie and Mandi. Nothing elaborate. Just something short and to the point, with each pretending to be the other, and asking to meet in person in a building that had been searched by arbiters a week ago, so it won't be under surveillance and is still empty.

Chase walks into the room with both Sheila and Gwen as I finish. I open my mouth to protest—they could get killed—but he stops me.

"They both know Arel well."

"But if they get caught…"

"I won't get caught," says Gwen in a stern tone, desperate to prove herself. "I know this city, and no one pays much attention to a small plebeian girl like me."

"She can deliver one of the messages and…." begins Chase.

"And I will deliver the other one," interrupts Sheila.

"She overheard me talking to Gwen and insisted on coming," Chase says.

"What about their chores? They'll be missed," I say.

"I will finish the laundry," says Chase, "and Sheila is being sent out to get a few supplies for the manor."

Still uneasy about the entire thing, I know I have little choice. If I deliver the messages, it will ruin what secrecy I have, but if they deliver them, both Mandi and Natalie will have no way of knowing that they come from me, and that it is a trap, or so I hope. Either way, it puts the odds in my favor.

Chase places his hands on my bare shoulders, their warmth filling me with comfort.

"They want to help, Noni. You're not alone, and you can't do everything on your own."

I give in and hand the messages to Chase, who gives the one for Mandi to Gwen, and the other to Sheila, who frowns when she sees what I used to create it.

"It was all I had," I apologize, but her lips remain pursed in disappointment, since my actions ruined a towel.

Chase opens the door and ushers them outside, and they run off, making very little noise so as not to attract unwanted attention.

"They will be fine," he says to me, to ease my worries. "I'll let you know when they return. For now, do your duty, and try not to worry."

We embrace once more before he slips out of my room, leaving me to get dressed and face what the day has to offer, so I remove all emotion from my face, determined to not give anything away. Today, I am just another arbiter, but tonight, I intend to get some answers.

Chapter 29

Mandi's Secret

Crouched behind a pile of rotted wood and crumbling brick, I wait in the darkness for both Mandi and Natalie to arrive, assuming they fall for my ruse, while the incessant drip of water into a puddle—that has formed in a patch of cracked and sunken cement with a few rusty nails stuck in its center—hit my ears, providing the only sense of companionship on this mission.

Chase wanted to come, but I told him no. If it turns out to be a trap, if they turn the tables on me, I need to know that he is okay and will be able to watch over Gwen and Sheila, because if both Mandi and Natalie choose to bring other arbiters, I will be executed for certain. But, if they do come alone, I need them to be able to trust me, which will be difficult enough, considering that I have set them up. My muscles start to cramp from the position I am in, but I ignore the burning desire to move, to stretch, to ease their discomfort and provide some sort of relief. Sitting still is a skill that arbiters are supposed to excel at. Musky air stifles my lungs as the aged smell of burnt metal, gunpowder, and soaked wood permeates the atmosphere, filling it to the point where the idea of fresh air is nothing but a dream, but I breathe it anyway, knowing there is nothing else I can do, but try not to cough while I wait.

Minutes turn to hours, or so it seems, while my impatience grows. Perhaps they both have decided not to come. Maybe they both know it is a trap. People don't often handwrite anything, and maybe that was the tipoff. I cannot stay here for much longer. If no one arrives, if my plan is a failure, like so many of my plans, then I will need to leave, knowing that I will never get the answers I seek, a knowledge that will haunt me for many nights to come.

Just as I am about to give up waiting and go back to the manor, a door creaks, not a loud monotone sort of creak as though the wind had caught it, but a slow, deliberate movement as though someone does not want to be noticed, and is being cautious. I try peeking around the pole that is in front of me, but my muscles refuse to move, having gotten used to their cramped position. A lone shape moves closer to my position, but not too close, being careful to remain quiet, and the unease of its movements tell me that it is not certain about the decision it had made. I crane my neck to get a better look and can just make out that it is Natalie; her white uniform is covered by a dark overthrow to try and mask it as she moves through the night.

"Mandi?" she whispers, but not too loud so as not attract anybody. Even though the buildings have been searched in the past, and the former occupants evicted, that doesn't mean there isn't an arbiter or two on patrol outside.

"Mandi!" the harsh whisper scratches my ear drums, making me cringe.

Where is Mandi? Did she decide not to come? As though in answer to my question, Mandi steps out of a pile of woodwork. How long has she been here? Was she here before I arrived? Or did she sneak in without my notice? I scold myself for not being more alert, but also remember that Mandi has been an arbiter for many years, and silence, prowess, and concealment are traits that are taught to arbiters. Some excel at them better than others, and Mandi must be one who surpassed all of them.

"I thought I had told you not to contact me," Mandi says with frustration. "It is too dangerous."

"You contacted me," Natalie replies, showing Mandi the piece of towel that I had written my note onto.

Mandi snatches it from her hand and throws it on the floor, setting it on fire with a lighter.

"You should have destroyed this the moment you received it!"

An image of her burning the note she had received fills my mind, and I imagine that is probably what she did so that no one else could read it.

"You didn't write the note?" Natalie asks.

"No," says Mandi, "which means someone else did."

Both look around, backing away from one another, ready to run if necessary, meaning that the time for me to reveal myself has come.

"I wrote it," I say, my voice filling the space between us and sounding more confident than I feel, as I step out from behind the pile of wood and bricks.

They both take a step back from me.

"Noni," Mandi says with surprise. "What are you…"

"I want some answers," I say.

"I have no idea what you are talking about," says Mandi.

"Cut the bullshit," I tell her. "I know you two are up to something. Too many times I have seen you two together, passing packages or notes, meeting in secret, and making every effort to not be noticed."

"Apparently we didn't do good enough of a job," Mandi says.

"I want to know what you two are up to," I say.

"We outnumber you," Mandi says.

"But only one of you is a trained arbiter, and both you and Molers taught me well."

Inside, my nerves scream at me to not push it, but I must appear confident in my ability to handle this situation; otherwise, all of this is for nothing. Bluffing is a huge part of winning.

"So, we have," Mandi says.

"We should go," says Natalie, inching away, but I stop her.

"Are you responsible for the bombings?"

"No!" Natalie's voice echoes around us, and she hunkers, afraid that someone might be outside to hear us.

"Then who is?" I demand.

"It is not us," says Mandi. "We are part of a small operation that works to smuggle people out of Arel."

"What about the attack on me on the railcar?" I ask.

"What?" says Mandi. "I heard there was an incident, but I didn't know that it involved you."

"What about the symbol that keeps appearing everywhere? And I saw both of you right before a bomb went off. Don't stand there and lie to me!"

"We are not lying," says Natalie, trying to calm me down. "I am a nurse, sworn to help people. I would never get involved in anything that would cause harm."

"There are rumors," Mandi chimes in, "of a group, a rebellion of sorts, but I think they are more than that, who wants to overthrow the Arelian government. Their tactics are reprehensible. They do not care whom they hurt, but we are not a part of them."

"How do I know that?" I ask.

Mandi takes a step toward me, and I take one back, keeping a distance between the both of us.

"Noni, you know me."

"Not well enough."

"Have I ever done anything to make you believe that I would intentionally harm another, just for the sake of hurting them?"

I think back at the training facility and all the times she stopped a plebeian from receiving a senseless beating, or the times she seemed unenthusiastic about the Arelian mantra, or how she scolded recruits who chose to use their position to bully another. As an instructor, she was tough and unforgiving, but she was always fair.

"I refuse to have anything to do with whomever is instigating these terrorist attacks," Mandi says. "And so does Natalie."

"There are only three of us," Natalie adds. "All we do is help get people who want to leave out of the city. Once out, they are on their own. But it is a choice they make."

Which is what I have done as well. I think back on the people I have helped leave and wonder how they are doing and if they made it to where they wanted to go. I may never know. In fact, I know I will never know their fate. Such is the way of life.

"Who's the third?" I ask.

Natalie gives me a questioning look.

"You said the three of you."

Daggers shoot from Mandi's eyes at Natalie for having given me an extra bit of information.

"Doctor Sahir," Natalie replies. "He fakes the death certificates, and I get the information to Mandi, who gets them out. Her clearance gives her an advantage."

"But it is getting more difficult," Mandi says. "Because of the recent attacks, my movements are being watched more and more. I'm sure you've noticed."

I have. Amal keeps a constant eye on me, which makes my extracurricular activities difficult, and Molers, well, he is always suspicious of others and looking for an opportunity to advance himself.

"I only came here," Natalie says, "because I have three people who want out. I thought…"

"I can get them out," I say, not sure what I am doing, and the words are out of my mouth before I have a chance to think about them.

"What?" Both Mandi and Natalie stare at me in disbelief.

"I've been doing it for a while now," I say.

"On your own?" asks Mandi.

"Yes," I reply, refusing to tell them about Luther, or even Chase.

Mandi gives me a doubtful look, but does not question me. It's not as though I am not telling the truth. Up until the last group, I had been on my own.

"We may have to tell them that they cannot get out," Mandi says to Natalie.

"No!" Natalie refuses to listen. "They need to get out. One is a breeder. She cannot go on for much longer, and the other two work in the medical center, but have made the mistake of questioning an order. If they don't get out, they will be executed!"

"And outside the wall, they may die as well," Mandi says. "It is too dangerous. If we get caught…"

"I thought you said that your only function was to help them leave. After that they are on their own," I say. "I can get them out."

"And what do you want in exchange?" Mandi asks.

"Honesty," I reply.

"That is a high price," she says.

"But it is my price," I say.

"And how do you know you can trust us?" challenges Mandi.

"How do you know you can trust me?" I answer.

"We don't have time for this," Natalie interjects.

"Send the same messenger to me within a week and I will get you the information you need. If you fail, you will be on your own."

What else is new?

"Understood," I tell her.

"We should leave. Natalie, you go first," says Mandi.

Natalie leaves without question, sneaking out the door and disappearing into the dark, with her overthrow covering her medical uniform quite well, allowing her to blend in.

"If you get caught, I will deny this meeting every happened," Mandi says.

"To save yourself," I reply.

"Not myself, but what I am fighting for."

"And what is that?"

"The individual." Mandi peeks out the door, but before she leaves, she turns to me and says, "I'm starting to think that I don't really know you, Noni."

"The feeling is mutual," I tell her, and she leaves, going in a different direction than Natalie.

I wait a couple of minutes before slipping outside and making my way back to the manor, wondering what I have gotten myself into.

Chapter 30

Consequences

Once again, I tuck my wristband under the mattress and put on Amal's, which Sheila brought to me earlier. Amal wasn't at supper this evening—something that I thought was a bit strange because he never misses a meal—and instead, had been in his room. When asked how she got the wristband, Sheila said that she had snuck into his room and took it off the desk in there, and that I needn't worry about Amal finding her because he had been in a deep sleep. I wonder if he hadn't been feeling well. Earlier today, he did look a little pale, so the possibility that he had caught a small illness is there. Either way, when he returned from his day patrol, he went straight to his room, and must have gone straight to bed, giving Sheila the perfect opportunity to steal his wristband. I do worry about Sheila helping me so much, but she insists, and there was no keeping tonight's proposed excursion a secret from her when Chase asked Gwen to report to Mandi for a message.

The door to my room slides open and Chase hurries in. I didn't want him to come along at first, afraid that, if something goes wrong, he will be hurt, but Chase insisted, and when I had first told him about the previous people I had snuck out, I had said that he could help me in the future, and now I must make good on my promise.

"We cannot go out that way," Chase says. "Molers is watching the main floor."

Of course, he is. Molers has been looking for anything suspicious since he arrived, almost as though he wanted something terrible to happen so that he would have something negative to report to the council about Commander Vye.

"We'll go out the window," I say, after checking Chase to make sure he has no identifying marks on him. "Where are Gwen and Sheila?"

"Gwen is in her room, safe. Sheila is outside, waiting for us."

My heart sinks. I want her to be safe and to not put herself in danger, but…

"She'll be fine," Chase says, as though he can read my thoughts. "She wants to help, and you can't do this alone."

He's right, but the thought of others putting themselves in danger for me sickens me.

"I just…"

"We'll be back before you know it. I told you, I'm not letting you do this alone."

Knowing that there is no winning this argument, I head to the window and open it with care, looking out at the green quad outside, and ease my way out, feet first, doing my best to make no noise. As I dangle from the window ledge, with my feet hanging in the air, a flash of lighting streaks across the night sky and thunder explodes overhead, causing my chest to vibrate as its tremendous bang hurts my ears, and as I let go, rain dumps from the sky. I land in the already soaked grass—it has only been raining for seconds—and tuck and roll, so as to absorb the impact and get out of the way before Chase drops down beside me. We hurry into the bushes and wait for Sheila's signal, but stop the moment we see Molers step outside and pace from the back door to the fence. What is he up to? Does he know we are here?

More lightning and more thunder fill the night air, and the torrential rain continues to pound the earth with its fury, masking any noise that Chase and I make. We watch as Molers steps toward us, and we both sink even further into the bushes, their fine needles poking through my clothing and pricking my skin with their sappy points, but before he gets any closer, a clapping sound comes from around the corner of the building. He jerks in the direction of the sound. Painful seconds tick by as we wait for Molers to decide what he will do next. He stalks away, unphased by the rain beating down on him, and goes around the corner. Soon after he disappears, I spot Sheila's face and she waves Chase and me onward. We both speed off across the grass and to the loose bar in the fence, squeezing our way through and hurrying down the street before anyone notices us.

The torrential rain saturates my ears with its white noise as we race down the flooded pavement, our feet splashing with every step, but muted by the onslaught of the rain itself. We duck down alleys and narrow gaps between brick buildings as we head for the same place where I had Mandi and Natalie meet with me. Considering it is still closed off, Mandi thought it was the best place to hide the people she wants smuggled out of Arel. I hope that she has not set a trap for me the way I had set one for her. Bits of my hair stick to my face as the rain pastes it against my skin, and I try to brush it off with the back of my hand, but only succeed at making it form a zigzagged pattern that covers my eyes. Chase stops and points in the distance. Through the wall of rain lurks a shadow, pacing the square, while trying to pretend that he does not care about the rain. I motion for Chase to turn a corner, and we snake our way past two residential buildings, relieved that nature has decided to mask our tracks. Painful minutes pass, and we make a few turns, until we arrive at the sequestered buildings. Pleased that the darkness surrounds us, and that no lights shine in any of the windows around us, I open the door, peeking inside for any sign of a trap, but the stilled silence, broken only by a fast-paced drip from the leaky roof, greets me, so I hurry inside with Chase right behind me.

"Mandi?" I hiss into the dusty air, my heart racing as horrid thoughts race through my mind, each worse than the one before. "Mandi!"

"Over here," comes a strong voice, and Mandi steps out from the shadows, surprising me in the same manner I had surprised her week earlier, and followed by three people, each dressed in dark clothing. One is a middle-aged woman, and looks to be near the end of her childbearing years, who, despite her dark skin tone, looks pale, as though she has been ill and is just recovering. As she steps further into the open, I notice her protruding abdomen and realize that she must have just given birth, and it must have been a difficult one. A man hurries to her when she steps backward and looks as though she might pass out, and holds her, steadying her, and the small smile on her lips informs him of her appreciation.

"Come," Mandi says to the fourth person in the room.

He continues to hide behind a pillar, unwilling to come forward. "I can't. It's too risky."

"Now." Mandi's firm tone forces him into the open.

"Who is he?" the frightened man demands, pointing at Chase.

"He's with me," I answer, using the same firm tone that Mandi had just used and the man quiets down. For an orderly at the medical center, he seems to be quick to frighten, or perhaps he is having second thoughts about escaping.

Mandi looks at all three of them.

"She and her cohort will lead you out of the city. Do as she says."

"We should leave while it's still raining," I say just as another crack of thunder roars overhead.

Chase leads the woman and two men outside, but before I can leave, Mandi snatches my arm and forces me to look at her.

"Do not cross me."

"I always keep my word," I tell her. "You should know that by now."

She lets go of my arm, and I hurry outside into the rain once more and hurry after Chase as he leads them away from the abandoned building and to a pile of trash cans, waiting for me. I squat next to him, ignoring the mixed odor of rotted food with the sweet smell of rain, as I scan the streets for any signs of arbiters on patrol, but see nothing. The rain must be keeping them at bay. Even though we are supposed to ignore the elements, some arbiters detest the rain and will hide from it when it pours, like it is now, which, for the moment, is to my advantage.

"Now!" I whisper.

We all jump from behind the garbage cans and race down the street with Chase, and one of the orderlies helps the woman run as the rain's thick curtain conceals us, rounding the edge of another building before anyone can spot us. Panting, I look at my charges, wondering how I am going to get them there, as the woman's frightened face stares back at me. Picturing the layout of the eastern sector in my mind, I chart the best route to the tunnel Luther had pointed out to me in what seems so long ago now. We will have to take the streets, but if the rain holds out, we should be able to slip by unnoticed, if we are fast.

"Can you help her?" I ask Chase and the orderly seated next to him.

They both nod, while the other orderly, the one who has grown cold feet, scans our surroundings in agitation.

"Follow me, and stay close," I tell them.

I bolt from behind the building as the rain stabs my face, sending burning sensations that linger after pricking my cheeks, charging down the sidewalks, before veering across another street and hugging the side of a building as I hurry down another walk. Despite my hurried movements, I keep my eyes peeled for any signs of arbiters on patrol, but the heaviness of the rain grows stronger as it beats down upon us, meaning that any arbiters assigned to night patrol will be hiding under awnings or inside someone's home uninvited. It doesn't matter. As long as they are not able to see us, we will continue to go unheeded. Drenched, my clothes tighten their hold on me, weighing me down and threatening to slow my movements, but I push onwards, while always aware of the people behind me. We're almost there. Another turn, and another, and I spot the area where the cover to the tunnel is.

I urge them to pick up their pace as water pours down my face, forming its own waterfall, but I ignore the discomfort; I have to, for their sake. My boots sink into the water of the flooded streets, forming ripples and pools as they go, refusing to stop or to be slowed down by nature, and before I can crash into empty food crates over the manhole, I drop to the ground and slide on my side to a complete stop. The others hunker around me.

"Help me with this," I say, and they each lean against the crate, pushing it to the side, revealing the manhole, and without waiting to be told, they each lift a side of the cover, until it uncovers the dark tunnel underneath. I wave them into it, and one by one, we climb down the rusted ladder, with me in the rear, until we drop down into waist deep water, and I force myself to stifle a yelp as the frigid liquid envelops me, penetrating me to my very core.

Panic starts to overtake me as the water surrounds me, holding me as though it means to imprison me with a foreboding air, as I do not recall the tunnel being this filled with water before, but was instead bone dry. Abandoned these tunnels may be, but they are still functioning as drains, and with all the rain that pours out of the sky, these tunnels are about to overflow. Though I am already soaked, this besmirched liquid creeps into places I'd rather it not go, making me feel soiled as it fills my boots and seeps between the bands of my underclothes. I force the uncomfortable feeling out of my mind, focusing on the task at hand, because, if my suspicions are correct, we will end up under water if we don't hurry.

My feet scoot across the uneven ground from all the dirt that has built up within as I slosh my way past everyone, doing my best to remember the map Luther had shown me when I first entered this desolate place, and head down the tunnel, as the others follow after me. Chase flicks on a tiny light, and I have no idea where he got it from, but I am glad that he thought to bring one, as we wade through the murky water. With each step, the water seems to get higher, but I swallow back the insipid fear that rises within me and stroke my arms through the water, half swimming, half wading as the current takes me, and I make my way further into the darkness, remembering my time here earlier and which turns to take, and which ones to avoid.

The woman slips and falls underneath the water, screaming as she does.

"Help her!" I hiss at the others, and the man that had been assisting her the entire night throws his arm out to catch her and lifts her head out of the water.

"It's getting deeper," she says with a shiver.

That it is, and I don't like it.

"Keep moving," I say, doing my best to not slow down.

Water ripples past me as I inch my way further into the tunnel, feeling the sides with my hands, but my fingers slip each time I try to grab hold of it—the moisture has made the slime worse—while I search for the ladder that I used the last time I was here, with the soft glow of Chase's light bouncing in front of me as he holds it high above his head, swimming with one arm. It's got to be here. I know it is. The fear that I went the wrong way, that I got lost and doomed us all to a fate of drowning settles into my mind, overtaking it, as I push myself through the water, searching in a semi-frantic state, while trying to not frighten the people with me. Maybe it's further. The water now covers the tips of my breasts and my lungs strain for air as the knowledge that soon there will be no gap between the surface of the water and the ceiling if this continues fills me. My face smacks into the edge of the tunnel, and as I spin around in the water, I realize that I am in of a domed area, but where is the ladder? It should—wait! What is that?

"Shine your light that way," I tell Chase, and he does, allowing me to see small ripples as the water brushes against the sides of a grime encrusted ladder.

I kick my feet in the water, propelling myself to the ladder and cling to it as though it is a life preserver, and in this case, it is. I start to climb up it, but Chase pushes me out of the way and snakes up the ladder with ease, pressing his shoulders against the cover and pushing against it until it opens. It pops free with ease, compared to the last time I was here, and a wall of rain plunges into the dark abyss I am in as he holds his hand out to me, but I wave the woman forward. Relieved, she takes his hand and he hauls her out of the water, helping her through the hole and into the world above. I wave one of the orderlies forward and he hurries up the ladder, but was almost knocked back into the water by the overeagerness of his colleague, who scrambles up the other side and out of the hole.

As they disappear, I clamber out of the water and to the top. My eyes try to scan the landscape, but the fierceness of the pouring rain makes visibility impossible, but from what I can tell, this is the same place I had come out of the last time I was here.

"The trees are that way," I yell so as to be heard over the roar of the rain. "Go straight and you'll be fine. From there, you are on your own."

"You're not coming with us?" says the orderly that was too eager to get out of the tunnels.

"No," I reply.

The man looks at me with a mixture of panic and incredulity.

"But, how are we…"

"You should have thought of that before wanting to be smuggled out," I interrupt him. "Either take your chances out there, or take your chances within Arel." I point at the water below me within the tunnel.

The man glances at it for a moment and runs off toward the tree line.

"Good luck," I say to the other man and the woman.

They both smile at me, a thankful, but uncertain smile before hurrying away to the tree line, disappearing beyond the curtain of rain the pounds the earth around me, forming pools large enough to bathe in. Knowing what awaits me underneath, I take a deep breath and let go of the sides of the manhole, plunging into the water below. My head pops through the surface as Chase replaces the cover and jumps in beside me, while the tips of my toes bounce along the tunnel floor as the water forces me to bob up and down, warning me that my worst fear has been realized. The water is rising fast.

Together, Chase and I push against the water as we swim back to where we had come in, our progress impeded by the current that now works against us. Each breath is a struggle as water seeps into my mouth, forcing me into a convulsive cough as it tries to go down my airway and coats my tongue with its gritty and metallic texture, putting the taste of spoiled stew and urine in my mouth. A ring of orange floats past me, sinking to the bottom, leaving a rippling glow beneath me, as I realize that Chase has dropped his light in an effort to make it back to the opening. My hands slam against the walls of the tunnel, searching for anything that can be used as a handhold, and the tips of my fingers burn as all I find is the rough edges of concrete digging into my skin from my worthless efforts. My head hits the celling. Turning my face up, I swallow a lungful of air, knowing that I have little time until this pocket of oxygen is gone for good, and my fear of drowning latches onto me, crippling me and forcing me to plunge beneath the water and into its inky darkness of silt and sewage, but before I sink too far down, strong hands seize me, ripping me free of the oppressive water and forcing my head back above the surface.

"Hang onto me," Chase says as I gasp for air.

I grip his waist, kicking with my feet in a futile effort to fight the current that grows stronger by the minute.

"The current is too strong!" I yell.

"Trust me," Chase says, and despite the darkness, I know he looks into my eyes with his gray ones, doing his best to encourage me.

Trusting him, I cling to him as his arms move through the water with a speed I didn't know he could muster, and together, we kick our way through the water, with him as my guide, pulling me after him, and my fear dissipates. Each second feels like an hour as the current pushes against us, encouraging us to give up, but both Chase and I refuse; we both need to get back to Gwen—I refuse to let her lose her brother for a second time—and Sheila. My muscles tire and want to quit, but Chase's continued efforts spur me onward, and I push forward as water ripples past me, almost like a massage, as though beckoning me to let it carry me away into nothingness.

"Hold your breath!" Chase yells, and his voice seems distant even though he is next to me.

We reach a dip in the ceiling, and there is no other way through, except to swim under water. Once again, my fear of drowning rises, threatening to overtake me, but Chase grips my hand in encouragement, and I suck in some air before plowing beneath the surface. My lungs want to explode as I hold onto the air within them while swimming as hard as I can with the current mocking my efforts, but I refuse to quit. I must not quit. Failure is death. My arms and legs move in unison to Chase's movements as we push our way through the water and to the opening. Almost there. We have to almost be there.

A few bubbles escape my mouth as my lungs burn and start to convulse, demanding to let go of their contents, but I will them not to, despite the pain in my chest as my head pounds, feeling as though a clamp has been placed around it, but I am unable to hold my breath any longer, and my mouth bursts open, expelling all the air in my lungs, and reflex takes over as I inhale and choke on the water. Convulsing takes over my body, but before I slip away, Chase grabs me and shoves me through the hole and into the street above. My head pops out of the manhole as a series of coughs and gasps over take me, but I manage to use the last of my strength to haul myself out of the hole and onto the pavement as the rain pelts my skin, admonishing me for trying to be heroic.

For a moment, I lie there, allowing the rain to beat me as I take in one deep breath after another, until Chase's hand grips my stomach, forcing me to remember him, and I lean over the side of the hole, grabbing his arm and pull on him until he is free of the tunnel. We both sit in the rain, looking at one another, ignoring the water pouring down the sides of the buildings, forming their own waterfalls, and the tiny rivers that snake their way past us, annoyed that we have blocked their path.

"I'm sorry," I say, apologizing for being a burden.

"There is no shame in needing someone," Chase replies.

Before I know it, my lips are on his, thankful that he insisted on coming along and that he was there to help me when I needed it most, and he holds me close, pleased that we are together.

"We need to get back," he says when we separate.

I nod. We don't have much time, and we cannot get caught out here when the rain stops. We plop the manhole cover back in place and hurry through the streets, taking one turn after another, using the lesser known alleyways as our path back to the manor so as to avoid any arbiters on duty, until we reach the fence surrounding the manor. Chase removes the loose bar in the fence and waves me through before following after me. I hunker in a bush, spotting my window, deciding on the best path to get there, and almost make a run for it, when I stop. Amal searches the ground for something, the same something I have around my wrist. I point him out to Chase and show him the wristband.

"We have to get this back to him," I whisper.

Chase takes the band from around my wrist.

"When it's clear, make a run for it."

"Be careful," I tell him.

He places a gentle hand on my cheek in reassurance and darts off into another bush with the wristband that Sheila had taken from Amal. I watch as Chase sneaks over to Amal and creeps behind him, dropping the wristband into the grass in front of Amal's feet, before hurrying inside the manor, obscured by the rain. Amal picks it up, confused as to how it got there, but pleased that he has found it, and disappears. Leaving me alone in the rain.

Now or never.

Taking my chance, I bolt from the bush I am hiding in and race for the manor, but before I get far, hands seize me and throw me into the soggy grass, knocking the wind out of me. Gasping, I get to my knees, but before I can get up, a boot rams into my stomach, forcing me to take a sharp breath, as I cough up bits of stomach acid before lying on my back in misery. Molers leers over me. Turning my head, I spot Chase's face, peeking around a corner, but I shake my head, hoping that he heeds my message. He saved me in the tunnels, and now it is my turn to protect him. Molers closes in and I jut my foot out, catching him in the shin and forcing him to stumble as I roll out of the way of another kick. Crouching low, I spring at him, grabbing him around the knees and knocking him down, but before I can do anything else, he kicks me away from him and jumps on me, pinning me to the ground as his hands go for my throat and squeeze. Frantic, I flail my arms around, searching for anything I can use as a weapon, but there is nothing as he closes my airway and I struggle, desperate for air.

"I knew you were up to something," he whispers into my ear before hauling me to my feet with his hand still around my throat.

My feet drag across the marshy grass as Molers drags me inside, kicking the doors open before throwing me to the floor, where I roll across it before ramming into a table, knocking it over on top of myself. Coughing, I try to think of a story, of a way out of this, but nothing comes to mind as I lie helpless on the rug on the floor, drenching it with my soggy clothes.

"Everyone up!" yells Molers. "I've caught a traitor!"

Doors to rooms open as feet pound down the stairs to see what all the commotion is about, only to find a triumphant Molers hovering over an arbiter that has only had her commission for little over a year.

"What is the meaning of all this?" demands Commander Vye as she enters the room, and her disheveled uniform indicates that she had shoved it on in a hurry so as not to allow others to see her in her night clothes.

"I've caught a traitor," sneers Molers.

Commander Vye looks at him before glancing in my direction as I continue to writhe in pain and cough up spit. Renal appears beside her, and for a moment, I see a mixture of sympathy and surprise in his eyes before it's replaced by a scowl. I must be a complete disappointment to him, and in a way, I do not blame him for his disgust.

Feet shuffle across the wood floor, scraping tiny pebbles that stick in the cracks between the floorboards, as arbiters gather around me—some rubbing sleep from their eyes, some wrapping towels around themselves, as fresh water from an interrupted shower drip from their knees and elbows, while others look infuriated at having such a disgusting sight in their midst—waiting to be told what to do next, to receive their new orders, or salivating at the prospect of witnessing another's punishment. I glare at each of them, daring them to challenge me and my actions, and I spot Amal among them, gloating over my predicament, when a black blur swishes past my field of vision before something slams into my mouth, knocking my head back into the wall, with bits of crumpling wallpaper falling away and dusting my drenched hair, and an intense pain grips my entire face, interrupted only by the feeling of something rattling in my mouth.

Dazed, I raise myself up on shaky arms that threaten to buckle beneath me at any second, while trying to get my eyes to focus as unconsciousness reaches out for me, trying to bind me to its will, but I ignore it, willing myself to remain awake as I spit out a mouthful of blood onto the foot of the man that had kicked me, laughing as a single, white tooth lands upon the reflective, black surface of his boot. I crane my head and stare straight into Molers' eyes.

"Is that all you've got," I say in a low voice with blood running down both sides of my chin.

I do not wait to be told to get up and stay put. Not tonight. Tonight, whatever befalls me will be my choice and my will. I bend my knee, lifting my foot up, placing it flat on the floor, and push with my other leg, until I am standing straight and proud. For a second, I waver as a wave of light-headedness passes over me, beckoning me to sleep, to give in, but I refuse, as I focus my gaze onto the dark abysses known as Molers' eyes. He raises his fist, and I prepare myself for what I know comes next, but nothing happens. As Molers swings, Commander Vye starts for him, but Renal, with a speed I never witnessed before, pushes her to the side, stopping her, before appearing next to Molers, catching his fist in midair.

"You've made your point," Renal growls at Molers.

"I wonder," whispers Molers to him, "do we have two traitors tonight?"

"If you want a real challenge," replies Renal in a whisper of his own, "just say the word."

Molers jerks his fist free and steps back.

"Now," Commander Vye demands, "what is the meaning of this?"

"Commander," Molers says, struggling to sound respectful, but Renal's presence forces him to, and I am reminded of the day Molers tried to choke me to death and how Renal stopped them, and how, ever since, Molers has been wary of him, and once again, I wonder if Renal is a marshal, "I found Arbiter Noni out after hours. This is not the first time she has snuck out."

His words confirm that he has been spying on me, and I bet it was Amal who did his dirty work.

"Being out on the grounds after curfew is hardly cause for the display you chose to put on," says Commander Vye.

"I believe Arbiter Noni has been sneaking into the city at night and smuggling people out," says Molers.

"Evidence?" demands Commander Vye.

"Look at her. She is defiant. She smells of sewage. And she consorts with plebeians."

"Is that it?" scoffs Commander Vye. "I know of her nights with a certain plebeian, but…"

"So, you have allowed her to have relations with scum," accuses Molers.

"By order of President Tapiwa herself," Commander Vye counters in a stern voice. "Are you questioning her orders?"

Molers rethinks his tactics.

"What about her bruises and their unknown origin? The attacks, the riots, they do not account for all of it, but if she were—"

"—smuggling people out of the city that could account for some of it," finishes Commander Vye.

She turns toward me and scrutinizes my presence. Truth is, Molers needs no proof of my disloyalty. An accusation is proof enough in Arel, but Commander Vye demands it, and I do not know why. I have betrayed her trust, and shame gnaws at me because of it. Despite her hard-ass ways, Commander Vye believed in me, or saw something that she admired, and I have put her in a terrible position. Yet, I couldn't abandon the others depending on me to get them out. Such is the nature of Arel: it puts two people against one another as it thrives on conflict and fear in order to remain in control.

"The Master Arbiter is correct," I say. "There is a traitor in our midst"—I glance at Amal—"and I have been watching him. That is why I was out of bed after curfew. I watched him leave and was waiting for his return."

Amal starts to protest, but before he can get a word out, Renal seizes him and drags him forward.

"He has been sneaking out into the city under the guise of night and sneaking back in before sunup. I was in the middle of tracking him when Molers attacked me."

"This is ridiculous!" Amal protests.

"Check his wristband if you don't believe me," I say.

Renal seizes Amal's wrist and removes his wristband.

"It's all a lie!" screams Amal. "She's lying!"

"There was another arrested earlier," says Molers, "for the same crime, and it's believed this individual had an accomplice in the eastern sector and from this manor. Maybe that person should be brought here."

"And how are we to believe this detainee?" asks Commander Vye.

"I know you are aware that Arel has ways of getting information, even from those trained to resist," growls Molers.

Commander Vye purses her lips before agreeing with him. "Very well. Bring this individual here, so that we can get to the bottom of this."

Molers salutes and stalks away with a smirk on his face, thinking that he has me trapped, and to be honest, he very well may. Who is this person they caught? Luther? I hope not. Luther and I do not always see eye to eye, but he deserves a better fate.

"Take Arbiter Noni and Amal to their quarters," Commander Vye says, taking command of the situation, and I cringe under her hawk-like gaze, as two arbiters take me and Amal by the arms and steer us to the stairs.

In an instant, I spot two pale faces poking out of a crack as the door leading to the plebeian quarters swings open, and I shake my head at both Sheila and Gwen, wanting nothing more than for them, and Chase, to be safe. They shrink back into the darkness and close the door, for which I am relieved. They are safe, for now. My feet stumble on the steps as the arbiters drag me up them, not caring it I fall, and before I know it, we reach the door to my room. It slides open and they throw me inside, allowing me to crash onto the floor as the door slides closed and locks in place, refusing to allow me to pass through.

Dark thoughts overtake my mind. Who did they capture? I can only imagine the torture that they put this person through. Feeling exhausted, and my face still reeling from the impact of Molers' kick,

I crawl across the floor and to the cot with its covers pulled taut, just like when I arrived here on my first day in the eastern sector, and haul myself up onto the mattress and their short springs, stretching out on it as I lay on my back. I feel a bruise forming on my stomach as I run my tongue over my teeth, pausing when it sinks into the new gap from the tooth Molers had knocked out of my mouth. How much time passes as I lie here, I do not know, but it feels like an eternity moseys by, taking its time as it allows me to stew in my own thoughts, each one worse than the last.

The engine of a transport pulls up, and my eyes flutter open, telling me that I must have passed out, despite my attempts to remain awake. Doors open and close, and I know what comes next as boots pound up the stairs, heading straight for my door. It opens. Arbiters rush in and seize me before I have a chance to sit up, and drag me into the hallway toward the stairs. I try to move my feet, but they refuse to work, too exhausted to obey my commands, as the arbiters holding onto me haul me down the stairs and to the foyer, where a slumped figure in cuffs sits in the middle of the floor, guarded by arbiters. The arbiters carrying me throw me on the floor next to the slumped figure, followed by Amal. My heart skips a few beats as the moment of truth rears its ugly head at me, taunting me.

"Tell us," orders Commander Vye of the slumped figure, "who is your accomplice?"

The figure moves as matted hair escapes its hold, plastering to the person's chin, before sitting up and showing a face I almost don't recognize: Mandi. She got caught. Why did I force her to meet with me that night? She knew she was being watched and she met with me anyway, because I pretended to be Natalie, because I wanted answers. Because of me, she now lies in the middle of the floor at the manor, her face so beaten that it will never pass for human again, and her uniform torn to the point where it appears to be nothing more than rags thrown together in a pathetic attempt to clothe her. I bite my tongue to keep form gasping as she opens her one good eye, the other sunken in as though it had been ripped out, and her mouth so swollen that, when she tries to speak, her words are slurred and blend together, making it impossible to decipher them. What did they do to her? And it's all because of me.

I steal a quick glance at Molers, who stands triumphant over us all, knowing full well who Mandi's real accomplice is and enjoying every minute of it.

"Tell us!" an arbiter screams, punching Mandi in the face, and I want to lash out, to demand that they stop torturing her, but, to my shame, I don't.

"All right," Mandi whispers, relenting to their incessant demands, and I can only imagine the horror she was forced to endure from the moment of her capture to now, "I'll tell you what you want."

"You had an accomplice?" demands Molers, relishing the power he has over her.

"Yes," whispers Mandi in a harsh voice that sounds like she hasn't had water for days.

"Tell us who it is!" Molers commands, savoring his moment of victory as his eyes settle on me, certain of what she will say. He either figured it out, or sees an opportunity to be rid of me.

"Him," Mandi points a broken finger at Amal.

"What? No!" Amal screams in terror. "I never—it's all a lie!"

"He is my accomplice," Mandi says, her voice growing stronger as she commits to her story. "We would meet, in secret. I would bring him names of those who wanted to leave and he would smuggle them out. That is what he was doing for me tonight."

Renal leans in to Commander Vye, holding Amal's wristband.

"His wristband shows that he has been sneaking out for some time now, and that he was in an abandoned tunnel tonight."

"No!" shrieks Amal in terror. "I never left! I lost my wristband! It wasn't me! I swear!"

Amal's piercing screams echo off the walls as arbiters drag him away to a transport, while Molers' gaze stays fixed upon me, forcing me to keep my face impassive so as not to reveal my surprise by Mandi's actions, even though, deep inside, I am perplexed and wonder why she lied. I tricked her into revealing herself. She should want to take me down with her, to get revenge, but instead, she spares me.

"You lie," Molers says to Mandi as he grabs her by the hair and yanks her head back.

Mandi laughs at him. "I have named my accomplice."

Molers raises his hand to her, but she stops him.

"Careful, Molers," she whispers, "sometimes, those who revel in the power they have over others live to regret it."

Arbiters seize Mandi and haul her away, and I am unable to move as I stare after her, wondering what her motive for tonight was, wondering why she let me live. Out of all the instructors I had at the training facility, Mandi was the only one who tried to be fair, who showed kindness, and who looked out for her recruits, and even in the end, she looked out for me. No, it cannot end this way for her. I cannot let her lie for me. I deserve to be punished alongside her.

I shift my leg and start to stand up, to run after her, when a firm hand presses down upon my shoulder, holding me in pace, as Renal appears behind me, refusing to allow me to undo Mandi's sacrifice. Does he know? Or is he just preventing me from doing something rash?

"It appears we are done here," Renal says, staring at Molers, forcing him to remove his gaze from me.

"You were only half-right tonight," says Commander Vye to Molers. "You had the wrong traitor."

She stalks out of the foyer and to her office, sealing the door behind her, while Renal glares at Molers, giving an unspoken command. One by one, the arbiters in the room disperse, leaving me alone in a tumultuous wave of guilt and relief as the lights turn off, plunging me into darkness, while my eyes remain fixed on Molers' form, until he disappears around a corner, but I refuse to move, to go back to my room, as I remain kneeling on the floor with the edge of a cracked board digging into my knees.

A gentle hand touches my shoulder as a familiar voice whispers my name, taking great care to not attract attention. I jerk away before realizing it is Chase. How long have I remained here? Chase says nothing, but holds his hand out to me. I let him lift me to my feet and lead me away, being as quiet as we can. When we reach my room, I move away from his comforting embrace and to the window, staring out at the wall and the reflection of a resolute person hovering over it: my reflection. Molers may have won tonight, but I swear that Mandi's sacrifice will not be in vain. I do not know how I will honor her, but I will.

I... No. He will not be allowed peace.

Noni's story will conclude in book three: Entombed.

Get the Entire Series

Having spent her entire life secluded in the Martial Diplomatic Corps, Noni passes the final test, achieving the coveted position as arbiter of Arel. Placed under the tutelage of a seasoned veteran, Noni will see her city for the first time and learn that not everything is as she had been taught to believe.

Available at major retailers.

About the Author

Janet McNulty is a self-published author, practicing what she calls the most expensive hobby one can engage in.

In 2011, she released Legends Lost Amborese, which was published under the pen name of Nova Rose. Ms. McNulty has since published three novels in the Legends Lost series: Tesnayr and Galdin.

Ms. McNulty has gone on to publish three more books series in the last seven years: The Mellow Summers Series, The Dystopia Trilogy, and The Solaris Saga.

Currently, Ms. McNulty is working on the next book in her new dystopian series: The Enchained Trilogy.

More books by Janet McNulty

The Solaris Saga

Solaris Seethes
Solaris Seeks
Solaris Strays
Solaris Soars

Also available in audio.

Every myth has a beginning.

After escaping the destruction of her home planet, Lanyr, with the help of the mysterious Solaris, Rynah must put her faith in an ancient legend. Never one to believe in stories and legends, she is forced to follow the ancient tales of her people: tales that also seem to predict her current situation.

Forced to unite with four unlikely heroes from an unknown planet (the philosopher, the warrior, the lover, the inventor) in order to save the Lanyran people, Rynah and Solaris embark on an adventure that will shatter everything Rynah once believed.

The Mellow Summers Series

Sugar And Spice And Not So Nice
Frogs, Snails, And A Lot Of Wails
An Apple A Day Keeps Murder Away
Three Little Ghosts
Oh Holy Ghost
Where Trouble Roams
Two Ghosts Haunt A Grove
Trick Or Treat Or Murder
Roses Are Red…He's Dead
Double, Double Nothing But Trouble
Ring Around The Rosy Not Another Ghosty
Hickory Dickory Dock The Ghost In The Clock
Violet Are Blue More Trouble Brews
Hey Diddle Diddle The Zombie In The Middle
Easy As Pie Until Someone Dies

Mellow Summers moves to Vermont to attend college, accompanied by her friend Jackie. They soon find themselves running into ghosts and one mystery after another.

Some titles also available in audio.

The Dystopia Trilogy

Dystopia (Book 1)
Tempered Steel (Book 2)
Liberty's Torch (Book 3)

**Imagine living in a world where
everything you do is controlled.**

Dana Ginary lives in a world where every aspect of her life is
controlled by the Dystopian Government. Forced to work in
Waste Management, her life becomes a nightmare with hunger
and survival is her only constant. Before she knows it, she is
caught up in a resistance movement and exiled from Dystopia,
forced to find her way in the barren wastelands. While there,
she must learn to live independently and discover how far she
is willing to go to live and achieve freedom.

Available in audio.

The Legends Lost Series

Published under Nova Rose

Tesnayr
Amborese
Galdin

Enter the Lands of Tesnayr and join on an epic fantasy adventure that spans over 1,500 years.

Begin with Tesnayr, the first king of the five lands as he unites the against a savage foe bent on their destruction.

Next, Join Amborese as she fights reclaim the throne after her family was forced to flee from it.

Thinking peace has finally entered the land, follow Galdin as he returns to Tesnayr to find it greatly hanged. Barbarians, led by a mysterious sorcerer, burn and destroy as they go. And only Galdin can stop them if he chooses to accept his fate.

Grandpa's Stories

My grandfather grew up in Arizona during the 1920s and 1930s. One week after the attack on Pearl Harbor he joined the Navy. During the summer of 2012, my mother visited him and recorded his stories about growing up, World War II, and his time as an employee at the Pacific Bell Telephone Company. This is the history of the 20th century as he lived it. These recordings make up this book. These are his words.

Something for the Little Ones

The Dragon Who series

The Dragon Who was Afraid of the Dark
The Dragon Who Went to the Moon
The Dragon Who Found a Monster Party
The Dragon Who Found a Spider in His Shoe
The Dragon Who Explored the Sea
The Dragon Who Caught a Cold

The Fairy Who series

The Fairy Who Lost a Tooth
The Fairy Who Got Lost

The Mr. Chili series

Mr. Chili's Chili
Mr. Chili Goes To School
Mr. Chili's Halloween
Mr. Chili's Christmas

Others

Mrs. Duck and the Dragon
The Hungry Washing Machine
Rhymes-a-lot
Are You the Monster Under My Bed?
How Do You Catch An Alien

www.ingramcontent.com/pod-product-compliance
Lightning Source LLC
Chambersburg PA
CBHW020825030726
47496CB00001B/101